A DANGEROUS FOSSIL

JOHN J. DELANEY

A JURASSIC JEMMA MYSTERY

For Pauline

PLESIOSAURUS MACROCEPHALUS

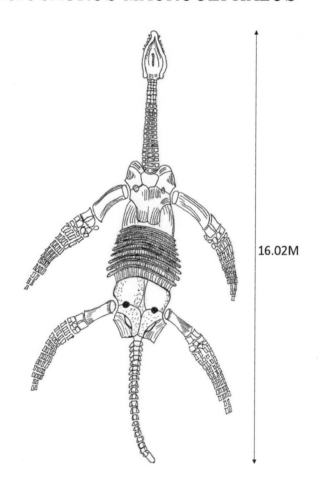

16.02M

Chapter 1

Jemma Thorne pointed her head torch along the shore. In the flickering light, she could see that a section of the cliff had collapsed during the previous night's storm. Her dog growled at a pile of debris on the beach.

After checking where he was looking, she went over to examine the landslip, shining her torch over the stones and spotting a piece of dark bone sticking out of the mud.

'What's there, Dino?'

The smell of wet seaweed assaulted her nostrils as she knelt on the damp sand and moved some of the larger stones.

'Wow, a jawbone and a big one at that!' Jemma's heart beat faster. 'Might be a plesiosaur, you clever dog. At least this makes getting up so early worth the effort'.

She had always been inspired by Mary Anning, who had lived in nearby Lyme Regis around two hundred years ago. It was Mary who'd discovered some of the first fossilised ichthyosaurs and plesiosaurs. Since then, more fossils of the Jurassic marine reptiles had been found locally, but none as spectacular as Mary's plesiosaur, on display in the Natural History Museum. With its long neck and tail, large skull and double set of paddles, it had enthralled Jemma on a school trip when she was ten.

She opened her rucksack, took out her trowel and scraped away more of the rock. She'd brought her full digging kit, including a shovel, brush and bags.

Staring at the bone, Dino licked his lips. She tutted at the dog. 'This one's not for you, but if it's as good as it looks, I'll buy you something tasty from the butchers.'

In the light from her torch, Jemma recorded the first few measurements and photographed the skull where it lay partially exposed.

Her eyes kept returning to the cliff towering above them and a tear formed in her eye as she looked at Dino. 'That's the spot where Alice fell. This rain had better stop or the whole lot could come down.'

The cliff face seemed stable, so she made a quick mental risk assessment and decided it seemed safe enough to carry on. The exposed fossil was in significant danger if the bones weren't removed before the tide returned.

Waves crashed behind her as she knelt on the exposed beach. Dino, her border collie, watched, his tail no longer wagging in the pouring rain. The wind still whistled off the sea, despite it being much calmer than before. During the night, the noise had woken her several times.

In the post-storm greyness, it was hard to imagine holidaymakers picnicking on the beach and enjoying ice-creams in the sun. Despite her years of experience, she never felt safe working on a beach in stormy weather, with the sea crashing behind her and the rain soaked cliffs rearing up in front. During a brief respite from the rain, she removed a glove and tried to make a call, sheltering from the wind blowing in from the sea.

Dino looked up at her as if to say, 'Don't like this. Home please?'

Jemma laughed. 'Sorry, you wanted to come. No backing out now. There's lots of work to do.'

He got bored with fossil hunting and wandered off, sniffing and scratching as he went.

Jemma finally got a signal and called one of her contacts. It rang out and was eventually answered.

'Hello?'

'Hello, Billy, I need some help, please. Any plans today?'

A male voice croaked, 'No, I er... what's the time?'

'Five o'clock.'

'What? It's the middle of the night?' he said.

'If I'd called you at ten, you'd still say that.'

'I'm not that bad Auntie Jem. What d'you want?'

She couldn't help grinning. 'I've found something brilliant on the beach.'

'What?'

'A big skull. Might be a plesiosaur.'

He paused. 'A plesio-what?'

'A plesiosaur. Two hundred million years old.'

Billy yawned. 'Cool. You want me to come down now?'

'Please. Will you bring your handcart, some sacks and a shovel?'

'S'pose so, but you owe me breakfast.'

'You're on. If this is a full skeleton, I'll buy you dinner as well. We need more help though. Can you think of anybody who might help?'

'Some of me mates might. See you in a bit.'

'Oh, ask your mum to let Freddie know please, he can come down after school.'

'Will do. Bye, Auntie Jem.'

'Bye, Billy, see you in a bit.'

Jemma squinted across the beach and smiled when

she couldn't see any other torches. Storms were rare in September, and she hoped she'd arrived before any other fossil hunters. The rivalry between them often meant there were several out searching after any storm. She respected most other palaeontologists, but some did a lot of damage to the cliffs, putting themselves, and others, in danger from rock falls.

After she knelt back down, she dug into the pile of broken rock with her shovel. The Blue Lias layer was quite soft so she could dig without too much trouble. As she took measurements, she entered them in her notebook. The light improved so she took more photos with her phone.

Behind the skull, she found more bones. The size of the vertebrae suggested a massive creature, perhaps over ten metres long. Her heart raced as she thought through the implications of what might be buried. A plesiosaur like this would be a major find for Lulcombe, which had been in the shadow of its Jurassic Coast neighbours for many years.

She assessed the waves. As the tide went out they'd retreated well down the damp beach, but would return later.

As she stared at the sea she could imagine how it was two hundred million years ago, when the amazing giant marine reptiles patrolled the oceans. They would have eaten fish and clams, using their long necks and sharp teeth to catch prey.

She jumped back to the present and shouted at Dino, who was sheltering under a scrubby bush trying to stay dry. 'Do you realise you could be more famous than Pickles?'

'Hi, Auntie Jem. Who's Pickles?' Jemma hadn't seen or heard her nephew approach so his voice made her jump.

'Hello, Billy. He's the dog who found the 1966 World Cup after it was stolen. He even became a film star.' Her legs ached, so she stood and stretched.

Her nephew leant on the handcart he'd pushed along the beach. A strong nineteen-year-old, he was well-built with a shock of dark hair that flopped in his eyes.

'How's the gap year going?' she asked.

'Brill, so far. Earning some money as well.'

Jemma laughed. 'Well, you can earn a bit more today, and boost your fitness with some weightlifting.'

Stamping his feet to keep warm, he pulled his coat tighter. 'Always happy to turn out when you need some muscle.'

'Cheers, Billy. Shame Freddie's got to go to school.'

'Yep, the little runt loves fossil hunting with you.'

'Don't be cruel; he'll be as big as you one day and then he'll start pushing you around. By the way, sorry for the early call and thanks for coming so quickly.' She pointed to the skull. 'This is it.'

He moved closer. 'Wow. Impressive! Is a plesiosaur the giant dolphin with a mouthful of sharp teeth?'

She shook her head. 'No, they're ichthyosaurs. A plesiosaur is a long-necked creature like the supposed Loch Ness Monster.'

He whistled. 'What a beauty. Is it valuable?'

'No idea. If it turns out to be a full skeleton, it could be megabucks. What I've seen so far is in better condition than the one Mary Anning found.'

He gave Jemma a cheeky grin. 'You gonna sell it?'

She shook her head. 'No way! It's going to be the centrepiece of the museum extension. Lots of visitors will want to see this. It'll really put Lulcombe on the map.'

Picking up his shovel, he glanced at his watch. 'It won't be long before the tide comes in and destroys anything that's left. There could be a hell of a lot to dig out before the waves come back.' With a flourish, he stuck the shovel into the loose rock near the skull.

Jemma grimaced. 'Gently, gently. It does need moving but I want to take measurements and photos as we dig. If this is complete, it'll take some work. Did you have a think if any of your mates might come down and shift some rocks?'

'Bet some of the lads from footie will help, especially if you pay them a few quid.'

'How about fifty quid for the day?' she asked.

'Cool. I'll ring round in a bit. How many do you need?'

A frown crossed her face, as she thought for a moment. 'At least six and I can try to get some local hunters to help as well.'

'OK.'

As the first weak strip of daylight appeared over the sea, they continued digging. Once fully extracted from the rock, they wrapped the skull in cloth and together they managed to lift the whole package onto the handcart.

A while later Billy stood and took out his mobile. 'I'll see who's up.' After jabbing at it unsuccessfully, he frowned. 'The signal's crap here, I'll try further along.' He wandered off, holding it to his ear as he went.

Jemma carried on with the digging, measuring and photographing. The rain had stopped and the sun peeped out through the clouds. She hoped it would stay miserable as it would limit the holidaymakers turning up asking questions. As she dug, she found some more bones that she thought could be a front flipper.

Within half an hour, three lads arrived. Billy looked at Jemma. 'Sorry, I think these are the only ones.

She pulled a face. 'Oh, well, we'll have to manage.'

After Billy introduced them, Jemma organised everybody

into two teams to move rocks and loose scree away from the massive fossil.

She did most of the digging herself, trying to balance careful excavation and measurement with the shortening timescale. The ever-destructive sea would soon come back in and cover everything. Any bones left would be broken up if they weren't removed by the end of the afternoon.

Jemma stood and looked over at her nephew.

'Billy, can you pop up to the workshop and get the van and some other stuff please?'

'No probs. What do you need?'

'Some wooden planks, more sacks, Plaster of Paris, buckets, rope and stakes to keep any bystanders away.'

'OK. Got that. Back in a bit.'

He wandered off along the beach and returned twenty minutes later, laden down with the items Jemma had asked for.

As they worked, the wind dropped, so that even the gulls ventured over the beach for food. Eventually, some vertebrae and part of the front flippers were out of the rock. They wrapped them in field jackets made from Plaster of Paris and sacking before the helpers transported them to the van. Billy took the first load up to the workshop and laid the findings out on the floor, placing them in the order of the pencil numbers.

Around midday, Jemma's stomach started rumbling. 'I'm starving. Anybody fancy fetching some chips? I forgot breakfast this morning. We'll have to keep working while we eat though as we're tight for time.'

Ryan, one of the other helpers, clambered up. 'You're a hard taskmaster, Jemma, I'll go. Me back's killing me with all this lifting.' He straightened out his long legs like

11

a geriatric flamingo.

'Someone of your age shouldn't moan about their back,' Jemma said. She handed him some money. 'Can you get five bags of chips and five Cokes, but don't tell Gareth from the café what we're doing? He always sticks his nose into any activity on the beach. I don't know why, he's never collected fossils.'

Jemma watched him head off down the beach but then yelled after him. 'Can you bring some water for Dino please?'

'Will do.'

Billy stood next to Jemma, waiting for her to pass him the next bone. 'Are we going to get it all out?'

She shrugged. 'We've got to, Billy. We can't let any of this be destroyed.'

They stared at the waves. The tide had turned and was making its menacing way relentlessly back up the beach. Her heart beat faster as she started digging more quickly.

Chapter 2

The sun emerged as Ryan arrived back at the dig with his goodies.

'Grub's up!' he shouted.

Billy came over and helped himself to some chips and a can. 'Cheers mate, I'm starving.

Jemma walked over and took a bag of chips. 'Any salt?'

Ryan passed her the bag. 'Some in the bottom.'

She retrieved a small packet of salt and tore the corner off, trying not to drop her chips which she had temporarily cradled in the crook of her arm. She salted her chips and put the empty packet in her rucksack. As she deeply inhaled the scented steam rising from her lunch, she salivated. Holding a hot chip carefully between her fingers she blew on it as she scanned the beach. 'Was Gareth there?'

Ryan started on his own food. 'Afraid so, he was behind the counter. He was desperate to know what we're all up to, but I didn't tell him anything.'

'That's good.'

'The bad news is that he's coming along later to check up on what's going on,' he said.

Jemma frowned. 'Bugger! Everyone will know we're digging. Hopefully, the rope cordon will keep him and anybody else away.'

'Oh,' Jake began eating a chip, 'he also offered me a tenner if I let him know what's happening. Why's he so nosy?'

She thought for a moment. 'I don't know. Maybe someone pays him to tip them off about who's working on the beach. That's it, he must be a fossilling spy.'

'Who'd be bothered enough to pay him?' Ryan asked.

'Could be a rival collector.'

Dino lapped up his water and worked his way around the group begging for spare chips. The gulls circled and checked out the alfresco diners, always ready for a smash and grab attack. The team demolished the food in a short time, and Ryan screwed up his wrapper. 'Give us yer rubbish and I'll take it to the bin.'

That was a dangerous thing to say, as another four chip wrappers went flying in his direction. As he picked them up, he laughed. 'Very funny.' He took them off to one of the silver litter bins guarding the beach like bored Daleks.

Jemma checked her watch and said to Billy, 'We're not making as much progress as I hoped. It's one o'clock already and the tide's coming in so quickly. I wonder if any of the local hunters are available. Perhaps Vincent will help, he's often out on digs.' Holding up her phone, she thumbed through her contacts and called one. 'Hi, Vincent, it's Jemma.'

'Hello, Jemma. You OK?'

'Yes, I'm fine. Are you free to take part in a dig?'

'What've you found?' Vincent said.

The drizzle started again so Jemma turned her back to it and pulled her hood over the phone. She continued. 'A plesiosaur. It might be complete, if I'm lucky.'

'Wow. I'm up for that. Where are you?'

'Lulcombe West Beach,' she said.

'Right. Do you need anybody else?'

She thought for a moment. 'Another helper or two would be good. If you can get anyone else, please, that would be brilliant?'

'I'll try.'

'Thanks, Vincent.'

'No worries. Cheers, Jemma.'

***

Twenty minutes later, two more figures strode along the beach carrying shovels and big rucksacks.

'Afternoon, Jem, where's the monster?' Vincent shouted.

She stopped digging and stood to shake hands. 'Hi, thanks for coming.'

'Couldn't miss this,' he replied. He was sixty-two and tall, with light brown grey-flecked hair. Like Jemma, he was a trustee of Lulcombe Museum.

She then spotted who was behind him and tried to smile. 'Oh, hello, Sally.'

'Hello, boss.'

The smile left Jemma's face. 'Just Jemma, please, we're not at uni now so there's no need for boss. Not that you call me boss there.'

Sally dropped her rucksack. 'OK. Hello…Jemma.'

Jemma smirked. 'You're looking glamorous as ever.'

Sally replied with a smile that didn't reach her eyes. 'I wouldn't say glamorous but I do my best.' She looked down her nose at Jemma. 'I'm afraid the weather-worn, bedraggled appearance is not for me.'

Jemma scowled at the slim Irish thirty-six-year-old who wore an immaculate field outfit and had her long red hair in a ponytail. *Why do I never look like that when I'm out working? I must retaliate somehow.* 'I always think the dirtier I am, the harder I've worked,' she finally responded.

Vincent butted in before things escalated. 'Do I qualify as glamorous as well?' He did a quick twirl.

Jemma laughed. 'I'd say more a distinguished ex-military look.'

He stroked his grey-flecked moustache. 'At my age, I'll settle for that.'

Sally checked the excavation. 'I'm jealous. Struck lucky again, Jem?'

'Yep, although Dino found the skull.'

Hearing his name, Dino came running over wagging his tail, hoping for some more food, or at least some attention.

Sally bent to stroke him and he rolled on his back expectantly. 'You're a clever boy.' She scratched his tummy and glanced up at Jemma. 'Any lectures today?'

Jemma resumed her digging and didn't look up. 'No, none 'til Monday. The marking never goes away, but I can attack the pile at the weekend.'

Sally stood and pulled her coat tighter. 'Not enough hours in the day for a fossil hunting lecturer who works in a museum as well.'

Jemma refused to rise to the taunt. 'You know what they say. No rest for the wicked.'

Vincent knelt next to her. 'What stage are you at?'

'The skull, two front flippers, some vertebrae and the rib cage are out, all wrapped in field jackets and in the van.'

Vincent took out his tools. 'Where do you want me?'

'On the other side please, and Sally, can you find the end

of the tail?' Jemma pointed to the rocks nearest the cliffs. 'Probably over near the cliff.'

Sally sneered. 'Typical. I get to start at the arse end.'

Jemma ignored her and carried on digging.

'Where did you find the skull?' Vincent asked.

'Over there by the white stick.'

Sally's eyes widened. 'My God, must be fifteen metres long.'

'Could be bigger,' Jemma said.

Sally whistled, 'That's incredible, but there's a lot left to excavate. We'd better crack on.'

She went over to the pile of rocks. 'Have you undertaken your risk assessment, Jemma?'

Jemma retorted. 'Yes, I've done it mentally, but not written anything out yet. We're under a lot of time pressure with the tide turning, you know.'

Sally held her hands up. 'OK. Keep your hair on. I was only checking.

Kneeling on the sand, Vincent started digging and brushing away the loose stone and debris. 'Don't worry. What you've done is fine. After all, the sea's on its way back in.'

Nodding her head, Jemma agreed. 'My thoughts entirely. Don't want to risk any wave damage to the fossil.'

Sally walked to the far end of the rockfall under the cliff and peered up at the overhang above her. 'You reckon this is safe to work under?'

Jemma glanced up at the cliffs. 'Hopefully.'

'Just get digging,' Vincent snapped. 'We should be fine, as long as the rain doesn't start again.'

Sally sneered. 'It's dangerous to cut corners. That's how accidents happen.'

Vincent turned to her. 'I'm beginning to wish I hadn't asked you to come.'

Jemma stopped digging. 'Can we just get on, please? The tide'll reach us soon.'

With a shrug, Sally knelt on the damp sand, delving into the landslip with her trowel.

Around two o'clock, the skies cleared and Jemma glanced over at the waves as she tried to work out how much was left to dig out.

Alongside her, Vincent put down his shovel and stretched. 'How much longer do you think we need?'

She thought for a moment. 'We've got at least a couple of hours before the water gets back up here.'

'Can we manage?' said Vincent.

'Might be tight,' Jemma hesitated. 'Working against an incoming tide is so stressful. Even with two hours left, I can't stop looking at the waves every few minutes.'

He laughed. 'Same here.'

They both went quiet and carried on digging with renewed vigour.

One of the helpers had to go as they had prior plans. Billy tried without success to persuade some others to come and help. He put his phone back in his pocket. 'There are some bloody lazy people out there,' he said. 'Will we be OK, Auntie Jem?'

She glanced back at the waves. 'I don't know. The water's getting closer. It'll get dangerous if we stay on the beach too long.' Then she saw a man in a long raincoat picking his way over the rocks. 'Oh, goody, Gareth's here for a nosy.'

Gareth approached and attempted to peer around the diggers obstructing his view. 'This is interesting. Have you discovered something exciting?'

Sometimes that question really annoyed her, and she snapped, 'Just digging around in a rock fall.'

He leant over the rope. 'Can I come closer and see what you've found?'

'Sorry, I wouldn't mind, but we have to follow the West Dorset Fossil Collecting Code of Conduct. The whole area has to be roped off, you know, in case of any further falls. If you were killed in a landslip, I might be sued.'

Gareth licked his lips. 'I bet you're finding some great fossils. These lads have been backwards and forwards with the cart all morning. I tried to get a look, but you'd wrapped everything in blankets.'

Jemma rammed her shovel in the sand. 'Only a few bones so far. Sorry, can't stop. The tide'll be back in shortly. Bye, Gareth.'

He scowled and watched quietly for five minutes as several of the lads moved between him and the excavations blocking his view. Eventually, he stuck his hands in his pockets and stomped away down the beach.

Vincent looked over at Jemma. 'Who was that then?'

'Gareth from the Beach Café.'

They watched as he trudged back along the beach. Vincent turned back to his digging. 'Where do you know him from?'

'He was in my class at school. He asked me out a couple of times, but I thought he was obnoxious,' she said.

'I get that.'

Jemma rubbed her hands together. 'It's the way that he wrings his hands when he's talking. So creepy.'

'Just like Uriah Heap from the Dickens novel.'

'Got him in one,' she said.

'What's he after?' Vincent asked.

'I don't know. Maybe somebody's paying him for info as he's desperate to know what's going on.'

Chapter 3

Brad 'Indiana' Jones sat in his hotel room in Poole reading the New York Times. The luxury room was enormous with a massive bed, a sofa, chairs and a wall of windows that reached from floor to ceiling. The views out towards Brownsea Island were stunning, but he was more interested in the news from back home.

He was browsing the Dow Jones when the phone rang. 'Hello.'

'Hi, Brad, this is Gareth.....from Lulcombe Beach Café. I've obtained some information you might find interesting.'

Brad scratched his chin. 'What ya got?'

'It seems like Jemma from the museum has found something exciting on Lulcombe West Beach. She's been busy all day in the rain, and she's got some lads doing her lugging. They've made a lot of journeys up and down with a handcart.'

'What a surprise, 'Jurassic' Jemma Thorne.' He chuckled to himself. 'Haven't heard that name in a while. What's she found?'

'No idea. They clammed up and wouldn't tell me. Also, they put a cordon around the dig, which stopped me seeing anything. Must be an important find as there were two other fossil hunters with her as well.'

'It's good you called. Ask some more questions. Find out what's going on, please. Those diggers will end up in a bar somewhere. Pump an extra beer or two into 'em to loosen their tongues. I'll come down to Lulcombe and see for myself.'

'I take it this information might be valuable?'

Brad could imagine the dollar signs spinning in Gareth's eyes. He sighed. 'An envelope will be dropped off at the café later. Keep an eye on them, will you?'

'Yes, of course. Will do.'

Brad ended the call. *Well, well, well. Sounds like Jurassic Jemma has struck gold.* That was the nickname she'd been given when they were both at university over twenty years ago. The memory of the three years they spent together made him smile. They had started out as classmates on the same course and quickly became lovers. As one of the wealthier students, Brad had his own apartment which gave them the privacy they didn't get in Jemma's shared room in the halls of residence.

As he packed his suitcase, hat and field bag, he hummed the theme tune to *Raiders of the Lost Ark.*

***

Back on the coast at three o'clock the rain started again, which quickly became colder as the tide neared. The helpers trudged up and down with shoulders slumped and damp hair stuck to their heads.

Billy yawned. 'How much longer, Auntie Jem?'

Jemma thought for a moment. 'We've still got a few more metres of the tail to dig out, although the waves are getting a bit close. Shouldn't be much longer.'

Vincent stood and walked down towards the sea. 'The water's up to the skull marker stick, so we must speed up, or we won't remove the lot.'

Sally glanced up from her part of the excavation. 'I'm worried about the cliff now the rain's started again. You ought to redo your risk assessment.'

Jemma tried to reassure her. 'I can't spare the time now. Not long, Sally, we're almost there.'

Sally looked over 'You do realise this section of the beach is about to be entirely cut off by the tide.'

'I've been hunting on this beach since I was six,' Jemma replied patiently. 'So yes, I'm fully aware of that.'

At that moment, a smaller figure came running along the beach. 'Hello, Auntie Jem.'

Freddie was a small, fair-haired eleven-year-old and nothing like his brother Billy who towered above him. A lover of nature and fossils, heaven for him was a day out with his aunt. His favourite finds were coprolites, or fossilised dinosaur shit as he called them if his mum wasn't around.

A smile crossed her face as Jemma tousled her nephew's hair. 'Hello, Freddie, thanks for coming.'

'Mum wouldn't let me come this morning.'

'She didn't want you to miss school.'

He grinned. 'This would've been educational.'

Jemma smiled. 'Still a no.'

'Mum still stopped me coming, even when I told her that you had said it was OK.'

She frowned. 'I did no such thing.'

'I thought you told Billy to come straight down,' he said.

'That was him, not you.'

23

He shrugged. 'Oh, well. Worth a go. Ellie here?'

'I didn't ask her. She's busy at college.'

'You'll be in trouble.'

Jemma shrugged. 'She's not usually that bothered about getting dirty and digging up fossils.'

'Sure she's your daughter?'

'Oh, yes.'

Freddie glanced around at the scene. 'Where's the plesiosaur? Can we call it Plessie?'

'Great name. Most of the skeleton's out. We're on the last section now, but the tide is coming in quickly, so we better carry on. Here,' she held out a trowel, 'grab this and help me with the digging, please.'

As he lifted a piece of bone, Billy frowned. 'How come the brat gets a trowel but I have to do the heavy carrying?'

Jemma laughed. 'You're stronger than him and he can't drive.'

Freddie puffed out his chest. 'Can so. Who drove the van a bit in the big car park?'

She grinned. 'Thought that was our secret, Freddie.'

Sally intervened. 'I'm sure it's lovely to have a family chat, but the cliff's dripping with water again. Can we finish please so I can get away from here?'

The work continued frantically as the sea lapped the section being cleared. Jemma stopped measuring and just dug like mad. The helpers grabbed the bones from her and loaded them onto the handcart but they struggled to manoeuvre it over the stones so they left it by the van and used their arms to carry the next batch.

Then a larger wave splashed into the hole where Jemma was digging. She panicked and jumped. 'Bloody hell! We need to build a wall of rocks to protect this last bit.'

From where she was working, Sally shouted over to Jemma, 'You're not King Canute, you know, we should leave now. We're in danger of getting cut off. Can't we give up with this section and come back tomorrow?'

What a lightweight. Jemma frowned. 'No way, it'd be destroyed by tomorrow. We're nearly done. We can't give up now we're so close.' She felt exhausted but was determined to move all of the fossil before the sea commenced its demolition job.

Vincent placed some bones straight into a sack. 'This is going to take some sorting out in the workshop.' He handed some more sacks to the lads for them to carry off, as the waves crashed around their feet.

Jemma worked in a pool of cold seawater, which the waves kept topping up. As she struggled with the last few bones, she saw Sally stand and put her tools back in her bag. 'You done, Sally?'

Sally looked down at her filthy clothes. 'Yep. I've finished the tail section. Time to get off the beach before we're all cut off.'

'Thanks, Sally,' Jemma said. 'I'm almost done here too.'

A larger wave came splashing in and knocked Jemma over. She got up spitting out water and waited for the wave to retreat before pulling out the last piece of bone. She climbed back to her feet, 'Job done. Everybody off the beach. Stay close to the top on the way back as the rocks will be slippery and we don't want anyone washed into the sea. Freddie, will you help me take the tools back, please?'

'Yeah, course I will,' he replied.

The tired, wet workers carried the remaining sacks back to the van. Billy went with them to open it and help load them up.

'Thank God, we're done.' Sally shook her coat. 'This is filthy and my boots are full of water. Come on, Vincent, let's go and have a drink in the Anchor.'

'Good idea,' he said and they walked off together.

Jemma waved to everybody. 'Thanks for the help,' but her words were blown away by the wind. She had a last look round before leaving. Even in the rain the beach looked beautiful.

As the muddy workers retreated down the beach, she turned to Freddie. 'Do you think the landlord will let them in?'

He laughed. 'I bet he's used to sandy tourists and wet dogs.'

'Talking of dogs, where's Dino?' Jemma asked.

Freddie pointed. 'He's sniffing around at the base of the cliff.'

From where she stood, she could see his tail sticking up. 'Come on, Dino! We're off.'

Dino ignored her to carry on investigating interesting smells.

She shouted again. 'Dino, I'm not messing about. We need to go.'

Her dog's selective deafness seemed to have returned.

'Bloody stay there then. Drown for all I care.'

Jemma and Freddie took down the rope cordon and grabbed the last few tools. As she put them in her rucksack, she saw that the others had reached the car park at the end. 'Wow, they can shift themselves when the pub's calling.'

Freddie laughed. 'Time for us to follow.'

Jemma picked her way along the top of the shingle and Freddie followed behind. 'You OK?' She kept an eye on the waves breaking ever higher up the beach.

'Yes,' he said. 'I'd say I'm ready for a shower.'

A wave crashed right in front of where they were walking so they hung back and dashed across before the next one could break.

Jemma shouted over her shoulder, 'Dino, come on, keep up.'

Just then there was a rumble and a loud crashing noise as a nearby section of the cliff collapsed onto the beach.

She grabbed Freddie's hand. 'Run.'

They scrambled over the rocks away from the falling stones. A few smaller pieces flew through the air and hit them on the legs. Once they were clear of the dust they turned and saw a new pile of debris behind them.

There was a large mound of rocks, mud and smaller stones, all mixed together and piled up on the beach.

Jemma had turned pale. 'My God! That's a massive chunk of the cliffs that's come down. I'm glad Sally wasn't here to see that or I'd never hear the last of it.'

Freddie realised he was still holding her hand and pulled away embarrassed. 'I've never seen a rockfall that big before.'

She turned and looked around. 'We'd better shift ourselves in case there are any more slips.'

Freddie panted. 'I can't believe how close that was. If we'd been standing where you found the fossil, we'd have been flattened.'

'I didn't find it, Dino did.' Jemma looked at Freddie in horror. She screamed, 'Dino!'

Chapter 4

The porch of the Anchor Inn quickly filled with boots and coats as Ryan and the other lads stripped off their wet gear. It was a popular pub, frequented by both locals and tourists. Simply furnished, it had several nautical artefacts fixed to the wood-panelled walls. Fishing nets hung from the ceilings and an enormous iron anchor covered the main wall opposite the bar.

The rotund landlord wandered over to serve them, his red nose suggesting a liking for his own victuals. 'Not dripping all over the floor, are we lads?'

Ryan protested. 'No, we left our wet stuff in the porch. Four pints of best please.'

'Coming up.'

None of the team had noticed Gareth sitting in a wooden alcove. Crablike, he sidled over. 'Here, let me buy those. Hard workers deserve a pint.' The lads thanked him and took their drinks, welcoming the first sips after their tiring work. Gareth paid and lifted his glass. 'Cheers. To fantastic dinosaurs.'

'Wasn't exactly a dinosaur,' Harry explained. 'Technically-'

Ryan interrupted. 'Not worth speculating; we don't know what Jem's dug up until she tells us. We were shifting some rocks for her. Until she cleans them up, nobody knows what's in them.'

After a short pause, Harry nodded. 'Oh, yes, right.'

Gareth pressed further. 'Surely you're curious about what she found, aren't you?'

'She'll tell us when she's ready, and don't call me Shirley,' Ryan smiled.

The lads chose a small table and didn't leave any room for Gareth. He looked for a chair but there weren't any free near to the digging team. Vincent and Sally sat at a small table in the corner deep in conversation. Gareth wandered over and sat at the table next to them.

The digging team had just finished their first pints when a loud rumble shook the place.

'Bloody hell,' Ryan said. 'I'm glad we're off the beach if the thunder's started.'

Harry put down his empty glass. 'Doesn't matter now we're in here. Another pint for everyone?'

As he spoke, the pub door swung open and a man rushed in. 'The cliff's collapsed and there are people nearby. Can someone call the police, the signal's rubbish?'

Ryan jumped up. 'Jemma!'

The landlord grabbed the phone. 'You lot see if you can help. I'll call 999.'

They left their glasses, grabbed their coats, wrestled into their wet boots and ran back to the beach. Behind the bar, the landlord was already talking to the emergency services.

***

The cloud of dust settled and Jemma picked her way back towards the landslip. 'Stay back Freddie,' she yelled. 'Don't move.' She scrambled onto the loose rocks in a complete panic. 'Dino! Dino!' she screamed.

Freddie called after her, anxiety making his voice higher than normal. 'Come back Auntie Jem, it's too dangerous.'

She didn't turn around. 'I'm OK. Stay where it's dry. Can you spot Dino?'

Freddie pointed. 'I think I saw him on the other side, but you'll never get round now, the sea's too far up.'

Jemma waded through the waves trying to negotiate the rockfall. 'I can scramble past it here, the water's still shallow.'

Halfway round a wave hit, knocked her off her feet, and threw her under, spluttering and gasping. She struggled to stand in her heavy boots and clothing but a hand grabbed her arm and helped her up. The taste of salty water filled her mouth. She spat it out. 'Go back, Freddie, you should have stayed where you were.'

'There's no way I'd let you drown. Quick, up the far side, before the next wave hits.'

They half swam, half scrambled up the other side of the landslip. Dripping with cold water and seaweed, they shivered. The landslip was one of the largest she'd ever seen. She'd witnessed the power of the sea many times and it never ceased to amaze her how destructive it could be. She snapped back to the search.

'Dino.' Jemma's voice quavered as she dug into the massive pile of rocks with her bare hands. 'Where are you?'

Freddie reached for her arm and shook her. 'No good, Auntie Jem. If he's underneath that lot, he's dead. Let's head back and dry off before we get hypowhatsitsname. I can't stop shaking.'

'But I've got to keep trying.' She wept, still scrabbling and throwing stones behind her.

He persisted. 'If we don't go now, it'll be too late. The sea's getting rougher, and we'll never clamber back over.'

Jemma ceased digging and stood. 'I can't leave Dino, I have to help him.'

Freddie glanced at the approaching waves. 'We've got to go.'

'I didn't help Alice,' she said.

'Who?'

'Doesn't matter. You shouldn't have followed me here.'

'Well, I did, so let's get back.'

She concentrated on the spot where the rockfall met the sea. 'Not sure we'd get round now so we need to climb over it somehow. Here, I'll help you up.' She tried to help him climb the obstruction, but he kept slipping back down onto the heap of mud, rock and sand.

For a moment he stood panting. 'Not a chance. Can we try the cliffs at the back?'

She stared up at them. 'I don't want to go anywhere near the cliffs, it's just too dangerous and we've seen what can happen.'

Freddie pointed. 'Isn't it safer at the base? It's further away from the sea, and we might be able to see over the rockfall and wave to someone.'

'No joy,' Jemma said. 'The waves always crash against the bottom of the cliffs at high tide. We've got to climb over the landslip. There isn't enough time to wait for help. Even if somebody calls out the lifeboat, it wouldn't get here before the waves reach the top.' She checked her phone, which seemed to have survived its dip in the sea, but there was no signal.

Freddie grabbed her arm. 'How about I climb on your shoulders and try to wave for someone.'

'You might be a bit big for me but we can give it a go.' As she spoke, the end of a rope flew over the rocks and came to rest by their feet. She pointed to it. 'Quick, stick your foot in that loop and give it a pull.'

He pushed his foot inside, pulled the rope and waited for it to tighten before moving up the slippery side and disappearing over the pile of rock. The rope flew back over and Jemma smiled as she put her foot in the loop, giving it two quick tugs. It went tight and she started lifting off the ground. She felt so happy as she was pulled up the side of the rockfall but then her progress halted and she hung there, three feet off the ground. Her tired leg shook as she tried to stay upright holding the rope.

Suddenly, she began sliding back down towards the water, so she clutched at the loose rocks but couldn't get a grip and finished back where she started. She almost wept as she landed in knee-high water and the rope slackened.

'What's happening,' she shouted but, with the noise of the wind and waves, she couldn't hear any reply.

As she waited, the rope suddenly moved but her boot had slipped out of the loop which disappeared upwards. She reached for it but, without her foot in the loop, she couldn't hold on and slipped back down into the water with burning hands. Freed of its burden the rope disappeared over the top.

Jemma leant against the rockfall and waited, shivering, until the rope came back over again.

This time she wedged her boot straight into the loop, pulled the rope twice and she was lifted up the rockfall. As she went over the top she could see the heads of Billy, Ryan and Freddie as they strained to pull her up. She slid down the other side straight into the arms of Billy and Ryan, who stopped her landing face down in the water.

Billy helped her up. 'That was bloody close. Glad the others came to help; I was struggling to pull you over with just Freddie helping. Come on, quick, let's go.'

They all scrambled back along the ever-decreasing beach as the waves forced them further beneath the cliffs.

The benches in front of the café were a welcome sight and they all collapsed on the concrete.

Jemma hugged Billy and Freddie. 'Thanks, guys,' she said. 'That was a bit close. I should've sent you back with the others, Freddie.'

He wiped away a tear. 'But then I wouldn't have been around to pull you from the sea when you went under.'

Jemma groaned. 'I'm gonna be in such trouble with your mum when she hears.'

A cheeky grin crossed Freddie's face. 'I won't tell her and I'm sure Billy'll keep quiet. We'll just say we got muddy digging.'

A police car raced up as they slumped on the seats, stopping in the car park with its blue lights flashing. A young-looking policeman jumped out and approached carrying a bag.

'Are you all OK? The coastguard and lifeboat are on standby, and an ambulance is on its way. Is there anybody still on the beach?'

'Yes, Dino.' Freddie tried not to cry.

The policeman reached for his handset. 'OK, I'll call for help. Who's Deano, an adult or a child?'

'Dino's a dog,' Jemma responded. 'He might be buried in the landslide.' The tears started again, and she sunk her head into her hands and sniffled.

The policeman spoke on his radio. 'No people left on the beach. All safely out of the way. Stand down the lifeboat and coastguard.'

'But Dino's still lost,' Freddie jumped up. 'You can't just leave him there. Can't the lifeboat rescue him?'

The constable placed his hand on Freddie's shoulder. 'Sorry, young man, it's much too dangerous for anyone to go back for your dog, especially if he's under all the rocks.'

Jemma sagged back into her seat. 'He's my dog.'

'Sorry, miss.'

She realised she was shaking uncontrollably, a combination of dampness, cold and emotion. The policeman took a silver blanket from the bag he was carrying and handed it to her.

'Here's a blanket. Keep yourself warm.'

'Thanks.' She put it around her shoulders and rested her head on her knees.

Just then she heard a commotion in front of the Beach Café and someone shouted about having their chips stolen.

Bloody seagulls. Her head sagged into her hands again.

Freddie yelped. 'Auntie Jemma. Look.'

She jumped up just in time to see a black dog running towards them with a mouthful of white chip papers. Her eyes widened as she bent down to stroke him. 'Dino!'

The soggy dog looked up at her as if to say, 'What's the matter? They'd finished with them.'

Freddie ran over and rubbed Dino's neck.

'I take it the missing animal is back?' The policeman made some notes in his notepad.

Jemma turned away from stroking Dino. 'Yes, yes, and I think he's OK. I thought he'd suffered the same fate as Tray.'

'Who's Tray?' the policeman asked.

'Mary Anning's dog,' she responded.

He appeared confused. 'Is Mary still on the beach?'

Jemma laughed. 'I don't think so. She lived in the eighteen hundreds.'

'Oh. That's OK then. How about you, miss, and the others? Do any of you need checking out? Any head or back injuries?'

Jemma glanced at Freddie, who shook his head. 'All's good, thanks. Cancel the ambulance. We've only got a few scratches and bruises, nothing a soak in a hot bath won't sort out.'

The policeman pocketed his notebook and spoke into his radio.

Ryan stood. 'My pint's calling me, Jemma, can we go back to The Anchor now? No more drama.'

She smiled. 'Yes, you go. Thanks for everything.'

The lads headed off to the pub and the policeman returned to his patrol car and drove off.

'Well, if it isn't Jurassic Jemma back in the thick of things again. You look like a part-drowned superhero.' The instantly recognisable voice gave Jemma a jolt and, as she turned, a tall man in a brown fedora was walking up the steps.

'Brad.' Her heart raced. 'What are you doing here?'

He sprawled out on the bench. 'I'm living in England for a while. Had a bit of a misunderstanding with the authorities in the States about a fossil. Thought it would be interesting to come and check things out over here. Snazzy silver cape, by the way. Is this Jurassic Jemma's new style?'

Billy came over and stood above them. 'OK, Auntie Jem?'

'Yes, I'm fine. Billy, this is Brad 'Indiana' Jones; we were at university together a lifetime ago. Brad, this is my nephew Billy and that's my other nephew, Freddie.'

'Hi, Brad.' Freddie glanced up from stroking Dino, who was lapping up the attention. 'Where's the whip?'

'Hi, Freddie, I must have left it in the car. I remember your mom from way back. How's she doing?'

'She's good, but don't tell her what's happened, will you? We don't want Auntie Jem to be in trouble with Mum.'

'Well, I don't know what's happened yet but if I do meet Sue, I'm not talking.' He winked at Freddie.

Jemma watched them in a bit of a daze. Brad's American accent seemed so strange on a wet Dorset beach. He was well over six feet tall with shoulder-length brown hair. The years had treated him well and, with his trim build, he'd kept himself pretty fit. *I must look an absolute wreck.* There was a moment's silence as she drifted off.

Brad's voice broke into her daydreaming. 'What'd ya find?'

Back in the real world, she raised an eyebrow. 'Wow, news travels fast. A huge plesiosaur.'

Brad thought for a moment. 'Who owns it?'

'It was below the high-water mark, so technically it's finders keepers. However, important fossils have to be offered to a museum first. Anyway, how did you know we were here?'

He tapped his nose. 'I have my sources.'

'Gareth didn't contact you by any chance, did he?'

'First rule of fossil hunting. Never reveal your sources.' He smirked and peered at the café. 'Is this Gareth's place?'

'Yes, this is it.'

'I need to drop off an envelope for him.'

'You just revealed your source.'

'But I didn't reveal everything.'

Jemma felt herself drifting back into dream world.

As they talked, Sally and Vincent were approaching from across the car park. Jemma rolled her eyes and groaned.

Sally stood in front of Jemma with her arms crossed.

'Trying to have a quiet drink in the pub and there's a commotion on the beach. Guess who's involved? Jemma! I thought you'd done a proper risk assessment. It doesn't appear to have been particularly effective, does it? Almost drowned you and your nephew, and wiped out some of the football team by the sound of things.'

'Someone's been exaggerating,' Jemma said. 'Everybody's fine. It was the extra rain that brought down a different section of the cliffs.'

Sally persisted. 'I said we should have finished sooner. I bet the university won't be happy when they find out what scrapes their head of Geology and Palaeontology has been involved in.'

Jemma seethed. 'Hopefully, they won't hear about it.'

'I might just decide it is in the interests of student and staff safety to bring them up to speed with what happened today. I'm sure that would help them with any future decision making.'

Jemma lost it. 'Sally, will you just pi-'

Brad stepped across in front of her. 'And who is this beautiful young lady?'

Sally blushed and started babbling. 'What?...Who?... Er...'

Jemma silently thanked Brad for the distraction technique, especially as she had a shovel in her hand. 'Sally O'Keefe, meet Brad Jones, also known as Indiana because that's where he's from.'

At that, Sally started acting like a shy sixteen-year-old girl with a crush on a sixth former.

He took her hand and kissed it. 'Enchanteé. Nice to meet you.'

Billy tapped Freddie on the shoulder and mimed putting his fingers down his throat and being sick.

Sally gazed at Brad. 'What brings an American fossil hunter to Dorset?'

'Oh, I'm over in the UK for a while to acquire some specimens. Unfortunately, my collection has been decimated recently.'

She touched his arm. 'Oh, no, have you had things stolen?'

Brad put his hand over hers. 'Sort of. The whole collection is being examined by the Feds.'

Sally's eyes widened. 'Did you steal them?'

'No, I found a dinosaur on government land and they got a bit possessive.'

Billy stood. 'God, I'm smelly, I'm having a shower before going to the pub. Shall I take your van back up to the workshop now, Auntie Jem?'

Jemma yawned. 'I'll drive it back, thanks, Billy; I need a relaxing soak myself.'

Freddie stood and walked over. 'I'll help you unload the vans. Come on, Dino.'

Dino shook himself off, showering Sally with sand, mud and water.

'Dirty dog!' She wiped herself down.

Brad took Sally's arm. 'Come on Sally, I'm sure you can point me in the direction of a local hotel?'

She stopped wiping her trousers and looked into Brad's eyes. 'Of course. I'd love to.'

As they left, Brad turned back to Jemma. 'I'll be in touch.'

'Cheers you two.' She watched jealously as the pair walked away.

Billy grimaced. 'Is he creepy, or what?'

'Some folks think he's charming, I know I did years ago!'

'Is he an old boyfriend?'

'Yes, long time ago though.'

'Mum will love to hear that one of your old boyfriends has come back on the scene. Bet Dave'll be jealous!'

Jemma wagged her finger at him. 'Stop stirring things, Billy Heath! No need to go blabbing to anyone, especially Dave.

Billy laughed. 'I think that's enough dinosaur lugging for one day.'

Freddie scoffed. 'It's not a dinosaur, it's a marine reptile. Like the Loch Ness monster is supposed to look, although that doesn't exist.'

'Might do,' Billy said and folded his arms.

'No, it doesn't.' Freddie laughed. 'Loch Ness doesn't meet the sea, so a marine reptile couldn't survive in the freshwater.'

Jemma grinned. 'If you two have finished arguing, I'm off. Come on, Freddie.'

Vincent turned to leave as well. 'Are you planning to display this at the museum?'

'Yes. It could save us.'

'It needs something to get the visitor numbers up.' Vincent said. 'We've been struggling and running out of money for years. It'd look good in a new building up the hill.'

She sighed. 'Don't start on about that again. We can't sell the site.'

Vincent frowned. 'But we're in danger of going bust.'

'This find will help,' she said. 'We won't need to sell.'

'Surely, a sale would give us a new building and some spare money as well?'

'Look, my family has been involved with this museum for a long time.' Jemma paused. 'Lots of my Grandad's finds are in there. If we moved to a smaller, modern building, half of them couldn't be displayed, especially if we try to fit this beast in.'

He turned. 'Oh well, just give it some thought.'

'I have done,' she said, 'and the answer's no.'

He shrugged and walked off. 'See you around Jemma.'

'Cheers Vincent.' She nudged Freddie. 'Come on, let's go.'

They trudged over to her scruffy Ford Transit and got in. The smell of wet dog and damp coats filled the van but it was peaceful after the noise of the wind and waves. She drove away and, a few minutes later, arrived home.

Jemma's cottage sat on a hill overlooking the sea in Lulcombe. It was an old semi-detached property with breath taking views of the woods which led down to the Beach Car Park. Beyond the trees, the blue expanse of the English Channel stretched into the distance.

Feeling exhausted, she backed her van up to the large shed she used as her workshop then turned to Freddie. 'Right, let's unload first and then I'm having a long bath.' Opening the workshop door, she examined the enormous pile of rocks, bones and sacks that covered the entire floor. 'Lots of work needed to prepare Plessie for display.'

He grinned. 'I'll help. It'll be half-term soon and I've got weekends free as well.'

She tousled his hair. 'Cheers, matey. I might even teach you how to use an air chisel, but you need to wear goggles and a mask.'

Freddie grinned. 'You're on!'

The last few sacks were quickly unloaded and, after they were done, Jemma locked the shed. 'Thanks, you're a star,' she told Freddie. 'Tell Billy I'll sort some money for him and his mates.'

'I don't want any, I just love helping.'

'You'll end up a fossil hunter yet and then I'll be in such trouble with your mum.'

He shook his head. 'She won't mind.'

He headed off down the path. 'See you later, Auntie Jem. Thanks for letting me help.'

She smiled. 'Thanks, and don't forget, not a word to Mum about having to be rescued!'

'OK, cheers.' He disappeared down the road.

She shouted Dino from the garden and he trotted up without his usual enthusiasm. 'What's up? Are you knackered?' Dino wandered up to the back door and sniffed at the step. She unlocked the door and let him in. He walked straight over to his bed and curled up. 'Not hungry then? I'll sort out some food for you in a bit.' The warmth of the kitchen had a soporific effect on her as well. She put her rucksack down and stretched her tired arms.

Just then, Dino jumped up and started growling at the back door.

Jemma walked over and stroked his head. 'What's up, boy?'

He continued growling with his hackles up. As she opened the door he rushed out and started sniffing round by the bins.

'Stop messing about. There's nothing there. Is it a cat or a fox you can smell?' Jemma checked the garden and couldn't see anything strange, but on her way back to the door she spotted some footprints in the soil at the end of the lawn nearest to the house.

She bent down to look closely. 'Who's been traipsing over the garden, Dino? I don't recognise those boots; they're bigger than Dave's.'

Dino jumped and barked towards the end of the garden. 'Who's there?' she shouted.

There was no answer so she called Dino and went back inside. As she locked the door she shivered. *Has somebody been prowling around?*

Chapter 5

D.S. Dave Gill walked into Swanbourne Police HQ with a file full of case notes. The headquarters were a soulless concrete monstrosity that felt dated, even though they were only fifteen years old. No attempt had been made to brighten the grubby, magnolia-painted public areas, other than a few faded posters advising people to watch their speed and not lock dogs inside hot cars. The reception desk was covered with boxes waiting to go to storage.

The desk sergeant looked up. 'Afternoon Dave, I've been waiting for you.'

'Hello, sarge. What's happening?'

'One of the constables came back from an incident on the beach involving your lady friend.'

'Who, Jemma?'

'Yes, it seems she came a bit of a cropper in a landslide down on Lulcombe Beach.'

Dave dropped his files on the counter. 'What? Oh, no. Is she OK?'

'Yes, I think she's fine. Almost drowned and lost her dog for a while, but seems OK.'

'Is she in hospital?' Dave asked.

'No, the ambulance was stood down.'

Dave frowned. 'Why didn't anyone call me?'

'Check your phone.'

Dave pulled his mobile out and saw several missed calls.

'Ah, I put it on silent when I was talking to a witness. Must have forgotten to unmute it.'

The sergeant grinned. 'Modern technology, huh!'

'Yeah. Do you know any more?' Dave asked.

'The PC said the drama was over by the time he got there. Sounds like Jemma and a young lad had to be rescued. A landslip on the beach cut them off with the tide coming in. They had a missing dog as well but he turned up.'

'Bet that's her nephew, Freddie and her dog, Dino.' Dave tutted. 'Trust Jemma to be in the wars. I'm always reminding her to look after herself but she never listens.'

'You two serious?'

'Yep, pretty serious.' Dave unmuted his phone and tried to ring Jemma. 'Turned off. I'll try again in a bit. Cheers, sarge.'

'See you, Dave, I hope she's OK.'

'So do I.'

Dave walked through to his office. *I'll try Jemma again in a minute.* He'd been going out with her for two years and was on the verge of moving into her place. However, she was fiercely independent and didn't like any fuss. There were times when he just wanted to look after her. That never ended well.

***

The heat from the Aga was very welcome as Jemma sat in her kitchen. Her limbs ached and she felt exhausted after the long day on the beach. A short nap would be welcome but as it was six o'clock, she knew that if she slept now then she wouldn't fancy going out later.

A pair of eyes were burning into her back and, when she turned around, Dino was standing by his empty bowl watching her hopefully.

'Sorry, Dino. Hungry now? I think you deserve something tasty so I'll fetch you a bone from the butchers tomorrow. You'll have to make do with a pouch tonight though.' She poured him some food out, which he wolfed down. 'Slowly, you'll be sick!'

Leaving Dino trying to lick the pattern off his bowl, she switched on her phone that had been turned off for hours, and which revealed messages from her daughter Ellie, her sister Sue and Dave. As she went to press redial, the mobile rang. It was Ellie.

'Hello, Els, how you doing?'

An almost hysterical voice answered. 'What do you mean "how ya doing?" You nearly drowned! I've been worried sick, Mum, ringing and getting no reply!'

'I'm fine. Nothing to worry about. Who said I nearly drowned?'

'Dave. A colleague of his at the station told him about your near-miss with a collapsing cliff and getting cut off by the tide.'

'He had no right to go telling everybody, especially Dave. Now he'll be fussing over me.'

'The policeman didn't know you were Dave's girlfriend, but his sergeant knew who you were. Have you called him yet? He's been trying to reach you.'

'No, you rang first. I'll ring him in a minute.'

'Is Dino alright? Dave told me he disappeared in the landslide.'

'He's fine. Bit of a panic for a few minutes, but he's here next to me, troughing his food.'

'You sure you're OK?'

Jemma sighed. 'Yeah, I'm great. Just a bit tired after a long day.'

'What'd you find?'

In the tension of the cliff collapse and rescue, Jemma had almost forgotten the day's fantastic find. 'A massive plesiosaur. Really well preserved.'

'Worth a lot?'

'Is that all everyone thinks about? It might be worth a bit but I won't be selling her. She's going on display in the museum.'

Ellie laughed. 'Oh, well, bang goes my new car. You could've rung me earlier. Auntie Sue told me Dino found a giant fossil.'

'Sorry Els, I was in such a state of shock when Dino spotted it. We were racing against time to get all the bones out and it was a college day today so I didn't bother you.'

'I'd have been happy to help.'

'I didn't want you to miss anything important.'

Ellie raised her voice. 'Auntie Sue said Billy had been down all day and Freddie went down after school. Yours truly left out again! A good mum would think of her daughter first.'

'You obviously don't think of me as a good mum. I'm sorry, I'll make it up to you!'

'Bloody typical. You think more of your nephews than you do of me.' The call finished abruptly as Jemma was about to say, 'Love you.'

'Teenage girls!' Jemma shouted at her phone. She rang Dave who answered immediately.

'Jem, are you OK?'

'Yes, I'm fine.'

'Were you on the beach when the cliff collapsed?'

'Yes, but I'm good, just a few scratches and a bit muddy.'

'I've been really worried since I heard about what had happened. I always thought you were scared of cliffs.'

Jemma paused. 'I am but…'

'You sure you're OK?

'Yes, honestly. I didn't go near the cliffs.'

'I believe you. You still alright to go for a meal tonight? You can tell me the full story. Table's booked at the Anchor,' he said.

'Yes, I don't want a late night though, I'm totally whacked.'

'OK, Jem. Pick you up around half seven.'

'See you later.'

Jemma rang off and checked her other texts. Her sister, Sue, had sent one, hoping she was uninjured after her 'escapade', and could they talk.

As she ached so much, she ignored the message and put her phone on charge. Dino finished cleaning his bowl and curled up in his bed, the excitement of the day having been too much for him.

She grabbed a bottle of wine, went upstairs and ran a bath. The ancient claw-footed enamel bath occupied most of her small bathroom. She added some bath salts for her aches and poured herself a glass of wine. Every muscle complained as she collapsed into the suds, drank the wine and closed her eyes.

Sometime later she awoke spluttering and coughing having swallowed a mouthful of water.

Bloody hell, I've almost drowned twice in one day. The bath had gone cold and the bubbles dissolved. *What was that noise?* The doorbell rang again.

Climbing out, she wrapped herself in a towel and with another small one around her head, she went downstairs to open up. On the doorstep, Dave stood holding some flowers.

'Evening, they're lovely. Thanks,' Jemma said as she took the flowers. 'It's about time you had your own key though, I was just enjoying a bath. I'll find you a spare one from the drawer.'

He came in and hugged her. 'My own key. Wow. That's a big move.'

He grinned and snatched at the towel. After it fell to the floor, he pulled Jemma in for a long kiss.

'We don't have to go out.' A glint appeared in his eye. 'Shall we eat later, or I could cancel the table?'

'In your dreams!' Jemma laughed. 'I'm really knackered. My head would hit the pillow and I'd fall asleep straight away. Let's leave it until the morning?'

'Cool.'

Dino wandered in to see what was happening.

Dave bent down and scratched his ear. 'So you're the fossil finding star, Dino.'

'He did find the first bit of the skull. Where did you hear that?' Jemma asked.

'Ellie rang me after she spoke to you.'

She grinned. 'The jungle telegraph works well around here.'

'It's only because people care about you. Sometimes you're so obsessed with your fossils, you forget to tell them what's going on.'

'But I love the excitement!'

'I know. Like what I do in a way.'

'What?'

'I dig and delve to solve a case. You dig and delve to find your fossils.'

She smiled. 'So I'm not a palaeontologist, I'm a rock detective.'

'That could be the title of your new TV show when you're famous; *The Rock Detective*.'

'Like the sound of that. Anyway, I can't stand here naked chatting all night.'

Dave perched on the table. 'I'm not complaining.'

'I better get dressed.' She picked up the towel and went back upstairs to her bedroom, every step an effort for her exhausted legs.

Dave followed her up the stairs admiring the view with a smile on his face.

After fishing out some of her best underwear, she sat on the chair by the dresser. 'Chuck me the blue dress off the wardrobe, will you please?'

'Wow, Jemma in a dress, I'm highly honoured!'

'Keep quiet, or I'll go in my digging trousers.'

Dave grinned and threw it over.

She slipped into her underwear, scarcely able to lift her feet off the ground. 'I'm in Ellie's bad books for not asking her to help with the dig.'

'I didn't think she had much of an interest in fossils,' he said.

'Nor me. Whenever she came along in the last few years she complained about the dirt and broken nails.'

He shrugged. 'Oh well. Never can do right with teenagers.'

'Too true.' After she'd dressed and put on some makeup, she checked herself in the mirror. 'That'll have to do.'

Dave smiled. 'Looking good to me.'

'I'm surprised after what I've been through today.'

'It sounds pretty eventful.'

'It's been incredible. I've got a good feeling about this find, I reckon it's gonna lead to some great things.

Chapter 6

Down in The Anchor, the evening trade kicked off with the usual mix of locals relaxing after a hard day's work as well as tourists relaxing after a hard day's holiday making.

In one corner some fishermen complained about the previous night's storm that kept their boats in the harbour.

A small group of ramblers discussed the highlights of their walk and had a drink after finishing another stage of the South West Coast Path. No wild camping or huge rucksacks for them, just fifteen miles to the next B&B, with their luggage sent on in a van each day.

The 'Beach Team' was getting rowdier as the drinks kept flowing. The story of the great rescue was being embellished with every re-telling, more so now that some girls were sitting at a table next to the lads.

Billy was talking to Kerry, an attractive blonde girl he knew from school, and she was listening attentively to every word. 'So, Jemma and Freddie were up to their waists in the sea. Luckily, I'd fetched a rope from the van before I ran back along the beach.'

Kerry leant closer. 'So, you ran towards the landslip?'

He put his hand on her arm. 'I only did what I had to do.'

'Oh, how brave.' Kerry didn't move his hand and

continued listening.

'I saw they'd be underwater and drowning in a few moments, so I used a rope to rescue Freddie. It was pretty risky but I managed it.'

'You must be so strong.' Kerry squeezed his bicep, which he was already flexing.

'All those arm sessions at the gym.'

'Go on, what happened next?' She drained her glass and put it down next to Billy.

'What you drinking?'

'Vodka, please, but finish your story first.'

'Then I rescued Jemma. That was more dangerous but I soon pulled her over.'

Ryan leant over and butted in. 'He needed the rest of us to help pull her over because he's such a weed.'

Billy thumped his shoulder playfully. 'Push off. Stick with your own conversation.'

Kerry ignored Ryan. 'Go on.'

He continued, 'Well, a few of the others helped drag Jemma over, but I'd have found a way on my own if needed.'

'Wow. A real-life hero!' She rattled the glass. 'With tonic please, no ice.'

Billy took the glass and approached the bar, followed by a barrage of winks and snide comments.

'You're in there, mate.'

'Oooh, feel my muscles!'

As Billy waited to be served he could see Gareth from the cafe sitting on his own, his worn suit jacket with leather elbow patches making him look like a nineteen-seventies maths teacher on his day off. He stood and approached Billy.

'What did you find on the beach today?'

Billy tried to get the barmaid's attention. 'Don't know.'

He leant closer to Billy. 'But you must know what Jemma found.'

Billy stepped away, desperate to be served and escape the questions. 'Jemma asked us to carry some rocks along the beach, she didn't tell us what they were.'

Gareth downed his drink and slammed the empty glass on the bar. 'Look, I need to know what you found. It's important.'

Billy looked at him. 'Why? Is somebody paying you to tell them what fossil hunters have found on the beach or something?'

Gareth glanced down at his shoes. 'A man has to make a living, you know.'

'Well you're not learning anything from me,' Billy said.

Gareth huffed and grabbed his coat. 'I'll have to ask her myself.'

Billy watched him go. 'Thanks for the drinks.'

Gareth ignored him and left.

***

Dave parked his car in the Anchor car park, and wandered towards the pub with Jemma. The lights of Lulcombe were dimmed by the mist rolling in from the sea. Jemma shivered as they went in.

'Getting busy in here,' Dave remarked.

Jemma smiled and pointed across the bar. 'It is, but I can still hear the lads over there.'

They walked through the crowded room and went over to the lad's table. A cheer went up.

'Our famous fossil hunter, Jurassic Jemma!' Ryan said.

'Evening, you lot,' Jemma replied. 'Still got some energy left for a drink or two?'

Laughs all round. 'Always!'

Jemma handed Ryan a twenty-pound note. 'There you are. Where's Billy?'

'Thanks.' Ryan pointed to a table, where Billy was sitting with his arm around Kerry's shoulders. 'He's there.'

Jemma wandered over to the table. 'Hello, Billy. Who's your friend?'

'Hi, Jem, this is Kerry. Kerry, this is my aunt, Jemma Thorne.'

'Oh, you're the one whose life Billy saved this afternoon,' she said.

Jemma glanced at Billy who winked at her. She turned back to Kerry. 'Oh, yes. He certainly helped me out of a tight spot when the tide came in.'

'Isn't he brave?' Kerry took no prompting to squeeze Billy's bicep again.

'Yes, he's a strong lad.' Jemma smiled at the adoration in Kerry's eyes. 'Do you live locally?'

'Yes. I live in Lulcombe. I work at the Cliff Hotel as a maid.'

Dave checked his watch. 'Come on, Jem, we'd better go up.'

Jemma waved at the group. 'Bye, lads, and thanks for all you did today.'

He took her hand, and they went up the stairs to the first floor.

The spacious restaurant was half-full as they took their seats. Voices floated up from the downstairs bar but it was a peaceful room. After ordering drinks, a waitress in the standard uniform of black skirt and white blouse gave them menus.

Jemma studied hers intently, not realising how hungry

she was and she almost slobbered as she examined the list of dishes. 'I think a nice rump is calling me.'

Dave grinned. 'Happened to me earlier.'

'Cheeky!'

'Yep. Definitely was.'

'What are you having?'

He thought for a bit longer. 'Mmm, reckon the steak and ale pie sounds yummy.'

'No starter?'

'No, I might manage a pudding though.'

'OK.'

Their drinks arrived and they ordered the food. After the waitress left, they picked up their glasses and clinked them together.

Jemma put down her glass. 'I had a shock on the beach.'

'What, finding a giant fossil and almost drowning?'

'No. An old flame turned up.'

'Not crazy Phil?' he said.

'No. Not him, Brad Jones, or Indiana as they used to call him.'

'Isn't he the guy who went to America and broke your heart?'

She paused. 'He didn't break my heart; he went home and wanted me to go with him.'

'Didn't you fancy it?'

'No, there were too many discoveries to be made in Dorset. So much still to find. Look at what we dug out today!'

Dave sipped his drink. 'What's he doing back in England?'

'He's after some quality specimens.'

'Thought there'd be plenty in America.'

'He's also in trouble with the Feds over a fossil,' she said.

'Wow,' Dave said. 'He doesn't mess about, does he?

They're serious folks.'

'Sounds like they certainly scared him off.'

'Has he been back since you both finished uni?'

'He came over once after I married Liam.' She paused for a moment. 'When Liam found out that Brad was in the country he had a word with him and persuaded him to go home to America. Liam would never tell me what he said, but it did the trick. I haven't seen Brad for nineteen years, and then he showed up today!'

Dave rubbed his chin. 'If he causes you any problems, I can always get my mate in Special Branch to check him out. Quite fancy arresting an American.'

'Forget him, bet I won't see him again. He went off arm in arm with Sally, so she's probably got her claws into him by now.'

'Sally from the uni? I thought you hated her.'

Jemma shrugged. 'I do a bit.'

'What was she doing there?'

'Vincent asked if I wanted anybody else to help. I never dreamt he'd ask her.'

'What's the problem between you and Sally?' he asked.

'Nothing much. It goes back to when the job came up for the head of geology and palaeontology. I got it but Sally had applied as well and thought the job should be hers.'

'But she still works there?'

'Yes. She took a part-time lecturer's job, so technically I'm her boss.'

Dave sipped his drink. 'Is she OK with that?'

'Outwardly yes, but she continually makes snide comments. She says that she doesn't know how I can do my job properly with everything going on.'

'She's got a point, Jem.'

'Don't you start.'

'Is she from Dorset?'

'No, she's Irish, with a hot temper to match her red hair,' she said.

'Troublemaker then?'

'I hope not, I just don't trust her. She's threatened to go blabbing to the management about the drama on the beach.'

Dave frowned. 'She wouldn't do that, surely.'

'Oh, I don't know.'

The food arrived and the conversation halted while they ate. Jemma was ravenous as she'd had no breakfast and only a bag of chips while on the beach. Dave always seemed to be hungry and ate everything put in front of him.

After they finished the main course Jemma seemed to zone out and her eyes became distant.

He touched her hand. 'Penny for them?'

She jumped. 'Sorry. Gorming out a bit.'

'Dreaming about Indiana Jones?'

'No, I was thinking about how lucky I am to have you.'

He narrowed his eyes. 'What are you after?'

'You're the detective, you work it out,' she rubbed her foot against his leg under the table.

'I thought you were tired.'

Jemma smiled. 'I am, but not too tired for a nightcap and an early night.'

'No dessert?'

'No, I'd explode. How about we go straight home for a brandy and....bed.'

Dave wiped his mouth on his serviette. 'Sounds yummy.'

He paid the bill and they walked back to his car before driving to Jemma's. When they arrived at her cottage, they watched as Dino rushed around the garden, sniffing at the bushes in the darkness.

Jemma placed her arms around Dave. 'Dino was barking like mad earlier and there were some footprints in the mud by the bins.'

He took out his phone and turned on the flashlight. 'Whereabouts?'

She pointed. 'Over there.'

He checked out the footprints and took a photo. 'Could they be the dustmen?'

'I don't think so,' she said. 'They came yesterday to empty the black bin but left it at the kerb on the front.' She shouted, 'Dino.' The dog came bounding in, she locked up and then stood with Dave in the kitchen.

He gave her a hug and a kiss. 'Any lectures tomorrow?'

'No, none 'til Monday, so we can have a lie-in. Are you off tomorrow?'

'Yep, I'm ready for a day off.'

He poured two brandies, handing one to Jemma who took his hand and led him up the staircase.

***

Across Lulcombe in the Cliff Hotel, Brad Jones lay in a sumptuous king-sized double bed with a glass of wine and a contented expression on his face. The room was luxurious with large french doors opening out to a balcony with a sea view. The spacious hot tub had been put to good use and was very welcome after having spent a few hours in the rain.

'I know I asked for a hotel recommendation,' a smile creased his face, 'but I wasn't expecting full service.'

Sally O'Keefe reached over for her glass of wine and took a long drink before lying back down next to Brad. 'I'm only doing my bit for Anglo-American relations. I like this place but I bet the room cost a fortune.'

He ran the back of his hand gently over her breasts. 'Worth every cent, especially with you to share it. I suppose that's one benefit of having wealthy folks. I can afford the best of everything.'

She took another sip of champagne. 'Lucky you. I could certainly get used to this lifestyle.' He put his hands behind his head. 'Did you see the plesiosaur that Jemma found?'

Sally put down her glass. 'What? Oh, I only saw bits of it. I was given the dignified job of removing the tail section. Thanks a million, Jemma Thorne.'

'How did the landslide happen?' he said. 'Was Jemma digging in the cliffs?'

'Oh, no. Mrs Thorne would never do anything like that.'

'Is she a stickler for the rules these days?'

'No. She's petrified of cliffs,' she said. 'Anyway, enough talk of Jemma, back to us and what we're going to do next.'

She placed her glass on the side table and turned to face him. 'Hope you're not too jet-lagged. I fancy some more entente cordiale.'

'My God, woman, you're insatiable.' He smiled as she rolled over and straddled him, kissing his chest and moving down towards his stomach.

***

The smell of the sea filled her nostrils as Jemma knelt on the ground and dug with her small trowel. The grass was soft and easy to kneel on. Water seeped into the knees of her trousers, but she ignored the dampness as she concentrated on her find. She'd spotted the small piece of fossilised jawbone earlier and had raced home to get her digging equipment. It was a shame that Alice and Phil had also come along because they could be so annoying when she wanted to concentrate. She was the studious one and they just wanted to play and mess about.

At the highest point of the coastal footpath her school friend, Phil, sat on a bench, fascinated by the fishing boats out at sea. Her sister, Alice, was picking flowers further along the meadow, oblivious to the fact that she was very near to the top of the towering cliffs. She edged closer and closer to the edge, reaching for the flowers that grew over the lip.

'Alice…'

Chapter 7

The next morning the sun shone in a clear blue sky with a clarity you only seem to find on the coast. It was much calmer. The only signs of the previous day's storm were the landslips on the beach and the shingle piled up on the car park.

***

In the Cliff Hotel, Brad and Sally were showering. He passed her the luxurious soap. 'Glad I booked two nights or they'd be kicking me out soon.'

She soaped herself under the power spray. 'I've got nothing planned today so we can either just stay in the room or I'll take you round the sights of West Dorset.'

Brad came out of the shower dripping onto the plush rug and reached for the towel. 'Oh, I know this area pretty well. Two summers here fossil hunting, but that was over twenty years ago when I dated Jemma.'

Sally glared at him. 'You and Jemma went out?'

'Yeah, way back. We were kids at university. I tried to get her to come back to the States with me when the course finished. I guess she loved Dorset too much.'

The shower stopped and Sally frowned as she peered round the door. 'I didn't know that you two had a history.'

'It was a long time ago. I tried to come back for her a few years later, but she was married and her thug of a husband threatened me. Yesterday was the first time I'd seen her in years.'

She stepped out of the shower and wrapped a towel around her hair. 'Oh well, all old history then.' She stood naked as she towelled herself off. 'Anyway back to us and now, what do you fancy doing today? Nothing?'

Brad could tell she spent time at the gym keeping herself trim and he certainly appreciated her efforts. He sat on the bed, holding his towel, watching her. 'Gonna visit some local collectors and discuss the museum with Jemma.'

Sally's face darkened. 'Jemma?'

'Yes. She's head of the trustees. I want to help her prepare the find. I'm desperate to see it.'

She threw down her towel. 'OK, I can come with you today. After that, we can grab dinner somewhere posh before coming back to ruin some more bedsheets.'

'Now, Sally...'

'Yes?'

'Last night was fantastic, but...' Brad decided what to say next. 'That was all. I'm not looking for anything heavy. I'll be going back to the States soon and don't want any tearful goodbyes. I prefer to negotiate on my own and I'm sure Jemma won't be happy if I turn up with you.'

Sally scowled at him. 'You're after bloody Jemma again, aren't you?'

Brad shrugged. 'No, my interest is purely professional. I had an awesome evening, but need some space today.'

'Some space, some space!' Sally's voice rose higher. 'You

arrogant Yank.'

'Perhaps you'd better leave.'

'Right, I'm off.'

Sally dressed without a word and, wearing the previous day's muddy trousers, picked up her rucksack and left the room, slamming the door behind her.

'Bye, Sally,' Brad said to the closed door. He dropped his towel on his bed and started sorting through his clothes deciding what to wear.

***

The blonde maid watched from the open door of the adjacent room. Sally stood outside Brad's room with clenched fists and shouted. 'Jemma bloody Thorne.' After a moment, she stormed off to the lifts, stabbing at the brass button with her finger as she tried to make it arrive quicker.

Kerry, the maid, watched her attack the call button. *I wonder what Jemma has done to her to make her that mad. It'll be my turn to tell Billy a few stories later.* She picked up the room phone and rang reception.

'Good morning, Cliff Hotel. How may I help?'

'Hello, Kerry here on floor three. Who are the occupants of Room 303, please? I want to knock and check if they need the room cleaned and I prefer to use names.'

The receptionist checked her system. 'That would be a Mr Bradley Jones. Arrived last night with a lady for two nights.'

'Thanks, I'll try the door.'

Kerry pulled out her mobile, went into Notes, added the name, put her phone away and smiled. She knocked on the door of Room 303 and waited.

The door flew open and a naked man threw a coat out at her. He froze as the realisation hit him that he'd made an embarrassing mistake. He went red and glanced around for something to cover himself.

Kerry handed him the coat back, which he used to restore his dignity.

He stammered. 'Sorry, miss, can you please come back later?'

As she tried not to laugh, a thought crossed her mind. *Not in bad shape for an old man.*

She struggled to hold in her laughter, but answered. 'Of course, Mr Jones, I'll come back in a while.'

He slammed the door shut.

She turned and pushed her trolley back down the corridor before starting to giggle. She stepped into an empty room, brought out her phone and rang Billy's number, only added the night before.

'Hi, Kerry.'

'Hello, Billy, you'll never guess what's happened in the hotel this morning.'

He got all the gory details, but without her opinion of Brad.

***

Later that morning Jemma took Dave through her long garden down to her workshop. She had a small patio then a square of lawn that led to a path. On either side were some overgrown vegetable beds and larger bushes. At the end was Jemma's workshop with a separate drive back to the road.

A blackbird sang in the cool sunshine proclaiming its territory. Dino followed them but was soon distracted by lots of smells. As they walked down the path, they had to keep to the side to avoid the wet bushes.

Dave grinned. 'Garden needs some work.'

'You volunteering?'

'I'll have a go if you want. Grub them all out?'

'No, most of them are perennials and bushes for the butterflies and bees. They just need a prune.'

'OK, I'll try on my next day off.'

'I might be able to help, but Plessie's going to take a lot of time from now on.'

Jemma walked up to the workshop door and unlocked two padlocks before inserting the key in the main lock.

Dave smiled. 'Good to see some decent security.'

'Fossils can be worth a lot of money.'

'I bet Plessie's worth a few quid.'

'Yep. I can't ever remember a complete plesiosaur coming onto the market, so I've no idea. She's priceless, really, as she's irreplaceable.'

He stepped inside. 'You're lucky to have this place. If only I could find space to stand somewhere.'

Jemma followed him in. 'It means I can work on the fossils and store them all in here. Stops getting the house all dusty. Just be careful where you step.'

Rocks covered the floor while sacks and various parcels of white plaster filled the shelves. Jemma moved some stuff to make space. 'Not much unwrapped yet as everything is in sacking or plaster field jackets, but you can get some idea of the scale.'

'Wow. It's enormous. You've got some work to do to sort this lot out.'

She knelt and opened a long sack. 'This is the skull. I wrapped this first because the rain stopped me using plaster.' As she unwrapped the sacking, sand dropped off. 'Here, give me a lift please?' They lifted the package onto the workbench. 'Isn't she beautiful,' Jemma said. 'I think the skeleton is female because of the layout of the pelvic bones.'

'Not because she'll take ages to get ready?'

She laughed and punched his arm. 'As if.'

'Is the room at the museum big enough to house her?'

She sighed. 'Not yet, but we're hoping the extension can go ahead now.'

'How are they going to pay for that?'

'A new Lottery Heritage Fund grant. Approved in principle last month. They just wanted more proof that we'd got enough exhibits for the project to be worthwhile.'

Dave looked down. 'This monster should prove that. I bet she'll fill the extension on her own.'

A grin crossed Jemma's face. 'Yes, I can imagine a display running the full length of the back wall, facing the entrance. What a spectacular way to get your first glimpse. A dark corridor opening out into a well-lit viewing area.'

'So, this find will be great for the museum,' he said.

'A complete game-changer. Hopefully, I can now persuade the trustees to reject the offer to sell the site for development.'

'Oh, yeah, you mentioned that a few weeks ago. Serious offer?'

'Yes,' she said. 'Some of them want to cash the site in and move to a new smaller building, but I don't agree.'

'Wouldn't a new building be better, especially with Plessie to house?'

Jemma frowned. 'No, there's a great deal of history wrapped up in our museum. To move to a shed up by the car park wouldn't be the same.'

Dave picked up a piece of bone and peered at it. 'Who are the developers? I'm sure you told me, but I can't remember.'

'Their company is Fletcher Brothers Property Development Limited. Run by two local men, brothers called Reggie and Keith Fletcher. I don't know much about them, but I think they made lots of money in London and decided to come back to Lulcombe for some reason. They built the High Fields Estate up the hill, although I put in an objection to the planning, which was upheld. That meant they couldn't cut down the larger trees.'

Dave grinned. 'I bet you were poplar.'

Jemma groaned. 'That's bad enough to be a dad joke! I went along to the meeting with the council tree officer. I got some serious stares from the Fletchers. We won though and the trees stayed. Now they want to build an enormous hotel, casino and spa resort in town. Wouldn't be right.'

He thought for a moment. 'If they built on the museum site, would the development come right up to the bottom of your garden?'

'Not far off. They sent a letter to me, Chrissie next door and the two other neighbours asking if we wanted to sell up, but we burnt them.'

'What do the local council think?'

Jemma pretended to spit. 'Bloody council! I heard they fell over themselves to help the developers. Offered to contribute part of the car park and let them cut down the woodland between these houses and the beach.'

He made some notes on his pad. 'Tell you what. I'll do a bit of delving into the Fletcher brothers. Just in case they have some skeletons in their closet. Find out who you're dealing with.'

'You won't end up in trouble, will you?'

'No, I'll just say an unnamed source suggested they might be worth investigating.'

'I'm hoping nothing will happen now that Plessie has turned up to save the museum.'

A serious look crossed his face. 'You have to be careful dealing with big property developers. Some of them can be unscrupulous about anybody who gets in their way.'

***

Later that afternoon Dave went home to do some washing. Jemma sorted and labelled a few of the sacks. As she loaded some photos onto her laptop, her mobile rang. She didn't recognise the number but still answered.

'Hello?'

'Hi, Jem, Brad.'

'Brad...Oh. What do you want?'

'How pleasant.'

'Sorry. Lots to do.'

'OK, I'll be quick. Can I ask you a couple of questions?'

'Is that one of them?'

'Touchy this morning, huh?'

'That's your two questions, are we done?'

'Hang on! First, an offer. Would you sell me your plesiosaur?'

'No way.'

'I'll go as high as six figures. That's in pounds not dollars.'

'Still no way.'

'I thought you'd say that. OK then. Second question, can I buy you dinner?'

Jemma retorted. 'No to that as well.'

'Calm down, give me a chance to explain myself. I was thinking of becoming a benefactor to the museum.'

Jemma sat back in her seat and tried to second guess his intentions. 'What are you after?'

'You don't have a very high opinion of me, do you?'

'No.'

Brad persisted. 'If you're a trustee you need to take seriously any offers of help.'

She wiped her sweaty palms on her jeans. 'I'll ask again, what are you after?'

'Nothing. I'm thinking of buying a house in Lulcombe and I'd like to help out at the museum.'

She sighed and conceded. 'I suppose I better let you explain what you're thinking.'

'Lunch tomorrow at the museum, one o'clock?'

'OK. See you then.' Jemma ended the call.

Alone in her workshop, her palms had gone all sweaty, despite the lack of heating. She wiped them on her apron. *Why does that man have such an effect on me, even after all this time?*

Chapter 8

After spending most of the morning marking assignments and planning her next lecture, Jemma wandered to the museum around noon. Lulcombe Museum was a typical Victorian building, a mixture of red brick and Purbeck stone. It stood on its own on a large site at the bottom of the steep hill that ran up from the harbour. An imposing building, it dominated the view from the town out towards the sea.

Outside, two men were taking photographs and making notes on a clipboard. Jemma walked over and, as she got closer, she recognised them as the Fletcher brothers, who were trying to buy the museum site.

'Good afternoon, gentlemen, can I help you? I'm one of the trustees.'

The smaller man looked up from his clipboard, 'Oh, I know who you are Mrs. Thorne. No thank you, we're fine. I'm just collecting some information for a planning application.'

'We're not selling the museum, you know?'

'Oh, I'm sure you will when the price is right. Good day to you.' They walked off towards the town.

As Jemma watched them leave she shivered. There was

something about the Fletcher brothers she didn't like. Very polite, but with disguised threats.

She turned, entered the foyer and looked round. Her mind drifted back to coming here as a young girl to see the fossil displays. It was her favourite place as a youngster and she often pestered her parents to bring her.

I can't let this place get torn down. I've always been so excited every time I come in. My whole life is tied up in the building and exhibits.

She snapped out of her daydreams and walked into reception. There was a hubbub of excitement around the staff as they saw who had come in.

The museum manager, Anna Jenkins, bounced over to Jemma. She was a petite lady, always full of energy and was wearing her hair short in a Peter Pan style cut that made her appear much younger than her thirty-two years.

'Congratulations, Jemma. Sounds like an incredible find!'

'Thanks, Anna. Just in the right place at the right time.'

'Or Dino was.'

'OK, I concede that. He's going to be a famous dog.'

Anna grinned. 'When do you think the plesiosaur will be ready?'

'Oh, it'll be a while.' Jemma thought for a moment. 'Probably three months. We've got to prepare the room and there's a lot to do to extract the bones from the rock and clean them for mounting.'

'Can't wait,' Anna said. 'I bet there'll be massive crowds when it goes on display.'

Jemma smiled. 'At least we're getting the grant now, so we can finish the extension.'

'You wanna cuppa?'

'I'm OK, thanks. I'm meeting someone in the café at one o'clock for some lunch.'

'Anybody interesting?'

Jemma laughed. 'Nosy madam, aren't you?'

'If you don't ask…'

'I'm seeing a potential donor.'

'Fingers crossed with signing them up then,' Anna said. 'See you later.'

'Cheers.'

Jemma pottered around doing a few jobs, but her mind kept wandering. It annoyed her that she was so excited about lunch with Brad. She'd thought she was over him, but hearing his voice on the beach yesterday had brought all the memories flooding back.

They had three happy years together while at university. Then Brad asked her to go with him to America and she just wasn't ready for that. She didn't want that level of commitment and had much more hunting to do in the UK. However, even though she hadn't seen him for a long time, she still had feelings for him.

At a quarter to one, she entered the café, avoiding the quieter tables in their alcoves and sat at a table by the door and the sales counter. Sipping her orange juice, she checked the emails on her phone. When a hand touched her shoulder, she jumped. 'Bloody hell, Brad, don't do that!'

'Sorry, Jem, didn't mean to startle you. Let me start again.' He walked out of the café, immediately turned around and came back in before returning to Jemma's table.

'Well, Mrs Thorne.' He spoke in a formal voice. 'Good day to you.'

'Afternoon, Mr Jones.'

Jemma thought she kept her composure well, but, as Brad held out his hand to shake hers, she thought she felt sparks flying down her arm.

'Good to meet you in more glamorous circumstances than last time,' he said, obviously referring to her being covered in mud on the beach.

As Jemma checked her clothes, she wondered if she'd overdone the glamour a bit. A white blouse over smart jeans should appear purely professional, but it seemed Brad couldn't keep his eyes off her. Perhaps the red lipstick was a mistake. She rarely wore any and didn't know what possessed her to apply it this morning. Luckily, Dave had left before she started getting ready.

She flapped a dismissive hand.

'Oh, these are a just few things I threw on earlier. Anyway,' she handed Brad a laminated menu, 'what are you having?'

He glanced at Jemma and smiled. 'Classy.'

Her heart rate shot up and she blushed. 'Thank you... Oh, you mean the menu!'

'Only in a sarcastic way, but you are classy as well.'

Ignoring his reply, she went back to reading the menu. 'I fancy lasagne.'

'And I'll have egg and chips, one of my favourites. Never tastes the same in the States.'

'To drink?'

He checked out the choices. 'Coke, please. Regular.'

Jemma stood, went to the counter, and ordered the meals and drinks. When she returned to the table, Brad took his wallet out.

'Here, let me pay.'

'Don't worry,' Jemma replied. 'My treat. Now, what are you after?'

'How would you like a sizeable donation towards the costs of housing your new fossil?'

'Oh, that's generous of you. Donations are always welcome. How much?'

'Five thousand dollars.'

'Wow!'

'Also, do you need a volunteer to help?'

They sat at a table with their drinks. 'That would be useful. Anything in particular?' she asked.

'I can help prepare the plesiosaur for display.'

'Bound to be dirty work.'

'I don't mind eating some dust.'

Jemma thought for a moment. *Perhaps I should give him the benefit of the doubt and let him help.* She leant back in her chair. 'I suppose I could use some help in my workshop and also here, to get Plessie ready to display.'

Brad gave her one of his killer smiles. 'It would be like old times. Indiana Jones and Jurassic Jemma working together!'

Jemma suddenly found the menu interesting. 'A lot of water has passed under the bridge since then.'

'Did you ever regret not coming back to the States with me?'

'What? Erm... No. I perhaps wondered occasionally how different my life would be, but no regrets.'

Their meals arrived and they ate them in silence. Brad seemed to gulp his down while Jemma picked at hers, trying not to keep glancing at him while he ate. After they'd finished, Brad drained his Coke and slammed his glass down. 'I hear you're making out with a cop now.'

Jemma's eyes widened. 'Well, sort of. Dave's a DS in the local force.'

'DS?'

'A Detective Sergeant. He works on the more important crimes.'

'Are you happy?'

'Yes,' Jemma snapped. 'Look. If we're going to work together, can we just keep everything on a strictly professional basis?'

He held his hands up. 'Fine by me. When can I start?'

'I've got a few days lecturing and catching up with my students. How about Monday of next week?'

'Great, thanks, Jem.'

'OK then, can you come to my workshop at nine o'clock? It's on...'

'I know where it is. A little bird told me where you live, so I drove past earlier.'

'Right.'

'How about a quick guided tour of the museum? I bet it's changed a lot in the last twenty years.'

Jemma shrugged. 'OK. I suppose. Follow me.' She carried their plates and glasses to the trolley and walked out, Brad followed her into reception.

As she swung her arm around, she pointed at the dark wooden display cases on the polished floor. 'Everything downstairs features the natural world.' They walked up the spiral stairs and Jemma could feel herself getting warm.

Brad smiled. 'I love this staircase. It reminds me of an unravelled ammonite.'

Jemma glanced back over her shoulder and found that Brad was staring at her rear. He quickly looked away to the paintings on the wall. 'I think that was the intention when it was built,' she said. They reached the top floor and Jemma stopped. 'Upstairs we have everything to do with man and his exploits over the years.'

Brad sniffed. 'It just smells of age. Objects from long ago. Nothing much has changed in twenty years. I love it.'

After being in close proximity to Brad for some time, Jemma felt that her skin was getting redder and redder. *I hope he doesn't think I'm blushing. Time to cut the tour short.* She turned to go back downstairs. 'It's got to be a quick tour today as I've got a lot to do this afternoon. See you on Monday morning.'

'Wow, that was quick. You don't get much for five thousand dollars these days.'

Jemma frowned at him. 'I'm sorry, but I only put aside an hour for a quick lunch.'

'OK. See ya Monday.'

She watched as he left by the main door.

***

Jemma was sitting at her kitchen table when her daughter, Ellie, came in. She wore a duffle coat with jeans, boots and a woolly jumper. Like her mother Ellie was tall but, unlike Jemma, she had long red hair.

They hugged. 'Hi, Mum, you OK?'

'Yes, I'm great, thanks. Still so excited about finding Plessie.'

'You and your bloody fossils. They're always the first thing you think about, although I admit this latest one is pretty cool.'

Jemma smiled. 'It certainly is. How's college going?'

Ellie dropped her bag to the floor. 'I'm enjoying it. I'm so glad I chose nursing.'

Jemma looked at her. 'I thought you'd like it. You were always looking after injured things when you were little. Maybe the course is bringing it all back to the surface.'

'Yeah, maybe. Any chance of dumping some washing?'

'Course you can. Is Becky too busy at school to use a washing machine?'

Her daughter mock punched her on the arm. 'Mum, you're awful! She's twenty-five and a beautician. She's not still at school.'

'I'm only kidding.' Jemma grinned. 'Getting on OK at your dad's?'

'Yes, I'm fine. I'm in my room working most of the time. That way, I stay away from the lovebirds.'

Jemma was shocked when Liam left her for a younger woman and, initially, was very bitter. However, she had gradually come to accept that her marriage to Liam was effectively over before he met Becky. Now she just loved taking any opportunity to poke fun at her ex and his young girlfriend.

She grinned. 'Is your dad still making a fool of himself with a woman twenty years younger than him?'

'A bit, but they're happy, which is more than you and Dad were for the last few years before you split.'

Jemma made cats' claws with her hands. 'Ouch!'

Ellie frowned. 'Well, you were always arguing.'

'I'm sorry, he couldn't cope with my lifestyle, and then he met Lolita.'

'Mum!'

'OK, I'll stop!'

As Ellie knelt and sorted her washing, Jemma thought her holdall must be a Tardis. The amount that came out of such a small bag defied the laws of physics.

She watched her daughter and wondered where it all went wrong with Liam. They seemed to drift further and further apart with their own interests and poor Ellie was caught in the middle.

At least I'm happy now with Dave. I just hope Brad doesn't try anything to rock the boat.

***

Later that day, Jemma's phone rang. She didn't recognise the number but answered anyway.

'Hello, Jemma Thorne.'

'Hi, Jemma, I'm Jane Goodwin from the *Sunday Browser Magazine*. We're planning a series of articles about women in science, and we saw some news pieces about you finding a monster dinosaur on a Dorset beach.'

'A plesiosaur, but carry on.'

'We want to do a feature on you and your work. We'll offer a fee to you or a donation to the museum you run.'

'I'm only one of the trustees. I help out a bit, but I don't run it.'

'Oh, we can sort out the details on the day, but are you happy to take part?'

'Love to, might encourage more girls to do science in general and geology in particular. A donation for the museum would be fine, thanks.'

'When are you free? How about Thursday or Friday, or any day next week?'

Jemma flicked through her tatty diary. 'Next Tuesday? I haven't got any university work that day, and you might be able to get a sneak preview and photo of Plessie's skull.'

'Oh, can't we photograph you with the whole fossil?'

'Sorry, she's not ready yet. There isn't enough room in my workshop to lay it all out, and the new display area at the museum isn't finished.'

'OK, just the skull will do. Shall we meet at your home?'

'Yes, fine.'

'What's your address?'

Jemma hesitated, nervous about giving out personal details after her recent concerns.

'No, tell you what,' she said. 'Let's use the training room at the museum and I'll ask someone to help me bring the skull in. That way, you can take a photo of it.'

'Next Tuesday it is. Is ten o'clock OK?'

'Fine, see you then. Bye, Jane.'

'Bye, Jemma.'

Jemma put down her phone. *That's interesting. This could lead to all sorts of things.*

Chapter 9

Jemma spent the weekend with Dave and Ellie. They took Dino for some long walks and Ellie helped Jemma to organise her photos and field notes. However much she tried to concentrate on what she was doing though, her mind kept drifting back to Brad.

Ellie's voice broke into her daydream. 'Anybody in there, Mum.'

'What? Oh. Sorry, Els, I'm a bit tired.'

'Well just chill or have a bath or something.'

'That's a good idea. Will do.'

Dave went a bit quiet when Jemma told him Brad intended to help, but he soon seemed to forget about it, or so she hoped.

The highlight of the weekend turned out to be a meal at her sister's. Jemma and Sue had always been close, especially since their sister Alice died in a tragic accident thirty years before. Her nephews, Billy and Freddie, loved their hands-on auntie, and she'd always encouraged them to go with her when she went hunting fossils.

Billy provided some laughs as he retold the story of his new girlfriend, and what she'd observed at the Cliff Hotel.

When she stopped laughing, Jemma recapped. 'So

basically, Sally stormed off, blamed me for something and Brad flashed his privates at a cleaner?'

Ellie blushed. 'Mum!'

'Spot on,' Billy said.

Dave found it hilarious as well. 'Lucky we haven't seen a headline in the Lulcombe News, "American visitor flashes maid in posh hotel". I know, I could arrest him for indecent exposure.'

Jemma couldn't stop giggling. 'I bet he'd claim diplomatic immunity. We'd better keep an eye out for an enraged Sally as well, no telling what she might do to me!'

'And Brad,' Dave added.

'Yes,' Jemma said. 'You never know!'

She found herself thinking about Brad and Sally sleeping together and suddenly felt very warm. She hoped that Dave didn't notice her blushing and went to the toilet to splash her face with cold water.

After they returned home, they opened a bottle of wine, sat cuddling on the sofa and watched a film on TV. As they relaxed, Dave held Jemma's calloused hands.

'These are a right mess.'

'Yeah, I don't often work with gloves on. You lose some of the texture of the rock.'

'How about I treat you to a manicure?'

'Are you serious, a manicure? Me? That would be a waste of time. I'd only break my nails or bite them within a day. I know we've been going out for two years, but there are times when I think you don't really know me at all.'

He grinned. 'Every day's a school day.' He pretended to write on his notepad. 'No manicures for Jemma.'

As they snuggled, he turned to her. 'I meant to say, I did a bit of delving into the Fletcher brothers.'

Jemma jumped. 'I was nodding off! What did you find out?'

'Well, they might be a bit shady. Their father used to own the old quarry on Axminster Road. That shut down and they moved away. One of the DCs thought the names rang a bell from when he worked in London. He checked with one of his old colleagues. There were rumours some property developers called Fletcher diversified into different areas, namely drugs and prostitution. However, they left in a hurry when one of the big players thought they were overstepping the mark on his manor.'

'Is it the same two brothers?'

'He didn't know. They were only rumours and the brothers disappeared.'

'Probably different guys, it's a common name. Always need lots of arrows.'

'What? Oh yes, fletchers. Anyway, I'll keep my ears open, but their Lulcombe operation seems kosher.'

Jemma shrugged. 'Oh well, thanks for trying.'

***

Monday morning came and Jemma and Dave sat together eating breakfast.

Dave sipped his tea. 'All geared up for a last crusade with Indiana Jones?'

Jemma felt herself go slightly red. 'Yes, of course. It'll be good to get some free help from somebody who knows what they're doing.'

'I bet he knows full well what he's doing.'

Jemma looked across at him. 'What do you mean by that?'

Dave grinned. 'Nothing, I'm only winding you up.'

Jemma put down her spoon. 'Well don't. Seriously though, I'm so glad you're OK with me working with Brad.'

Dave stood and kissed her on the head. 'Have I got any option? He better keep his hands to himself in the confined space of the workshop or he'll have me to contend with. I trust you to keep him at a safe distance.'

He grabbed his coat and keys and opened the back door. 'See you tonight.'

'See you later.'

At nine o'clock Brad walked into the workshop.

She checked the clock. 'Punctual. Good start.'

He grinned. 'Thanks, boss.'

'Can you grab an air chisel and remove some of the excess stone from the skull, please?'

He gave a quick blast on the chisel. 'Will do.'

It was useful to have another experienced fossil preparer and together they made steady progress. Brad concentrated on the work, so she relaxed. There were no embarrassing references to the past and she resisted the temptation to mention Brad's exhibitionism at the hotel.

After a while, they took a break and Jemma poured them both a glass of cold water from the small fridge in the corner. 'Here, have a swig to wash the dirt away?' she said.

'Rock dust never tasted so good.'

'Where are you staying now, still at the hotel?'

'No. I've rented a cottage in Lulcombe,' he said. 'I hope to buy one somewhere.'

'Good luck sorting something out. Finding a place around here can be a nightmare.'

Brad and Jemma stood in her workshop looking at the skeleton, which had been partially cleaned and arranged on the floor in various sections.

She beamed. 'I reckon she'll be well over sixteen metres when she's finished.'

'You've got an impressive baby, Mrs Thorne.'

'Isn't she? The largest ever found in the UK.'

He put his hand on her shoulder. 'The whole display wall will be magnificent when she's mounted.'

Jemma took a deep breath and leant away so his hand dropped off. 'I can't wait.'

He took a step back. 'How are things going at the museum?'

'Pretty good,' she replied. 'The building work on the extension is flying along and the application's been approved.'

'Have they sent the grant money over?'

'Yes. Straight to the bank after I sent some pictures of Plessie.'

'Be great to see it finished.'

Jemma went over to the bench. 'Come on, let's crack on. Lots of polishing still to do.'

Brad put on his gloves. 'Yep.' They went back to work and after a couple of hours he paused and put down his chisel. 'I had a flashback when we were on the beach after you found Plessie.'

Jemma glanced over. 'What?'

'I remembered the hot summer night when we went skinny-dipping and then crept up into the sand dunes.'

She smiled, 'I thought you were being ultra-professional. They were good times though. I remember the sand getting everywhere!'

Brad laughed. 'And that was one picnic blanket that we never used again. Happy times, hey!'

Jemma looked into his eyes. 'Happy times, but oh so long ago. We've all moved on from those days.'

He looked serious for a moment. 'Have we?'

She gulped. 'Yes, we have,' and turned back to the piece of stone she was cleaning.

Brad resumed his work with the air chisel.

***

Later that evening Jemma and Dave sat in her kitchen after they'd finished their dinner.

'I meant to say. It's probably stupid, but I keep imagining someone's been watching me.'

'What?' Dave asked. 'Have you seen somebody?'

'No. It's weird. It was just a feeling there was someone over in the woods or the field.'

'Why didn't you tell me before?'

She shrugged. 'I thought you'd accuse me of being paranoid.'

'I wondered why you started shutting the curtains upstairs. Do you want me to go over there and check around before I go to work?'

'No, don't bother. I'll keep an eye out and let you know if I actually see anybody.'

***

The watcher lay motionless in the long grass by the trees, controlling his breathing as he'd been taught when he was training.

After focussing the binoculars, he watched as Dave left for work. He was much happier when he knew she was on her own. He smiled as Jemma locked the workshop and returned to the house. Using such powerful lenses, she seemed to be right in front of him.

It was good to be back in her life, even if only from a distance and he was sure she'd love to have him back if she'd just dump the detective.

Suddenly she turned and stared straight at him and he dropped the binoculars in case she caught sight of them. As his heart was racing, he went through his breathing exercises to reduce it. He kept his head down for a few minutes and lifted them again. She'd gone inside so he watched the windows. His heart beat faster again as the light went on in her bedroom, but disappointment washed over him when the curtains closed.

For a while now she'd been closing them whenever she went to her room.

Did she see me? He immediately discounted the idea. Nobody would ever see him when he was concentrating.

Packing away his binoculars, he rolled up his mat and slinked away through the trees. That would have to do for today.

Chapter 10

On Tuesday morning Jemma woke early as she'd asked Brad to help take the skull into the museum for her interview with the Sunday Browser journalist. At nine o'clock she heard his SUV pull up. She went out to meet him and stood by his truck. 'Still doing your bit to pollute the planet driving this gas guzzler, I see.'

'Yeah.' He laughed. 'Although I bet it chucks out fewer toxic fumes than your beat-up old van.'

'OK, I give in.' She wore her field outfit of a khaki shirt, green shorts and heavy walking boots.

After arriving, they carried Plessie's skull into the meeting room, placing it on a table in front of a display board with some of the museum's other exhibits.

'What are you hoping to achieve from the interview?' Brad asked.

'I haven't given it a lot of thought. Mainly publicity for this place, I suppose. Some photos in a national Sunday glossy magazine won't do any harm.'

'It'll give you some exposure as well.'

She frowned. 'I'm not bothered about publicity.'

'OK then. Good luck.'

'Are you staying?'

He grabbed his coat. 'No, I'm going back to the workshop. Lots to do on Plessie.'

Jemma smiled. 'Dedication.'

'Me all over.' He glanced at her as he walked out.

***

Jane Goodwin, the journalist from the magazine, turned up with her photographer at ten. They entered the museum's meeting room and sat round the large oval table. The polished surface was well worn and bore the scars of a long working life. The whole room smelt of old wood, one of the characteristics of the museum that Jemma loved. They took some photographs of Jemma with Plessie's skull before beginning the interview.

Jemma had formed a mental picture of Jane after their telephone chat and expected a smart-looking professional journalist in a business suit. Instead, she rocked a new-age hippie look. Her hair swung around in a ponytail of dreadlocks, and she wore a kaftan-style blouse with colourful baggy trousers and sandals.

Anna brought in a tray of tea, coffee and a jug of water. Jemma sat with Jane who took out her notepad and voice recorder and the interview began.

'Hello, Jemma, or should I call you Jurassic Jemma?'

'Call me what you like as long as we generate some publicity for the museum.'

Jane continued. 'A sort of Indiana Jones in her field.'

'Not really, he's an archaeologist; I'm a palaeontologist, more like a contemporary Mary Anning.'

'I saw a film about her. Didn't she struggle to be taken seriously in Victorian England?'

'True. She discovered, identified and sketched some of the best plesiosaurs and ichthyosaurs ever found. Unfortunately, the gentlemen of the British Geological Society took the credit.'

Jane continued. 'I read a quote that she was the wrong sex, the wrong class and not educated enough for the scientific world at the time.'

'Yes, she was fully self-taught but ignored by the Society.'

'Has it been tough for you to become a top lecturer in a man's world?'

Jemma considered the question. 'Perhaps a bit more difficult than for a male student. However, the dusty walls of academia have long since been breached by the fairer sex.'

Jane grinned. 'Love that quote.'

She turned another page in her notepad. 'How did you first become interested in fossils?'

Jemma sipped her water. 'I used to go out fossil hunting with my grandad. He was quite a collector in his day and many of his finds are in Lulcombe Museum.'

'How old were you when you started?'

'Around six or seven.'

'I read in an old article that your twin sister, Alice, died in a tragic accident on Lulcombe Cliffs.'

Jemma went quiet. 'That was a long time ago.'

'What happened?'

Jemma's voice tightened. 'Sorry, I don't like to talk about that.'

Jane put down her pen and persevered. 'I don't mind going off the record. It'll help me get a picture of the real Jemma.'

Jemma snapped. 'Just leave it or the interview's over.'

Jane held her hands up. 'Sorry. Let's move on. Can you tell me something about your latest find?'

'Down to being in the right place at the right time, after a storm the night before. The waves brought down a section of the cliff where we found her.'

'Her?'

'Yes, we can tell by the pelvic bones.' Jemma gave Jane some more background information about Plessie and the time flew by.

Jane turned another page. 'Is it true you almost drowned when you were digging Plessie out?'

Jemma frowned. 'No. A load of fuss over nothing. I just needed a bit of a hand to scramble over a slippery rock fall.'

'Are there any more monsters in those cliffs?'

Jemma shrugged and had another drink of tea. 'Could be, nobody knows. I'm taking part in a survey of the clifftop meadow using GPR which might reveal something interesting.'

'What's GPR?'

'Ground Penetrating Radar. The recording is a pilot episode of a new TV show being filmed in conjunction with the archaeology department from Swanbourne University.'

'I hope you find something worthwhile. How much is Plessie worth?'

Jemma put down her cup. 'Hard to say. It's irrelevant, apart from insurance, as she's going on display at the museum for all to enjoy and isn't for sale.'

'You're not tempted to sell and go off fossil hunting, are you?'

'No, I love what I'm doing.'

'The papers said that it was your dog, Dino, who found Plessie. Is that true?'

Jemma smiled. 'Sort of. He found the first bone sticking out of the rockfall, so I went to investigate.'

'And spotted Plessie?'

'Yes.'

'Tell me more about the museum.'

Jemma gave her a potted history of the museum and Jane's notepad soon filled.

'How is it financed?' Jane asked.

'Funding is always difficult as we've never charged an entry fee. I suppose we're a bit vulnerable as we're not a wealthy museum and rely on donations and legacies.'

'I heard the building might be knocked down to build a hotel. Is that true?'

Jemma frowned. 'No, the trustees had an approach to sell the site to some property developers. They wanted us to move to a warehouse up the hill by the upper car park. Hopefully, Plessie's discovery will put a stop to those ideas. This is a traditional museum that has been near the seafront for over one hundred and sixty years and it should stay there.'

Jane persevered. 'But aren't some of your fellow trustees in favour of moving to a new, purpose-built place with modern facilities?'

Jemma narrowed her eyes at Jane. 'I'm not sure where you're getting your information from. I suppose some of them would like to swap to a shed with flashing lights and interactive displays. To me that sounds like Disneyland with fossils.' By now Jemma was starting to tire of the questions.

Jane looked at her notes. 'How much have you been offered for the whole site?'

'Sorry,' Jemma checked her watch, 'that's confidential.'

The journalist shuffled through her notes. 'OK, thanks. Should be plenty for the article. One last question. What is the one thing that you find so fascinating about fossils?'

Jemma stood and stretched. 'Whenever I split open a rock and find a fossil inside, I know that no one else has seen it in two hundred million years.'

'Perfect.' Jane shut her notebook, turned off the recorder and packed them in her bag. 'The piece will be in a week on Sunday.'

Jemma shook her hand. 'Thanks for the interest in Plessie. She'll be a celebrity yet.'

They went out to the car park where a few brave holidaymakers were lacing up their boots ready for a bracing walk. Seagulls waddled around like slightly obese men in grey suits with their hands clasped behind their backs.

Jane's photographer was sitting on the wall eating an ice cream and glanced over sheepishly. 'I'd have bought you one, but you didn't tell me how long you'd be inside and it would've melted.'

'Thanks for nothing.' Jane laughed as she walked to the car.

As he followed, an opportunist seagull swooped down and snatched the whole ice cream from his hand.

'You bugger.' He began running after it until he realised it was a waste of time. He stopped and strolled back over to Jane and Jemma who were in hysterics as he tried to regain some dignity in the face of the unexpected avian assault.

Jemma giggled. 'First rule of the seaside, don't leave any food on display.'

Jane and her photographer, still grumbling, climbed into the car and drove away.

Jemma waved before walking back up the hill towards her cottage.

***

She looked over at Alice. Nobody would guess we're twins. I'm tall and a scruffy tomboy. You're delicate and ethereal.

The sun shimmered. In the summer warmth, small blue butterflies flitted back and forth on the clifftop. Kittiwakes flew around overhead, their mewing cries sounding like a flock of flying cats. The sea was calm. The waves only whispered as they broke on the beach.

Alice was picking handfuls of thrift, a common flower which grew in profusion along the clifftop. Jemma carried on digging and wished her sister would stop bothering her about the 'pretty flowers'.

Suddenly, Alice's panicked cry cut through the blissful serenity. 'Help, Jemma, help!'

Chapter 11

The next morning Dave came round for breakfast after finishing work. He often called in early when he was on a night shift, then went home for a sleep, before coming back later in the day. The smell of bacon filled Jemma's kitchen as they drank their tea.

Jemma sipped her tea. 'I got that feeling again last night that I was being watched.'

'What?' He put his toast down. 'Did you spot anybody outside?'

She shook her head. 'No, I didn't see anybody. It was just a strange sensation that somebody was watching.'

'Whereabouts?'

'After I locked the workshop, I looked over at the woods between the house and the sea. I thought I saw a light in the trees.'

'Will you show me before I go?' Dave asked.

'Yeah, of course.'

After finishing breakfast, they put on their boots and took Dino for a walk across the fields behind her house. Jemma showed Dave where she thought she'd seen a light.

He checked out the spot. 'No sign of anybody, although the grass under those trees has been flattened down a bit.'

'Thanks for checking,' she said.

He shrugged. 'No worries. Could be anything. A footpath runs through here and somebody could have been having a picnic.'

She breathed out. 'Hopefully it was nothing, but I'm getting a bit jumpy.'

***

Jemma's cottage was set back from the road. Like most of the cottages in Lulcombe, it was old and small, built in an age when home was somewhere people ate and slept without much time for leisure. She had a long, thin garden that led down to the fields behind.

When Jemma came in from her workshop, her neighbour Chrissie was fetching in some washing. She came to the fence as Jemma walked up the path. They were the same age and had a similar build, so much so that Dave thought they could be sisters.

Chrissie smiled. 'Are you winning with your monster?'

'Yes, he's doing a lot to help.'

She laughed. 'I meant the fossil!'

'Oh, I thought you meant Brad. Yes, everything's going well. It's such a filthy job using an air chisel to strip the stone away from the skeleton. Even with a mask, you end up eating rock dust all day.'

'Rather you than me. Anyway, who's this Brad fella that you take into your shed every morning?'

'He's an old friend who volunteered to help me clean the bones.'

'I'd clean his bone any day.' Chrissie licked her lips. 'When he took his shirt off to shake the dust out, wow!

95

He's well ripped.'

Jemma laughed. 'You are awful! I'll introduce you one day. He needs a girlfriend.'

'He's not spoken for?'

'Don't think so. He had a brief fling with Sally from the uni, but he upset her.'

'How did he do that?'

'I think she was getting very heavy after a one-night stand.'

Chrissie sighed. 'Is that all he's after then?'

'I've no idea. She was just a bit intense for him.'

'Oh well, might be worth giving him my number if you can be bothered,' Chrissie said.

Jemma smiled. 'OK, I'll pass it on.'

'Tell you what, are you free tonight? Fancy a glass of wine and you can tell me more about Brad?'

Jemma grinned. 'Good idea. I seem to have been busy for so long that we haven't had a chance to chat since you moved in. How long have you lived here?'

'Just over a year.'

'No! That's flown by. I feel awful now that we've not had a drink together.'

'Don't worry. I'm just as bad.'

Jemma checked her watch. 'I need a shower to wash off the day's grime. Dave's working 'til ten, so how about seven o'clock at mine?'

Chrissie picked up her washing basket. 'Perfect. Catch you later. It might be mild enough to try sitting outside on the patio.'

Jemma looked nervously towards the woods. 'Yes, I suppose we could. Might be too cold though.'

Around seven Jemma heard a knock at the back door.

Through the opaque glass she could make out a figure holding up a bottle.

Jemma let her in. 'Well, warm enough outside?'

Chrissie glanced at the sky. 'Yeah, the sky's clear now. Might get cold later, but we can move inside if we need to.'

Jemma opened the wine, filled two glasses, and they sat by her small circular patio table where they could gaze out over the sea reflecting the last light from the sky. The wind had dropped so it still felt mild.

'I never get tired of this view,' said Chrissie.

Jemma smiled. 'Fantastic, isn't it?'

'Cheers,' Chrissie raised her glass, 'to dusty hunks.'

'To dusty hunks, especially if they save me some work.'

Chrissie leant closer. 'Tell me about him.'

Jemma placed her glass on the table. 'Brad's an American guy I met at uni, and we went out for three years.'

'So, he's your ex?'

'I suppose so, but we're colleagues now.' Jemma's mind wandered off. *But would I like him to be more than a colleague? Stop it. Now!*

Chrissie smirked. 'Do you still fancy him?'

Jemma felt herself going red. 'Er, no. That was all a long time ago.'

'You don't sound convinced. I reckon there's still a bit of a flame burning in there somewhere.'

'No way. I must admit that he's still an attractive man, but I'm with Dave now, so I'm not interested.'

They continued talking about boyfriends. Jemma told her about dumping her first boyfriend, Phil, to go out with Brad at university, followed by Liam and Dave. As the wine flowed, they laughed more and more.

'Is that Jemma's timeline of fellas?'

'Yes, full disclosure. What about you? Anybody on the horizon?'

'No, nobody special unless your Yank fancies the girl next door. I met a bloke at seventeen. We married at nineteen, and we split ten years later when I caught him with a girl from the Co-op. I wouldn't mind, but she worked on the meat counter and served me loads of times.'

Jemma giggled, the wine taking effect. 'Sounds like she served him as well.'

Chrissie spluttered on her drink and burst out laughing. 'Too right! I always said I divorced him because he put his dick in a bacon slicer.' She carried on laughing so hard that she almost forgot to take a breath.

'And breathe,' Jemma said. 'You OK?'

'Bloody marvellous.' Chrissie giggled. 'It's been ages since I laughed this much.'

Jemma took another sip of wine. 'Yep, same here.'

Chrissie's eyes narrowed. 'Is Ellie Brad's daughter?'

Jemma jumped. 'What? Oh no, she's Liam's. She was born four years after Brad went home.'

'Oh. It's just that I think she looks like Brad.'

Jemma swallowed. 'I never noticed that.'

They sat in silence for a few moments looking at the stars twinkling above them.

'It's a shame about the lights on the Beach Car Park.' Jemma mused. 'Ever since they put them up, we don't see the Milky Way very often. How come all the so-called improvements seem to make things worse?' There was no reply, and she thought Chrissie had fallen asleep.

Chrissie jumped a little. 'Sorry, miles away. I'm so glad I came to live in Lulcombe. I love it here by the sea. Why do you live here?'

'I was born here, but the main reason I've stayed is the strata.'

'What's that, a posh restaurant?'

'No, the different layers of rock along the Jurassic Coast. Strata means layer in Latin. That's where we get the word "street" from. It refers to the many layers that went into making a Roman road.'

'Never knew that. Learn something new every day.'

'The strata here are great for a geologist and fossil hunter. Some of them are two hundred and fifty million years old and unique globally, so this section of the coast has been awarded World Heritage Site status.'

'It all sounds like my love life.'

'What?'

'Totally extinct and happened years ago.'

Jemma laughed. 'Wait until you meet Brad!'

'I'm not holding my breath... So, you like the local strata. Just like the fellas in your life, lots of layers!'

Unused to the wine, Jemma giggled harder. 'Trouble is, whenever I dig to find a new bloke, the sides collapse and an old one drops back into the hole!'

Chrissie tutted. 'Lucky you, I bet your life has lots of layers. Maybe with some dark secrets buried in your strata.'

Jemma shivered and went quiet for a moment. 'Yep, some of those, but we're not going down that road.'

Chrissie wrapped her arms tightly around herself. 'Sorry if I said something wrong. Always opening my mouth and sticking my foot in. We were so relaxed.'

Jemma touched her arm, which felt cold in the night air. 'Don't worry. Some things happened years ago that I don't want to talk about. Anyway, I'm tired and don't want a late night. I'll probably be asleep by the time Dave gets back.'

Chrissie stood and hugged her. 'Thanks for a lovely evening, Jemma. Hope you didn't mind all the questions.'

'It was good,' Jemma said. 'We must do it again soon.'

'Sounds like a plan!' Chrissie picked up the empty glasses and tottered back home.

Jemma stood by the back door and watched her go. Her eyes scanned the treeline and, in the bright moonlight, she thought she saw someone standing by the trees. She shivered and rushed back inside. As she went in Dino went outside to water a few bushes, but she remained at the kitchen window, her eyes fixed on the suspicious outline.

As she stared, she was sure she saw the dark figure turn and disappear from view.

Chapter 12

The following day Jemma was at the university with lectures and student meetings. The day flew by and the wine and disturbed sleep from the night before had left no ill effects.

After driving home, she was thankful to be going into her cottage without her hair being full of rock dust. The daylight was fading as she parked and went round the back of her house. She glimpsed something bright over in the trees and froze. It may have been nothing, but it was another hour until Dave finished, and she felt too scared to inspect the woods on her own.

Dino came bounding out as the door opened, his tail wagging like mad, so she stroked him. He didn't like being on his own, even though Chrissie had taken him out for a walk at lunchtime. Jemma let him have a run around the garden and watched while he explored his favourite smells. She kept an eye on the woods but didn't see anything else.

***

Dave came home around five.

'I'm sure someone was in the woods again,' said Jemma.

He opened the kitchen door. 'Come on Dino, let's go.'

With Dino running around, he walked over to the trees. 'You're useless as a tracker dog, can't you sniff anybody out?'

Unfortunately, Dino preferred chasing squirrels.

Dave found the spot that had previously appeared flattened and was still well-trodden. In the soft mud he spotted three holes in a triangular pattern, so he knelt and took a picture with his phone.

Possibly a tripod for a telescope or maybe a camping stove. Either way, best not worry Jemma.

There weren't any further signs, so he called Dino and walked back to the house.

***

Jemma looked up as he came in. 'See anything?'

'No, nothing new. I know, if you're worried about being watched how about a CCTV system?'

'How much will that cost?'

'Don't worry, I'll pay. It can be an early Christmas present.'

She kissed him. 'Thanks. That'll make me feel a lot safer.'

Looking out of the window, Jemma spotted Chrissie walking down her garden path so she went outside.

'Thanks for taking Dino out at lunchtime.'

'You're welcome, any time. All OK today?'

'Yes, I'm good. Quick question, have you seen anybody down in the woods watching the house?'

'Oh, my God! Has somebody been watching us?'

'Don't think so, I just thought there was somebody in the trees a couple of times,' Jemma remarked. 'Probably nothing.'

'Don't freak me out,' Chrissie said. 'It can be scary living on your own, but I've always felt safe here.'

'Nah, don't worry, Dave's going to arrange some CCTV. Plessie's worth a few quid, so it won't do any harm to beef up security.'

Chrissie winked. 'As long as the camera doesn't point towards my topless sunbathing spot.'

Jemma raised an eyebrow. 'Better not tell him or he'll be zooming in.'

***

The following afternoon a van turned up. A man with a ladder got out and installed two cameras, front and back, with a recorder and small monitor that he set up in Jemma's utility room.

After five minutes of instructions on how to work the system, her eyes glazed over.

He laughed. 'Don't worry. Dave'll know how to work it. All simple really.'

***

The talk of stalkers made Jemma nervous. Sitting on the patio with a cup of tea, she watched the trees herself. Somewhere, out in the woods, she was convinced that somebody was watching her. She kept telling herself that she was worrying about nothing, but was still very nervous outside on her own.

When Dave came back from work, he showered and joined her outside. For some extra security, he set up a door cam for her front door with a feed that linked to Jemma's phone and to his as well.

He joked, 'At least now I can keep an eye on all your fancy men coming and going.'

'Yes, you can.' Jemma wondered if he was joking.

'A weird idea,' he said, 'but do you think Brad might be the watcher?'

'Brad?'

'Yes, perhaps this whole, "helping with the fossil" thing is a plan to work his way back into your life, and working with you for a few days isn't enough for him.'

Jemma shook her head. 'I'm not sure. He seems to be on his best behaviour and is way more interested in Plessie than me. After turning up, he works hard all day and then leaves. It's been a godsend having another helper who doesn't want paying.'

'Watch him closely, will you, I don't trust him? Try asking him what he did yesterday afternoon, and the day before.'

She sighed. 'OK, I'll try to find out what he's been up to. Although, if he was watching me, he wouldn't exactly tell me.'

When Brad turned up the next morning, he took his cup of coffee and headed out to the workshop, followed by Jemma.

She put some music on. 'Anything you fancy?'

Brad shrugged, 'No, you choose.'

Reaching over for a CD she fed it into the player. 'How about 'The Mess I Made' by Kezia Gill? She's a top UK country star.'

He picked up his air chisel. 'Sounds good.'

Jemma tried to look nonchalant as she glanced at him. 'Have you been doing much over the last few days?'

'Not really. Took a run on Tuesday afternoon after I finished here, and yesterday I walked along the coast.'

'On your own?'

'Yeah. Why?'

She shrugged. 'No reason. I wondered how you were getting on.'

'All good. The house in Lulcombe is awesome and I might be able to buy it.'

'Good. Seen much of Sally?'

A bitter laugh. 'I don't think I'm flavour of the month with that one. She dragged me into bed at the hotel she found, but acted weird when I didn't want to hang around with her the next day.'

Jemma thought for a moment. 'There's been a strange atmosphere at work as well. Maybe she's jealous you're helping me with Plessie.'

He grinned. 'A very intense woman. Where I come from, she'd be called a bunny boiler.'

'I remember that film,' Jemma said. 'I suppose she could be watching me.'

'Stalking! You think she's that mad?'

'I don't know. She's certainly a bit volatile and she doesn't like me.'

Brad smiled. 'Yeah, I got that message.'

That evening after dinner, Jemma sat with Dave watching TV. Her sitting room was cosy and warm, but her mind wasn't on the film flickering on the screen.

She snuggled up to him. 'I spoke to Brad earlier, and he went running on Tuesday. Yesterday, he went for a long walk along the coast path.'

'Any proof?'

'I couldn't ask him for evidence, but it can't be him. However, he made me wonder if Sally O'Keefe could be the stalker.'

Dave turned to face her. 'What? Sally from the uni?'

'Yes, they spent the night together after he arrived in Lulcombe. Turns out she wanted more than a one-night stand.'

'Do you think she might be watching you?'

Jemma shivered. 'I don't know. She could be, I suppose.'

Dave sipped his beer. 'We'll have to keep an eye on the CCTV footage.'

***

The following day, Jemma received a phone call that took her mind off stalkers.

It was from a fossil agent she'd dealt with before. Jeremy Lovell had a business in London and only ever considered the top geological specimens. When he spoke, Jemma thought he sounded like a posh BBC announcer from the nineteen-fifties.

'Good morning, Jemma, Jeremy Lovell.'

'Hello, Jeremy. How are things?'

'Wonderful darling, but always better with the commission from a substantial transaction.'

Jemma always thought Jeremy was rather stuck up and didn't like his attitude so she got straight to the point. 'What are you after? Buying or selling?'

'Buying this time, or rather one of my clients is.'

'Who's that?'

'Sorry,' he said. 'This is a confidential approach.'

'Fire away,' Jemma said, guessing what he wanted.

'Well, I have a wealthy collector client who wishes to offer you one hundred and twenty-five thousand pounds for the plesiosaur you found recently.'

'Wow,' she gasped. 'But she's not even fully prepared yet.'

'No problem, he'd wait until you were finished before buying.'

Jemma sighed. 'Sorry, Jeremy, but she's not for sale at any price.'

'Might even go to one-fifty.'

'The answer's still no. Plessie is going to be the focal point for the new extension at Lulcombe museum and will put the town firmly on the fossil hunting map.'

'Plessie!' Jeremy spat the word as if it had left a nasty taste in his mouth. 'Oh, how Disney! You're missing a major opportunity, you know. It isn't often a fossil of this quality comes to the market.'

'That's why I want to display it at Lulcombe Museum,' she said.

'It's such a waste putting something like that on show in a tiny provincial museum.'

Jemma seethed, 'But with Plessie in a new exhibition Lulcombe will become a major player. Anyway, Jeremy, I've got to go. Bye.' She ended the call.

He always played on his silver-spoon upbringing, but was still a buyer and seller, like the dealers on the stalls at the Fossil Festival.

***

Alice shouted. 'Come and see these flowers, Jemma, they're so pretty.'

'I'm busy.'

'Go on, they're lovely.'

'I'm not interested in flowers. I'm busy with a fossil.'

'I'll pick some and bring them over. It won't take long.'

'OK. Just don't go near the edge...... Alice...'

The last word turned into a scream as Dave took her in his arms.

'Jemma? You OK?'

She sat up drenched in sweat and held him. 'I'm fine,' she sobbed.

'If you want to talk about Alice, I'm here,' he said.

'I know you are.' She hugged him tighter. 'Thanks. I better have a shower, I'm soaked.'

She walked through to the bathroom. *How can I stop these nightmares?*

Chapter 13

The next few weeks flew past with Jemma and Brad working hard to finish Plessie and mount her on the newly painted wall of the museum extension. It was a painstaking job to separate the pieces of fossilised bone from the stone that encased them and then take a plaster cast of each one. The bones then had to be photographed and catalogued for the scientific records.

As they fixed up the final piece of the tail, all the hard work was nearly over.

Brad held the last piece in position. 'That's it, can you tighten the mounts?'

'I'll try, but it's a bit awkward.'

'Put your hand under my arm and you'll be able to reach it.'

Jemma leant against his back and tried to reach the mount.

He grinned. 'It's getting hot in here.'

Jemma blushed and tried to move away from him. She'd tried to stay professional while they worked, not easy when she still found him so attractive.

'Only joking, you lean all you want,' he said.

As she tightened the mount her nostrils filled with

Brad's scent, a mixture of aftershave and sweat. 'OK, let go,' said Jemma.

He carefully released the section and stood back to admire the full display. The sixteen-metre beast was mounted horizontally on the rear wall of the new room. 'Magnificent.'

'Isn't she?' Jemma grinned. 'Thanks for all your help.'

They hugged awkwardly, Brad holding the hug longer than Jemma was expecting. She pulled away and took out her phone to take some photos.

As they stood in front of the display, he grinned. 'Job done?'

Jemma shook her head. 'Oh, no, you know I've been taking plaster casts of all the bones?'

'Yes...'

'I need to make a resin copy of every bone, so we've got a complete spare Plessie.'

'Isn't that a waste of time?'

'No, I want a full-size replica then we can take her out to local schools and other museums.'

'I can see it now. *Plessie on Tour.*'

'Just imagine the kids' faces.' Jemma swept the floor under the display as Brad took the empty boxes out to the storeroom.

He returned and picked up his jacket. 'That's me done for today. Back to an empty house.'

Jemma frowned. 'Not made any friends yet?'

He shrugged, 'No. I've not really had time.'

Jemma grinned. 'I'll have to introduce you to Chrissie.'

'Who's Chrissie?'

'My next-door neighbour. She saw you by the workshop the other day.'

'What's she like?'

'She's lovely, very attractive as well.'

'Sounds interesting. Do you think she might be up for a drink or a meal?'

Jemma pulled out her phone. 'Here, I'll give you her number. Give her a call and you can arrange something.'

***

A few days later Jemma called next door at Chrissie's. Her cottage was similar to Jemma's but, as the other half of the semi-detached property, it was a mirror image, which Jemma found confusing. The door opened and Chrissie stood framed in a towel.

'Hi, Jemma,' she hugged her.

'Hello. Wondered how the prep was going for your big date with Brad?'

'Too many choices! Come in and you can help.'

'I have no fashion sense, but I can try!' Jemma laughed. She followed Chrissie inside and closed the door. Chrissie ran up the stairs with Jemma following more slowly up the narrow staircase. As she entered the low-ceilinged bedroom, Chrissie was already holding up a little black dress and a longer red number with a split up the side.

Jemma smiled. 'All guns blazing.'

Chrissie grinned. 'Not been on a hot date in a while. Thanks for playing matchmaker by the way.'

'No problem. You both deserve a night out.'

'Which one do you reckon?'

'It's hard to tell without seeing them on.'

'That's easily remedied.' Chrissie, with no modesty at all, dropped her towel and wriggled into the black number.

'This one's my favourite. What do you think?'

Jemma checked her out. 'I hope you'll be wearing some underwear for your big date.'

Chrissie laughed. 'I might do. Depends how lucky I feel. What about the dress?'

'He'll have no chance! Where's he taking you?'

Chrissie twirled in front of the wardrobe mirror. 'Della's in Swanbourne, no less. I've heard it's really swanky.'

'So they say. Too pricey for me though.'

'Oh, well, it'll be worth his while.'

Jemma laughed. 'So you're not playing hard to get?'

'Nope. I need a bit of passion in my life.

Jemma grinned. 'I'll be off. Enjoy your night.'

'Will do, and thanks again for giving him my number.'

She swirled round and smiled at her reflection in the wardrobe mirror.

***

Brad arrived at Chrissie's at seven. He knocked on the door and it quickly opened. His first impression of her in a short black dress was, "wow".

He smiled. 'Hi, Chrissie, you look stunning. Very sophisticated with your hair up.'

'Thanks, Brad. You've scrubbed up well yourself.'

He'd gone with a slim-fitting white shirt, which showed off his tanned arms, chinos and brown boots. 'I think we've been played into a blind date, but can we relax and enjoy the evening? Here, these are for you.' He handed her a bunch of roses, which she accepted and smelled.

'They're lovely, thank you! Come in while I put them in water. What time's the reservation?'

'Seven-thirty. Plenty of time.'

Chrissie went to fetch a vase from a shelf in her kitchen. As she was struggling to reach up, he strode over to help.

He grinned as he lifted it down. 'One advantage of being tall.'

'Sure is, but mind your head on some of the door frames, especially upstairs,' Chrissie blushed. 'Not that I'm...'

His eyes lit up. 'No problem, I always watch out for beams in these quaint English places.'

After putting the flowers and water in the vase, Chrissie checked her lipstick in the mirror. 'I'm ready. Shall we go?'

They chatted on the way there and soon they were parking up at Della's with Brad's truck occupying two spaces in the car park. Again, Brad opened Chrissie's door for her.

She smiled. 'Quite the gentleman, I like this!'

'We're not totally uncouth in the States!'

'Glad to hear.'

The restaurant was very spacious and, through the large windows, the lights of Swanbourne twinkled in the darkness of a cloudy October night. The décor was plush but tasteful. Each table was covered in a pristine white tablecloth and set with a multitude of knives and forks. The green velour seats looked extremely comfortable. Most of the tables were occupied, but with carefully placed screens and plants, it didn't appear busy.

A maitre'd in a dinner jacket greeted them. 'Bon Soir Monsieur Jones, madam.'

Chrissie gave Brad a wry smile. 'You a regular?'

He grinned. 'May have eaten here a few times.'

'Is this where you bring all your lady friends?'

'No, you're the first.'

She laughed. 'Wow! Highly honoured!'

The maitre'd took Brad's jacket and showed them to their table.

Brad followed Chrissie across the dining room with his hand on the small of her back.

She turned back towards him. 'This is plush.'

He glanced around. 'Sure is. The amount of space between the tables is unusual; I hate places where you pretty much eat on top of each other.'

As they crossed the room, Brad was surprised to see Sally O'Keefe at a table with an older lady. She noticed him immediately and made a point of turning away. He ignored her and walked over to where a waiter was standing. Their table was in an alcove and lit by candles.

Chrissie lowered herself onto the chair as demurely as she could in her revealing dress. 'So romantic.'

Brad sat down opposite her. 'Food ain't bad either.'

A waitress brought the menus and wine list. 'What would you like to drink?'

'Gin and tonic for me please,' Chrissie said.

'Orange juice, please,' Brad added.

She left them to choose and went back to the bar.

Chrissie read the menu. 'I'm almost slobbering reading this.'

'Hard not to,' he agreed.

The waitress returned with their drinks. 'Are you ready to order or do you need more time?' she asked.

'Sorted,' Chrissie said. 'Scallops and steamed halibut, please.'

'Oysters and a rib-eye steak for me please, medium-rare,' Brad said.

They added a bottle of wine to their order and the waitress returned to the kitchen.

'You like seafood then?' Brad asked.

'Yes, I love fish and shellfish.'

'Me too.'

She gave him a cheeky grin. 'You know they're an aphrodisiac?'

'A complete fallacy. Last time I had a dozen oysters, only ten of them worked!'

She grinned. 'Promises, promises!'

Brad coloured. 'Sorry, I wasn't being presumptuous.'

She flashed him her best sexy smile. 'You're not. Relax, you're welcome to stay over tonight if you like. Don't worry about making the first move.'

He chuckled. 'English directness. I love it.'

'Life's too short to mess about.'

He held up his glass and tapped Chrissie's. 'Cheers, I'll drink to that. You never know what could happen next.'

He glanced over and saw Sally staring at them across the room. As he caught her eye, she turned away again. She didn't look happy, but Brad was determined to not let anything spoil his night.

Chrissie smiled at Brad. 'I bet it's been weird working with an old flame.'

He thought for a moment. 'No, not really. It's all very professional and Jemma seems happy with Dave.'

'That's good then, I've got nothing to be jealous of,' she said, 'unless you've got a girlfriend waiting on the front porch back home?'

'Fraid not. You don't have to share me with anyone.'

Chrissie picked up a knife and waved it with an evil grin. 'That's good because I don't share my toys with anyone.' They both laughed loudly and received some stares from their fellow diners. She placed down the knife and blushed.

The wine arrived, closely followed by the starters together with some warm slices of baguette that smelled irresistible. The conversation stopped while they attacked the shellfish and bread.

After they'd finished and the plates had been removed, they spoke about families and where they grew up. They could both tell a story, but were happy to listen as well. The conversation flowed freely and they relaxed in each other's company. The main courses arrived and, to their delight, they were as tasty as the starters.

The waitress returned. 'Is everything OK for you both?'

'Delicious!' Chrissie enthused.

'Awesome,' Brad added. 'Could we get a water refill please?' He picked up the wine bottle and moved to top up Chrissie's glass. 'I've had a glass and a half of wine,' he said. 'I'm driving, so that's enough for me. Hope you can finish the bottle.'

She drained her glass. 'Sure can.'

They giggled loudly and several of the other diners stared pointedly in their direction, including the older lady sitting with Sally.

Brad leant towards Chrissie, 'I wonder who the old girl is over there with Sally?'

Chrissie took a quick glance. 'No idea. Oh, is that Sally who grabbed you on the beach?'

'Yep. She doesn't look very happy.'

Chrissie returned Sally's stare. 'I'd take her down any day.'

Brad laughed. 'I bet folks would pay good money for a ringside seat.'

She guffawed. 'Better shush or we'll be thrown out.'

Brad held her hand. 'Well, I'm stuffed. I'm gonna skip dessert.'

She stroked his arm. 'How about we adjourn to mine?'

'Sounds like a plan.'

He asked for the bill, paid, and they left hand in hand. They carried on chatting on the drive back and soon pulled up outside Chrissie's. After she unlocked the door, they went into her sitting room, which was invitingly warm. She placed their coats over a chair and poured a single malt for Brad and a cognac for herself.

She added some extra wood to the logburner, dimmed the lights and turned on some music before sitting on the sofa. Brad slipped his arm around her and, as she snuggled up to him, he was in heaven.

After a while, Chrissie unfastened the buttons on Brad's shirt and rested her hand on his chest. His hands explored the material of her dress and undid the zip. She stood and, with a wiggle, it fell to the floor.

'Love the lingerie,' Brad said.

'Thanks.'

After helping Brad remove his shirt, her fingers played with the hair on his chest. He reached around her and with a one-handed flick, unfastened her silver lacy bra.

She grinned. 'Years of practice?'

He smiled. 'Luck! I usually fumble with two hands.' He took a condom from his jacket pocket.

After taking the packet, she opened it for him. 'I like a man who's well-prepared.'

'Only carry three with me though.'

'Don't worry. More upstairs, if needed. After all, we've got a lot of oysters to work through.'

He swallowed. 'No pressure.'

Soon, the rest of their clothes littered the floor and they made love frantically on the sofa before rolling onto the sheepskin rug in front of the log burner. Afterwards, they lay by the fire with the light from the flames flickering on their naked skin.

Chrissie lay in Brad's arms. 'That was lovely. It's been a while.'

Brad murmured. 'Very nice.'

They lay there for ages before Chrissie led Brad upstairs. 'Come on, plenty more oysters to go.'

He chuckled. 'I'll do my best.'

Chapter 14

The following morning was cold but bright. The weak sun battled to warm the air as it shone down from a pale blue sky. When Brad turned up whistling at the workshop, Jemma could tell the date with Chrissie had been a success.

'Did it go well last night?'

Brad smiled. 'Yep, and she makes a great breakfast.'

'That's good.' Jemma blushed so she turned away and tried concentrating on her work. *Lucky Chrissie*. 'Enjoy the meal?'

'Yeah. Awesome.' A grin spread across his face. 'The food was excellent, and guess who we saw at the restaurant?'

'No idea.'

'Sally O'Keefe with an older lady. Bet it was her mom.'

'Did she say hello?'

'No, but she kept looking at me with some serious stink-eye.'

Jemma laughed. 'Well done, you've stirred things up with her, so you better be careful. Hell hath no fury like a woman scorned.'

Brad smiled. 'Who cares?'

***

The day of the press opening arrived and at Jemma's house there was a lot of activity as everybody got ready. Ellie had come to stay as she had no lectures for a few days and was now chief fashion advisor.

Jemma sat patiently on a stool in her kitchen. 'I'm not used to having my hair done.'

'Be quiet and sit still. It's been ages since I tried to tame your hair.'

'You know, I can't remember having much trouble with your hair when you were young.'

Ellie put down the brush. 'That's because you were crap at all the mum stuff and left it to dad. Do you realise he was the one who taught me to braid my hair, while you were out hunting bloody fossils?'

Jemma went quiet. 'Sorry, Els, I should have given you more time.'

Ellie grabbed the brush and started back on her mum's hair with renewed vigour.

'Come on. We'd better get this done.'

'Ouch!' Jemma jumped. 'Go steady or I'll end up with chunks missing.'

Ellie laughed. 'Don't be such a wuss.'

Dave walked in. 'Is this the start of a new career as a hairdresser?'

Ellie snatched a hairdryer, pointed it at him and gave him a blast. He dropped down behind the sofa like he'd been shot.

'Don't get any dog hairs on your suit.' Jemma laughed.

He stood and brushed himself down. 'Sorry.'

'So nice to see the two of you dressed up smartly for a change.' Ellie put down the dryer. 'All done. I haven't got a mirror but it looks a lot better.'

'Thanks, Els.'

'Can I have a photo of you both by the back door before we go?' They stepped outside, and she took some pictures of them on her phone.

Posing for photos, Jemma couldn't help smiling. 'I'm so happy right now, this is lovely.'

Dave squeezed her hand. 'You're just basking in the glory of the find. Talking of which, are there many coming to the event today?'

'There have been around thirty applications for press passes so we should have a reasonable turnout. Don't think the museum has ever been so neat and tidy.'

Ellie slipped her phone back in her pocket. 'Knowing you, Mum, I bet you've been working all hours to get it ready.'

'Not really, I've mainly been sorting Plessie with Brad. The rest has been down to Anna and the cleaners.'

A deep American voice spoke behind them. 'Is this a private shoot or can anyone join in?'

'Morning, Brad,' said Jemma. 'Brad, this is my daughter, Ellie.'

He shook her hand. 'Hi, Ellie. Nice to meet you.'

'Hi, Brad.' Ellie said. 'What do you think of this smart couple?'

'Very elegant. Is Chrissie ready?'

'Reckon she should be,' she replied. 'I took her hair up earlier. She looks dead cool.'

The back door of the neighbouring house opened and Chrissie stepped outside. She leant over the fence and smiled.

'Wow. Stunning.' Brad reached over to kiss her.

'Careful with the hair and lipstick.' Chrissie laughed. 'It took Ellie ages to do.'

Ellie pulled her phone out again. 'Can you come round Chrissie, so I can grab some photos of you with Brad?'

As Jemma took Dino back inside and locked the door, Ellie took some more pictures.

Brad and Chrissie were kissing in most of the shots, and she tutted. 'Get a room, you two. You know, Chrissie, you look the spitting image of Mum with your hair like that.'

'Better keep an eye out for Dave then,' Chrissie giggled.

As Ellie watched Brad and Chrissie together, she turned to her mum. 'It's strange with Brad, Mum. I feel a real affinity with him, it's like I've known him for ages.'

Jemma put her arm around Ellie's shoulders. 'Oh, he's a real charmer that one.'

***

As Brad kissed Chrissie, a well-hidden watcher raised his binoculars to find out what was going on.

From where he lay he thought that Brad was kissing Jemma. *What? It can't be. What's he doing here with her?*

With shaking hands he pulled out his notepad and made a note of Brad's arrival time. He hadn't been expecting the American to show up. That wasn't part of his plan at all. Now he had two obstacles to prevent him from achieving his goal.

However much he tried, he couldn't watch, so he folded his mat and stormed off through the woodland before heading back to his campervan at the Lulcombe Camping and Caravanning Park.

***

Jemma and her entourage walked round to the museum, which looked very bright with multi-coloured bunting and extra displays.

They were all given name badges by the manager, Anna, and as she handed them out she said, 'If you all wear a badge, it's like we've got lots of staff.' She winked. 'We don't want to be too outnumbered by the press.'

Jemma had never seen the museum looking as good. As there were so many items in storage, they could rotate exhibits to give some variety. The staff had raided the stores to find extra fossil exhibits, including more items that had belonged to Jemma's grandad. Plessie was mounted on the wall and Brad had rigged up a long curtain that would drop down when the rope was pulled.

'Wow, Anna, you've been busy. This place looks great,' Jemma said.

Anna smiled, 'Looks good, doesn't it? I've had some help with the cleaning while you were working on Plessie.'

'Worth the effort!' Jemma checked the list of attendees and spotted a few she didn't know. 'Who's F Butcher?'

Anna checked her clipboard. 'Let me see. Here we are, Frank Butcher with a London address.'

Jemma frowned. 'Who's he?'

Anna glanced around. 'He collected his pass and is around somewhere. A tall bloke.'

'OK,' Jemma said. 'I'll have a word if I see him.'

Anna looked at her watch. 'Oh, it's about time.'

She tapped a glass to attract everybody's attention. 'And now, ladies and gentlemen, the moment you've been waiting for. I'd like to hand you to the chairman of our trustees, and the discoverer of the largest complete plesiosaur ever found in England, Jemma Thorne.'

There was a scattering of applause and a few whoops from friends and family. As Jemma approached the wall, an expectant hush fell over the room. Standing by the display, she reached for the rope. 'Thank you, everybody, for coming today. I'm sure many of you know I'm not one for long speeches, so we'll go straight to the countdown. Three...Two...One...Plessie!'

A pull on the rope and the red curtain dropped away to reveal the impressive skeleton that covered most of the back wall.

There were some sharp intakes of breath and wows before the room burst into a much louder applause. The spectators queued for a better look and the chance for a photo.

Jemma held up her hand. 'Photographs are fine but please, no flash photography.' She smiled as she watched the visitors gently jostling for a better view.

Ellie came over and gave her a hug. 'I'm so proud of you, Mum. You've been searching for a Plessie for years. Happy?'

Jemma wiped a tear from her eye. 'Ecstatic. I can't believe that she's finally finished and on display.'

'She's so impressive.' Ellie said.

***

The helpers were replenishing glasses whilst they mingled with the press and guests. Nobody paid any attention to a tall attendee in a bulky jacket with a pass partially hidden and who watched from the back. He wandered into one of the other galleries and, after checking he was alone, placed a small black object on top of one of the taller cabinets. After sauntering back to the crowded section, he slipped out of the entrance without saying goodbye to anyone.

***

After the last of the press and visitors left, Jemma went to talk to Anna and Vincent Lawrence, one of the other trustees.

Anna raised her glass. 'To Jurassic Jemma, the saviour of the museum.'

Jemma coloured slightly. 'I wouldn't say that.'

Vincent looked over. 'Plessie has certainly earned us some excellent publicity in the papers and on TV. I'd love to see her in a brand-new building up the hill.'

Jemma frowned. 'Don't start today. This is the proper place for a museum, not a shed in a car park.'

Anna held up a hand to keep them apart. 'Seconds out, round two,' she joked. 'Don't argue about selling today, please. This should be a happy occasion.'

'OK,' Vincent said. 'We'll save that for the next trustees meeting.'

Jemma sipped her drink. 'Nothing to discuss.'

He snapped, 'Seventy-five thousand reasons to talk!'

With that, she ignored him and went to chat with Dave and Ellie.

***

After watching her leave, Vincent checked the ceiling. 'Is the new alarm OK? The old one was being very temperamental.'

Anna replied, 'Yes, fine, no trouble so far.'

'Excellent,' he said. 'I was getting fed up of call outs. Am I on the rota this week?'

She thought for a moment. 'No. Jemma's down for three nights and, after that, my turn.'

***

That night, after everything had been locked up, a figure dressed in black walked around the outside of the museum carrying a remote-control unit. They turned it on and stood by one of the windows. Watching the screen, they manoeuvred the small drone they'd left on one of the cabinets. As it flew across the room, it triggered one of the new system's movement sensors.

When they saw the alarm light flashing, they returned the drone to its resting place and slunk away from the car park.

***

Jemma was asleep in bed when the phone rang. It was the alarm company with a call-out at the museum. The police had been notified and they wanted her to meet them at the front entrance with her keys.

She dressed and set off down the hill. Dave was snoring so she left him sleeping.

After meeting two policemen, she unlocked the doors and disabled the flashing control panel. They asked her to check if anything was amiss so she walked around before declaring everything was OK.

They radioed in the false alarm and Jemma locked up behind them.

***

The following night the dark figure waited until three o'clock before standing by the window for some nocturnal drone flying.

Jemma answered her phone and the controller asked her to meet up with the police. This time Dave woke up.

'Do you want me to come?' he mumbled.

'No, don't worry. Probably a fault with the new alarm. I'll ring the company to come and check the sensors. I'm getting sick of all these disturbed nights.'

She left for the museum and this time met with a different policeman. After checking the rooms she reset the alarm and walked home.

***

At two o'clock the following night, Jemma's phone rang, and she woke up with a start.

'Bloody alarm,' she fumed as she dressed.

Dave was staying at his own house that night as he had an early start, so she walked down on her own.

This time a different policeman turned up. Jemma watched him exit his car and approach. *He can't be more than twelve, I must be getting old.*

'Evening Mrs Thorne.'

'Evening Constable, sorry to drag you out.'

'No problem. The sergeant told me to remind you that if this is another false alarm, we won't be coming out to any other calls for a month.'

'We'll be "sin-binned" will we?'

'I'm afraid so,' he said. 'We take callouts seriously but we have limited resources.'

Jemma unlocked the door and together they wandered the museum, yet again finding nothing wrong and not spotting the small drone on top of the tall cabinet. After locking up, she followed him back to his patrol car.

'Oh well, I'm off the rota now for a week so it'll be Anna's turn tomorrow night if we have any other problems. I forgot to ring the alarm company, but I will later.'

'OK, Mrs Thorne, good night to you. Can I give you a lift home?'

'That's kind, but no thanks,' Jemma said. 'My house is only five minutes away.'

She stomped back up the hill, annoyed about having three nights' sleep disturbed by the faulty alarm. She undressed and slipped back into her bed, which had gone cold while she'd been away.

***

The next night Anna was fast asleep when her phone rang, and she jumped up. Three o'clock.

She answered and listened for a moment.

It was a call from the monitoring company. 'The alarm's going off again but, as there have been three false alarms, the police cover is cancelled.'

'OK,' Anna rubbed her eyes. 'Jemma warned me it might happen. She rang your company, but no one can get out until tomorrow.'

The lady wasn't sympathetic. 'That isn't down to us madam, we only monitor the systems. Can you take that up with the alarm suppliers?'

Anna sighed. 'Someone will when they turn up.' She put down the phone, dressed in some warm clothes and grabbed her keys. Her husband, Graham, was working in London, so at least it hadn't woken him up as well.

She drove down and parked up by the front door. She

unlocked it, turned on the lights and immobilised the alarm with her key. After toying with the idea of going straight home, she decided she'd better check the halls.

In the old part of the museum, everything was fine. Then she went to the new room, opened the double doors and her eyes widened at the sight that greeted her.

Two men in masks were lifting down sections of Plessie's skeleton and placing them on the floor by the open exit, where a van had been reversed up to the door.

She froze until finally she was able to turn and run.

One of the men was too quick and rugby tackled her to the ground.

She fell with a cry.

He held her down whilst securing her hands with cable ties. He dragged her over and tied her to the radiator, leaving her face down on the floor.

She lay there, her heart thumping, wondering how she could escape.

One of the men coughed and removed the mask to clear his throat, throwing it to the floor. Anna lifted her head and stared at him as she tried to recall where she'd seen him before.

The smaller man groaned. 'Oh, no, she's seen your face' He held out a large stone. 'Quick, you better cave her head in with this.'

Anna's eyes opened wide as she began to shake, and she tried edging away from the man whilst covering her head with her hands. 'I didn't see you. Please don't hurt me,' she begged.

The big man lifted the fossil and, as she looked up with pleading eyes, he brought it down with a sickening crunch and her whole world went black.

He dropped the stone and turned to look at the other man.

The smaller man yelled, 'Come on, grab the last bits of fossil and don't forget to retrieve the drone.'

The larger man dawdled over. 'OK. Never killed a girl before.'

'Oh well, good time to start.'

The big man grabbed the drone and they loaded up Plessie's bones before shutting the rear doors behind them. They drove away slowly, not turning their lights on until reaching the main road.

Anna lay motionless on the ground, a pool of blood spreading out from her head like a dark red wave.

Chapter 15

Jemma had arranged to meet the service engineer from the alarm company at ten o'clock, so she arrived at the museum at nine-forty-five. Surprisingly, the front door was unlocked and the lights on, but nobody was in reception. The deserted foyer possessed a cold chill and she shivered as she looked around.

'Hello,' she shouted. 'Anybody about?'

There was no answer so Jemma checked the shop and gallery, which were both empty but then she opened the doors to the new extension and a scene of devastation greeted her. Plessie was gone and some of the other cases had been overturned.

She stood there, shaking in shock. *Oh, no. All that work. Plessie was going to save us.*

Slowly stepping forward, Jemma saw a pair of white trainers sticking out from behind a cabinet. Running over, she suddenly stopped, her hands coming up to cover the silent scream that left her mouth as she found Anna sprawled on the floor in a pool of blood, her arms awkwardly tied to the radiator next to her.

Oh, my God, it's like Alice all over again.

For a brief moment her mind cast back to that fateful day

by the cliffs thirty years ago. She wrenched herself back to the awful reality, knelt by Anna and felt for a pulse. At first there was nothing until, finally, she managed to locate a faint beat.

The first thing she did was call the emergency services. The controller told her an ambulance would be there in ten minutes and advised her what to do. She felt sick from the sight of all the blood Anna had lost and tears ran down her face as she tried to remain calm.

Her first aid training from the University finally kicking in, she tugged off her jacket to wrap around Anna. She fetched the medical kit and her hands trembled as she fumbled with a dressing for Anna's head. There was a nasty gash covered in blood so she used some surgical tape to hold the patch in place. Other than the head wound, she couldn't find any other injuries, so she knelt with the unconscious woman until two ambulance men arrived to take over.

Two police officers also rushed in, their car's blue lights flashing through the window. One of them frantically scanned the room. 'What's happened?'

Jemma tried to calm herself. 'There's been a theft and Anna's been attacked.'

'What's her full name?'

'Anna Jenkins, she's the museum manager.'

'Has anything been stolen?'

'Yes, Plessie.'

'Plessie?' The officer poised with a pen and notepad.

'A fossilised plesiosaur skeleton I found a few months ago. It was mounted on the wall ready for the opening day on Saturday.'

'Value?'

'Someone offered one hundred and fifty thousand, which I turned down.'

She whistled. 'Wow, for a fossil!'

Jemma walked back to Anna and watched as the paramedics strapped her to a stretcher. 'Is she alright?'

'Touch and go. She's still alive but has a nasty wound, and she's lost a lot of blood.'

The town hall clock struck eleven as they wheeled Anna out to the ambulance, but Jemma didn't notice the time. The paramedics drove off, their sirens disturbing the gulls on the roof causing them to fly away.

Jemma shivered as she approached the policeman. 'Where are they taking her?'

'Don't know for certain, probably Swanbourne,' he said. 'Why would she be here?'

'Maybe the alarm went off again.'

'Why weren't the police here?'

'We had false alarms for the last three nights so the monitoring company stopped notifying them.'

The policeman noted this down on his pad. 'Maybe the culprits triggered them somehow to get the notifications stopped.'

Jemma shivered. 'You mean they could have been watching when I came down?'

'Possibly, although my guess would be they disappeared once they'd set the alarm off.'

A man in a dark blue uniform wandered into reception.

The policeman walked over to stop him. 'This is a crime scene, sir, you can't go in there, I'm afraid.'

'Oh, I'm here to check the alarm system.'

'A bit late for that,' Jemma remarked.

'Sorry, madam, I came as quickly as I could.'

She had a sudden flash of guilt. *The first problem would have been a few nights ago. I should have called them sooner. This wouldn't have happened if I'd remembered.*

The policewoman took his arm and led him back towards the door. 'Sir, this is a newly discovered serious crime scene. I'm sure somebody will be in touch to reschedule but for now I'm afraid you'll have to leave.'

'OK. I'll wait to be contacted.' He picked up his toolkit and left.

One of the officers radioed in the details, whilst his colleague used some fluorescent yellow tape to secure the area. She approached Jemma. 'How many people have been into the crime scene?'

Jemma thought for a moment. 'Two paramedics, the culprits and me.'

The policewoman made some notes. 'We'll need your fingerprints and a DNA sample, please.'

'That's fine,' Jemma said.

'Where exactly did you go in there?'

'I ran over to Anna, knelt next to her, fetched a first aid kit and stayed with her until the ambulance arrived.' She looked down at her bloody knees and shivered. As she leant against the wall she suddenly felt like she was going to faint.

'Are you OK, miss?' the policeman asked. 'Don't lean against the wall, please, in case there are fingerprints there.'

'Oh. I'm alright, but I need some fresh air. I feel a bit queasy.' Her head was spinning, so she stepped outside and sat on a step by the front entrance. 'That could have been me last night,' she said to no one in particular.

The policewoman came over. 'Do you know the victim's next of kin?'

'Yes, her husband's name is Graham. His number's in here.' She found it, held out her phone and the policewoman wrote it on her pad before going off to make the difficult call.

Jemma rang Dave but his phone went to voicemail so she left a message telling him what had happened.

Two more police officers arrived and placed crime scene tape over the door. By now several people had gathered and the officers began asking for witnesses.

Jemma sat with a cup of tea in the museum office as white-suited forensic technicians came and went. Her mind was in a whirl. Finding Plessie and losing Plessie. One day Anna was fine, the next day she was lying in a pool of blood.

She struggled to make sense of what had happened. Plessie was valuable, but to try and kill somebody over a fossil was unbelievable.

What the hell is happening?.

Chapter 16

Jemma unlocked her cottage and turned on the lights, which did nothing to dispel her gloom. Dino ran into the kitchen to be stroked before going out for a mad run around the garden. The landline rang.

'Hello.'

'Hello, Jemma, it's Vincent. I tried ringing your mobile but got no reply. Any further news?'

She swallowed. 'No. I contacted the hospital twice, but they wouldn't tell me anything.'

'Have you spoken to Dave? Does he know any more?'

'No, I left a message earlier, but he hasn't rung back yet.' She paused. 'I don't know if no news is good news.'

'Are we cancelling the opening on Saturday?'

'Yes, I'm afraid so. The whole museum is off-limits as a crime scene.'

He tutted. 'Just when we thought we might get back on our feet.'

'Yeah, it's a bit inconvenient for Anna as well!'

'Of course. Can you ring me if you hear any news?'

'Will do. Bye.'

It was a relief to hang up. She turned on her mobile and noticed some missed calls and messages.

She rang Dave first and he answered straight away. 'Hi, Jem, you OK?'

'I'm alright. I tried to call you earlier and left a message. Any news about Anna?'

'Nothing new. I was interviewing someone for a couple of hours so I muted my phone. I'm not on this case because I'm linked to a person of interest.'

'What? Who?'

He groaned. 'You, you eejit! They say I'm too close to a major witness, so can't be on the team.'

'Oh, I'm sorry.'

'Don't worry, not your fault, you've been through a lot already. When are you giving a formal statement?'

'Tomorrow morning at Police HQ.'

'Do you want a lift?'

'No, I'm good. We can chat tonight. I need to call Ellie and Sue.'

'OK, I'll be back around six.'

'Catch you later. Love you.'

'Love you.'

Next, Jemma rang Ellie and Sue, having long chats with each of them. She confirmed everything was OK and tried to put their minds at rest.

After setting her phone on charge, she realised she hadn't eaten since breakfast so she made some beans on toast but didn't really fancy them and just picked at a few. She felt sick and could still smell Anna's blood.

***

At Swanbourne Police HQ, a team had been assembled and was gathered in the incident room where a whiteboard had been erected on the wall. It was empty apart from a photo of Anna lying on the floor with two paramedics and a picture of Plessie before the theft.

DI Laura Day addressed her team. 'Good morning, everybody. An update after the nasty assault at the museum last night. The young lady involved, Anna Jenkins, is in a critical condition with a fractured skull and bleeding on her brain.'

DS Amrik Hussain put up his hand.

'Yes, Amrik?'

'Do they think she'll pull through, ma'am?'

'We don't know, I'm afraid,' Laura said. 'Anyway, I'm the Senior Investigating Officer and will report up to the Detective Superintendent. I need all of you on my team but DS Gill has to sit this one out as he's too close to our major witness.'

'Shagging the fossil lady,' Amrik said, prompting giggles around the room.

Laura scowled at him. 'Quiet please, Amrik, if you've nothing important to add.' She continued. 'As this is such a nasty assault and aggravated burglary, we're treating it as a murder case.' There were nods of understanding around the room. 'Initial tasks, I want two officers out taking statements in the vicinity of the incident and tracking down witnesses. They'll be checking any CCTV footage as well. Our principal witness, Jemma Thorne, is coming in tomorrow morning. DS Hussain and I will interview her and take her to the museum to double-check what's missing. Any questions?'

Everybody looked at each other but no one had anything further to add.

'OK.' She pointed to the whiteboard. 'Information on here. This is called Operation Fossil. Off you go.'

They all dispersed to start their tasks. Swanbourne didn't have many serious assaults, let alone attempted murders.

***

Later that afternoon, Jemma couldn't face doing any university work so instead she spent her time tidying up. Even Dino couldn't cheer her up when he put his head on her leg asking for a walk.

'OK, Dino.' She sighed. 'Let's go.'

They strolled down to the beach where the calm seas and blue skies gave no clues as to how rough the weather was when Jemma had found Plessie a few months earlier.

'I wonder where Plessie is now Dino.'

With a half-hearted throw, she skimmed a stone into the sea, but the water was too cold for Dino to go for a paddle. As they cut back across the fields from the coastal path, she couldn't help feeling nervous. She hadn't been into the woods at all since she thought someone might be watching her. Though she'd seen nothing else unusual, she still walked a bit faster until she reached her garden. All she could think about was the attack on Anna, the theft of Plessie and how they would affect the museum. Every now and then it hit her that she could have been the one assaulted by the thieves.

Dave pulled up in his car so she ran over to him. They kissed in silence and held each other tight.

Jemma started crying. 'How is she?'

He released her slightly. 'Last update wasn't hopeful. It's an important night for her.'

'I'm worried about Graham as well. I should ring him but he'll be at the hospital tonight,' she said.

'He knows everyone is thinking of them. It's down to the medical staff now and Anna herself.'

Jemma sniffed and wiped away the tears. 'Poor Anna. Come in, I fancy a cuppa. Shall we grab a takeaway for supper?'

'Yes, fine. The new Chinese place will deliver so how about something from them?'

'That'll do me.'

They chatted until their food arrived and ate it with a bottle of beer each. The television was on but they weren't concentrating so they went to bed. After undressing, Jemma peered through the bedroom curtains and scoured the treeline. She couldn't see any signs of life apart from a ghost-like barn owl that flew across the field.

***

The following morning the rain poured down as Jemma drove to Swanbourne. Dave had offered again to give her a lift, but she wanted to drive herself.

The freshly ploughed fields looked like brown corduroy, but Jemma hardly noticed them as she drove past. After parking outside Swanbourne Police HQ, she was shown to a dull interview room where she sat on a hard plastic chair beside a scratched wooden table with recording equipment.

***

In the incident room, Laura Day and Amrik Hussain were going through the evidence from the scene. Laura was the older of the two, medium height with short dark hair. Amrik was tall and heavily built, with dark brown hair and a full beard.

Amrik looked at the names on the whiteboard. 'Have you met Jemma Thorne, ma'am?'

Laura thought for a moment. 'No, I know that Dave's been going out with her, and I passed her once on the beach, but we've never spoken. I chatted to the victim, Anna, several times when I took the children to the museum.'

He screwed his nose up. 'Boring things museums, aren't they?'

She replied. 'No, my kids love Lulcombe because of the fossils.'

'I believe you. What do you want to ask Jemma, ma'am?'

Laura checked her notes, 'I want to go through the events leading up to your discovery of Anna's assault.'

Amrik wrote on his pad. 'Anything else?'

'We need to get to the bottom of why Anna was there,' she said. 'This seems like a well-planned operation, which only went wrong when poor Anna Jenkins disturbed them.'

They studied the crime scene photos, printed some for the whiteboard and prepared for the interview with Jemma.

***

After Jemma had been sitting in the interview room for around five minutes, the two detectives joined her. Laura shook Jemma's hand. 'Good morning, Mrs Thorne, I'm DI Laura Day and this is DS Amrik Hussain.'

Jemma shook Amrik's hand. 'Call me Jemma,' she said. 'Sorry to meet in such circumstances.'

'Yes,' Laura said. 'It must have been a terrible shock to discover Mrs Jenkins as you did.'

Outwardly, Jemma tried to stay focused but she couldn't

erase the picture of Anna, lying in a pool of blood, from her mind. 'Awful. Any more news?'

'No, she's still in a critical condition, I'm afraid,' Laura said. 'Can you talk us through everything that happened after you arrived at the museum? We'll be recording this interview, so please take your time and give us as much detail as you can. No fact is irrelevant, no matter how small.'

After pouring a glass of water, Jemma recollected the events of the previous morning from arriving, discovering the theft of Plessie, and finding Anna on the floor. She was used to lecturing her students so despite the circumstances was able to speak steadily and confidently. She had an excellent memory and eye for detail.

Jemma spoke for more than half an hour, with Laura and Amrik asking an occasional question to clarify some points. After she'd finished, they asked more background questions.

Laura leant back in her chair and stretched. 'Do you want a break, Jemma?'

'No, I'm used to talking for a couple of hours in lectures, so I'm happy to keep going if we can?'

'Yes, fine,' Amrik said. 'Can you think of anybody who would want your plesiosaur badly enough to try to steal it?'

Jemma considered the question. 'Not really, although I received a call from a London-based fossil dealer wanting to acquire Plessie on behalf of a client.'

Laura glanced up from her notes. 'Who was the client?'

'He wouldn't say.'

'Who was the dealer?' Laura said.

'His name's Jeremy Lovell, I've known him a long time and always thought he was a reputable guy.'

Laura smiled. 'We'll organise a chat with Mr Lovell and lean on him to reveal his customer.'

Amrik added, 'Did anyone else show any particular interest in Plessie?'

Jemma deliberated for a moment about whether to mention Brad's initial phone call. She was sure the theft had nothing to do with him but thought she should say something. 'I also had a phone call a while ago from an American fossil hunter called Brad Jones offering to buy Plessie, but I'm not sure he was that keen. He did come and help us out on a volunteer basis to prepare the fossil for display, so I'm sure he wouldn't be involved in any theft.' *Oh dear, I'll be in trouble with Brad if the police contact him.*

'Right,' Laura said. 'Anything else?'

'Don't think so,' Jemma racked her brain for anything important. 'Obviously, we received a lot of general enquiries after the article in the *Sunday Browser Magazine*. We had a reasonable turnout for the press day.'

'Any suspicious characters turn up?'

'Well, Gareth from the café came, but he's just a nosy bugger.'

'What's his full name?'

'Gareth Wilkins. He runs the Beach Café in Lulcombe. Some collectors pay him to tell them who's digging where.'

Amrik wrote down the details. 'We'll check him out. Can you come up with a list of people who attended the open day, please?'

Jemma made a note on her pad. 'Of course, I can.'

'Thanks. Anything else out of the ordinary?'

Jemma pondered whether to mention her feelings of being watched. There was always a slight chance those feelings were somehow linked to the theft. *What if Anna's attackers had been watching her for some reason?* She decided she was being paranoid. 'No, I can't think of anything.'

Laura sipped her water. 'Thanks, Jemma. That was helpful and can't have been easy. Would you mind meeting us at the museum and going around to confirm what's missing?'

'Yes, no problem. Do you want to go now?'

Laura smiled. 'If you're OK, that would be fantastic. We can follow you.'

Jemma met Laura and Amrik at the museum and walked round with them. Other than Plessie, all that she could see was missing was the large ammonite the culprit had used to assault Anna.

As she walked through the eerily silent and dark museum it seemed like a horror version of the film *Night at The Museum*. She hoped that none of their exhibits would come to life as she walked past.

All through the new extension, the metallic smell of blood invaded her nostrils. *Who did that to Anna?*

Chapter 17

As Laura walked into the tired interview room at Swanbourne Police HQ, Amrik handed her a coffee.

'Thanks, Amrik. From the machine?'

'Fraid so, ma'am.'

'Oh well. I love to live life dangerously.' She stood with him and waited for the team to take their seats. 'If you watch them closely, Amrik, you'll see that the most punctual and eager always grab the best seats. The last-minute arrivals all end up either on the grotty seats or standing. That says a lot about the character of the team.'

'So it does, ma'am,' he said, smiling at his boss.

Laura addressed the team. 'OK then, let's crack on. I'll give you an update.' She stepped up to the whiteboard. 'So, to recap, Anna Jenkins is thirty-two and the manager of Lulcombe museum. She answered an alarm call at three a.m. on Friday and went to the museum. The police hadn't been notified by the monitoring company due to persistent false alarms. We believe the perpetrators caused those. It's possible that she disturbed a burglar or burglars. They caught her and tied her up with cable ties before beating her viciously with a rock, which was found on the floor next to her.'

'An ammonite, ma'am,' Amrik added.

'Thank you, DS Hussain. A sixteen-metre-long fossil that had been mounted on the wall was stolen. A plesiosaur, before DS Hussain corrects me again!'

Amrik smiled smugly.

'Mrs Jenkins was discovered by Jemma Thorne at nine-thirty the next morning with severe head injuries caused by being hit with a large st...' she glanced at Amrik, 'Ammonite.' The young DS grinned again. 'Mrs Thorne had gone in for a prearranged meeting with an engineer from the alarm company.'

A hand went up. 'Excuse me, ma'am.'

'Yes?'

'Did the alarm people find out how the false alarms were triggered?'

'The engineer wasn't sure, but he thought it was the same sensor each time. There were some marks in the dust on top of a tall cabinet near the sensor, but forensics haven't been able to identify what caused them. Amrik, can you summarise the forensic findings, please?'

He stood. 'Of course, ma'am. Extensive examination of the scene showed the following. Firstly, the ammonite used as a weapon, which weighed two point eight kilos, had no fingerprints or DNA apart from the victim's, so it appears that the culprit wore gloves.' He paused to sip his water.

'We found a discarded black balaclava on the floor with some traces of DNA not belonging to the victim. One of the culprits seems to have left their hood on the ground.' He looked at his notes. 'I've just had a thought, ma'am. What if one of them took off his hood and realised Mrs Jenkins had seen his face, so carried out the assault.'

She thought for a moment. 'Possible, Amrik, but we

can't say for certain. We recovered some DNA but haven't got a match from the database. At least it's on the system in case we arrest anybody.'

Amrik continued. 'The culprits drove a white van. We spotted a number plate on some CCTV footage, which led us to a removals company in Honiton. Unfortunately, the vehicle had been stolen the day before the incident. It turned up today, abandoned in a car park in Shaftesbury.'

'Any forensic findings, Amrik?' Laura asked.

He continued. 'They found some fingerprints and DNA traces but these turned out to belong to employees of the removals firm. We've not located any CCTV images that show the occupants of the van, so that's a dead-end, ma'am.'

'Thank you. Can you summarise any follow-ups from the interview with Jemma Thorne?'

He walked over to the whiteboard, which contained some photographs. 'Following our discussion with Mrs Thorne, we identified three people who had shown an excessive interest in the plesiosaur, or Plessie as it's nicknamed.' He pointed to a picture of a man standing outside a café. 'This is Gareth Wilkins, the proprietor of the Beach Café in Lulcombe. We spoke with Mr Wilkins and, as his premises overlook the sea, he's been paid by a number of fossil hunters to keep them informed of the conditions and any activity on the beach. According to his wife, Gareth was asleep until they got up at five, preparing to open up for breakfast.'

Laura interjected. 'We won't discard him as a suspect but he's not at the top of the list.'

Amrik drew a cross through his photo and pointed to another. 'This is Bradley Jones, an American citizen who entered the country a month before Jemma Thorne found

Plessie. We checked with the US authorities and he has no criminal record in the States. However, they are currently investigating him over the alleged removal of fossils from Federal land.' He chuckled. 'They were interested to know his whereabouts, as they thought he was on holiday in Canada. So, he started out as a real person of interest, but, when we checked him out, he has a reasonably strong alibi.' There was a pause while he reviewed his notes. 'Apparently, he was enjoying the company of a lady called Christine Jones, Jemma Thorne's next-door neighbour. When we contacted Mrs Jones about Brad's whereabouts, she told us they'd spent the whole evening together. Her actual words were, "He was definitely with me, at it like rabbits all night we were"'

The room erupted into laughter which momentarily broke the tension.

Amrik waited for the noise to subside. 'We did check with Jemma, and she confirmed Christine is reliable and that also, in her words, "Good for her, go Chrissie!"'

More chuckles.

'So again, Brad Jones is not at the top of our list of suspects.' He drew a cross through that photo.

He pointed to a third picture. 'This is Jeremy Lovell, an upmarket fossil dealer from London who deals in expensive specimens. We tried a lot of persuasion and even threats about visits from the VAT man and the tax man but he still refused to give us the name of his client. He doesn't have a criminal record and has an alibi for the night of the incident. We're sure he's not connected to the theft but we'll leave him on the board for now. Any questions so far?'

He glanced around the team.

'No? OK, I'll continue. Jemma gave me a list of the

people who attended the press day at the museum four days before the robbery. After checking everybody on the list, we discounted them all, except one. A person called Frank Butcher. He gave an address but said he'd collect his pass on the day. When I checked, the name and address were both false.' He sipped his water, allowing Laura an opportunity to read out some details from an internet search.

'Frank Butcher was a character in EastEnders,' she said. 'Have we got any CCTV or eyewitnesses who saw the man?'

Amrik glanced at his notes. 'Sorry, ma'am, nobody remembered him. Jemma recalled that Anna met him and gave him a pass. There's no CCTV inside the museum and we've not spotted anything unusual from any of the footage in the local streets.' He pointed to a card on the board with Frank Butcher written on it and a question mark. 'This person could be important so we'll keep trying to identify him. That's everything, ma'am.'

Laura nodded. 'Well, I think that's all for today. No real suspects, no ongoing vehicle leads. Not a lot at the moment, so we've got to step things up. I want all fossil dealers contacted, including Mr Lovell, and asked to notify us if they hear anything. I want checks of all CCTVs in Lulcombe, Shaftesbury and everywhere in between. Come on team, give me something! Thank you, off you go!'

She found the lack of progress so far with no real leads or credible suspects frustrating. There hadn't been many murder cases since she became a DI and she was desperate for it to end with a conviction. She walked out of the incident room and left behind the usual hubbub of post-meeting chat.

***

The High Dependency Unit of Swanbourne Royal Hospital was quiet as Jemma entered. She spoke to the nurse in reception and asked for Anna Jenkins. She was sent to an area with a couple of red plastic chairs outside a side room. After sitting down for a few minutes, Graham came out, and the two of them hugged. He was a handsome man with short dark hair turning grey by his ears. He looked pale and had aged considerably since she'd last seen him, his current ordeal giving him a haggard appearance.

Jemma fought back her tears. 'How is she?'

'Not good,' he said. 'She hasn't regained consciousness and is in a medically induced coma. They're concerned that, if she survives, she might be badly brain-damaged.'

'Oh, Graham, I'm so sorry,' she said. 'Can I sit with her for a bit, give you a break?'

'Yes, please, but I'm afraid she's not thrilling company. She just lies there with the machines bleeping. Maybe the café is still open and I can find something to eat. I've not eaten in twelve hours.'

'Go on, you need to keep your strength up. I'll be fine.'

Graham left and Jemma entered the room.

It was shocking to see Anna with her head bandaged and such a pale face. She lay on the bed with tubes and wires connecting her to life. An array of machines crowded the bedside and recorded her vital functions. Her chest rose and fell with the pumping of the ventilator.

Jemma hated hospitals, something about the constant smell of disinfectant and illness. Swanbourne Hospital was relatively new but still it felt depressing to her.

She perched on the chair beside the bed and reached over to hold Anna's cool, lifeless hand. 'Stay with us Anna, you'll be fine. We'll find Plessie, get the new extension finished and there'll be thousands of visitors.' Tears flowed as she sat with Anna. 'It should have been me who disturbed them, not you. This is all down to my stupid obsession with fossils. If I hadn't found that bloody plesiosaur then you wouldn't be lying here.'

She sat in silence for a while as her mind wandered back.

'I never got the chance to sit with Alice, you know. I only saw her from the top of the cliff. I wanted to go and see her, just to say goodbye one last time but they wouldn't let me after they retrieved the body. It was my fault that she fell. Everything bad that happens is my fault.'

She wiped her eyes and kept talking, alternating between telling her random gossip and sitting in silence. After an hour, Graham returned and sat beside her.

He touched Jemma's arm. 'You OK?'

'Not too bad. How are you bearing up?' she asked.

'So so,' he replied. 'Any signs from her?'

Jemma tried to smile. 'My hand got a squeeze when I told her the latest about Chrissie and Brad.'

Graham took Jemma's hand. 'Oh, it happens occasionally. The nurse said it was an involuntary muscle spasm and not to get too excited, so I didn't.'

Jemma stood and replaced Anna's hand gently back on the bedsheets. She was upset to see her in this state but was glad that she'd visited. She wiped a tear from her eye. 'We're all thinking of you both.'

Graham's voice cracked, 'I know you are.'

She left, keen to get away from the smells, the noises, and the artificial light.

***

Jemma arrived home, showered and stood in a towel looking out of her bedroom window. With the lights off, she hoped that nobody could see inside. She still worried about a possible stalker and usually closed the curtains whenever she entered her room at night.

When she settled down and tried to sleep, her mind kept replaying the image of Anna's head on the museum floor in a massive pool of blood.

Chapter 18

The following morning, a lone figure hid in his bivouac. After almost being spotted a while back, he'd been much more careful, varying his approach route and avoiding busy times of day. The path behind his vantage point was usually quiet but he had made a camouflaged bivvy to help stay hidden. The smell of bracken filled the shelter.

Through the telescope, he could see right into Jemma's bedroom. 'Come on. Come on,' he whispered, 'open your curtains before you get dressed.'

There was no sign of the American. When Brad kissed Jemma before the museum press event, he'd been so confused. Since then, Brad had gone into the workshop a few times, though hadn't kissed her again.

One by one he stretched his muscles like he'd been trained to do on long surveillances, watched and waited.

***

Jemma sat in her kitchen and had a light lunch. The events of the last couple of days had drained her but she knew she should eat properly, even though she didn't fancy anything. Dino looked up from his favourite spot, the warm rug in front of the Aga. Jemma rubbed his head and he lay back down.

Her phone rang and Brad's name flashed up on the screen. Since finishing Plessie they hadn't been working together as much. However, she now planned asking him to help her prepare a resin copy of the bones so they would have something to display when the police allowed them to reopen. Hopefully, that would be soon, once they were allowed back into the building.

She pressed answer. 'Hello, Brad.'

'Jemma,' he replied.

'You OK?'

'We need to talk. Can I come over now?'

'Yes,' Jemma sounded confused. 'What's the matter?'

'I'll explain when I get there. See you in ten.' He hung up.

Jemma wondered why Brad was short with her, but suddenly realised the police must have been in touch.

A few minutes later Brad knocked on her back door, and she let him in.

***

In the woods, the watcher's heart beat a little faster as he saw the American enter Jemma's house. Oh, to have a sniper rifle aimed in that direction. It would be perfect to make Brad's head explode like a watermelon.

He released his breath; he'd simply wait for the right opportunity.

***

Jemma offered Brad a coffee but he refused. He sat on one of her kitchen chairs and folded his arms.

'What's up?' she said.

'You ratted on me to the cops,' he snapped.

'Woah, I didn't rat on you. The police asked me who showed an interest in Plessie, so I said you wanted to buy her.'

'Well, they grilled me more than a burger on the Fourth of July, thanks to you. I thought they were gonna take me into the basement and bring the waterboard in.'

Jemma sighed. 'English police aren't like that.'

Brad ignored her. 'They also asked the US authorities about me.'

'And?' Jemma asked.

'Let's just say I'm not the flavour of the month with the Feds. They thought I was on vacation in an RV in Canada. Instead, I put it in the long-term parking lot and flew to England for a while, 'til the heat dies down.'

'Are you in trouble with them?' Jemma asked.

Brad shrugged. 'Not much. Anyway, that doesn't matter. They didn't know I was here until you told them.'

'I'm sorry but I had to tell the truth.'

'Just don't mention my name again.'

'I won't.'

Brad stormed out and slammed the front door behind him, shaking the plates on her kitchen dresser.

She stroked Dino. 'Oh, well, I might just have made a museum volunteer walk out.' She shrugged. 'Men, hey! At least we got his donation first.'

Dino rushed around wagging his tail at the word 'Walk.'

Jemma smiled. 'Sorry, Dino. Haven't got time for a W. A. L. K. right now. Dave'll be here soon.'

She started preparing the evening meal. Dave loved lasagne, especially Jemma's homemade version, one of the few things she cooked well.

***

Beneath the trees, the watcher packed away his kit but couldn't find his binoculars in the dark. He turned his torch on to try and find them.

***

Dave parked up and walked around the back of Jemma's house. He liked to stand in Jemma's garden and watch the lights of the boats on the distant sea. It had taken him a while to get used to living by the coast, after moving from Derbyshire ten years ago. He'd lived there for over thirty years and loved the rugged splendour of the Peak District. As he looked at the woods, he spotted a faint red light.

He knocked on her window. 'Jemma, quick, pass me a torch, I've seen something in the trees.'

She passed it to him and watched as he sprinted off over the field. 'Be careful!' she shouted.

***

Seeing Dave running over the field, the watcher realised he'd made a mistake turning the light on. Grabbing his telescope and bivouac cover, he took off along the path.

As he'd been sitting in the dark for a while, his night vision was excellent, so he made easy progress through the woods, running across the wet meadow, past the row of cottages and crossing the road to the Hill Farm Campsite.

He dropped to a fast walk and soon arrived back at his campervan, panting from his efforts. *It pays to stay fit.*

Thoughts of Jemma flashed through his head so he

flicked through the photos on his phone.

***

By the time Dave ran across the field to the woods, there was nobody around. It was darker than he'd expected and he'd needed a few moments to get his bearings.

He shone his torch around where he stood, and this time he spotted a patch where the bracken had been cleared and a shallow depression dug out.

Taking out his phone, he rang the station to call it in and request a tracker dog. Next he called Jemma to tell her to lock the door until he got back.

Fifteen minutes later two uniformed officers arrived. Dave flashed his badge and told them what he'd seen and found so far.

'Is the tracker dog coming?' he asked.

The policeman spoke into his handset, listened and turned to Dave. 'Sorry, sir, the dog's on a job over in Swanage so won't be able to come tonight. With the rain due later, there'll be no chance of picking up any scents tomorrow.'

'Bugger!' Dave showed them the bivvy spot.

One of the constables pointed to an object in the bracken. 'Here's something.'

Dave walked over and saw a pair of powerful binoculars on the ground. 'Can you send these for fingerprinting please?' he asked.

The PC took some nitrile gloves and an evidence bag from his belt and sealed the binoculars inside. They continued searching but couldn't find anything else.

Dave took some photos of the bivvy spot on his phone

and they followed him back to Jemma's house.

'Tea or coffee, lads?' he asked.

'Love to sir, but shift ends in half an hour and we need to write this up before we finish.'

He shook their hands. 'Thanks. I'll check about the binoculars tomorrow in case they find any fingerprints.' He knocked on Jemma's door.

After checking the CCTV monitor, she let him in.

Dave said, 'It's OK. They might find some fingerprints on the binoculars they found.'

'What binoculars?' Jemma asked. 'Has he been looking at me through them?'

He held her hand. 'We found some on the ground. It looks like whoever's been watching used them on the house. Don't worry, we'll catch the bastard. Do you think it could be Brad?'

'I'm sure it isn't him. He called round earlier to moan because I gave his name to the police.'

'What?'

'I told the two detectives he rang me and offered to buy Plessie, so they gave him quite a grilling.'

Dave grunted. 'Serves him right for splashing his dollars around.'

'Maybe, but I don't think he could have got round to the woods after he left.'

'How about I ask the uniforms to call in and check his boots,' Dave suggested.

'No, don't. He'd kill me if the cops turned up again.'

'That doesn't matter. Jemma, this is serious.'

'I know, but it can't be Brad. Can it?'

Chapter 19

The next morning, Dave went into Swanbourne Police HQ. He stayed on the ground floor to check any follow-up from the previous night's call-out.

The desk sergeant glanced up as he walked in. 'Morning, Dave.'

'Morning, sarge. What's the latest on the incident in Lulcombe last night?'

'Give me a minute and I'll fire up the system.' He clicked the computer mouse and waited. 'How long have you worked in Dorset, Dave.'

Dave thought for a moment. 'It's coming up to ten years soon. Why?'

'Your Derbyshire accent comes through every now and then. I can't understand what you're saying some of the time.'

Dave laughed. 'I'll have to bring in one of the police interpreters.'

'Here we are, it seems they got a clear fingerprint off the binoculars and...' He read the notes on the screen, 'oh, bad news. No matches on the criminal system so there's no chance of finding him that way.'

'Bugger and bollocks!' Dave snarled.

'Sorry mate, they've sent the details off for checking on other databases, but nothing so far. At least the print is on record now, in case they arrest a suspect.'

'Back to the drawing board,' Dave replied.

***

Jemma's phone rang. It was Dave.

'No joy on the fingerprints,' he said. 'They found a decent one but it doesn't show up on any of their systems. You seem to think it can't be Brad but it might be worth double-checking his prints to eliminate him. Have you got them on anything or shall we pull him in?'

'What did he touch?' She thought for a moment. 'I know. There are some tools in the workshop he's been using without gloves. Would one of those be useful?'

'Perfect! Remind me later and I'll borrow some.'

She put down her mobile and thought about Brad. Surely, it couldn't be him. At that moment, the back door flew open and Ellie came rushing in.

She dropped her bag, ran over and they hugged. 'Mum, so sorry about Anna. How is she?'

The thought of Anna almost made Jemma cry again and she had to swallow back the tears. 'No more news. I went to visit her yesterday and she's not good. They've put her in a medically induced coma to give her more hope of survival.'

'Oh, Mum.' Ellie sobbed. 'But she's lovely, and she's always been there!'

'She's worked at the museum for sixteen years so she's always been around while you were growing up.' Jemma didn't want Ellie to worry too much about Anna so she tried some distraction therapy. 'And how are you? College going well?'

Ellie grabbed her stuff. 'Yeah, brill.'

'Do you want to eat with us tonight?'

'Yes, please.'

'I bought steak if you fancy some?'

'Sounds lovely. You got plenty?'

'It'll stretch to three, no problem. I'll put the kettle on. I bet you've got loads more washing.'

Ellie grinned. 'Only a bit.'

When Dave came home, they refrained from any talk about Anna, Plessie, or the possible stalker. Jemma had told Ellie the basics and to watch herself and close the curtains.

They enjoyed their meal and afterwards watched *The Commitments*, a film they all liked.

***

The next morning at ten past eight Dave's mobile rang, the caller ID displaying DI Day.

'Ma'am.'

'Morning, Dave. Sorry to disturb you when you're not on duty but I have some bad news.'

'What?'

'I'm afraid we have to escalate the museum case to a murder enquiry. Anna Jenkins died during the night.'

Chapter 20

Across the town, Brad stretched his hamstrings before the five-mile run he did every morning, his fluorescent yellow running kit and green trainers out of place on a dismal grey Dorset morning. But he didn't care. Better to be seen by any drivers out on the narrow country roads where he ran the first part of his route. Most people drove steadily on the narrower sections, but some went way too fast.

As he ran down a single-track road, a car came up behind him. He glanced over his shoulder and saw a Land Rover Discovery filling the road. Running faster, he intended to reach the next gateway and let it past.

As he continued, the vehicle increased its speed until it closed in on him.

Again, Brad checked over his shoulder and decided to slow down. As he did, the vehicle slowed too so it remained the same distance behind.

Slowing to a walk, he considered squeezing into the side to let it past but unfortunately the road was too narrow. Instead, he stopped, turned round to face the Land Rover and pointed to a farm gate further along the road. The driver gave him a thumbs-up from the open side window.

Brad started running again and decided to make for

the opening.

Suddenly the revving increased and before he had a chance to step onto the verge, something crashed into him from behind, throwing him into the air. With a thud, he landed on the tarmac, and then blackness.

**

Laura Day was working through her emails when her phone rang. It was the desk sergeant.

'Hello, ma'am.'

'Morning, sarge. How can I help?'

'One of your suspects in the museum case has been involved in an incident. Hit and run while out jogging.'

'Who?'

'A Bradley Jones.'

She sank further into her chair. 'Is he badly injured?'

'Don't know ma'am. Two uniforms are on their way to meet the ambulance and check the scene, but I thought I'd better tell you.'

'Thanks, sarge. You can never tell if these things are connected.' She ended the call and dialled an internal number. 'Amrik, Brad Jones was hit earlier by a car near Lulcombe. Can you go down and see if there are any connections with the murder and theft?'

'Yes ma'am. How is he?' Amrik asked.

'No idea, we only received the call a few minutes ago.'

**

Down in Lulcombe the ambulance arrived and attended to the victim. Two uniformed officers had closed the road and were measuring tyre marks.

Amrik parked and got out of the patrol car, donning his cap as he approached the traffic officers. 'How's the victim?'

'Unconscious. He was in a bad way when they loaded him up.'

He took some details but nobody at the scene knew anything else so he worked his way along the road, ringing doorbells as he went.

At the fifth house, he struck lucky when the elderly owner stepped out before he even had a chance to knock. The man was dressed smartly, had the bearing of an ex-military man and twirled his handlebar moustache as he stood there.

'I wondered when your lot would arrive.'

Amrik took out his notebook. 'Morning, sir. We're investigating a hit-and-run.'

'I'm not surprised, the speed he was going.'

'Who?'

'The bloke driving the big black four-by-four that came screaming past earlier.'

'Did you see the driver?' Amrik asked.

'No, but I saw the number plate. One of those personalised ones with AJH and three numbers. Bugger drove by too quickly for me to see properly.'

Amrik radioed in and found out that a black Land Rover had been reported missing from Hill Farm in Lulcombe two hours before. Half an hour later, a vehicle matching that description was spotted in the Beach Car Park at Lulcombe. He drove down and found the Discovery with its nearside front bumper and wing dented.

He donned his gloves and opened the vehicle to check inside but unable to find anything, he called in a forensic team to search for fingerprints.

When the team arrived, they found the car had been wiped down well, though they were able finally to lift a full print from the handbrake. After they photographed and scanned it in, an immediate match came up with the fingerprint from the binoculars in the 'Peeping Tom' incident.

***

Jemma wanted to stay in bed but Dave said it would be better if she was up and occupied. Anything to distract her from thinking about Anna.

'Come on, Jem, you've got to get up and have some breakfast.' All he got was a grunt from under the sheets. 'I'll cook some bacon.'

Another grunt.

'It'll be ready in fifteen minutes so don't let it go cold. You need to keep your strength up.'

Jemma pulled the covers higher as he walked downstairs.

Ten minutes later Jemma pottered into the kitchen in her dressing gown. She snuffled into a tissue. Dave had the bacon sizzling and Ellie was in charge of the toast and tea.

'Sit down, Mum, it's almost ready.'

'I don't want much.'

Dave brought over a plate of bacon. 'Here, have what you fancy. I'm sure Ellie will mop up any you don't want.'

Ellie set a mug of tea and some toast in front of her mum.

'Wow, this must be a first. An Ellie and Dave co-production.' Jemma said.

He laughed. 'Don't knock it, might not happen again.' He sat down with his own tea and took some bacon and toast.

Jemma picked up the newspaper but saw a headline about Anna and dropped it as if it was hot.

He held her hand. 'We'll get the bastards who did this. Stay strong.'

She smiled a smile that didn't reach her eyes. 'I'll try Dave, I'll try.'

***

Dave's phone rang. It was DI Day again.

'Afternoon, Dave.'

'Afternoon, ma'am. Any developments?'

'No, but we've had another incident.'

He hesitated. 'What's happened?'

'Brad Jones was the victim of a hit-and-run this morning along a narrow road, two miles out of Lulcombe.'

'Brad! How is he?'

'He's got several breaks but they think he'll pull through. A black Land Rover ran into him from behind. Due to the nature of his injuries, the investigators think that at the time he was sprinting, and the impact propelled him into a hedge.'

'Have they got the driver?'

'No, but there's something interesting. The Land Rover turned up in the Beach Car Park and Forensics retrieved a fingerprint from the handbrake. It isn't on the criminal system, but it matches the one from the binoculars in your 'Peeping Tom' incident last week.'

Dave gasped. 'What? How?'

'Well, whoever was watching Jemma also used the vehicle to mow down Mr Jones.'

'That's incredible!' Dave exclaimed. 'Who the hell is doing this?'

As he spoke, Jemma walked in and listened.

He placed his hand over the receiver. 'Sit down. I'll only be a minute.'

She sat quietly, picking at her nails.

Laura continued. 'Would you mind asking Jemma if she can think of anybody who might want to do such a thing?'

'I thought I couldn't be on the case,' he said. 'A close relationship with a material witness.'

'Ah, yes, that. Unfortunately, we're stretched already. Nobody's available at any neighbouring forces, so we think you should join the investigation.'

'We?'

Laura paused. 'Well, I do.'

'Right, if you're happy to sign things off, ma'am.'

'Needs must. See you in the morning.'

'OK, ma'am. Bye.'

Dave ended the call and sat next to Jemma. 'More bad news, I'm afraid.'

***

Jemma chewed the inside of her lip as Dave told her about Brad. Ellie came in so he told her as well. Jemma sat with her head in her hands, Dave and Ellie either side of her.

'Brad'll pull through, he's strong.' Ellie said, fighting back her tears.

Jemma sat up with a start. 'I've just thought, has anyone told Chrissie?'

Dave pulled out his phone. 'I'll check at the station.'

She started to put on her shoes. 'I'd better go and tell her.'

'Wait a minute 'til I find out if she knows or not.' Dave stepped outside and returned a few minutes later.

'Someone called her earlier,' he confirmed. 'They found his list of contacts and he'd called her number quite a few times over the last few weeks.'

'OK,' Jemma said. 'At least it won't be a surprise for her.'

'The strange thing though is that they've also contacted his wife in America.'

'His what?'

'His wife. When they went to his house and checked through his belongings, they found her listed as next of kin on his passport.'

'That's strange,' she said. 'Did they speak to her?'

'Yes,' Dave said. 'But she complained about the call. Turns out when they rang, it was three a.m. in LA. She didn't seem that bothered and told them she and Brad were separated. They no longer keep in touch.'

'The old dog. Fancy keeping that quiet! Oh, I better go and see Chrissie.'

Ellie stood up. 'Do you want me to come as well?'

Jemma touched her arm. 'I'm OK, I won't be long.' She walked next door and knocked on the back door. It opened revealing Chrissie in her dressing gown.

'Hi, Jem.'

'Hi, Chrissie, you OK?'

'Yes, I'm fine. Brad's the broken one.'

'Have you seen him yet?'

'Yes, I went straight down when they called me, but he's still unconscious.'

'What did they say?'

Chrissie wiped her eyes with a tissue. 'They said he was serious but stable. I think that means they're not sure, but he's not getting any worse.'

'That's hopeful, isn't it?'

'Might be, I don't know. How are you bearing up?'

Jemma shrugged. 'I'm OK. It's all a bit bewildering with Anna's murder and now Brad's accident.'

'It wasn't an accident.'

'That's what they think. What's more, it was the same person who has been watching my house from the woods.'

Chrissie flopped down into a kitchen chair. 'No! But who?'

'No idea. Some strange folk out there, Chrissie.'

'Too bloody right.'

'OK, catch up soon. We'll have a drink together, the four of us, once Brad's out of hospital.'

'That's a date or a double date. Thanks for coming round, Jem.'

'Bye.'

Jemma returned home.

***

The rest of the day went by in a blur; Jemma spoke to Anna's husband, Graham, and then sat with Ellie in the kitchen.

'You OK, Mum?'

Jemma shrugged. 'OK, I suppose. I've been better.'

'How's Graham?'

'Just about coping. He's been hit hard and is in a state of shock. I kept apologising to him but he said it wasn't my fault.'

'How can it be your fault?'

'It's my obsession with fossil hunting that's put people in danger. If I hadn't found Plessie then Anna would still be alive.'

'That's just silly. You can't blame yourself.' She hugged her mum.

Jemma rested her head on Ellie's shoulder and her mind wandered back thirty years.

And if I hadn't been digging out a fossil Alice would never have gone over that cliff.

***

That evening Jemma received a phone call from Vincent Lawrence asking if she could attend a meeting of museum trustees the following day.

'Not really,' she complained. 'Is it important?'

'Yes, it is.' He swallowed. 'We need to talk about replacing Anna, the public opening and also an increased offer to buy the site from the property developers.'

Jemma snapped. 'Can't we just leave it? Anna's died, Brad's lying in hospital and I'm trying to build a replica Plessie.'

He spoke quietly, 'I'm sorry, Jemma, but there are some important decisions we've got to make.'

She sighed, 'OK, what time?'

'Ten o'clock at the Town Hall. They won't let us back into the museum yet.'

'OK, I'll be there.'

Jemma felt everything was piling up on her so she took two paracetamol, and went to bed.

***

Jemma ignored Alice's shout and wished she'd stop messing about. A real attention seeker, Alice always tried to get people to run around after her or look at the boring things she found. Jemma returned to working on the fossilised fish that materialised before her eyes.

She heard Phil shout down from his vantage point. 'Jemma, quick. Alice is hanging on a branch over the cliff!'

As she looked up, the world appeared to be going in slow motion.

Phil ran down the hillside, his arms pumping. Even the gulls seemed to have stopped flying and hung motionless in the sky.

Jemma scrambled up and ran along the cliff edge to the area where she'd last seen Alice, but couldn't see her. Halfway down the path, Phil pointed to a spot on her right. As she turned, she heard a fading scream…

Chapter 21

'Hello, Brad, are you awake?'

Brad could make out a woman's voice, muffled and faint. Not one he recognised. Right on the edge of his consciousness, the words didn't seem to mean anything. Every bit of him ached but he didn't feel any real pain.

After a while, he forced his eyelids apart, and the light crept in as he focused on his surroundings. He lay in a white room with curtains hanging around the bed. A tube from a drip disappeared into his arm.

He turned his head to look sideways and... Whooah! World spinning! Instead, he returned to staring straight ahead and eventually the room stopped turning. His other arm throbbed in a plaster.

'Gently, Brad,' the voice said. 'I'm your nurse. Go steady and don't make any sudden movements.'

He closed his eyes and tried to summon the energy to speak. 'Wherrhh am eye?' His tongue felt thick and didn't belong in his mouth. The words wouldn't come out as he intended but she still understood him.

'You're in Swanbourne Hospital because you were in an accident. A vehicle hit you but didn't stop. You've been unconscious for two days. Everything will be a bit woozy.'

The words gave Brad a flashback. Running along the road and hearing a vehicle behind him, going faster and then slower. Finally being hit and thrown into the air and then, blackness.

He tried again. 'Whortts wrang?'

'You broke your arm, leg and several ribs. You also have extensive bruising. Pretty lucky. No damage to any internal organs and everything that's broken should heal.'

'Fanng you. Zat's good.'

'Welcome back to the land of the living. Just relax and don't overdo things. No sudden movements, please, as you're connected to the machines. I must go, but there's a call button by your left hand in case you need anything.'

Without moving his head, he looked around the room trying to acquaint himself with his surroundings. A bunch of colourful flowers were sitting in a vase on his bedside table along with a couple of cards. He reached for the nearest one but got shooting pains through his whole body. Giving up, he closed his eyes and returned to his morphine-induced slumber.

**

The next day Jemma left Ellie having a lie-in and breakfasted with Dave before he left for the station. As it was dry, she walked down for the meeting at the museum.

The town hall was an old building that served many functions from a meeting room to table tennis club. The main hall contained a rectangular table with six chairs. Some of the trustees were already seated with mugs of grey tea. Jemma joined them but couldn't face the over-stewed liquid so she took a bottle of water instead.

They chatted for a while about the terrible occurrences with Anna and Brad and then got down to business, agreeing to start interviewing for a new manager and signing the forms for Anna's pension and death-in-service payout to go to her husband, Graham.

Jemma, as the chairman, looked at the next item proposed by Vincent. She frowned and folded her arms. 'The motion is that the museum sells its site to Fletcher Brothers Property Development Ltd. Can you give us the latest details please, Vincent?'

He picked up a letter. 'The offer has been increased to one-hundred thousand pounds, plus a purpose-built museum, south of the Axminster Road car park. Personally, I think we should accept this offer as that amount would guarantee our financial security for a long time.'

One of the other trustees, Wendy, raised her hand.

'Yes, Wendy?' Vincent asked.

'We don't know a great deal about the Fletcher Brothers. Do you have any more information?'

'They're a development company,' he replied. 'Operated in London for some years, and recently built the High Fields Estate in Lulcombe.'

'And destroyed part of an ancient woodland in the process,' Jemma added.

Vincent scowled. 'But they created one hundred houses for local people to buy, such as Anna Jenkins, who lived in one.'

'However, lots of them are now holiday homes,' Wendy said.

Jemma added. 'I did a bit of research and heard rumours they were involved in some shady goings-on in London.'

Vincent snapped, 'I don't pay any attention to rumours, only facts.'

She persisted. 'The existing building is steeped in history and location, so it's important we stay. Especially as we applied for, received and spent a seventy-five thousand pounds Heritage Grant to extend the building.'

Wendy added. 'Which we would need to pay back if we sell the site within five years.'

'Thank you, Wendy,' Jemma said. 'I'd forgotten. That wouldn't leave us with much. The extension is complete and I'm sure we'll have lots of visitors once we reopen.'

Vincent harrumphed. 'But those extra people would've been coming to see Jemma's plesiosaur. If it's not displayed, I bet they won't come and...'

Jemma interrupted, 'I've had an idea about that. I took a plaster cast of every single bone from the skeleton and made a resin copy. We can reassemble those and mount them in place of Plessie. Only temporarily, of course, until she's back on the wall.'

He frowned. 'If ever.'

Jemma continued. 'Hopefully, she'll be back one day; she'll be too hot for the dealers.'

'The fossil won't come on to the market.' Vincent grunted. 'An unscrupulous private collector will snap it up. Plenty of those about.'

Jemma ignored him. 'It would be terrible for Lulcombe if they built a massive hotel, spa and casino dominating the western half of town. The museum would be lost along with most of the Beach Car Park and many mature trees. We can't destroy this important part of our heritage. I've been going to the museum since I could walk, there's so much history in the building.' Her voice raised. 'It would be wrong for me and wrong for Lulcombe. We need to keep it running where it is. It's what Anna would have wanted.' By the time she finished she was almost shouting. 'It can't close, it can't close. We've got to fight to keep it where it is.' She slammed the table with her fist, making everybody jump, and stared at the shocked faces gathered around. 'Sorry, everybody, but it's something that I'm very passionate about.'

'Don't worry, Jemma, we understand,' said Wendy.

Vincent stared at her. 'Isn't your opposition just because the view from your cottage might be affected?'

Jemma stiffened. 'I resent what you're implying. I will only vote for what I think is right for the museum. Anyway, back to the agenda. Any comments from anybody else?'

They discussed the matter further and voted. Three trustees went against selling the site, three voted in favour, which meant the decision came down to the chairman's casting vote, so Jemma confirmed the motion had been defeated and couldn't be put forward again for three months. Vincent sighed and screwed up the agenda in his hand.

Next, they discussed when to re-open and decided they should do so with Jemma's replica Plessie as soon as possible.

Jemma added, 'The Natural History Museum did well with their diplodocus in the foyer. That was a copy.'

Then they considered an application by Sally O'Keefe to join the board of trustees. Only Vincent supported the motion, mainly because Sally also wanted a shiny new building. The others voted against it.

Vincent said. 'What's the position about Plessie's insurance?'

Jemma thought for a moment. 'I'm not sure, I think Anna added Plessie to the policy because she asked me for a rough idea of her value.'

His face brightened. 'What did you tell her?'

'One hundred and fifty thousand.'

'So, should we receive that back from the insurance company?'

'Possibly, if they agree with the valuation and everything else is OK, but I'd much rather we got Plessie back instead.'

With no more business, the meeting closed and they all left.

As she walked home, Jemma wondered why Vincent was so keen for the museum move to go ahead. *Maybe he's on a commission from the developers to help oil the wheels.*

***

At that moment Vincent was making a call on his mobile. The call was answered.

'Yes?'

'Hello. It's Vincent from the museum.'

'Good news, I take it?'

'Ah, well, not good news I'm afraid. They don't want to sell.'

'I thought you said you could swing it.'

Vincent hesitated, 'I said I might be able to help. Unfortunately, the lady trustees are traditionalists who want to keep the old site.'

'And?'

'The chairman, Jemma Thorne had the casting vote and defeated the proposal.'

'Jemma Thorne! Well, well. I must admit, Vincent, that I'm very disappointed. Very disappointed indeed. There will obviously be no payment after this failure.'

Vincent swallowed, 'I'll try again in three months' time.'

'That may be too late.'

The call ended leaving Vincent staring at the screen.

Chapter 22

Jemma travelled straight from the meeting to Swanbourne Hospital to check on Brad. He'd recovered consciousness and they were allowing visitors. On the way, she picked up some grapes and a fossil collecting magazine so he wouldn't be bored.

Walking into the ward, she glanced sadly at the door to the Intensive Care Department, where she'd visited Anna not long ago. Her eyes filled with tears when she read the name of the room's current occupant. *I hope they do better than Anna.*

The Musculoskeletal ward had four beds that were all occupied by patients with varying injuries. The bed she passed first had a man whose face was wrapped in bandages like the invisible man.

The usual smells of antiseptic and illness hit her nostrils as she breathed in the clinical air.

Brad was sitting up in bed wearing a set of headphones, his gaunt face a marked contrast to his usual tanned, outdoors appearance. With eyes shut, he was singing along to some music. Jemma knew the song. *Old Time Rock and Roll* by Bob Seger, one of Brad's favourite performers.

She touched his arm, the one not in plaster and he jumped, grimacing. 'Ouch!'

Jemma winced. 'Sorry, didn't mean to hurt you.'

'Don't worry, everything hurts at the moment.'

'How are you?' She handed him the grapes and magazines. 'I thought you might like these.'

'Thanks. I'm still in a lot of pain, but I'm alive. They said I only survived because I was sprinting when the Land Rover hit me. It ended up being more of a glancing blow. If I'd have been running towards it, then, splat!'

Jemma went pale. 'Yuk! Did they say how long you'll be in for?'

'A few weeks. Don't think their stock of morphine will last very long. I'm in la-la-land most of the time.'

'Will you recover fully?'

'I won't be doing any marathons but I should be OK.'

They talked for a while about metal pins, Chrissie and hospital food. Jemma suddenly remembered, 'Oh! The policeman mentioned he contacted your wife. You didn't tell me you're married.'

'I'm not, we're separated. It didn't last long. We'll get divorced one day when Pop's lawyers sort it out.'

They carried on chatting but, just as Brad's eyes were starting to close, Jemma leant on his arm again.

'Ow!' he jumped, 'my arm!'

Jemma lifted her hands up. 'Sorry, Brad, I won't touch you anywhere!'

'Call me Indy.'

'What?'

'You used to call me Indy.'

'That was years ago.'

'Go on.'

'OK. Sorry, Indy, I won't touch you anywhere.'

'I don't hurt everywhere.'

'Right, where doesn't it hurt?'

'My right shoulder.'

All of a sudden, Jemma had an urge to kiss his shoulder. Against all of her instincts she did. *Oh my God, what am I doing?*

He pointed to his forehead. 'Here.'

She smiled, leant over gently and kissed him on his forehead.

With a grin he pointed to his lips. 'This isn't too bad.'

Jemma leant in and kissed him gently on the lips. She didn't mean to do it, but it happened anyway. He responded for a moment but then went limp and she realised he'd fallen asleep.

'Brad?'

No response.

'Indy.'

Still no response. Jemma stood and looked down at him. *I can't believe what I've just done. I hope he's so drugged up on morphine that he doesn't remember anything.*

She turned and rushed from the ward.

After arriving home, her phone rang. The screen showed it was Barbara Hunter, the middle-aged local lady who ran the Lulcombe Fossil Festival.

The festival celebrated Lulcombe's status as a fossil hunting location. The weekend of stalls, walks, exhibitions and hands-on science brought people into the town when there weren't many holidaymakers around.

Jemma found Barbara a daunting lady. A tall woman, some people said she looked and acted like Margot from *The Good Life*, a seventies sitcom. She'd run the Fossil Festival for many years and usually got what she wanted.

Jemma answered. 'Hi, Barbara.'

'Hello Jemma, how are you?'

'I'm OK, thanks. How can I help?'

'Well, a bit delicate really. I thought about all that's happened to you and the museum recently.' She paused.

Jemma waited. 'And?'

'If you don't feel up to having a stall this year then I wouldn't mind in the slightest. I'd happily refund your deposit.'

Jemma seethed inside but stayed polite. 'So kind of you,' she replied, 'but we have to carry on.'

'Oh,' Barbara paused, 'you wouldn't be letting us down if you gave it a miss this year. I'm sure you'd be better just relaxing. We've got the perfect replacement.'

'What? Who?'

'A Miss O'Keefe from the university. I'm sure you know her. She said she'd be happy to come up with her own fossil stand. After all, she was part of the team that discovered Plessie. She also volunteered to give a Fossils of Lulcombe talk as you probably wouldn't be up to it.'

Jemma bristled. 'What?'

'Yes, she'd be happy to give the talk you usually give.'

Jemma wondered what Sally was after. 'You can tell Miss O'Keefe I am perfectly capable of looking after the museum stall and delivering a speech on my favourite topic. And she was not part of the team that discovered Plessie. She just helped me to dig it out.'

'Oh, smashing, super! I'm so pleased. Between ourselves, you know I found her rather brash. Not from round here, is she?'

Jemma smiled. 'No, she's not.'

'OK. That's lovely. See you on set up day!'

She rang off and Jemma relaxed. It would be good to concentrate on the Festival and try to forget about everything else that was going on. She hoped it would be a good weekend, without any unwanted drama.

Chapter 23

On the day of Anna's funeral, Jemma sat in her kitchen with Dave waiting for Ellie to come down. She wore a black dress with a dark blue cardigan while Dave was in a black suit and white shirt. They waited in silence.

'Are you up to this?' he said, squeezing her hand.

She shrugged. 'I've got to be.'

'I'm worried about you.'

'I'll be better once today is over,' she said. 'Hopefully, things will be back to normal soon.'

'They will, once we catch the culprit.'

'That would be great.'

'And remember, don't bottle things up,' he said. 'If you feel like a good cry, go for it.'

She leant over and kissed him. 'Thanks.' Her face went red when she realised she was thinking of Brad as she kissed Dave. *Pull yourself together woman.*

Ellie walked in. 'Really, I leave you two for a few minutes and you're snogging like teens on a first date!'

Jemma laughed. 'Nothing wrong with that. Are you ready Els?'

'Yes.' Ellie replied.

'OK then, let's go,' Dave said. 'Oh, is Brad going to be

there?'

Jemma picked up her handbag. 'No, he's not fit to travel yet.'

She locked up and they left.

***

Dave parked at the crematorium and gazed around. 'I hate this place.'

'Me too.' Jemma said. 'Hope this is our only visit for a long time.' They went in, took their seats and Jemma spotted the red hair of Sally O'Keefe a couple of rows in front. 'What's she doing here?' she whispered to Dave.

He shrugged. 'It's a free country. Perhaps she knew Anna from the museum.'

Jemma frowned. 'I don't think so.'

Ellie turned to face them. 'Shush, you two, it's starting.'

The ceremony flew past and Jemma managed to hold back the tears until Anna's husband, Graham, gave a eulogy. He spoke with a clear voice that threatened to crack as his emotions came to the surface. 'Anna was a very lucky lady. She left school and started working at the museum. It turned out to be the job she loved. After starting out as a receptionist she eventually became manager and was so happy in her work.' He let out a shaky breath as he composed himself to continue. 'She was the love of my life and I am honoured that she was my wife for over ten years. We'd been hoping to start a family soon. She'd have been the most incredible mother.'

By now there were few dry eyes and Jemma sobbed on Dave's shoulder.

He whispered. 'Let those tears out for Anna.'

She wiped her eyes. 'They're not just for Anna, they're for everything that's gone on recently.'

Dave held her tighter.

After the service, they went to a local pub for the wake. The Royal Oak in Swanbourne was a large place with a function room that was currently packed with mourners.

As they walked in, they were given teas and coffees, or pointed towards the bar if they needed something stronger. Jemma was trying to gather herself, speaking to Graham and some of the museum staff, when Sally interrupted.

'Ah, just the person I wanted to speak to.'

'Hello, Sally. Sorry, I'm talking to Graham.' She angled her body away from Sally and back to Graham.

Sally stood still for a moment but then moved, smiling, between Jemma and Graham. She smiled at him. 'Excuse me, I need to have a word with Jemma about work and it's really important.'

His cheeks turned red. 'Don't worry, Jemma. I'll do a bit of mingling.'

Sally slipped her arm around Jemma's shoulders. 'Right, I need a word about my hours and responsibilities.'

Jemma pushed her hand off and glared at her. 'That's so rude. I was talking to Graham and that's more important than anything you have to say. I can't believe you want to talk about work now, at Anna's wake!'

'I never have a chance to chat at the uni.'

'I'm sorry, but I can't get my head around that sort of stuff today.' She turned away from Sally and walked over to where Dave was standing with Ellie.

'You all right, Jemma?' he asked.

'I'm seething. I can't believe that awful woman wanted

to discuss her role at uni at a time like this.'

Ellie glanced across at Sally. 'Watch out, she's coming over.'

Sally strode closer and stood so her face was nearly up against Jemma's. She raised her voice. 'Don't you dare walk away from me. I need to discuss important things with you and you're never in your office when you should be.'

Jemma was so shocked that her mouth fell open while around the room, the other mourners stopped their conversations to stare at the two women.

Jemma gathered herself and shouted back, 'I have never come across anybody as rude and unprofessional as you. You are totally out of order. This is a funeral, for God's sake. Now, just piss off.'

Sally turned and stormed off. Two men holding pints at the bar applauded as she left.

Jemma looked around as she felt her face burning. 'Sorry, everybody, she's not with me.'

Chapter 24

The first day of the Fossil Festival arrived and Lulcombe was bathed in warm autumn sunshine. The streets heaved with visitors and locals. The event was sponsored by Fletcher Brothers Property Development Ltd. After the success of their housing estate, High Fields, they were now trying to drum up some publicity and support for their hotel, casino and spa resort plans for Lulcombe. Jemma was not happy about their high profile but the Festival couldn't be choosy about corporate sponsors as there weren't that many.

Jemma and Dave took down the copy of Plessie's skull, which was going to be the star exhibit of their stall at the event. After a struggle, they managed to get the head on the stand.

Jemma exhaled. 'I know this is resin but there's still some weight to it.'

'Sure is,' Dave said. 'When are you hoping to reopen the museum?'

'Next weekend if the police let us. Our new manager has started. You might meet her later.'

'Shame the full replica isn't here today.'

'Too large to move and leave on this table,' she said.

Dave zipped up his coat. 'I'm off. Catch you later. Hope you have a busy day.'

'See you tonight.' They kissed and he left.

The festival attracted the usual mix of tourists, locals and collectors. More people had turned up this year due to the Plessie article in *The Sunday Browser,* as well as the notoriety surrounding the whole theft and murder investigation.

Jemma didn't like the glossy display in the entrance to the town hall. The board displayed an advert for the Fletcher's project. She had hoped their interest would wane after the trustee's vote. However, the Fletcher Brothers appeared to be persistent people.

Manning the museum stall, many people were interested in the replica skull and wanted to ask questions, some sensible, others not.

On Saturday afternoon, Jemma gave her talk on the fossils of Lulcombe in the sports hall of the leisure centre. She explained about the ammonites, belemnites and crinoids that could be found on the beach. Moving on to her latest find, she used some impressive slides showing Plessie in all her glory before the theft. The presentation also included photos of parts of the skeleton in situ in the rockfall before she removed them.

While Jemma spoke, she spotted a face at the back of the hall that she thought she recognised. After a pause, she grabbed her glass of water and glanced back at the same spot but the person had gone.

While she continued with the lecture, uncertainty played on her mind. Could she have seen her old boyfriend, Phil Brown, standing at the back? Afterwards, as she went back to the stand, she convinced herself she'd imagined the whole thing.

***

The festival wound up for the day and Dave returned to help Jemma move the skull back to her workshop.

'Fun day?' he asked.

'Yes, lots of visitors and an incredible interest in Plessie, even the replica!'

'Should improve museum visitor numbers, once you re-open.'

Jemma grinned. 'Yep!'

'Brad still in hospital?' he asked.

'Yes. He'll be in for a bit longer yet.'

'Is he going to be OK?'

'Yes, but he's gone a bit quiet and introverted since the accident.' She paused. 'You ask a lot of questions about him, don't you?'

He shrugged. 'Do I? I just like to know what he's up to, as I don't trust him and his intentions.'

She picked up a box. 'Oh, well. By the way, a weird thing happened today.'

Dave glanced up. 'What?'

'During my lecture, I thought I saw Phil Brown standing in the hall.'

'What? The guy you went out with at school?'

'Yes.'

'Where?'

'At the back. I only glimpsed him, or a person who looked like him, for a moment. I didn't see him again afterwards.'

'What's he doing in Lulcombe?'

'No idea.' She thought for a moment. 'Unless he's the person who's been watching me.'

'I'll check him out tomorrow when I'm at work,' Dave said.

'OK, thanks.'

They loaded up the skull and drove it back to Jemma's workshop before having some food, a bottle of wine and an early night.

***

The next morning Dave was sitting at his desk at the station, the surface a colourful mess of notepads, bits of paper and sticky notes. Accessing various online databases, he searched for anything about Phil Brown and found the usual basic information, though nothing detailed. The Police National Computer contained no details about him and neither did he have any motoring offences on his licence other than a speeding endorsement many years earlier.

He tried obtaining Phil's army records without success, so he decided to call an old friend who worked in Special Branch. He picked up his mobile and scrolled down until he reached a number for Max Ellis, an old friend from Police College. Max had taken a different career path and was recruited for Special Branch. Dave never knew much about his work. Max joked that if he told Dave exactly what he did, he'd have to kill him. Hopefully, he was joking, but he did seem to be involved in some serious secret stuff.

The number rang out for a while and, when he thought the answerphone message was about to cut in, a voice answered breathlessly.

'Yes?'

'Max?'

'Who's this?'

'Dave Gill.'

The voice relaxed. 'Oh hello! Long-time no speak.

How're things?'

'Excellent, thanks. How about you?'

'I'm OK, thanks. How can I help?' Max never chatted much and always went straight to the point.

'My girlfriend has been worried about someone watching her and an old boyfriend showed up unexpectedly today. Whoever was watching her left a fingerprint on a pair of binoculars and also on a car they used in a hit and run. I tried to check out her old boyfriend in case he's involved but his fingerprints aren't on the system. He was in the army so I hoped you could do me favour and tap into the military database?'

Max paused, 'I shouldn't. These things leave a digital trace and I could get into trouble if I don't have a good reason.'

'Isn't being a possible stalker a good reason?'

'Those aren't the sort of things I deal with.'

'OK, don't worry then. I'll keep searching.' Dave said.

'Tell you what, let me have some details and I'll see what I can do.'

'Cheers, Max, I owe you a pint next time you're anywhere near Dorset!'

'I'll take you up on that. Could do with a few days by the sea. What've you got?'

Dave gave him Phil Brown's information. 'Thanks, mate, you're a star.'

'OK. I'll have a go. What's your email?'

Dave told him and rang off. He was desperate to solve this case. He'd been a DS for ten years and was planning to start the exams and try for an Inspector's job.

***

That morning Jemma was on the stand again and kept an eye out for Phil. Around ten o'clock she had a visit from the event's main sponsors, Reggie and Keith Fletcher. They checked out the stall and Reggie asked some questions about Plessie and the museum. He didn't mention their previous encounter over the trees on the Highfields Estate.

For brothers, they were quite different in appearance. Reggie was short and wiry; his brother was taller with brown hair and built like a prop forward.

Reggie gave Jemma a smile that made her squirm. 'I hear you didn't like our latest offer for the site.'

'That's right. I don't think a move would be a benefit for the town.'

'Your prerogative. We'll have to come up with a better price.'

'Doesn't matter how much, I won't support any sale. If we moved to your new shed, we'd have less space for exhibits and we'd have to lose some staff. It's not going to happen.'

'We'll see about that. You'll find that we are people who are used to getting what we want and don't stop until we do.'

Jemma sneered. 'You didn't get to cut down the big trees on your last development, did you?'

Reggie made a dismissive gesture with his hand as if swatting an imaginary wasp. 'A minor inconvenience. Anyway, we must go. Bye, Miss Thorne.'

Jemma shivered and turned to talk to another visitor at the stand, shoving the discussion from her mind. Near to closing time, she found an envelope on the stall she hadn't noticed before, with *Jemma - Private* written on the outside. She picked it up, opened it and found a handwritten note inside:

Hi, Jemma,

I'm coming back for you. Dump the detective and the Yank and be mine again. I'm sure you'd hate your old secret to be revealed; especially now you're a celebrity in all the papers. Would you like everybody to know that you lied about what really happened thirty years ago?

At the bottom, it had a P with a cross.

She looked around the room in a panic. Phil had been in the room and had been near enough to leave a note on her stand without her spotting him.

Her eyes teared up as she thought about what the note referred to. She'd lived with the guilt for so long and still dreamt about the events when she was thirteen. She'd tried to forget that there was somebody else there that day. Someone who knew everything and was willing to blackmail her. She folded the note and stuck it in her pocket.

Dave turned up. 'OK, babe?'

She was so wound up about the letter that she couldn't hug him back with her usual gusto. 'Yes, I'm fine, but I'm whacked. I fancy a bath and bed.'

He grinned. 'Sounds interesting.'

'On my own.'

'Oh,' his smile faded.

'Come on, let's stick this stuff in the van.'

'By the way, you might be right about Phil Brown,' he said. 'He joined the army and, after leaving nine years later, went to live in Australia, before coming home three months ago. Not much trace of him since.'

Jemma rolled up a poster. 'Oh, maybe I didn't see him. Probably my vivid imagination.'

'He's got a vehicle in his name, a mobile home, so I put an alert out in case he drives it past any cameras.'

'Don't go to any trouble.' Jemma continued packing

things away. 'I've convinced myself the person I spotted didn't look like Phil.'

'You sure?'

Her face darkened. 'Yes. Can we just pack up and go.'

'Look, I've been trained to detect when someone's lying and I can tell you're hiding something.'

'I'm not one of your suspects. Just stop hassling me.' She stormed off.

Upon arriving home and unpacking, she decided to ring Ellie to tell her to be careful but after searching her bag she was unable to find her mobile. Dave called her number and it rang out before going to the answerphone message.

'Can't we try Find My Phone?' he asked.

She stared at him. 'What?'

'An app to track missing phones.'

'New one on me,' she snapped.

'Won't be any use then.' He tried to stay calm.

'I reckon some toe-rag stole my mobile at the festival. I'm sure I left it on the stall at some point.'

'Could it have been Phil?'

'I suppose so, if it was him. But why would he want it?'

'I dunno. Maybe he'll sell it somewhere. If you have to buy a new one, make sure you install the app. Freddie'll set everything up for you.'

She grumbled a comment about horses bolting and stable doors, but Dave ignored her.

She tried ringing the town hall to check if one had been found. When they told her a phone had been handed in, she smiled but then they asked her what kind of phone she'd lost. Unfortunately, the one that had been found was a different make.

The next day Jemma drove up to Swanbourne to visit the mobile phone shop. She endured a mind-boggling hour of questions, explanations and filling in forms on computer screens. The salesman knew a lot about his products and enjoyed showing them off, and afterwards, she came out as the proud owner of a complicated new smartphone.

Arriving home, she opened the bag, took out the phone and read the instructions. Ten minutes later she reached for her landline and dialled a number.

'Two one six, eight nine seven.'

'Hello, Sue, is Freddie there?'

'Goodness, straight to business. No small talk with my sis is there?'

'Sorry, are you all OK?'

'I'm only joking.' She shouted, 'Freddie, Auntie Jem for you.'

Another pause. 'He's here.'

'Hi, Auntie Jem. Whatcha want?'

'Hello Freddie, I lost my phone so I bought a new one but I'm confused already. Can you help me, please, and set up a tracker in case I lose it again?'

'No problem. Now?'

'Please. If that's OK.'

'It's fine. I'll be round in a bit.'

Ten minutes later the back door opened and Dino went mad. Freddie bent down to stroke the dog who was almost knocking him off his feet. Jemma walked through to the kitchen to find Dino desperately trying to press himself further into Freddie's legs, as though he'd never received any attention in his life. She laughed at the pair of them. 'Thanks for coming.'

Freddie sat at the table and picked up the box the phone came in. 'What've you done so far?'

Jemma grinned sheepishly. 'Well, I put it on charge.'

He rolled his eyes. 'Oh, well, that's something. Give it here.'

She handed him the phone and left him with the instructions. Fifteen minutes later he shouted that he'd finished and asked her what device she wanted the tracker on.

She came back into the kitchen. 'In English this time. Can I have the question again please?'

He smiled. 'Your phone is now ready with a tracking app in case you lose it again. I need to set up which device will be the one doing the tracking if it's lost.'

Jemma was still a bit confused. 'What are the options?'

'I could add Dave's phone or mine.'

'Your phone would be brilliant, please. Dave's always so busy.'

'OK.' Freddie went back to the mobile settings. Two minutes later everything was sorted. 'All set up.' He handed the phone over to Jemma. 'If you ever lose it, let me know and I can track it.'

'Brilliant, my IT hero.'

'You're welcome. Right, I better be off, got to finish my homework.'

'When's it got to be done for?'

'Tomorrow morning, but I've got loads of time tonight before bedtime and it'll only take a few minutes.'

'So, let me check I understand this. If I lose my phone I must ring and tell you?'

'Yes,' he said.

'But if I lose my phone, how can I call you?'

'Oh, Auntie Jem, you're hopeless. Don't be so old.'

She hugged him. 'Thanks mate. Don't know what I'd do without you. Cheers.'

He reddened. 'No problem. Catch you soon.'

***

The man sat at a desk in a shabby office staring at a mobile phone. He made notes on a pad and muttered, 'Oh dear, Jemma, fancy not having a password on your phone. Anyone can read your messages and e-mails and find the numbers for all your contacts. Now, who might be useful?'

He scrolled down the list. 'Well, let's add Dave for a start,' he said as he wrote down the number, 'and Ellie, Chrissie, Mum and Dad. Oh, things keep getting better and better.'

He chuckled and read some of Jemma's e-mails. *There's so much useful information here. This'll make things much easier.*

Chapter 25

Jemma stood by the edge of the cliff looking down at the body on the beach, hundreds of feet below. Her head spun and tears flowed.

'Alice!' She stared down at the long hair being swirled around by the waves.

A male voice broke into her consciousness. 'You should've come when she shouted,' he said.

She turned to face Phil as he stood next to her gazing down at Alice's body.

'Why did you ignore her when she called for help?' he taunted her.

Jemma felt like a knife was being twisted in her gut. 'I thought she was messing around. She was always after attention. I didn't know she was in any trouble!'

Phil grinned and wrung his hands. 'Well I heard her call for help, and you just carried on digging. Now, what are we going to do about that?'

Jemma was confused. 'What are we going to do about what?'

'The fact I know you ignored all of Alice's cries for help. She shouted for you but you ignored her. How awful. Now, shall I tell everybody what happened, or say Alice slipped and fell?'

Jemma looked at Phil with tears in her eyes. 'Please say she slipped and fell and I'll do the same.'

'Right, I'll do that, but don't forget you owe me and one day I'll come knocking on your door. One day.'

'No!' Jemma woke up screaming and found herself in Dave's arms.

'Jemma! Everything's alright, you're safe with me,' he said, as he held her close.

She sniffed. 'I've got to sort myself out and stop these nightmares.'

Dave lifted her face so she was looking at him. 'Can't you try to be a bit less independent and accept that I care about you and want to look after you?'

'I'll try,' she said.

She rested her head on his chest. *How can my life be such a mess? I feel so guilty. Guilt about Alice. Guilt over Anna. Guilt over Brad. So many problems because of me and my bloody fossils.*

***

In Swanbourne Police HQ the team members were all busy with their tasks in the open plan office. Heads bobbed up and down over the dividers as ideas and results were discussed.

Dave sat at his post-it-note covered terminal and read the email from Max Ellis, his friend in Special Branch, who'd sent a full record for Philip Roy Brown, including a separate file with fingerprints. Dave sent a reply thanking him and loaded the images onto the Police National Computer.

The screen went blank for a few moments and... Bingo!

A match flashed up between Phil's army fingerprint and the unknown culprit whose print came from the binoculars and the Land Rover.

He punched at the air. 'Got you, you bastard! Max, you're a star.'

Amrik came rolling round to Dave's cubicle on his wheeled chair. 'Who you calling a bastard?'

'Great news! We have a match and a name for the print found on the handbrake of the hit-and-run car.'

'Who is it?'

'A bloke called Phil Brown, an ex-army guy who used to go out with Jemma years ago.'

'Any address?'

'No known address at the moment.' He typed in some more details. 'But he has a vehicle registered to a place in Dorchester that's owned by a lady called Carol Brown. Looking at her age, she might be his mother or an aunt.'

'Is he still around?'

'He could be. Jemma thought she saw him at her lecture in the leisure centre on Saturday.'

Amrik wrote in his notebook. 'Is he dangerous?'

Dave frowned. 'Well, he mowed Brad Jones down with a stolen Land Rover. I'd say he passes the "Am I dangerous" test with flying colours. Are you free to come with me to check out the woods again, but from the south this time? If he's about, he won't spot us coming.'

They went out to a patrol car and sped off towards Lulcombe with the blue lights flashing. As Dave drove, Amrik updated DI Day with their plans.

'Could he be armed?' she asked.

Amrik glanced at Dave who shook his head. 'Don't think so. He's ex-army, but there's nothing on the firearms record, so hopefully not.'

'OK, be careful. Surveillance only. If there's any suggestion that he has a gun, call in and we'll get the Armed Response Unit out. Do not engage.' The line went quiet.

Dave smiled. 'Didn't quite catch the last bit. Terrible

reception round here, you know.'

Amrik tapped his extendable baton. 'I know. Awful.'

On the way to Lulcombe, Dave rang Jemma hands-free and told her to stay inside with the door locked. He explained the fingerprint results and what they planned to do before he ended the call.

Dave thought as he drove. 'Do you think there's any link between the hit-and-run, the theft and Anna's murder?'

Amrik considered the question. 'Can't spot one. Didn't they retrieve some DNA from the balaclava at the scene?'

'Oh, yes, I'd forgotten. Might be useful if we catch Phil.'

'What else do we know about him?'

As he drove, Dave told Amrik everything he knew. After parking at the Beach Car Park, they strode towards the woods.

***

The man lay in his camouflaged bivouac and watched Jemma's house through a telescope on a small tripod. Nothing much had happened today, other than fifteen minutes ago, when Jemma came out from her workshop and went into the house. Since then he hadn't seen her apart from when she went round closing all the curtains.

He'd been a bit concerned his surveillance operation might have been compromised when her policeman friend had come running across the field. It annoyed him that he had to leave in a hurry, losing his binoculars, so he now was forced to use his telescope instead.

Suddenly, a twig cracked underfoot nearby, so he pulled his scope back under the camouflaged tarpaulin of the bivvy.

He only needed a few seconds to relax his breathing, knowing it would be almost impossible to spot him as long as he didn't move.

***

Dave and Amrik followed the path searching for any signs of disturbance. The undergrowth had grown back and showed no signs of anybody returning.

They checked up and down along the section where the best views of Jemma's cottage were found, but couldn't spot anything interesting.

Dave sniffed. *What's that? A weak odour of stale sweat.* Looking over at Amrik, he counted three, two, one with his fingers. Reaching one, he shouted, 'Nothing here, but the dogs will arrive in five minutes. They'll sniff him out.'

Just then a commotion broke out in front of them and an area of the forest floor covered in bracken erupted when a man dressed in camouflage gear leapt up and took off down the woodland path.

Even though Dave and Amrik were tensed up and ready, the sudden movement still made them jump, especially as he came from a spot six feet from where they stood.

With the element of surprise, the watcher had a good head start but they were soon in pursuit running along the path. Unfortunately, the culprit was wiry and fast and they struggled to run in stab vests and boots. When Dave reached a fork, he stopped and listened, breathing heavily. Amrik caught up and panted beside him.

'Which way did he go?'

Dave shrugged. 'Choice of three. The ground's dry so we won't find any footprints. Let's call in the cavalry. A dog would be useful, a helicopter brilliant, but I bet there's no chance of one turning up for this. Choppers cost too much to keep in the air.'

'Shall we split up?' Amrik suggested.

'Remember what DI Day told us, we shouldn't engage so I better call it in.' The radio crackled when he pressed the talk button. 'DS Gill to base.'

'Receiving.'

'In pursuit of a lone male in camouflage gear who we disturbed in the woods south of Seaton Road in Lulcombe. We followed him through the woods but lost him at a fork. We will not engage, repeat, we will not engage, as the suspect is wanted in connection with an earlier incident.'

'Any sign of firearms?'

'Negative. Any dog or helicopter units available?'

'Don't think you'll get the chopper up for a hit-and-run but we can try. What possible choices does he have?'

Dave checked around. 'He could've taken the Coast Path, continued west across the fields or gone north towards the houses on Seaton Road.'

'OK. Follow him at a distance, and keep reporting in.'

Amrik checked the paths. 'Now, which way to go?'

Dave pretended to toss a coin and checked the back of his hand. 'I reckon he's gone north. The Coast Path is quite busy with walkers and the track through the field is very open. More hiding places in the sheds and gardens beside Seaton Road.'

'Let's go,' Amrik said.

Dave handed him the radio. 'Here, hold this for a minute, will you? I need to let Jem know what's happening.'

***

The watcher cleared the last of the trees and decided to cut between the houses onto Seaton Road. He walked up the stream, crossing to the other side and smiled. *Might confuse the dogs*. As there was nobody else nearby, he removed his camouflage jacket and switched to a gentle jog.

He crossed over and jogged up the drive to the Hill Farm Caravan and Camping site. He kept looking at his watch to make it appear to any onlookers that he'd been running.

Losing the telescope, as well as the binoculars, had annoyed him. He'd love to get at the policeman who'd disturbed him and made him drop them but he hadn't seen who it was. His meagre funds wouldn't stretch to buy any new ones so he'd have to do without. Maybe he might find an opportunity to steal one from a careless birdwatcher who left his car unattended. His money would only cover a few more weeks at the campsite and some basic food supplies, so he'd need a plan B soon.

After showering, he changed into some bright shorts and a vest and ran out again along Seaton Road.

***

Jemma was busy marking assignments when she heard a knock at the back door. *Thank goodness, Dave's back.*

She went to answer. 'That you, Dave?'

A quiet reply. 'Yeah.'

She breathed out and unlocked the door. 'Oh, God!'

A man shoved her back inside and closed the door. 'Hello, Jem. How are you doing after all these years?'

She sat down in a state of shock. 'Phil, why are you here?' She recognised him easily, although his hair appeared much shorter than when she went out with him. A chill ran through her as he smiled and rubbed his hands together.

'It's lovely to see my darling Jem.'

She sagged back in her chair. 'Well, your darling Jem doesn't want to see you.'

'No way to speak to the love of your life!'

Jemma shook as she stared at him. 'Go away, Phil. Now. Please, I won't tell anyone you came.'

'That's my girl. Tell you what. How about lending me some money to tide me over for a while? Things are a bit tight at the moment and I could do with a top-up.'

Jemma went to the shelves, took down a tin and counted out the notes. 'Here. One hundred and eighty quid. Every penny in the house. Now, leave and don't come back!'

'Now, my love.'

'I'm not your love.'

'You will be soon. I'll be off but don't forget, not a word to anyone or I'll go public with what really happened on the cliff with Alice.'

Tears gathered in her eyes. 'Will you go now, Phil, please? I won't say you've been here?'

He shoved the money in his pocket and turned to walk out the door. 'Bye, Jemma, see you soon.'

***

There was no sign of Phil as Dave and Amrik walked along the field next to Seaton Road. They checked for any signs of disturbances until the dog handler arrived and radioed through to them. Another backup team parked in the Beach Car Park and cut back through towards the woods. Dave went over to them and explained where they'd already searched.

Dave and Amrik took the handler to the bivvy, so the dog could try finding a scent.

'No helicopter?' Dave asked him.

'No, only me and Wilbur, I'm afraid.'

Amrik knelt to stroke the dog but he was already sniffing around the bivouac.

The handler lifted the cover and Wilbur dived underneath, twisting around and barking. He pulled Wilbur's lead to get him back out, held the material to his nose and gave him a treat from a bag in his pocket.

'Scent, Wilbur, go find!'

The dog barked and started off along the path, dragging his handler behind him.

Amrik grinned at Dave. 'Woof woof?' he said.

'Woof,' Dave replied and they jogged off after the duo, Wilbur following the smell and taking the north fork. Dave nudged Amrik. 'Told you so.'

The trail led across the field until they reached a small stream. Wilbur stopped and appeared to lose the scent, leading his handler up and down the stream on both sides but being unable to find the trail again.

Dave had an idea and called to the dog handler, 'The suspect is army trained so may know how to disguise his tracks. What if he walked a long way through the water before setting off again?'

'We're trained to go a hundred metres upstream and downstream sir, but it's worth a go.' He headed north along the water. Two hundred and fifty metres upstream they found a waterfall and, beside it, Wilbur became excited again, and led them off across the field.

'Here we go again,' Dave said. They followed, radioing in their position and progress.

The procession led by Wilbur reached Seaton Road. After a gap in the traffic, they crossed the road near the Hill Farm Campsite. Wilbur abruptly turned ninety degrees and headed back towards Lulcombe.

Dave and Amrik followed, looking around in all directions. As they approached Jemma's house, Wilbur wanted to cross back again, so his handler let him lead. He sniffed his way up her drive and to her back door where he stopped and indicated.

Dave frowned at Amrik. 'He's been here. Quick, I'll ring her.' He called Jemma. 'Hi, Jem, are you OK?'

'Yes, I'm fine.'

'Alone?'

'Yes.'

'We're by your back door and the sniffer dog's getting excited. We think Phil's been outside. Can you open up?'

'No problem.'

Jemma ran out and shut the door behind her.

'Are you sure you're OK? he asked.

'Yes, I'm good,' she said.

Wilbur wanted to go into Jemma's kitchen.

'Hold, Wilbur,' his handler commanded. 'Can we go in, Jemma?'

'No. Don't bother,' she said. 'Nobody else is here. I bet he can smell Dino or the dinner cooking.'

He protested, 'But he's never distracted by food or dog smells.'

'OK, but don't go in. Dino's shut in the sitting room and he'll go mad if another dog comes inside. I've been in the kitchen all the while, so I'd have seen if anybody came in.'

Dave opened the door and peered inside but all he saw was an empty room so he turned to leave. 'Come on, let's retrace our steps. See you later, Jem.'

***

As Jemma closed the door, her head spun, and she sat down at the table again. She hated lying to Dave and the others but she couldn't risk Phil blabbing to the police or the press.

***

Wilbur led them back along the path away from Lulcombe. When he arrived at the drive to the campsite he kept turning backwards and forwards. At first, he wanted to go back across the road, but then he pulled towards the site. Dave's heart beat faster as he sensed they were getting closer to their quarry.

After choosing the drive, they followed Wilbur until he came to the entrance. The field was quiet as they walked in and searched the place. As usual for the winter, there were only a few cars beside the static caravans. A lone campervan with an electric hook-up stood on a patch of hard standing at the end. They stepped back out of sight of the van.

Amrik glanced at Dave. 'Did you make a note of the reg number of the vehicle owned by Phil Brown?'

Dave opened his notebook and read out a registration number, which was identical to the campervan parked near to them.

They radioed for the backup team to come to the campsite. Once the other officers arrived, they decided to check if anybody was home.

Dave and Amrik crept up to the front door while the other two PCs scurried around the back and crouched below the window line. Amrik frowned at him. 'Booby traps?'

Dave pointed. 'Cover me with your baton from the other side. I'll knock and step back.'

Amrik nodded. 'OK. Bodycam on.'

Dave knocked on the door and stepped back. It swung open. He shouted, 'Police! Come out and put your hands above your head.'

A man in bright shorts and a running top stepped out of the campervan and smiled. 'Good afternoon, gentlemen, how can I assist?'

'Philip Roy Brown?' Dave asked.

The man smirked. 'That is the name chosen for me by my parents.'

'Philip Roy Brown, I'm arresting you on suspicion of causing serious injury by dangerous or careless driving. You do not have to say anything, but it may harm your defence if you do not mention when questioned, something which you later rely on in court. Anything you do say may be given in evidence.'

Dave pulled out his handcuffs and Phil held out his hands with a grin. One of the PCs led him away and locked him in the back of the patrol car. While Amrik radioed in an update, Dave knelt to stroke the dog.

'Well done, Wilbur, top job!' He glanced up at the young handler. 'And you too.'

He smiled. 'Thank you, sir, he seemed like a pussycat when you arrested him.'

Dave shrugged. 'Didn't think the arrest would be so easy but he seemed quite happy to get in the car. We'll leave the camper for the forensic mob. I'm knackered.'

He strolled back to where Amrik was talking to the other PC. 'Can you go and take Brown in for booking please?' He turned to another young officer standing by the campervan.

'You're on guard duty, I'm afraid. The forensic team will be here shortly. Don't go in the van will you, just in case.'

'Sir.'

Dave started back for the Beach Car Park where they'd left the car, ringing Jemma as he did. 'Hi, Jem.'

'Are you OK?'

'Yes, I'm fine. We've got Phil Brown. We arrested him at the campsite in a mobile home.'

She gasped, 'Any trouble?'

'Strangely, he behaved himself and didn't try to resist arrest. They're taking him to the station to be charged with the hit-and-run incident...to start with. We'll work out what else to throw at him about the invasion of privacy offences.'

'Don't bother.'

'Don't bother what?'

'I don't want to press charges about the Peeping Tom offence,' she said.

'Why?'

'With everything else going on, I wouldn't want to go to court as a witness. Just charge him with the hit-and-run, that'll do.'

Dave took a breath. 'OK, I suppose. If we only charge him with one thing, there's a danger he'll be straight out on bail. Hopefully, we can beef the charges up with some other driving offences.'

Jemma tried to stay calm. 'That's up to you.'

'Thought you'd be happy we got him.'

'I am. It's just that I'm so tired.'

'See you later?'

'Don't worry about tonight,' she said. 'I think I need an early night.'

He looked concerned. 'Anything wrong?'

210

She paused. 'No. Nothing.'

'OK,' Dave hesitated. 'You know you can talk to me if anything is worrying you. See you soon.'

After he rang off, he unlocked his patrol car and drove back to the station. He had an instinct for when people were lying to him but he couldn't talk to Jemma the way he would a suspect. As he drove, he wondered what was wrong with her and what she wasn't telling him.

Chapter 26

At Swanbourne Police HQ, the team processed Phil Brown and formally charged him with causing serious injury by dangerous driving, taking a vehicle without permission, driving without insurance and failure to stop after an accident.

They'd searched for any links with the assault on Anna and the theft of Plessie, but so far hadn't found anything. Laura Day planned to question Brown with Amrik Hussain.

As they walked along the corridor Amrik screwed up his nose. 'What's that terrible smell?'

Laura grimaced. 'Sarge told me that a drunk had thrown up big time in cell six and a clean-up team is due shortly.'

He held his nose as he gagged. 'It's awful.'

'It'll take days to get the smell out, we probably won't be using it for a while.'

They entered the interview room and found the suspect sitting with his feet up on the table. He got up as they entered. A young police constable was standing silently in the corner.

Phil eyed them both. 'Afternoon, officers, or should I call you something else?'

'Sit back down,' Laura said, 'and keep your feet off the table.'

'I don't want to sit down. I've been sitting for ages on these hard plastic chairs.'

'Just sit down.' Laura shouted.

Phil did as he was told and smirked. 'Oh, dear! Got out of bed the wrong side this morning, did we?'

She ignored his comments and sat opposite. It was one of the better interview rooms at the Police HQ. Unfortunately, the décor didn't benefit from the faded beige ceiling tiles and grubby magnolia walls. The wooden table was covered in scratches and carved initials and was bolted to the floor.

Amrik turned on the recorder. 'Thursday tenth of November, two-fifteen p.m. Detective Inspector Day and Detective Sergeant Hussain. Interview with Philip Roy Brown of no fixed abode.'

Phil interrupted. 'Doesn't my campervan count as a fixed abode? It's even plugged into the electric, I'll have you know.'

Laura's hand balled into a fist as she slid a sheet of paper across the table. 'You're charged with these offences. Do you understand the charges?'

Phil read the document and stretched out his legs. 'I do, but I have a question.'

'What is it?'

'Why is there such an awful smell of sweat and sickly disinfectant in here?'

Laura ignored his question. 'And you have twice declined legal assistance, is that so?'

'That is so. I can sort things out myself. I've read a book about law, you know.'

'OK, let's continue. On the third of November, you stole a black Land Rover Discovery from Hill Farm in Lulcombe. Do you admit that?'

'Well, I borrowed the vehicle for a drive, but I didn't steal anything.'

'You did not seek the owner's permission?'

'Correct, but I wasn't going to keep it.'

'And you hadn't taken out any insurance?'

'A minor administrative oversight.'

'That's not how we view things, I'm afraid. You then proceeded to drive along Seaton Road and deliberately drove into a male who was out for a run on the same road, causing him actual bodily harm. Do you admit that charge?'

'No. I was driving along the country lane in an easterly direction, and I was blinded by the sun. I felt a bump but thought I'd hit a deer or something. It didn't seem like a safe place to pull over, so I continued on my journey.'

'So basically you crashed into a jogger, left him to die by the roadside and drove off?'

Phil smirked, 'So you say.'

Laura wiped her sweaty hands on her trousers and continued. 'Where were you going?'

'Oh, a scenic drive along the coast. I'd been to Seaton and was on my way back.'

'So, you don't accept the charge of failure to stop after an accident?'

'No, I do not. I might agree to a lesser one of not stopping after a collision with an animal.'

Laura raised her eyebrows. *He seems to know a bit about the law. We might need to be careful with this one.* She persisted. 'But you deliberately drove into a person.'

'So you say.'

'Well, we're going to charge you with those four offences.'

Phil shrugged. 'Your prerogative, but I'd like it on record that I dispute some of them.'

Laura made more notes. 'OK, let's move on. What do you know about the theft of a fossil from Lulcombe and the murder of Anna Jenkins, the museum manager?'

'Oh, I know rather a lot about those things.'

Laura's heart beat faster as she stopped writing and stared at him. 'Go on.'

'Unfortunately, only what I read in the newspapers.'

'You are trying my patience, Mr Brown.'

'Why so tense DI Day? Are you not getting any?'

Laura clenched her hands under the table.

Amrik joined in. 'What were you doing on the night of the twenty-fourth of October?'

'Oh, the handsome one speaks as well.'

Amrik took a breath. 'As experienced officers, we've come across every compliment, insult and pick-up line, so please stop acting like a smart arse and answer the question.'

Phil's jaw clenched but he cleared his throat and soon regained his confident composure, winking at Laura. 'Oh, I'm sure you're very experienced. As for the twenty-fourth, I'd have been in my campervan at Lulcombe Campsite.'

Amrik followed up. 'On your own?'

'Yes, on my own.'

'Can anyone else confirm that?'

'Well, I called my mum on the phone around seven-thirty but I ring her every night. A boy has to look after his mother, you know.'

Amrik replied. 'Very commendable, Mr Brown. So, no alibi for the night in question.'

'So you say.'

'During the forensic examination of the museum crime scene, we recovered some DNA from an article of clothing we found.'

Phil pulled a face. 'Oh yuk! The culprit must have been excited?'

'Would you consent to giving us a sample of your DNA so we can eliminate you from our enquiries?'

'I'd be delighted to let this young lady obtain a sample of my DNA.' He clutched his groin and grinned. 'Any suggestions?'

Laura glared at the suspect as if she wanted to eliminate him from the planet.

Amrik rolled his eyes. 'A technician will take a swab from the inside of your mouth.'

'Oh, what a disappointment.'

'We'll be applying to keep you remanded on bail while we investigate further links to the murder and theft.'

'Not going to happen.'

Laura stiffened. 'I'm sorry, what's not going to happen?'

'There's no way you're going to keep me in for a few minor motoring offences.'

Laura stood, pushed back her chair and slammed her hands against the table startling both Phil and Amrik. 'Right, that's enough for now.'

Amrik poised his hand over the recorder's controls. 'DS Hussain terminating the interview at three-fifty-five.' He turned off the machine.

Laura told the constable in the corner, 'Take him back to the cells, with handcuffs. I think cell number six is free.'

He grinned. 'Yes, ma'am,' before cuffing the prisoner and leading him away.

Amrik grinned. 'Cell six. Seems like he really annoyed you. He's an unpleasant bastard, isn't he, ma'am?'

'Sure is. I'd love to pin the murder on him, but we can't find any link to him and there's no evidence, forensic or otherwise.'

'Shame we couldn't find some now, ma'am.'

'I'll pretend I didn't hear that. We're not in a seventies TV series. Oh, well, back to the drawing board for the museum murder. I'm disappointed, as I thought he might be involved.' She went to discuss the custody position with her boss.

'Laura, we can't remand Brown in custody for this type of motoring offence.'

'But sir, he's been spying on a woman and tried to murder Bradley Jones.'

'The nature and seriousness of the offences he's been charged with aren't enough to keep him locked up. It costs a lot to keep suspects in custody overnight. They need feeding and watching.'

'So you're suggesting we let him go?'

'Yes Laura, I am. There's no evidence to prove any links to any other crimes. If you find some, I'll rethink the situation.'

'Sir, I think we should keep him in. He could be a flight risk.'

He stroked his chin and after a pause, finally grunted. 'OK. I'll authorise you to confiscate his passport.'

'What about bail?'

'I'm not authorising a bail application.'

OK, sir, but I want it on record that I disagree with his release.'

'Noted. Anything else?'

She clenched her fists in her jacket pocket and replied stiffly. 'No, sir.'

***

217

When Dave found out about the release he was furious and stormed into Laura Day's office, slamming the door after him. 'What about Jemma?' he protested. 'She's been living in fear of a stalker for ages!'

'She can apply for an injunction.'

'But that could take weeks,' he snapped.

Laura tensed. 'Look, Dave, you're too personally involved. I've been worried this might happen. Do you want to be taken off the case?'

'No, but it's bloody stupid letting him go.'

'Dave, I thought you had hopes of becoming a DI in the near future. Is that so?'

'I do, ma'am.'

'Then don't ever raise your voice and swear at me again or you'll be looking at DC instead. Understood?'

'Yes.'

'Yes, what?'

'Yes, ma'am.'

Her face softened. 'Look, I'll ask any nearby patrol cars to keep an eye on Brown just to make sure he doesn't go near Jemma.'

'Thank you, ma'am.'

Laura turned back to her papers. 'OK Dave, back to work.'

Dave was keen on promotion but it was tempting to kick up more of a fuss over Phil's release. He knew, however, that he would never hear the end of it from Jemma if he committed career suicide because he was angry on her behalf. He walked off seething and hoped they wouldn't come to regret their lack of action.

Chapter 27

Phil Brown strolled out of the station and basked in the November sunshine, breathing in the crisp, cold air. Although he'd only been in there for four hours, he'd started to feel claustrophobic and the smell in his filthy cell had been sickening.

The sun was out but he shivered as he walked over to the bus stop and checked the timetable for buses to Lulcombe. He'd asked for a lift back to the campsite but the custody sergeant had just laughed at him. He kept his cool and left without another word, determined to be a well-behaved and helpful suspect.

A bus would be along in five minutes so he sat on a bench and watched the traffic go past. He was pleased with how the police interview had gone. The female had become really annoyed with him and was probably furious he'd been released. The law course he'd taken years before had been worth the effort.

Half an hour later, he strolled up the hill from the town centre back to his campervan and planned his next move. On the way out of Swanbourne, he'd passed the hospital and wondered if he should pay Brad a visit, maybe assess his injuries and, if the opportunity presented, perhaps do something to reverse his recovery, permanently.

That would just leave the policeman, Dave, in the way of his meticulous plans for getting back together with Jemma. The copper might be more difficult to dispose of, but it should be easy for a man of his talents. OK, guns were hard to source, but knives and even homemade garrottes weren't too much trouble. He clutched his radio's cable and imagined the sensation of wrapping it around Dave's neck, thrusting his knee into his back and pulling the wire tight. He thought of the sights and sounds of Dave's demise, the noises from his throat as the life slowly drained from him. He put down the lead and began cooking supper.

Many times over the years he'd attempted to forget Jemma but she'd always come back into his head.

During his spell in the army, he kept himself occupied and managed to put her to one side in his thoughts. After he left the forces, he decided to check up on her. When he found her, she was married with a child, so he backed off and went to live in Australia. He made a new start over there and, although he dated a few women, he always compared them to her. None of them ever quite measured up.

After returning to England, he again tried to find her. However, he spotted an article in a newspaper about the discovery of a fossil and everything came rushing back. He discovered she was in a relationship with a policeman, worse still, the annoying American was back on the scene. He'd need to do something about him first and then get rid of the copper.

***

That evening Jemma sat with Dave watching TV but she

couldn't concentrate on the programme at all.

He interrupted her thoughts. 'Penny for them?'

Jemma tried to smile. 'Not worth that much, believe me.'

'If there's anything you want to talk about, I'm here,' he said.

She cuddled up to him. At that moment, in a warm room with a cool beer in her hand, she almost told him Phil had come into her kitchen the previous day. Resisting the urge, she decided she couldn't do so without also explaining why she hadn't told him yesterday.

Thirty years of guilt about Alice had built within her to such a level that she was mortified about anybody ever finding out the truth about that day on the cliffs. Although she hadn't seen Phil for years, she was shocked by the hold he still possessed over her. It wasn't her fault; she didn't know what to do.

She jumped out of her daydreaming again as Dave stroked her face.

'Earth calling Jemma, come in please!'

'Sorry, I'm not very riveting company tonight, am I?'

He kissed her. 'Don't worry, we've had a mad few weeks. How about a holiday sometime so we can forget about all this.'

She nestled her head on his chest. 'That would be good. Things might quieten down a bit after Christmas before the new term starts at uni.'

'I've heard that before,' he said with a flat voice.

***

The following morning Phil walked down into Lulcombe and entered the hardware shop. An old-fashioned family store, it was an Aladdin's cave for DIY enthusiasts. Fifteen minutes later he came out with a length of dowel, a roll of wire and a sharp kitchen knife that he put straight into his rucksack. He then called at the grocers next door and bought a bag of grapes.

On the bus journey into Swanbourne, he cut a length of the wire, which he tied to two pieces of dowel to make a garrotte. Nobody was sitting anywhere near him so he did what he needed without fear of nosy passengers.

Having served in volatile regions, Phil had a feeling of invincibility, and he had no doubts about any of his plans. As far as he was concerned the police were stupid and, as long as he planned his moves with military precision, he'd succeed.

He'd already called the hospital to find the visiting times for Brad's ward and they'd also told him Mr Jones was in his own private room. Perfect.

Pulling his baseball cap down low he donned his sunglasses as he entered the hospital. Although he was excited, he controlled his breathing to keep his heartrate steady and to make sure he was operating efficiently. The reception area was quiet as he passed through. Taking his time, he stood and memorised the floor plan on the wall so he knew the location of Brad's room. He also worked out his best escape route, plus two alternatives in case contingencies were required.

***

As Phil walked along the corridor, Jemma parked her van in the car park. Grabbing a paperback from the passenger seat, she headed for the entrance to check on Brad.

***

Phil went up in the lift to the fourth floor, found the room with Brad's name on a door card and peered through the window.

Result! Nobody was in the room with him, and neither were any nurses lingering in the corridor. With the grapes in one hand, he kept his other hand in the rucksack he carried, ready to grab either the knife or the garrotte. He hoped Brad would be on a high-dependency machine that he could unplug or sabotage, however the window revealed the drip in Brad's arm but no other connections.

Damn!

One of the ceiling lights flickered annoyingly as he stepped into the room and approached the side of the bed. 'Brad, old buddy, how are you?'

Brad frowned and turned his head. 'Have we met?'

'Yes, I'm Jim. Don't you remember me? I've brought you some grapes.'

'No, I'm sorry, I haven't got a clue. You got the right Brad?'

'Of course, you're Bradley 'Indiana' Jones. I was at Swanbourne University with you.'

Brad sounded nervous. 'Nope. Take off your sunglasses, buddy, and show your face.'

'No can do, mate, the lights in here are too bright. Anyway, here's a nice surprise for you.' Phil reached into his rucksack and brought out the garrotte.

'What's that?'

'A special...'

***

Jemma pushed open the door, took one step into the ward and froze. 'What are you doing here?'

Startled, Phil looked up with wild eyes, a length of wire taut between his hands hovering an inch above Brad's throat.

Jemma screamed and hit the fire alarm on the wall. From down the corridor the siren blared and Phil scoured the room for another escape. The whole world slowed until the noise of footsteps grew louder.

Phil saw the half-open window, ran over and climbed out through the gap to stand on the ledge.

Jemma dashed over and opened the window, catching him on the arm. He overbalanced and slowly toppled off. There was a cry as he managed to grab the ledge with his fingers.

As Jemma watched through the glass his quivering fingertips turned white as they slowly slipped away. Then they were gone and Phil was plummeting three floors, his arms windmilling as he screamed before landing on the concrete walkway below.

Several people rushed over to his body but the medical bystanders instantly knew there was no cure for a smashed skull.

Jemma opened the window fully and quickly peered down before closing it and rushing over to Brad. 'Are you OK?'

Brad tried to put his arm around her but couldn't as it had a drip attached. 'Yeah, I'm fine. Thanks for that.'

A nurse rushed in with a security guard.

'What's going on?' the guard asked.

Jemma was shaking as she replied, 'A man called Phil Brown tried to kill Brad but I disturbed him. He climbed out of the window but he's... He fell. I think he's dead.'

The guard gaped before gathering himself and talking into his radio. The nurse checked on Brad, who appeared unhurt after his latest ordeal.

Brad held Jemma's hand. 'Whoever that was had it in for me in a big way. Difficult to defend yourself when everything is wrapped in a cast. Well, almost everything.'

Jemma sat down next to Brad with tears in her eyes. 'That was my old boyfriend, Phil Brown.'

'Who? The guy who followed you to uni?'

Jemma was shaking. 'Yes. If I'd been a few minutes later, he'd have killed you and might have escaped.'

'Never thought we'd see him again. Well, you took care of him, Jemma. You're a hero.'

She looked at him and wiped her eyes as she thought, *and my secret died with him*. She fumbled the phone out from her pocket and rang Dave to update him.

Within a short time, a fire engine arrived for its obligatory alarm call-out. Dave turned up with the police team and rushed up to the ward to comfort Jemma, who sat grimacing as she drank the hospital coffee. She put down the cup of thick brown sludge and hugged him tightly.

'How are you?' he asked. 'I'm getting fed up with asking now. I better have a card made!'

Jemma squeezed him tighter. 'I'm OK, but it was horrible. I opened the window and it knocked him off the ledge. He fell down and down with his arms flailing.'

Dave comforted her. 'Sounds like you saved Brad's life.' He put on a pair of gloves and picked up the garrotte from the floor by the bed, sealing it in an evidence bag.

Jemma turned pale. 'I spotted that when I came into the room. It was in his hands when he stood there. I thought I was too late!'

Dave put his arm around her. 'He won't be back.'

'But it was like Alice again.' Jemma said. He handed her a tissue from the box on the table. She sniffled into it. 'Thanks.'

A voice from behind made them both jump. 'Hello! Remember me? I nearly got strangled or decapitated or whatever a garrotte does.'

Jemma glanced down. 'You don't look too bad.'

'I have a nasty itch inside the cast on my leg.'

She laughed. 'Better bring a ruler in next time, so you can have a good scratch.'

'That would be heaven,' Brad said, 'and thanks again for saving my life.'

'He's the bastard who hit you with his car,' she said.

Brad shuffled into an upright position. 'But why would he want to kill me?'

Dave shrugged. 'Unless he's left some notes in his campervan, we might never know.'

Jemma sat in one of the chairs with her shoulders slumped. 'Maybe he wanted Brad out of the way so he could get back together with me.'

Dave thought for a moment. 'But what about me?'

'No idea. Maybe you were next on his list.'

'Probably best he ate the tarmac then.'

She stared at the floor. 'Yep, I think it was.'

***

Jemma stood on the cliff staring down at Alice's body on the rocks below. Blonde hair radiated out and gently rocked in the waves.

She shouted. 'Alice. You should have held on. I was coming. Alice…'

Chapter 28

The next morning Jemma stayed in bed with a throbbing headache while Dave went downstairs for breakfast. Before he left, he brought her a cup of tea and kissed her.

'Nothing to worry about now, he's gone,' he said, caressing her hair.

'Do you think he murdered Anna?'

'We don't know yet, we're trying to find any links. We'll solve it, I promise'

She grunted, pulling the duvet tighter to her chin and squeezing her eyes shut to help her ease the pain.

Dave kissed her forehead. 'I hope your head clears soon. I'll see you later, love you, Jem.'

'Love you too.'

Jemma sat with a cuppa and scrolled through her e-mails, but couldn't concentrate. Her mobile rang and the display showed Ellie. *Oh, bugger, I meant to call and ask about her driving test.* 'Hi, Ellie.'

'Hi, Mum. Guess what!'

'You passed?'

'Yep. I thought you were going to ring?'

'I intended to but I had a lie in.'

'I suppose you had a good reason, acting the hero at the hospital yesterday and saving Brad's life.'

'The way you go on, anybody would think I was a terrible mum.'

There was a short silence. 'No comment,' Ellie said.

Jemma was mortified by Ellie's reaction but tried to make a joke of it. 'You're rotten. How was the test?'

'Not bad. The examiner put me at ease and I didn't feel stressed at all.'

'Any tricky bits?'

'Only one. A dog ran out in front of the car so I had to slam the brakes on. He told me I coped really well and that would cover the emergency stop.'

'Well done, Els, I'm proud of you.'

'Thanks, Mum, and my other news is...'

'What?'

'Ta-dah! Dad's bought me a car!'

'He's what?'

'He's given me a red Fiesta.'

'Good of him.' Jemma's face clouded over. 'Can you come over and show me, when you're happy driving all the way here.'

'Oh, it's only fifteen miles, not a major trek! I promise to show you at the weekend. Bye Mum. Love you!'

'Love you, Els.'

Jemma shut down the call, seething at Liam for not discussing Ellie's car with her. Important decisions should have her input too. Previously she thought that she and Liam had made a reasonable job of bringing Ellie up to be a well-balanced girl. It seemed, however, that Ellie had some issues with her mother being absent so often.

She typed out a message; *I'd have liked to have been told that you were planning to buy Ellie a car. I could have given you something towards the cost.* She sent the text and awaited a reply.

The phone rang while she had it in her hand, which made her jump. She thought Liam might ring straight back. He grunted. 'Now what's the matter?'

'Nobody told me anything about the car buying plans. How's she going to run the bloody thing?'

'She's got a job lined up waitressing in a restaurant to help her with insurance and petrol,' he said.

'What? Isn't she concentrating on college?'

'She'll only be working a few nights a week.'

Jemma hesitated. 'Oh, she didn't tell me.'

'She wanted to discuss everything at the weekend. You've never got time to talk with her. You're involved so much with your precious fossils and all the other things going on in your hectic life.'

She snapped. 'Don't tell me how to bring up our daughter.'

Liam laughed, which annoyed her more. 'Bit late for that now, she's eighteen!'

She sighed, totally deflated. 'I suppose so. Tell her I'll contribute something towards the insurance.'

The next few days passed by in a blur of giving statements and driving backwards and forwards to Swanbourne. The police confirmed Jemma wouldn't face any charges over Phil's death. That was good news as she hadn't considered that she might.

The national press had latched on to the news and turned up in Lulcombe to try to take some photos to fill out their stories. Some persistent photographers accosted her arriving back home but she covered her head with her jacket and said nothing.

When Dave came home he went back outside and spoke to the people hanging around with cameras. Jemma could see him gesturing as he talked to them and then, with grim faces, they climbed into their cars and left.

She gave a wry smile as he came back in. 'How did you manage to send them packing that easily?'

'I threatened them with arrest for causing an obstruction on a narrow road and parking illegally. They soon scuttled.'

'Thanks, babe,' she said. 'I hope this will all quieten down now. I've had enough of bad things happening.'

'Welcome to my world,' he said.

She held his hand. 'At least we don't need to worry about Phil anymore.'

He thought for a moment. 'How did Phil think he'd get away with murdering Brad in a hospital, especially after the hit-and-run incident and charges?'

She stayed silent for a moment. 'Guess we'll never know what was going through his mind.'

'So weird, almost as if he thought he was untouchable. He put on some sunglasses and a baseball cap and thought nobody would recognise him.'

She shivered. 'Probably past the point of thinking logically. When I stared into his eyes in Brad's hospital room, there seemed to be a wild madness in there.'

'He must have been completely insane. A garrotte. For goodness' sake!' he said.

Her face darkened. 'Can we stop talking about this, please? I need to lose the image of him toppling off the ledge when I opened the window.'

'Good idea, subject closed. Let's take Dino for a walk.'

They walked across the fields hand in hand. Dino chased rabbits, which waited until the last moment before disappearing into their burrows, leaving a frustrated dog sniffing down the hole.

Jemma stopped and hesitated. 'I've got something to tell you.'

His eyebrows raised. 'What? Are you OK?'

'Yes, I'm fine but I need to tell you about Phil.'

'What about him?'

'He was blackmailing me.'

Dave gasped. 'What? How could he blackmail you?'

'It all goes back to when Alice fell off the cliffs.'

'But that was thirty years ago.'

Jemma bit her lip. 'She called for help but I was busy digging out a fossil and I thought she was messing about.'

'What's that got to do with Phil?'

She sniffed. 'He was there and he heard Alice call me.'

He squeezed her hand. 'But if she fell it can't have been your fault.'

Jemma began crying. 'It was my fault. I ignored her and she slipped.'

Dave hugged her. 'It wasn't your fault. How was he blackmailing you?'

'He left a note at the festival telling me to dump the policeman and go back to him.'

'The crazy bastard.'

'He also came into my kitchen the day you were following him.'

'I bloody knew something was up. What did he do?'

'Nothing. I gave him some money and he went.'

'Why didn't you tell me?'

'He said if I told anybody he'd reveal my secret.'

He squeezed her tighter. 'Nobody would've been bothered if he'd said that.'

'But I've felt so guilty for thirty years.'

'Don't worry, babe, it's all over now,' he said.

'Now I've told you, will you have to reveal it to the investigation?'

'I should but I'll keep it quiet. We'll just say you were being stalked by a jealous ex-boyfriend. The investigation will be closed pretty quickly and the coroner will accept that, I'm sure.'

Jemma's brow wrinkled. 'Isn't it a risk for you now I've told you?'

Dave shrugged. 'Hope not. Let's just keep it between ourselves.'

'OK.'

He looked in her eyes. 'And one more thing.'

'What?'

'No more secrets.'

She held him tightly, 'OK.'

Chapter 29

Early on Saturday morning, Jemma planned to take some of the replica bones down to the museum. The process of mounting 'Plessie 2' on the wall could begin. Dave and Billy were both working so Freddie agreed to help. He walked round to Jemma's to help her move some of the bones.

'Hello, Auntie Jem, are you ready?'

'Yes.' After she locked her back door, they headed down to the workshop, where all the bones were in numbered boxes so it wasn't a difficult job loading the van.

He picked up the last box and walked down the path to the van. 'Let's go.'

They drove straight to the museum. Jemma parked up, put on the handbrake and turned off the ignition. After they unloaded the boxes, she spent a while inside sorting through them. Soon, everything was ready to start the massive job of mounting Plessie on the wall.

She realised she needed more brackets so decided to ring the DIY shop in Seaton where she'd bought some before. 'Oh, where's my phone?' she asked with her hands in her pockets.

Freddie took out his mobile. 'Here I'll use my app to find out what you've done with it.'

He pressed a few buttons. 'One hundred metres due south.'

'Bet I left it in the van.' She passed him the keys. 'Be an angel and see if you can find it for me, please while I finish sorting?'

She was going through one of the boxes of bones when Freddie returned. 'Any good?'

'Yeah, I went straight to it. Weird thing though…'

'What?'

'There was a man lying under the front of your van.'

Her head jerked up. 'What?'

'He had his head under your bumper.'

'Is he alright? Does he need an ambulance?'

'No, he's fine. I asked him if he was OK and he crawled out. He said he'd dropped his phone and was looking for it. He had a mobile in his hand when he stood up.'

'What was he like?'

'He was tall. Even bigger than Billy, but he wore a woolly hat and a scarf, so I didn't really see his face.'

'Had you seen him before?'

'No. I noticed he wore big boots as they clip-clopped like a horse when he dashed off.'

'Very strange. I better check the van before we go.' She rang the shop to find out if they had any brackets in stock. They did so she told them she'd be right over. She locked the museum, and together they walked to her van. 'Where was that bloke?' she asked.

He pointed at the front nearside tyre. 'Under there.'

Jemma knelt and checked underneath the bumper. 'Can't see anything. I hope he didn't break his phone when he dropped it.'

The road to Seaton followed the line of the coast. Every

so often it dived down into a valley like the kingfishers that fished the streams it crossed. There was a long downhill section as they approached Seaton.

Freddie peered at the dashboard. 'How long have you had this van?'

'Oh, must be ten years or so.'

'But the clock reads thirty-five thousand miles. Is that all you've done?'

Jemma laughed. 'This old beast has done a few more than that. It's on its second time round, so more like one hundred and thirty-five thousand miles.'

'Wow, that's a lot.'

'Might be, but it's always been reliable and a great run around.'

'I suppose you'd wreck a new one with all the muddy rocks you chuck in the back.'

'You're not wrong.' She drove over the brow of the hill and commenced the long descent into Seaton. As she reached the first bend she pushed down on the brake and gasped when nothing happened.

She pumped harder, but still nothing. 'Holy shit. Hold on Freddie, I've got no brakes.'

He gripped the handle above his head, took a deep breath and went quiet.

Jemma skidded round the first curve but their speed increased nearing the second bend where a wooden guard rail was the only thing standing between them and a drop over the cliffs to the sea below.

She tried to change from fourth to third but the gearbox complained loudly and refused to shift. Only with an adrenaline-fuelled surge of strength and a loud grating could she wrench the gears into third, causing the engine to scream as it red-lined.

Reaching the next bend she grabbed the handbrake and tugged as hard as she could. 'Here, Freddie, help with this.'

With his efforts, they slowed a little but the wheels locked causing them to skid again as the wing grated along the wooden railing.

Jemma prayed the guard rail would hold as they scraped around the corner, dust clouded around them and the back wheel left the road. They skidded around without going over the edge and Jemma released the handbrake in an effort to start the wheels turning again.

She pulled the handbrake again but this time the vehicle didn't slow. Instead, its speed increased as the engine revved higher. Her knuckles were white on the steering wheel as she focussed on the road ahead, glad there was no traffic in front.

As they hurtled down the hill all Jemma could think about was the hairpin bend at the end, with only another wooden barrier between them and oblivion.

Suddenly, she remembered the emergency run-off halfway down the long straight section. As the entrance rapidly approached, she shouted, 'Brace yourself!'

Freddie held the handle tightly. 'OK!'

She wrenched the steering wheel to the left but they were moving too fast to aim straight into the emergency lane. Instead, the left wheels hit the sand, which slowed them down but spun the van so that it bounced out from the pit. The rear of the van crashed through the fence and they came to a halt with the back wheels hanging precariously over the edge of the cliff.

Chapter 30

Dave was working on his computer at Police HQ when his mobile rang. He looked at the display, it was Jemma. 'Hi, Jem, how ya...'

A panicked voice answered him. 'There's been an accident.'

'What? Where are you?'

'I'm in the van with Freddie. We've crashed and we're hanging over a cliff halfway down Seaton Hill.'

Dave ran out of his office and down the stairs. 'Have you called 999?'

'Yes, there's a fire engine on the way, but come quickly.'

'I'm on my way. Can you get out of the van?'

'I daren't move.'

'OK, stay still. I'm getting in my car now.'

He jumped into his car, slapped on a blue light and raced out of the car park with no regard for the speed limits.

***

In the front seat, Jemma and Freddie sat motionless as the van continued rocking, his tearful eyes fixed on her.

'What do we do?'

'Just stay still and don't move.'

'Can't we get out? I want to get out,' he whimpered.

'Just wait. Help's on its way.'

'I'm scared.'

She slowly reached over and held his hand. 'Me too. Are you OK otherwise? You aren't hurt?'

'I think so. I nearly shit myself though.'

The van suddenly lurched backwards and they both screamed as the front lifted up some more. They squeezed each other's hands tightly.

'Oh, my God, we're going to die!' Freddie wailed.

'Listen! Listen!' Jemma said sharply, trying to calm her terrified nephew. 'I can hear a siren, can you? That was quick.'

A fire engine parked by the road and four firemen rushed out. They assessed the situation and one of them pulled a winch from the front of the engine and ran over to the van.

As the front of the van was slightly off the ground, he was able to attach the hook to the front axle immediately. He pressed the control and tightened the cable.

With the vehicle now stabilised, two other firemen moved to the driver's and passenger's doors and grasped the handles. Freddie's door opened easily but Jemma's was more of a struggle and the fireman had to break away pieces of the fence before he could open it.

Jemma waited until both doors were open and the firemen held out their hands. 'OK Freddie, out now, quickly.'

They both climbed out at the same time and were each grabbed by a fireman who pulled them to safety.

With their weight out of the van, it lurched backwards but was held by the winch. The motor started up and the van was slowly dragged back towards the road.

The firemen checked them over. 'Are you both OK?'

Jemma began to tremble as the adrenaline wore off. 'Yeah, I think so. I'm a bit bruised from the seatbelt and we're both a bit shaken.'

'You did the right thing staying in the cab. You'd never have opened the driver's door and if the lad had got out of the passenger side then the van could have gone over.'

Jemma's legs gave way and she came to land heavily on the floor.

A fireman helped her to sit up, wrapped silver blankets around their shoulders and gave them each a bottle of water.

Jemma saw Dave pull up in his car and he ran over to hug her and Freddie.

'Are you both OK?' he asked.

'Just about,'Jemma said. 'Although the shakes have started.'

'That's just shock and the after-effects of an adrenaline surge.'

Jemma remained sitting. 'I bloody hate cliffs. It was like *The Italian Job.*'

'What caused the crash?'

'My brakes failed coming down the hill.'

Dave gasped. 'My God, you're so lucky!'

'Before we left the museum, Freddie spotted a man underneath my van. As he scrambled out he said something about dropping his phone. I'm worried he might have tampered with the brakes.'

'Bloody hell, Jem, what's going on? I'll ask the forensic guys to check it out. If this is deliberate it would be attempted murder.'

She gulped and looked at Freddie. 'Your mum will be banning you from coming anywhere near me!'

He tried to smile. 'She can try, I s'pose. Should I tell her about this?'

'Don't worry, I will. You OK?'

'Yes, my heart's slowed down a bit.'

Jemma smiled. 'You did well to stay cool and not move.'

Dave walked over to speak with the firemen, who were grim-faced as they surveyed the scene. He returned to Jemma and Freddie as an ambulance pulled up. 'They'll check you both over and then we can sort out statements.'

The paramedics examined them for any injuries or potential whiplash and pronounced them both OK.

Jemma thanked everyone who'd helped and collapsed into Dave's car, casting one last glance towards her van and the large gap it had left in the fence. Dave gave her keys to one of his colleagues before driving away. On the journey back to Lulcombe, Jemma and Freddie gave him more details of what had happened.

They arrived at Swanbourne and Dave took them inside to give statements to Amrik Hussain. Amrik was holding an electronic device with a tube in his hand. His cheeks turned red when he asked, 'Sorry, Jemma. You need to do a breath test. Standard procedure in RTAs.'

'In what?' Freddie asked.

'Road Traffic Accidents.'

Jemma reached over. 'No problem, I don't mind. It must be a couple of days since I had a glass of wine.'

He handed her the tube and Jemma blew for what felt like an eternity. As she thought she was going to collapse, he said, 'That's fine, stop.'

She gasped and drew in a deep breath. They waited for a few moments during which Jemma felt guilty even though she knew she shouldn't.

He read the result. 'All good. Dave should have taken a reading at the roadside, but we're OK doing it now.'

Jemma sat with Amrik who typed her statement straight onto his laptop and printed it out for her to sign.

He turned to Freddie. 'You need to come back with one of your parents to make your statement. You could also take a look through some photo albums to see if you recognise the man who was under Jemma's van.'

There was a knock on the door and Dave came in. 'The forensics guys checked your van and found the brake line had been partially cut through. Not much leaked out initially, but when you started braking and the pressure built up, it ruptured, and your brakes failed. Luckily the handbrake was an old-fashioned cable one, so it helped you to slow down.'

Jemma turned pale. 'Bloody hell. That means somebody's trying to kill me.'

Dave held her arm. 'Yes, I'm worried about how serious this is. We can't blame Phil as he is, to put it mildly, a bit dead.'

Freddie giggled. 'A bit dead.' When he caught the expressions on the adults' faces, he stopped grinning. 'Sorry.'

Dave regarded Jemma. 'We'll try to organise a couple of uniforms to keep an eye on you at home and when you're out, but you know what things are like with budgets.'

Jemma shivered. 'Thanks. I'm scared Dave. Do you think Freddie needs police protection? After all, he talked to the bloke who tampered with the brakes.'

Dave shook his head. 'Not happening, I'm afraid! I don't think the bosses will agree to that. Can you think of anybody who might bear a grudge against you, Jemma?'

'No, I can't think of any enemies... Apart from Sally O'Keefe. She certainly has a few problems with me.'

Amrik wrote Sally's name on his pad.

Dave asked Amrik, 'Are you all done?'

'Yes, until Freddie can get back in.' He turned to Jemma. 'So, you're both fine to go!'

***

Dave dropped Freddie off at his house and he ran inside. Jemma shouted after him. 'Tell your mum I'll speak to her later.'

'OK, Auntie Jemma, see ya!' He slipped into the house, seemingly unaffected by his ordeal in the passenger seat.

Jemma stared after him. 'The innocence of youth!'

Dave put his arm around her shoulders. 'No nightmares at that age.'

She thought of the numerous nightmares she had about Alice. 'He's lucky.'

Dave drove her home and they kissed in the car. 'Seriously, Jemma, can you carry out a basic safety regime? Vary your routine, keep a look out for any unusual patterns of behaviour around you, watch for cars or people following you and, when your van comes back, lock it in the garage.'

Jemma interrupted him. 'You're scaring me now.'

'Don't forget there'll be some uniforms dropping by later to keep an eye on you as well.'

Her face darkened. 'Bang goes my privacy. Again!'

'Only until we catch whoever is doing this. And I'll be home around seven.'

'OK. See you in a bit.'

They kissed, and she walked up to the door and let herself in.

Jemma sat at her kitchen table. Her hands shook as the delayed shock hit her. Dino padded closer and rested his head on her leg.

'Oh, Dino, what am I going to do? I can't take much more of this.' She stroked his head then walked over to the shelves. The bottle of whisky looked very inviting, so she poured herself a generous measure. Walking back to her chair with the glass and bottle, Dino watched her with doleful eyes.

She pointed her finger at him. 'Don't you go judging me. I deserve a drink after everything I've been through today. Why is this happening to me, Dino? Ever since I found Plessie everything has been horrible. I almost got Freddie killed for the second time. My whole world seems upside down. What's going on? And why do I still have feelings for Brad when Dave is so good for me?' She paused. 'You know, Dino; you're useless as a psychiatrist.'

Dino lifted his head and licked her arm.

She stroked his ear and took a swig from her glass. As the smoky liquid burnt her throat, she grimaced and drained the glass. Another glassful followed the first. She pushed the bottle away and put her head on her arms.

Chapter 31

Tuesday started dull with thick, dark clouds. Heavy rain was forecast and parts of the county were under a flood alert. Breakfast was quiet as Jemma and Dave ate their yoghurt and cereal whilst listening to the news.

'Busy day?' he asked.

Jemma sipped her tea. 'I've got some student assignments to read through and two lectures on campus this afternoon.'

He checked the time. 'Bloody hell! Better move.'

He leant over and kissed her. 'Now, don't forget to lock the door. And be careful.'

She snapped. 'I don't want to lock my door. It's so frustrating, hiding myself away. I need to live my life!'

'Up to you, but please be on the lookout for anything strange.'

As Dave climbed in his car, a police car pulled up with a young, uniformed constable in the driver's seat. He put his hand up to Dave, who wound down his window and had a quick chat before driving to Swanbourne.

***

Jemma couldn't concentrate on her work, so she put a CD

on, but even her favourite Bruce Springsteen album failed to reach the spot. She turned it off and returned to her assignments, determined to finish them. Halfway through the marking, her sister rang.

'Hello, Sue, you OK?'

Sue gave a bitter laugh. 'Yes, I'm fine, but what the hell's going on?'

'No idea. Somebody thought it might be funny to cut through the brake pipe on the van.'

'I don't think "funny" is the best word to use. Attempted murder would be a better description, with my son in the passenger seat! Although he's telling it like it was a thrilling ride.'

Jemma sighed. 'Look, I'm so sorry. You should keep Freddie away from me, at least for the moment. I'm not a safe person to be near.'

'Don't be daft. He wouldn't stay away, whatever I say.'

'I'm not doing any of this on purpose, Sue.' They chatted for a while and Jemma caught up with all the latest gossip.

Sue said, 'Sorry, got to go. Make sure you stay safe, OK?'

'Will do. Bye.'

'Bye.'

She shut off the call and went back to her marking. Looking through the window, she spotted Chrissie hanging her washing out on the line. Jemma walked out and called her over. 'How are you?'

'Not bad, Jems, how's it going with you?'

Jemma sighed. 'Been better. I need some happy news right now.'

Chrissie thought for a moment. 'Brad's recovering well, and he's hoping to come out next week. I'll be looking after him a fair bit though.'

Jemma grinned. 'That'll keep you busy.'

Chrissie checked her watch. 'Fancy a walk before lunch? Clear your head. I have some viewings this afternoon, so we can't be out too long.'

'Sorry, I've got too much to do today. Thanks anyway. I haven't even got time to take Dino out. Would you mind taking him, please?'

'No probs,' Chrissie said. 'Collect him at quarter past?'

Jemma smiled. 'Thanks. That'd be brill!'

Half an hour later, Chrissie opened her back door and said, 'I'm ready! Walkies, Dino?'

Dino jumped out of his basket, stuck his nose out of the door and returned.

'What's the matter with him?' Chrissie asked.

'The rain's starting so he's not that keen anymore.' Jemma saw what Chrissie was wearing. 'Do you want to borrow my waterproof coat in case it chucks it down? There's a stash of poo bags in the pockets. I usually take him on the coastal path; he loves that as he can chase the rabbits in the meadows behind the cliffs. He never catches them though,' she laughed.

'Yes, please. Saves me unlocking and getting mine.'

Jemma took down her waxed jacket and handed it over to her, along with the dog lead that hung next to it. 'Here you are.'

'Thanks. Come on Dino. Let's go!'

***

The moment Chrissie stepped out of the door, the rain started falling heavier, so she put the coat on, pulled up the hood and set off.

As she and Dino walked down Jemma's drive, the policeman in the patrol car opposite jumped in his seat and started the engine. As she passed, she smiled at him, and he made a double-take.

He settled back down and took out his sandwiches.

Chrissie put Dino on his lead and they made their way along Seaton Road, before turning right towards the harbour. Once they reached the Beach Car Park, she let Dino off for a run around. It was empty in the cold and wet conditions.

A solitary man entered the car park and walked past her towards the South West Coastal Path.

'Miserable weather!' She spoke at his back as he strode on.

'Sure is.' He didn't look back.

Another mad coastal walker and an unsociable sod too. She watched him as he climbed the cliff path and was soon out of view.

Chrissie let Dino run down on to the sand, though he soon decided it was too cold for a paddle and came trotting back.

'Come on, Dino.' She walked up the path herself. Her calves were pulling tight on the steep steps and she made a mental resolution to do something to get fitter.

She reached the meadow at the top and stood looking out to sea while Dino chased rabbits, real and imaginary. There was no sign of the walker who had passed her earlier. *He must be setting a fair pace. Bet he wants to reach his next hotel.*

She turned around and saw the man leaving the wooded area to the north of the cliff path. She smiled. *I bet he's had a pee.*

He returned to the path, head down in the drizzle and suddenly sprinted back down the slope. Her eyebrows raised as he ran towards her. As he rapidly approached, she froze and before she could react he grabbed hold of her jacket and propelled her towards the cliff edge.

Taken completely by surprise, she stumbled at the top of the cliff and let out a scream that faded to nothing in the wind and rain.

As they reached the edge the man gave one last shove and she went flying over and, with arms flailing, hurtled down to the rocks one hundred feet below.

***

The man got up and glanced around to see if anybody had observed his attack. Satisfied, he returned down the path at a steady walk, wiping the mud from his coat as best he could. The whole thing had only taken a few minutes and he had a smile on his face at a job well done.

***

Dino eventually got bored with sniffing down rabbit holes and wandered back to where Chrissie had been. Confused, he gazed up and down the path and, as he couldn't see her, he set off for home via the car park.

Chapter 32

Jemma sat at her kitchen table working through her lecture notes, which she had brightened with multi-coloured highlights. She was engrossed when she heard a scratching at the back door.

Sounds like Dino. She opened up.

Sure enough, a very wet Dino was standing there and pushed past her into the house.

Jemma stuck her head out. 'Chrissie?' she shouted. 'Has he beaten you home?'

Nothing.

'Where is she Dino?'

The dog dipped into his bowl of biscuits and soon demolished the lot, wagging his tail and then returned to the door.

Jemma took down an old bright blue cagoule she rarely used, put Dino on a spare lead and let him pull her along the pavement. The policeman glanced up from his phone and wound down his window.

'Nearly followed you earlier but it was your neighbour.'

'Yes, Chrissie. Which way did she go?'

He pointed down the road. 'Down there towards the beach. Why?'

'Something's a bit weird. Dino came back but Chrissie didn't.'

He grabbed his cap and overcoat and got out of the car. 'We'd better check up, hadn't we? Maybe she's not well. Have you got her number?'

Jemma mumbled. 'Never thought of that!'

She took out her phone and rang Chrissie but she got no ringing tone, just an unobtainable solid noise. 'Very strange. That mobile goes everywhere with her and she never turns it off.'

'Shall we follow the dog, miss?' He pointed. 'It wants to go that way.'

'Yes, good idea. Good boy, Dino. Off you go!'

Dino walked down the street sniffing at every other lamp post.

The wind blowing in from the sea swirled around the town, tumbling an empty coffee cup probably discarded by a tourist.

Dino led them down towards the harbour, through the Beach Car Park and onto the cliff path. He seemed to know his way and, now he wasn't distracted by lampposts, kept a reasonable pace. As they walked up the steep path to the cliff top, the young policeman panted heavily.

He's not used to this, Jemma thought. She pulled up her collar and tried to shelter from the chill wind and the stinging rain blowing in from the sea. She shivered and walked faster.

When they reached the grass at the top, Dino rediscovered the rabbit smells and Jemma let him off his lead. 'Where's Chrissie, Dino?' Jemma asked. 'Come on, find her!'

He ignored her and stuck his head down the nearest hole.

Jemma watched as the policeman checked around the meadow and spotted a leather dog lead on the grass.

He held it up. 'Is this anything, miss?'

She walked over, shaking as she got nearer to the cliffs. 'Yes, it's Dino's.' Her voice quavered.

'Stay there,' he said to Jemma and stepped closer to the edge. He pointed. 'There are some footprints in the mud and a long muddy skid over here.'

He peered over the edge and the colour drained from his face. 'There's a body down there. Stay where you are.'

Jemma cried out, 'Oh no, Alice fell from that spot!'

'Who?' He asked.

'Sorry, nothing.'

He took out his radio. 'Sixty-two to base, Sixty-two to base. I'm on the meadow at the top of the cliffs above Lulcombe West Beach and I can see a body on the rocks below.' He paused as he listened to the reply on the radio. 'No worries, she's here with me. We came out to search for her friend who'd taken the dog for a walk. Not confirmed, but the body appears to be her neighbour, Chrissie.' He glanced over at Jemma who was now crying and waved to attract her attention. 'Your friend's full name, please, Mrs Thorne?'

'Christine Martin. Chrissie to her friends.'

He returned to his radio. 'The person who has disappeared is a Christine Martin, a neighbour of Jemma Thorne's from Seaton Road.' Another pause. 'It's likely she didn't survive the fall. We might need the coastguard as the tide is quite high. OK. Out.'

Dino came trotting back and Jemma dropped to her knees on the wet grass to hug him as the tears flowed.

The young policeman put his radio away and helped Jemma to her feet. 'Come on, Mrs Thorne. Someone will be along to take you home. I need to stay here and secure the scene.' He led her back towards the Beach Car Park.

A few minutes later a female officer arrived to drive Jemma home, and then walked with her from the car to her front door. 'Are you OK, Mrs Thorne?'

Jemma tried to smile at her. 'Yes, I'm OK.'

'I need to go now, but there'll be another patrol car along shortly to take over the surveillance.' She headed back to her car and drove away.

Jemma shut and locked the door then sat in her chair by the kitchen fire. It had almost gone out so she added some more coal with shaking hands. Was Chrissie dead now as well? It was all so hard to believe. Dino padded closer and rested his head on her legs as if to say 'What's up?'

Her phone rang and she jumped. Dave! For a few seconds, she stared at the phone without touching it. Wiping her eyes, she blew her nose and answered. 'Hello, Dave.'

'Oh, my God, Jem. Are you alright?' he said.

'Sort of, but I feel in a state of shock. I only spoke to her before lunch and now she's gone. It is her, I assume?'

'Well, they haven't formally identified her yet, but it appears she had your waxed coat on.'

Jemma's voice went quiet. 'Will I need to ID her?'

'Her ex-husband is going to do it. She's got no other family members locally.'

'OK. I did wonder if they'd want me to do it.'

'You wouldn't want to do that, I assure you.'

Her hand shook as she held the phone. 'I'm worried, Dave, what time will you be home?'

'Around six. As long as you're home, you're safe, the officer outside will make sure of it. I know it's hard but try not to worry too much, OK? I'll catch you later. Love you.'

'Love you too.'

The call ended and Jemma sat in her kitchen, stunned and drained after the recent events. Reaching for the bottle of whisky, she poured herself a glass and sat down for another cry.

She was trembling as she took a sip from the glass.

It's all too much. Anna's death. The attack on Brad. Phil returning and dying right in front of me. Almost going over the cliff with Freddie. And now my dear friend Chrissie. Everything seems to be linked to me.

She drained the whisky glass and poured herself another.

***

Two men sat in a grubby office with the radio on waiting for the local news.

The shorter one smiled at the larger man and raised his bottle of beer. 'To a successful result. About time'

His brother lifted his bottle. 'I told you I'd sort it.' At that moment the bulletin began, so they set down their drinks and listened.

'The time is four o'clock on Radio Dorset and here is the news. Our breaking story is the death of a local woman in an accident on the cliffs near Lulcombe. It appears the woman was on the clifftop path walking a dog when she fell to her death. Police have not yet named the deceased other than to say she was a forty-two-year-old woman from Lulcombe.'

The two men picked up their drinks and clinked them together. The larger man grinned. 'To problems solved.'

The smaller man smirked back. 'Problems solved. I like that because I don't tolerate failure. What don't I tolerate?'

The larger man gulped. 'Failure!'

'It's been a struggle you know, ever since Dad died and I've had to look after my little brother.'

'I'm not little, I'm taller than you.'

'You might be the muscle but I'm the brains. Without me, you'd be nowhere. Where would you be?'

The larger man looked down at the table, 'Nowhere.'

***

At Lulcombe Police HQ the latest developments were being discussed by the team in the incident room. As they were working long hours, Laura had treated them to a big box of doughnuts. Everyone had got their sugar rush and they were all licking their fingers.

She took some wet wipes out of her bag and put them on the desk. 'Nobody touches the whiteboard or photos until they've wiped the sugar off.' She stood in front of the murder board looking at the pictures, maps and the lines linking them. 'There's something going on in Lulcombe and I want to find out what!'

Amrik glanced up from his notes. 'Maybe they're all coincidences, ma'am.'

'No, I'm sure they're not.' She pointed her finger at him. 'I don't like coincidences, Amrik. Lulcombe is usually a quiet place. To have a burglary, a murder, a hit-and-run, a brake tampering incident and now a cliff death in such a short space of time doesn't feel right at all.'

One of the constables held up her hand.

'Yes, Jill?'

'Hasn't the hit-and-run been solved, ma'am, with one old boyfriend of Jemma Thorne's running down another old boyfriend of hers?'

Amrik grinned. 'Her current one had better watch out!'

Laura glowered at him. 'Thank you for your words of wisdom, Amrik. I'm sure Dave will feel safer following the death of the culprit. That one has been solved, Jill but I don't know if it's linked to the latest event.'

'Couldn't it be suicide, ma'am or a tragic accident?' Jill asked

'We don't know,' Laura said. 'According to the people who knew her, the deceased didn't have any suicidal tendencies and had recently become happily involved with Bradley Jones, the victim in the hit-and-run incident.'

Amrik walked over to the whiteboard. 'Ma'am, the one person who is linked to everything and everybody is Jemma Thorne. She works at the museum where Anna Jenkins was attacked and she was being stalked by Phil Brown. He ran over one of her ex-boyfriends, Bradley Jones, who had been volunteering at the museum as well.'

He pointed to a photo. 'Jemma accidentally knocked Phil off a ledge and killed him, after he tried to murder Brad in hospital. Next, she went off the road after her van's brake pipe was deliberately cut. Finally, her next-door neighbour, Christine Martin, was found dead after taking Jemma's dog for a walk.'

Laura smiled. 'Well summarised, Amrik. You can understand why I don't like coincidences. These events have got to be connected somehow. Any more news from the clifftop forensic team?'

Amrik shook his head. 'No ma'am. There were some larger boot prints near the edge of the cliff mixed with Christine Martin's own footprints, but there were no witnesses. They can't say for certain if she fell by accident, or whether it might have been suicide or a deliberate act by a person or persons unknown. However, the presence of the larger boot prints does suggest foul play. Forensics are trying to identify the make of boot.'

Laura looked around the room. 'When's the post-mortem due?'

'Dave Gill is attending it and should be back soon.'

A few minutes later the incident room fell silent when Dave entered with a folder tucked under his arm. 'Talking about me?'

'Well, Dave, what's the outcome?' Laura asked.

'Inconclusive I'm afraid, ma'am.' He took out his notes. 'Death was due to multiple injuries consistent with a fall from over a hundred feet, and the worst thing...'

'What?'

'There was water in her lungs so she was alive for a while after landing.'

There were gasps around the room.

Dave returned to his notes. 'There's no evidence to suggest it might have been suicide and nothing to prove a deliberate act, so at the moment it'll go down as a tragic accident.'

Laura slipped on her jacket. 'So team, we've had two fatalities, a vehicle crash and a major theft. Come on. We need some results.'

They all picked up their mugs and wandered off back to their desks.

***

Jemma rang Ellie.

'Hello, Mum.'

'Hello, Els. You OK?'

'I'm fine. You?'

'Yes, I'm coping. Fancy some lunch today?'

Ellie paused. 'Do you think it's safe for you to go out?'

Jemma paused. 'Look, Ellie, I can't just hide myself away. I've got to try to live life as normally as I can, even if it is with a policeman following me.'

'Ok. If you think it's safe. I'm free half eleven 'til three.'

'Part-timer.'

'Ha-ha.'

Jemma thought for a moment. 'How about The Singing Kettle?'

Ellie smacked her lips. 'Sounds yummy. Love their cake.'

'Meet you there at quarter past twelve. They've only got a few tables so we need to be there pretty early.'

'OK with me. Cheers, Mum.'

'Bye.'

***

The sun made a rare appearance as Ellie and Jemma met outside the tiny tearoom. It was a quirky place with six tables squashed into the single room. Every bit of wall space was covered with shelves full of old kettles and teapots.

They walked in and Jemma sat facing away from the door but then remembered Dave's advice and moved to sit with her back to the wall. She'd seen a policeman parked across the street earlier but she couldn't see him now. *I must be getting paranoid.*

Ellie sat opposite and viewed the menu as well as the treats on offer before choosing a hot chocolate and piece of lemon cake. Jemma went for a cup of tea and fruit scone.

Ellie looked across at her mum. 'You OK?'

Jemma smiled thinly. 'I'm fine, thanks.'

'No, I mean how are you doing?'

'I'm managing, honest. It's been hard with Anna, Brad and now Chrissie, but I'm coping. I have to cope as I don't fancy the alternative.'

'Well, don't forget I'm here for you.'

Jemma held her hand across the table. 'Thanks. You know, I'm sorry I neglected you when you were younger and I was busy.'

'You didn't neglect me, Mum, it was just some of the girlie stuff that you weren't good at, like hair and makeup.'

'Sorry.'

'Don't worry. None of those things were important. I realised ages ago that you were different from other mums.'

Jemma looked hopeful. 'In a good way?'

Ellie laughed. 'Let's just say sometimes and leave it at that.'

'Why didn't you tell me about getting a job?'

Ellie shrugged. 'I was going to but you had a lot on your plate and I forgot.'

'I'm never too busy to talk to you.'

'Oh, but you are, Mum. You are.'

Jemma took her hand. 'No matter how busy I might seem, I've always got time for you.'

Ellie smiled. 'Thanks.'

The food arrived and they gasped at the size of the slice of cake on Ellie's plate. 'I'll never eat all this,' she laughed.

'I bet you do. You've always been a gannet where food's concerned.'

Soon the table was covered in crumbs. Ellie licked her lips. 'Mmm, that was lovely. By the way, Mum, are you busy on Monday? I've got a free day and thought we could do something together.'

Jemma looked over at her. 'Sorry, Els I'm working then. We're filming a pilot episode for a new TV show about fossil hunting using GPR.'

Ellie's eyes widened. 'Wow. Sounds cool! When's it going to be on?'

Jemma shrugged. 'No idea, it might never be shown if they don't like it, or if I'm rubbish at presenting. Tell you what, I can ask them if you could come as well. Might be boring but could be interesting.'

'That'd be fun! I don't often get the chance to come along when you're working.'

'Let me give Jackson a call.' Jemma took out her mobile and called a number. It was about to go through to messages when it was answered.

'Jackson Carter.'

After exchanging pleasantries Jemma quickly got to the point. 'You know the pilot we're filming next week, could I bring my daughter Ellie along? She'd love to watch the filming.'

'Is she eighteen?'

'Yes.'

'No problem then.' He laughed. 'Tell her to bring a shovel and she can help with the excavation.'

'That's great, thanks. We'll see you Monday!'

Jemma rang off and looked at Ellie. 'You probably heard yourself but that's OK.'

'Brilliant! I'll stay Sunday night so I'm ready. It'll be really exciting!'

Jemma smiled. 'Hopefully.'

Ellie paused. 'Just a thought. Will it be safe with certain maniacs out there?'

Jemma hugged her as they stood up to leave. 'I hope so. There will be lots of people around for the filming so nobody will be able to get near to us.'

***

That night Dave and Jemma snuggled down on the sofa. He had his arm around her as she cuddled up to him. The remnants of a half-eaten Chinese takeaway meal sat in front, the pots of sticky, colourful sauces thickening and congealing.

Jemma thought for a moment. 'The more I think about it, the more I think it must have been deliberate. Chrissie was so happy having met Brad. She'd never jump off a cliff. I can't think of any reason she'd venture near enough to the edge to accidentally fall off. But why? Why would anybody want to kill her?'

Dave wrung his hands together. 'I've had a thought. I hate to say this but what if it was a case of mistaken identity because Chrissie looked like you.'

She froze. 'You mean...'

'Yes. What if they were after you? It was your brakes that had been tampered with, and Chrissie was wearing your coat while she walked your dog.'

Tears filled her eyes. 'My God. Who could do such a thing? And why?'

'Have you fallen out with anybody?'

'No idea. Unless Sally's involved.'

Dave paused. 'I'm sure she's not, but we can check up on her. What are your plans for the next few days?'

'I'm in at the university tomorrow for lectures and working on Plessie over the weekend. The work's harder now Brad's not able to help. Oh, no. Brad!' She gasped. 'He doesn't know about Chrissie.'

Dave patted her hand. 'Don't worry, all sorted. One of our team called in to see him at the hospital to let him know.'

'How did he take it?'

'Shocked and upset. I think he really liked her.'

Jemma started crying again. 'What's happening? My life was so happy but now everything is falling apart.'

'Not everything Jem,' he said. 'Not everything.'

***

The two men were sitting in their squalid office when the local radio news came on.

'The person who died in yesterday's tragic accident at Lulcombe Beach has been named as Christine Martin, aged forty-two, a resident of Lulcombe.'

The larger man spluttered tea over his lap as the smaller man glared at him menacingly. 'You fool! How could you get the wrong woman?'

'Er... I don't know. It was her, I'm sure! She came out of Jemma's house, in Jemma's coat with Jemma's dog. She looked like her!'

'The only problem is it wasn't Jemma. Start working on a plan B! No. On second thoughts, you're going to do things my way. It said in the *Lulcombe News* that on Monday, Jemma's taking part in a televised survey of the clifftop meadow. Here's what you're going to do...'

Chapter 33

Chrissie's death had made headlines locally and even the inside pages of some national papers. On the day of her funeral, Jemma woke and showered early. Ellie came downstairs and joined her and Dave for breakfast. As Jemma tried without enthusiasm to finish her bacon sandwich, Ellie put her hand on her shoulder.

'You OK, Mum?'

'Yes, I'm fine.' Jemma stared down at her plate to hide the tears in her eyes.

Dave squeezed her hand. 'Don't be too brave today. We're here for you if you need a cry.'

Jemma reached over to Ellie with her other hand. 'Thanks, guys, I appreciate it.'

She glanced at the bottle of whisky on the kitchen shelf. *I need a quick drink to get through today. How can I sneak one without anybody seeing?*

She waited until Dave and Ellie had gone upstairs before taking a long swig. *Much better.*

A pack of mints sat on the side so she took one to disguise the smell of the whisky.

***

The drive up to Swanbourne crematorium was a sombre, quiet trip. All of them were worried about how the service would go. As they parked in the car park a taxi pulled up outside. The driver helped his passenger out and passed him a pair of crutches.

Jemma saw who it was and headed straight over. 'Brad, how are you doing?'

'I'm getting there.'

'I didn't know you were coming. You could've come with us.'

'I didn't decide until last night. My leg's been hurting but I've had plenty of pain meds.'

Jemma noticed Dave pointing at the door and his wrist. 'Come on, we need to go in.' She walked with Brad and they joined the others.

'Hello Brad,' Ellie said.

Dave and Brad grunted at each other 'Dave.'

'Brad. How're the injuries?'

'Improving.'

'Good.'

The embarrassingly stilted conversation ended as Dave held open the church door and everybody entered.

During the service Jemma kept floating in and out until *The Boxer* came on, introduced as one of Chrissie's favourite songs. She started crying and Dave took her hand. She noticed Brad wipe his eyes and she reached over to him with her other hand. Dave frowned but didn't say anything.

The rest of the funeral passed in a blur and soon Jemma found herself standing outside the crematorium talking to a few of Chrissie's work colleagues.

As Chrissie had no family present and only a few friends,

there was no wake planned. After a brief chat, Jemma was ready to go. She checked for Brad and saw him about to leave in a taxi.

'Dashing off without saying goodbye?' she said.

'I don't want to be in the way.'

'What?'

'Dave's been giving me the evil eye.'

'Don't be silly. He's OK.'

'Oh, well, I need some more pain meds anyway.' He got in the car and the driver collected his crutches.

Jemma felt like she should go and mother him at home but that wouldn't go down well with Dave. She watched him slowly position himself in the seat. 'Can you manage?'

'Yeah, I'm fine.' He closed the door and wound down the window. 'See you around, Jemma.'

'Bye, Brad. I'll come round and visit sometime.'

'That would be good. See ya.'

The taxi drove away and Jemma watched it go before walking back to her family.

Dave was hard to read. 'Is he OK?'

'Yes, he's in a lot of pain so he wanted to leave. Let's just go home and drink a toast to Chrissie?'

Dave drove while Jemma sat quietly next to him. 'You all right?' he said.

'Not bad. It's all getting a bit much. I just want it to end.'

They all returned to Jemma's and Dave went into the station. Ellie headed upstairs for a shower and then came down to sit with her mum in the kitchen. There was some music on the radio but neither of them noticed it.

'Fancy some tea and biscuits, Els?'

'Yeah, why not? Might cheer us up.' They sat quietly for a while with their mugs then Ellie spoke up. 'I'm glad that's all over.'

'I still can't believe she's gone.'

'I know, me too.'

They chatted for a while until Ellie disappeared up to her room.

After she'd gone, Jemma stared at the whisky bottle on the shelf. *One more glass won't do any harm.*

She poured a generous measure and sat at the table as the golden liquid burned her throat. When it was empty, she topped up her glass and not long after the room seemed to turn softer around the edges. With slightly shaking hands she picked up the glass and bottle and stumbled up to bed.

Chapter 34

Friday began as a beautiful crisp day; cold, but sunny. Jemma was between lectures when her phone rang.

She answered. 'Jemma Thorne.'

A male voice spoke. 'Hello, Miss Thorne, this is the *Dorset Echo*. We read a news article that said you and Swanbourne University are doing a GPR survey on Lulcombe clifftop meadow, so the South West Coastal Path will be temporarily closed and diverted. We'd like to publicise the closure as well.'

'Yes, fine. We're filming next Monday, nine 'til four, I think. Usually the quietest day for walkers so it shouldn't affect many people.'

'Thank you. Would it be in order for us to send a photographer along?'

'Can you check with the TV people please? No problem with me but they might not want other photographers about. If you want, I can find you their number.'

'Don't worry, we'll contact them directly.'

The call ended. *Strange. They didn't ask which company. How will they know who to contact?*

***

At Swanbourne Police HQ, Dave stood in Laura Day's office putting forward his case. One of the plusher offices, he was always amazed that her wooden desk was totally clear of clutter. She followed a policy of delegation that kept most files off her desk and encouraged her team to come to her with suggested solutions to any problems, so she could pick one and hand the case straight back to them. That's what Napoleon did with his generals, or so she told them.

'Yes, ma'am, I understand the cost issues, but I think Jemma needs round the clock protection. If she was the target of the cliff incident, she might still be in danger.'

Laura sighed. 'But we've already racked up a massive overtime bill with the surveillance we've put in place.'

Dave frowned. 'That's good, ma'am, but, when Chrissie Martin went over the cliff, she was wearing Jemma's coat and looked very much like her. The death may have been a case of mistaken identity so Jemma's life could still be at risk!'

She folded her arms, which he took as a bad sign. 'A lot of ifs, Dave. We don't have the manpower for full-time surveillance but I'll ask some of the uniforms to swing by and keep an eye out when they can.'

'Thanks.'

'Anything else?'

'No, ma'am.'

'OK then, off you go and carry on detecting.'

Dave left her office and returned to his desk. Amrik looked up from his pile of work.

'Any good?'

'Not really. DI Day is sending uniforms to park outside Jemma's as much as she can but there's no budget available for twenty-four hour protection.'

'Tell you what. If they're not available, we can take it in turns to park opposite Jemma's for a while.'

'Thanks, Amrik. That's good of you.'

'I'll sort it out with the others.'

'Thank them too, will you?'

***

Back in Lulcombe, the two men were discussing the plan for the following week and had a map spread out on the desk in front of them.

The shorter man pointed to the clifftop meadow. 'OK. On Sunday night you place the charges here and here. Add the detonators and you're all set. If you hide in the trees early on Monday morning, you can watch out for Jemma. It's a narrow field so she's bound to go somewhere near to the cliffs during the day. When she walks over to this section near the cliffs you press the firer and bang! Over she goes.'

The larger man nodded. 'Over the cliff!'

'Did you get everything on the list when you went to the quarry?'

He grinned. 'Yep. Nobody spotted me going in or out.'

'Are you sure the explosives will still be OK?'

'Yeah. They've been kept in a dry storeroom for years so they should be fine.'

'Good. So, you know what you're doing?'

The larger man read from his notepad. 'Yes, set the explosives and detonators on Sunday night. Go back early on Monday and hide in the woods with the remote-control firing device. Wait until Jemma stands between the charges and blow her away.'

The shorter man laughed. 'Boom! Oh, and by the way,

it wasn't such a bad thing you pushed the wrong woman off the cliff.'

'You what?'

'The lady you tried to teach to fly owned the house next door to Jemma Thorne so, now she's gone, we can try buying her house again.'

'So I'm not in your bad books anymore?'

'No, you're not.' The shorter man put his arm around the shoulders of his brother. 'Just don't make any mistakes on Monday or you'll have me to contend with.'

His brother cowered. 'I won't.'

***

Jemma sat in the house on her own and decided she ought to eat something, although she didn't have much of an appetite. However, the fridge was empty because with everything going on, she hadn't had the chance to go shopping. She grabbed her rucksack and headed down the hill to the small supermarket. As she left she told her police minder where she was going and he told her he would follow at a distance.

Lulcombe had not joined the ranks of Dorset towns that had allowed massive out-of-town supermarkets, so the local small shops did quite well. Jemma usually walked there when she could. Now the car park was full of space-hunting drivers, all circling like vultures in the vain hope of an elusive meal.

After wandering the aisles, she filled her trolley with enough stuff to keep her going for a while. The whisky section looked very inviting, so, with a guilty check to see if anybody was watching, she added a couple of bottles to her pile. As she turned into the final aisle, she collided with a trolley pushed by a small man who looked vaguely familiar.

The man turned with a snarl, before recognising her and giving a thin smile. 'Oh, Miss Thorne, I'm so sorry. Very careless of me.'

At that moment Jemma realised who he was, a small man with weasel-like features and short hair. It was one of the property developers who were trying to buy the museum site. She'd met him at the Fossil Festival and several times before, though she couldn't remember his first name so she hedged her bets. 'Afternoon, Mr Fletcher.'

'Please call me Reggie, Miss Thorne.'

'Everybody calls me Jemma.'

'Pleased to make your acquaintance again, I'm sorry to hear about your colleague at the museum.'

Jemma squirmed. 'Yes, such a shock. Anyway, I must be off as I've got to make lunch.'

'Of course, don't let me detain you further. Delighted to have seen you again, Jemma. I'm sure our paths will cross again soon, especially when the trustees agree to sell the museum site.'

Jemma frowned. 'That's not going to happen.'

He smirked. 'We can be very persuasive when we want to be.'

She gave a little shiver. 'I'm sorry, I'm in a hurry. Bye, Mr Fletcher.'

'Reggie.'

'Bye Reggie.'

She joined the queue at the till, glad to escape his presence. For some reason, she didn't feel comfortable talking to him. It might be the trouble he was causing with his development plans, or possibly she just didn't like him full stop.

As he walked back down the aisle, she could see him speaking into his mobile phone.

'Lovely day for the time of year, isn't it?'

Jemma jerked and turned to the checkout girl who was trying to make conversation. 'What? Sorry, miles away.'

'I said, lovely day for the time of year.'

'Yes, yes, it is,' Jemma said.

The girl on the till decided further conversation would be hard work, so returned to her conveyor with the beeps from the scanner for company.

As Jemma loaded her rucksack, she remembered she'd walked here so everything she bought would have to be carried back up the hill. She finished filling the rucksack, paid for two extra bags and her purchases but couldn't stop thinking about her meeting with Reggie Fletcher. *What will it take to stop the sale once and for all?* She worried that the replica Plessie wouldn't attract enough visitors to keep the museum running.

***

Jemma spent the weekend with Dave during which they took the remaining bones of "Plessie 2" to the museum and mounted them on the wall. After finishing, they surveyed the new display.

Dave held his arms out. 'All done, can't tell the difference.'

Jemma shook her head. 'I can. The resin bones are much lighter in colour than the originals but she still looks fantastic.'

'That should bring the punters rushing in, especially after the publicity the museum has received.'

'Some of it bad,' she said.

'They say there's no such thing as bad publicity. I bet there'll be a bumper demand for Plessie tickets, what with it being a murder scene.'

Jemma started tearing up again. 'I'd much rather have Anna still here.'

Dave put his arm around her. 'We all would, babe, but I'm sure she'd want you to carry on for the museum.'

'I know she would. By the way, we've heard back from the insurers about the claim for Plessie.'

He looked at her. 'And?'

'The bastards offered twenty-five thousand in full and final settlement.'

'What!' he said. 'That's nowhere near its value.'

'Yep, but that's what they think it's worth.'

He thought for a moment. 'Can't you appeal somewhere?'

'We need to investigate how to complain to the Insurance Ombudsman but haven't had time yet. The problem is there have been no complete plesiosaurs sold for over twenty years and the last one went for ten thousand.'

'What happens if Plessie turns up later?' he said.

Jemma shrugged. 'Don't know. I bet they get to keep her.'

'Why not wait for a while. I've got a feeling in my bones we'll find Plessie one day.'

'That would be brilliant, Dave, but I'm not hopeful.'

***

In the fading dusk of a miserable Sunday evening, Keith Fletcher parked in the Beach Car Park and unloaded his rucksack from the boot. As there were no cars about at this time of day, he hoped there would be nobody on the coast path that cut through the clifftop meadow. His brother had given him a walking pole and a map so he'd look like all the other serious walkers.

After locking his car he started along the path and headed up the hill. Shortly after arriving at the place marked on the map he again checked nobody was about. Once satisfied, he headed for the cliff edge and began digging with his trowel. Soon he had a hole the depth of a wine bottle so he buried the explosives and detonator before covering them with the soil and grass he'd taken out.

After re-reading Reggie's instructions, he measured out a hundred paces along the edge and dug another hole. The second batch of explosives was buried in that one along with another detonator.

Taking one final glimpse around the field, he sauntered back down the path. It had become much darker since he arrived, and on the last section he needed to use his torch.

He unlocked his car, dumped the rucksack in the boot and, pleased with his evening's efforts, drove home.

Chapter 35

The following Monday was forecast to be a reasonable day, windy and dry with some sunny intervals although, as winter bit, the wind felt much colder. The breeze was bitter at six-thirty a.m. when Keith parked in the centre of Lulcombe and walked to the woods overlooking the clifftop meadow. He didn't want to go near the Beach Car Park in case it had filled with the film crew and early morning dog walkers.

As he took a folding chair from his rucksack, he could hear the waves as they crashed against the base of the cliffs. With his binoculars round his neck and the remote control for the detonators in his hand, he sat behind some trees where he could observe what was happening. He felt relaxed at that moment, but knew he'd be so excited when he eventually got the chance to press the detonator.

***

Jemma needed to be at the meeting point by nine so Ellie stayed over Sunday night. It was hard encouraging her to crawl out of bed on the Monday morning as she had a typical teenager's love for the duvet. Eventually, Jemma managed to shift her, and they dressed, ate a light breakfast, and then headed down into Lulcombe. The police surveillance was very hit and miss, so Jemma was not surprised there was no one outside the house.

When they arrived at the car park, there were already several vehicles present, including a catering van laid on by the TV company for the whole team. Ellie's eyes lit up when she saw what was on offer.

Jemma nudged her with an elbow. 'Thought you didn't want much breakfast.'

'That was before I knew they were doing bacon sarnies!'

'So you've not gone veggie again then?'

'Ha ha.' Ellie had flirted with vegetarianism when she first started college but only lasted three days until she walked past a catering van and couldn't resist the smell of the bacon butties.

As they donned their boots and coats, Jackson Carter from the Swanbourne University archaeology team came over.

He smiled at Jemma. 'Good morning.'

'Morning, Jackson. This is Ellie.'

He shook her hand. 'Hi, Ellie.'

'Hello, Jackson. Thanks for letting me come.'

'No problem. Firstly, we need to take some shots with me and your mum to introduce things. Once we start filming with the GPR unit, you're welcome to walk with us. Hope you've brought your spade!'

She tapped her rucksack. 'Yep, in here.'

'Sorted.' He turned to Jemma. 'All ready?'

She locked her car. 'Yes, let's go.' They walked up the steep path towards the cliff meadow and as they reached the top, Jemma glanced at the edge. Her mouth became dry and she shivered. 'One thing, Jackson, I don't want to go anywhere near the edge.'

'Oh, yes, I heard about your neighbour. So tragic, I'm sorry.'

'I'm not good with drops and cliffs.'

'No worries, we can film everything well back. I'm looking forward to trying this.' Jackson jerked his head towards a machine on a stand beside them. It was shaped like a large capital H with an electrical unit on the middle section and a neck strap to make it more comfortable to carry.

Jemma peered closely at the dials. 'How does it work?'

He lifted it off its stand. 'By shooting electromagnetic waves down into the ground and measuring what is reflected back.'

Jemma screwed up her face. 'I think I get it.'

Jackson put it back. 'Do you know if it's ever been used seriously as a way to look for fossils?'

Jemma thought for a moment. 'Don't think so, I can't remember reading about it being used for fossil hunting, but it could work. It all depends on the different densities of the fossil compared with the rocks around them. It also varies with the sensitivity of the machine.'

'We can try alternative settings during the day, depending on what shows up on the screen.'

Ellie left for the catering van, intent on trying out some of the free goodies on offer.

Jemma glanced over at the TV crew getting their cameras and sound booms ready.

'What do you want me to do?'

'First, I'll introduce you and then we can chat before we start surveying.'

Jemma fiddled with her hair. 'I haven't done any television presenting before so I don't know what to do.'

Jackson smiled. 'No worries. After the introduction, you'll walk up and down with me, and we can talk about fossil hunting. We don't see anything on the computers until we've covered a fair amount of ground and uploaded the data. We can then bring in Ellie and talk to her about her famous mum.'

Jemma ignored the last comment.

The recording team indicated they were ready.

Jackson pulled a face at Jemma. 'Now comes the worst bit. The makeup artist will be doing her rounds with sponges and face powders. Don't worry. They just don't want any shiny faces on screen.'

Jemma smiled. 'OK.'

After the makeup girl finished, Jackson made his introduction to the camera and explained what they'd be doing. Jemma found the details interesting and was engrossed until she suddenly realised he'd just introduced her.

'Our fossil hunting scientific advisor for today's show is Jemma Thorne. Jemma is the head of geology and palaeontology at Swanbourne University. She's also a renowned fossil hunter and recently discovered the largest plesiosaur ever found in the UK. A replica of Plessie's skeleton is going on display in Lulcombe Museum where Jemma is a trustee. Hello, Jemma!'

'Hi, Jackson, good to be here.'

'So, Jemma, what do you think we might find today?'

'You never know, that's the beauty of fossil hunting. One day you find nothing, the next day you could find something incredible.'

'What do you regard as incredible?'

'All fossils, big or small. They paint a picture of the past and teach us how species evolved or became extinct.'

'What was it like finding the fantastic plesiosaur fossil you discovered earlier this year?'

Jemma smiled at the memory. 'Absolutely brilliant. A lifetime best for me and in such perfect condition.'

Jackson looked serious. 'So sorry it was stolen.'

Jemma's smile disappeared. 'Yes. We still hope to get it back one day, but we're carrying on with a life-sized replica.'

'OK, thanks. Jemma's daughter, Ellie, will be joining us shortly as we walk along with the GPR unit, so let's get moving. The field has been marked out with ropes to form one hundred metre squares and that's where we'll be surveying.'

Jackson and Jemma started walking around the selected area.

***

Over in the woods, Keith swore when he spotted where they'd started. The first patch they searched was quite a way back from the edge. At this rate, it would be a long day. Cursing to himself, he set down the remote control and watched intently.

***

Jemma enjoyed walking up and down with Jackson. He was good company and she soon forgot the camera was rolling and just chatted about her fossil hunting career. Jackson added a few stories of his own and the time flew by. Partway through surveying the first square, Ellie joined them. She seemed very contented and was licking her lips after her visit to the catering unit.

As they walked and chatted, Jackson talked about the principles of Ground Penetrating Radar. The technique had been used extensively in archaeology, as on the TV programme *Time Team*, but was unusual in vertebrate palaeontology. He explained how it worked and, after the technical bit, he asked Jemma, 'Why did the university suggest this meadow as a trial patch for the GPR investigation?'

She gestured to the cliffs. 'Lots of fossil remains have been discovered here and in the cliffs. When I was younger, I found a perfectly preserved fish over there and Plessie came from the beach below us.'

Jackson nodded. 'Such an incredible find!'

He turned to the camera. 'Of course, any major digging near to the edge would be too dangerous so hopefully, with the results of the GPR survey, we can look at targeted digs with some small test pits.'

Ellie joined in. 'When will the first results be available?'

'When we have finished each square, we go over to the mobile unit and download the data. The computer takes a few minutes to process everything and give us a plan with any anomalies showing as darker patterns. If anything interesting appears, it's out with the shovels.'

Ellie grinned. 'Wow. Cool!'

'Cool indeed.' Jemma smiled.

They finished the first square, which didn't reveal anything, so Jackson headed to another, much nearer the cliffs. Jemma didn't want to go anywhere near the edge so he walked with Ellie and talked to her about having a fossil hunter as a mother.

Jemma couldn't be completely sure but it almost sounded like Ellie was proud of her mum's achievements. That would be a first and an improvement in their relationship.

Jemma had always thought that Ellie hated her mum's interest in fossils, or her obsession as she had once called it in an outburst of teenage angst. Instead, Ellie was contributing to the programme and sounded interesting and knowledgeable.

Jemma followed their progress from a distance as they collected the readings from the next section of the meadow. Once they'd finished surveying the area, she wandered over to the gazebo where the laptop processed the data. The new data was uploaded and one of the team pressed the key to display the plan.

Jackson pointed at the monitor. 'I can see some interesting shapes a few inches under the surface on the far side. He turned to Jemma. 'I know you don't like being near the cliffs but can you supervise the excavation of a small pit please, so we can check the larger shadow in that square?'

She hesitated. 'I suppose so, but we shouldn't go anywhere near the edge.'

They walked over to the square by the cliffs. Jackson added some markers based on the display on the computer screen. Jemma felt concerned as some of the markers were within two metres of the edge of the cliffs.

After marking the area out, he and Ellie started digging while Jemma stood further back, telling them how to dig. Gradually, they cleared a shallow pit without finding anything. Part way down the dig, Jackson stood.

'I'll go and get a printout to make sure we're digging in the right place.'

'OK,' Ellie said. 'I'll keep going, I'm enjoying this.'

As Jackson walked back across the field, the cameraman zoomed in on Ellie digging away. She looked up. 'Mum! I might have found something! Come over here please?'

Jemma came a few paces closer as the cameraman moved around the far side of the hole, nearer the cliff edge, to film what Ellie had found. Although the weather was cold, Jemma's palms were sweaty as Ellie worked near to the edge.

'Hang on a minute, Ellie, it could be a fossilised bone but wait 'til Jackson gets back so you can show him on camera.'

***

Over in the woods, Keith observed proceedings with interest, smiling every time the team wandered nearer to the cliffs. All Jemma had to do was stand a bit closer so that she would be between the two explosions. For some reason she was holding back and not going as near to the edge as the others. He held the remote detonator, ready to press the button.

***

Jemma edged closer to the pit but started to sweat and shake. 'That's close enough. I can follow from here.'

Jackson was on his way back, bringing with him a printout.

***

Keith watched through his binoculars and tried to stop his hands from trembling. Jemma wasn't quite as far over as he wanted but she was almost near enough for the explosion to blow her away.

***

While they waited for Jackson, Ellie stepped out of the hole and stood looking out to sea holding her shovel. The cameraman came back round to get some footage of her with the view behind. As Ellie wandered further along the meadow, Jemma's mouth parched when she saw how close her daughter was to the edge.

'Come back, Ellie, please.'

'I'm fine. I'm two metres back.'

'Don't go any closer.'

At that moment, Ellie spotted something odd and stepped over to a pile of grass near to the edge of the markers. 'Something strange here, Mum. Looks like an antenna'

***

Keith saw where Ellie was looking and, panicking, he was unable to stop himself from pressing the button.

The detonators went off and there was a small explosion close to where Ellie was standing, which threw some debris into the air. The canister Keith buried one hundred metres in the other direction worked perfectly and there was a massive explosion that knocked Jemma, Ellie and the cameraman off their feet.

Before any of them could react, the ground between the two explosions began to crumble, and the section beneath Ellie collapsed and sent her over the edge.

Chapter 36

From the woods Keith could see the effect of the larger explosion and he frowned as he saw Jemma sitting on the ground, gaping at the point where her daughter had disappeared over the cliff.

'Shit! Reggie'll kill me!'

He realised there was nothing else that he could do and panicked, grabbed his folding chair and ran off through the trees.

***

Jackson and the rest of the TV team raced across the field. The cameraman was writhing on the grass grasping his ankle.

With tearful eyes, Jemma peered over to the spot Ellie had disappeared. *Not you too, Ellie, not you too.* Her body shook as she moved closer to the edge on her hands and knees. At that moment a voice floated over the cliff.

'Mum... Help.'

'Ellie?'

'I'm here, Mum! Quick!'

Jemma's brain told her to stay away from the cliffs but

instead her mother's instincts took over, and she spread herself and crawled until she lay close to where Ellie had gone over.

'Where are you?'

'I'm down here, hanging on to something just below the top. Ouch! I can't hang on much longer.'

Jemma inched her way towards the cliff. 'I can't do it. I can't go near the edge.'

'Help me, Mum, please.'

She screwed up her eyes and crawled right up to the edge. Her whole body shook as she gazed down.

Ellie was hanging a few feet below her, holding on to a tree root sticking out from the cliff. Jemma tried not to look beyond Ellie to where an angry sea assaulted the bottom of the cliffs, each wave striking the base like a huge hammer. 'Hold on, I'll try to reach down.'

Jemma leant out over the cliff and when Jackson arrived, he dropped to the floor and held her legs.

'Got you, Jemma. Can you reach her?'

'Not yet, I'm so close though! Anybody got a rope?'

He turned his head. 'Any ropes back there?'

Jemma wiggled herself further forwards and looked down at Ellie who seemed so close, but still so far away. Beneath them, another piece of cliff tumbled down, striking the rocks below with a massive crash.

Ellie screamed and tried to lift herself up, and as she raised her arm, her fingers brushed cruelly against Jemma's.

'Just a touch more, Els. You're nearly there. Let go with one hand, and try to reach mine.'

'I can't, Mum, I'll fall.'

'Go on, I'll grab you.'

Jemma's heart beat faster as she watched her daughter

trying to reach her hand. Ellie made another attempt and swung her arm up. Jemma reached down further. This time their hands overlapped, and they each grabbed the other's wrist with a firm grip.

'Got you. Hold on tight,' said Jemma

'Pull, Mum! Quick!'

Jemma called to Jackson. 'Drag us up now. I've got her.'

She held on firmly and he pulled on her leg. Some of the other members of the filming team arrived, grabbed Jemma and heaved.

Pain shot through Jemma's shoulder. 'Let go totally and grab my other hand.'

Ellie took a deep breath and released the root she'd been grasping, reached up and grabbed her mum's wrist so she was fully supported by Jemma's arms, locked hand to wrist.

Jackson and the others pulled harder and slowly Jemma and Ellie inched back up and onto the grass of the meadow. Scrambling back to solid ground, Ellie collapsed to her knees, weeping, before throwing her arms around her mum.

Jemma cried as well, her shoulders shaking as she sobbed. 'Oh, Els! I thought you were dead!'

'Sorry, Mum! I should have stayed away from the edge.'

'Don't worry, you're safe now. Let's move away from the cliffs.'

They stumbled back across the field and the TV team helped their cameraman back to the safety of their main tent. Suddenly, a large rumble shook the ground and the section of the cliff where they'd just been standing disappeared in a cloud of dust and debris.

'Wow. That was close!' Ellie sobbed.

The crew brought over cups of tea and tried to settle the nerves of everyone involved in the ill-fated TV show while Jackson checked everyone for injuries. He brushed himself down. 'What happened?'

Jemma let go of Ellie and took some deep breaths to calm herself. 'We heard a dull thump and some soil flew up next to where Ellie was standing. A couple of seconds later there was a much louder bang, like an explosion, further along the meadow.'

Sobs continued to shake Ellie's entire body. 'What caused the explosions?'

Jackson shrugged. 'No idea, but they both happened at the same time. If I had to guess I'd say somebody used explosives.'

'Why would anyone plant explosives by an unstable cliff?' Jemma asked.

Ellie started crying. 'It's you, Mum! Someone's still trying to kill you!'

Jemma gasped. 'But why? Why me?'

Just then they heard sirens in the Beach Car Park and, several minutes later, two paramedics and a policeman came jogging across the meadow. 'Everyone OK?' the first paramedic panted while attempting to get his breath back.

Jackson took charge. 'I think so.' He pointed at Ellie. 'This young lady has a few bruises and scratches, but she's a lucky girl.'

'Yes, I'm glad I grabbed that root or I'd have fallen,' Ellie said.

The policeman poised with his radio. 'What caused the collapse?'

Jackson pointed at the edge. 'We think somebody set off some explosives over there.'

'Explosives?' The policeman repeated. 'As in a bomb?'

'No idea,' Jemma explained. 'I heard a thud and then

a loud bang. Next thing we knew, the ground collapsed, taking Ellie with it, but I managed to grab her and hold on until the others came to help.'

Ellie glanced up. 'You're so brave, Mum. That must have been a real ordeal leaning out over the edge to reach me.'

'Doesn't matter.' Jemma put her arm around Ellie's shoulders and fought back the tears. 'You're OK now. That's all that matters.' Her brain raced as she tried to think again why anybody would want to kill her.

The policeman inched closer to the newly created edge, craning his neck to peer over. 'Whereabouts were the explosions?'

Jackson gestured to a spot further away. 'A few feet out but that bit crashed into the sea when the cliff disappeared.'

The policeman drew a quick sketch of the meadow by the site of the explosion. 'So I bet we've lost any evidence of what caused the collapse.'

'Fraid so,' Jemma said. 'The tide's high as well, so everything that fell down will have been washed away by the waves.'

The policeman turned back to Jemma. 'Why would anybody set off explosives near to where people were standing?'

Jemma swallowed. 'They're trying to kill me.'

The policeman's head jerked up. 'Who's trying to kill you?'

Jemma stared out to sea. 'I've no idea, but it's frightening.'

***

Keith Fletcher returned to the office he shared with his brother without attracting any attention to himself. The office was in a bland building on a quiet industrial estate. It contained two desks and several filing cabinets. Keith's brother, Reggie, was sitting at his desk with a police scanner.

Keith took a deep breath. 'I'm...'

'Shut up!' Reggie snapped. 'I'm listening!' He listened for a few minutes and then turned to his brother and ranted. 'The report said no serious injuries! What happened?'

Keith gulped. 'Everything went well until I pressed the firing button. Both detonators exploded but only one lot of explosives blew. The daughter went over the edge though, so she must be dead.'

Reggie spoke in a quiet voice. 'No. Serious. Injuries. That's what was on the police radio. They said a girl went over the cliff but was rescued by her mother. I'm beginning to think I need to sort Jemma out myself.'

'Give me another chance, please! I'll kill her next time!'

Reggie jumped up. 'Next time? There won't be a next time for you! It's like having a bloody dog and barking yourself!'

Keith shivered in his seat. Although he stood a good foot taller, his brother had always been the boss.

Reggie sat down and exhaled. 'OK, two things we're going to do. Firstly, we need to shift the fossil. Cash flow is a bit tight with what we've already spent on the hotel project and the bank's getting jittery.'

'How are we going to sell it?'

'I spoke to a bloke in London who deals in dodgy gear. He thought the best way would be to make contact with some collectors, ones who occasionally buy stolen items.'

'What will we get?'

'Well, he thought it might be worth about a hundred thousand, but, with the link to a murder, we might have to settle for fifty. With your success rate, I'm tempted to shift it and hire a professional hitman to get rid of Jemma.'

'I can do it.'

'We'll see about that.'

'What's the second thing?'

'Well, I've had an idea to grab Jemma's daughter and use her as bait to entice her mother into our trap.'

Keith smiled. 'When are we getting her?'

'We'll leave it for a few weeks until the heat dies down and then, once the students are back at college in the New Year, we'll make our move.'

'Sounds good, bro.'

***

While Jemma, Ellie and Jackson drank tea, the policeman and one of the film crew came walking across the field with a laptop.

'We were pointing the camera at Ellie, and you can see some grass and soil come shooting up vertically and then a much bigger explosion further along.'

The policeman studied the recording and called in on his radio. 'Sarge, yes, I've taken a lot of notes, but there's also some film of the two explosions that blew the cliff down. A small one and then a much larger one. We were lucky Ellie was standing near the smaller one.'

Ellie gasped and hugged her mum again.

The police officer continued. 'No, sarge, the actual sites of the explosions disappeared over the edge, so there's nothing left to see. Yes. OK.' He turned to the group. 'The station's organising a sniffer dog that's used to track explosives to check whether they can find any remnants.

We've called in The Bomb Disposal Squad from Aldershot in case there are any other devices. In the meantime, I suggest you all go home. If you could let me have your details please, before you go, that would be great, as we'll need to gather formal statements. If you could come to Swanbourne Police HQ sometime, that would be helpful.'

Jemma blinked her tears away. 'The rate I'm going I'll have a chair there with my name on the back.'

Ellie put her arm around her mum's sagging shoulders. 'Come on, Mum, let's go.'

They said their goodbyes to the filming team, and walked back down the path, before driving home in a state of shock.

After arriving back, Jemma made some tea and they sat at the kitchen table holding their mugs, gradually warming back up.

Jemma fetched the bottle of whisky and poured some into her mug. 'I need a hot toddy after all that. Want one?'

'Oh God no. I hate the stuff.' Ellie tried to fight her tears. 'That was so brave of you today; leaning out to rescue me.'

'I didn't think. Your voice came from over the edge and I had to focus on you and look over. It forced me to get on with it and grab your arm. I just kept thinking I never got the chance with Alice.'

'Thanks anyway. Mum, if you ever want to talk about what happened to her, I'm here.'

Jemma reached over, held Ellie and burst into tears. 'I was so close to her and I let her fall.' She sniffed. 'I could have saved her if I hadn't been so busy with a fossil.'

'What happened that day? You've never told me.'

Between sobs, Jemma continued. 'We were on the

clifftop meadow. I was digging out a fossilised fish while Alice picked some flowers. She shouted for help but I thought she was messing about. She messed about a lot, always after attention, so I ignored her.'

'So, you couldn't have been responsible.'

Jemma wiped her eyes. 'I was. If I'd run over straight away, I could've helped.'

'But if she was messing about it can't have been your fault.'

'I tried telling myself that for years Els, but I've always felt so guilty about what I didn't do. It was awful that Phil had been there. He kept threatening to tell everybody that I didn't help her before she fell.'

'Well, you don't need to worry about him anymore,' said Ellie.

Jemma fell silent for a moment. 'But I lied to so many people about what happened.'

'What about?'

'I never told anyone that she shouted for me to help her and I ignored her.'

Ellie squeezed her hand. 'You couldn't have done anything.'

'I know, but I ignored her!'

Ellie hugged her mum until the sobs eased off. 'I think you were brilliant today. You saved my life. You can't do anything about Alice after all these years.'

'I know.' She cried until Ellie's shoulder was damp from her tears.

'I learnt one thing today, Mum.'

'What was that?'

'I do sometimes come first.'

Jemma frowned. 'Of course you do. Why did you only learn that today?'

'Because you rescued me and forgot all about the fossil we'd found.'

'That's true.' Jemma paused. 'I wonder if any of it is still on the beach.'

'Oh, Mum.'

***

Later that afternoon the team of detectives at Swanbourne Police HQ checked over the evidence from the clifftop meadow. Laura Day studied the short piece of footage with the two explosions passed over to them by the TV crew and then surveyed the room.

'Any thoughts?'

Amrik chewed his pen. 'It appears to be a deliberate attempt to blow up the cliff and take Jemma as well. Somebody must really hate her.'

Laura turned to Dave. 'Did you ask Jemma if she has any idea who might be trying to kill her?'

He sipped his coffee. 'We've talked about it a lot but she can't think of anybody she's fallen out with or upset in any way. Can we organise some full-time protection for her because this is getting silly?'

Laura picked up her clipboard. 'Yes, the boss has approved a team of three for twenty-four-hour surveillance. We're not sure which budget the funds will come from yet but fingers crossed it won't be ours.'

Dave nodded. 'That's good, ma'am, hopefully, it won't be for long and we'll catch whoever it is pretty soon.'

'OK. Can you tell Jemma?'

'Will do. I bet she won't be happy. She's so independent.'

'I'm sure it will only be temporary.' Laura looked over

at Amrik. 'Any joy with the forensic team on the beach?'

'Some, ma'am. The tide was high when the cliff collapsed so some debris has been washed away, but at least it meant there was nobody on the sand when it came down. They've been digging around at the base and found a canister of Ammonium Nitrate Fuel Oil.'

Laura made some notes. 'Is that an explosive?'

'Yes, ma'am, commonly used in mines and quarries. It hadn't fully exploded so they retreated and brought the bomb disposal people in to make the remnants safe.'

'Are they still down on the beach?'

'Yes, the army stayed on to help, in case any more explosives were found.'

'What do they say about the ANFO?'

'It appears to be quite an old canister so the serial number is from before any that are on the records. Must be over fifteen years old.'

'Is that why it didn't explode?'

'Yes, ma'am. The bomb disposal officer said that if both lots had exploded at the same time, a much bigger section of the cliff would've collapsed and taken Ellie, Jemma and the cameraman.'

Dave gasped. 'Bloody hell... Sorry, ma'am.'

Laura smiled. 'Yes, they were rather lucky.' She checked around the team. 'Any other questions or comments?'

Amrik held up his hand.

'Yes?'

'How did they find out Jemma would be doing the survey in that particular spot?'

'I wondered that as well.' Laura went back to her notes. 'The details appeared in a Sunday magazine article about Jemma. It's a narrow field so there was a fair chance that they might go near the cliffs at some point during the survey. Also, Jemma received a phone call purporting to be from a newspaper, which we now think may have been the culprits. She gave them the exact times. They said they wanted to publicise the temporary closure of the public footpath across the clifftop meadow while surveying was going on.'

'Any joy with the phone number, ma'am.'

'No, Dave, they used a pay-as-you-go mobile with no records. A burner. Anybody got anything else?' She waited. Nobody spoke and she banged her hand on the table. 'Come on team, we need some results. We're no nearer to finding who's behind this than when we started. I'm going to be getting flak from above about our lack of progress and if I get flak then you get flak. Go and catch the bloody culprits!'

Chapter 37

As it was the last day of term before the Christmas break, Jemma had a busy day lined up at the university. The drive to work felt strange with a police car following and parking near her in the campus car park. She sat in her car for a few minutes to compose herself, not wanting to burst into tears in front of her class.

During her lectures, she fended off questions from her students about how she was and what was going on. After she finished her morning lecture, she headed to the staff room for a cup of tea. On the way, she bumped into Olivia Davis, the Vice-Chancellor.

'Oh hello, Jemma, I wanted to see you.'

'Hi, Olivia. You alright?'

'Yes, I'm fine, thanks. Could you spare me a few minutes, please? In my office.'

'OK. I'm about to grab a cuppa.'

'Don't worry. I'll organise some tea and coffee to be brought in. Any more lectures today?'

'No, I'm reading dissertations this morning and I have some student meetings this afternoon.'

'Perfect. Come on then.'

They walked along the corridor to Olivia's rather

sumptuous office and Jemma sat in one of the comfy armchairs by a low table. The office assaulted her senses with colours. Psychedelic artwork hung on the walls along with brightly coloured hand paintings, which must have been created by Olivia's children in messy play at school. Jemma leant back against the cushions, wondering what she'd done wrong.

Olivia was middle-aged with greying hair in a ponytail. She thought she was trendy and wore bright clothes to the point of being gaudy. They had always got on well and she'd been on the panel that originally appointed Jemma to her current role.

'How can I help?'

Olivia sat next to her and leant closer. 'How are you getting on?'

'Fine, thanks.'

'It's just, with everything going on, we're a bit worried about you.'

Jemma bristled with annoyance. 'I'm OK, and I'm still able to do my job properly. And who is the "we"?'

'Oh, the management team. There's been a suggestion that you take a couple of months off, unpaid, of course, to sort yourself out.'

'I don't need to do that. I can't leave my students in the lurch midway through term.'

'Don't worry. We have the perfect solution. Sally O'Keefe has volunteered to step in if we need any more lecturing or student mentoring input.'

Jemma seethed. 'Sally! Why is she sticking her nose in?'

Olivia smiled condescendingly. 'I'm sure she was just concerned for your students.'

'So, you've been discussing me? Isn't that against privacy

rules?'

'No, not talking about you. She happened to come and see me and offered to go full time temporarily, if required.'

Jemma's face darkened. 'No, I don't want any time off, thank you. With the deaths of Anna and Chrissie, I'm much happier working and keeping busy. It wouldn't help me to be moping around not working.'

'Well, that's your decision, but I must also point out that yesterday we received a formal complaint involving yourself and a minor. The letter alleges you did not carry out a thorough risk assessment on a fossil discovery when there was a cliff collapse.'

Jemma clenched her fists. 'We were on a private hunt, nothing to do with the university.'

'That may be so, but one of our other lecturers took part.'

'So, Sally's the whistle-blower? I should have known.'

'I can't reveal the identity of the complainant.'

'You don't need to. If you wish, I can submit a written reasoning for my decisions about the day's digging. Don't forget the dig led to the discovery of the most significant local fossil for one hundred and fifty years. And with no injuries.'

'Luckily!'

'With no injuries.' Jemma let out a deep breath. 'And I'm not taking any leave, paid or unpaid.'

'If that's the way you feel.'

'I'm afraid so.'

'In that case, I must give you the decision of the management team.'

Jemma sighed. 'What decision?'

Olivia paused. 'We feel we need to slightly reign in your activities.'

'Please tell me you're kidding?'

'Oh, no, Jemma, I'm deadly serious. There is an immediate ban on you leading any off-campus university trips involving students or other staff until further notice.'

'That's unfair! Fieldwork is an important part of their degrees.'

'I agree, which is why any necessary external work will be overseen by Miss O'Keefe.'

'Can I appeal this decision?'

'You can, but it must be in writing, and we'll consider your representations and reply within twenty-eight days.'

'This is bullshit.'

'Please don't use foul language, Jemma. Look, two of your close associates died in suspicious circumstances, with another badly injured in a hit-and-run.'

'But none were my fault.'

'I'm not disputing the facts but we have a police vehicle in our car park for your protection. I have to think about our students and staff. Once the culprits are caught, we can reconsider. Thanks, Jemma.'

Jemma shook with rage. If she said what she thought, she'd be sacked and Sally would've won.

She stood and left the room. 'Good day, Olivia!'

***

The meeting with Olivia left Jemma in a foul mood. She headed home and was just about to take it out on her poor van when she remembered her police escort and slowed down to the speed limit.

When she parked and opened the back door, Dino rushed out and jumped up at her. 'At least you still like me,' she said as she ruffled his back before walking into the kitchen to make a cup of tea and try to calm down.

The back door opened and Ellie walked in. 'Hi, Mum, when are we putting the tree up?'

'We're not.'

'What? We always have a tree.'

'Not this year.'

'I know you've had a bad few months but we've got to celebrate Christmas.'

'You can if you want. I'm not celebrating anything with Anna and Chrissie dead, not to mention a police guard parked outside.'

'I'll decorate it. You don't need to do anything.'

'Look! I don't want a bloody tree,' Jemma snapped and got up to leave.

Ellie stood facing her. 'Is that what you're going to be like all Christmas?'

Jemma turned round. 'Sod bloody Christmas, it's cancelled.'

Ellie had tears in her eyes. 'I know you've been under pressure Mum, but we're all here for you.'

Jemma headed upstairs. 'Just leave me alone.'

Ellie shouted up after her. 'Merry Christmas to you too. I'm off back to Dad's for a few days. It might be more cheerful there.'

***

Dave walked into the kitchen and found Ellie sitting alone. 'Is everything OK? I heard raised voices.'

'It's just Mum being miserable. I know she's really upset but she doesn't want a tree. I think she just wants to cancel Christmas so I'm going to stay at Dad's for a while.'

'Take it easy on her, please, Ellie.'

'I'm trying but she needs to snap out of the gloom.'

'It's not that easy. She probably needs some time on her own.'

'I know. I'll disappear for a bit 'til she wants me around again.'

Dave nodded. 'I might end up having to work some extra shifts myself with everything that's been happening.'

'You might be better off at work,' she said.

'I know but I'm torn between giving Jemma some space and time on her own and being here for her when she needs to talk. At least I'll be popular with some of my colleagues with young families and I'll earn an extra few quid. That's probably better than hanging around here if Jemma doesn't want any company.' He grabbed his lunch and coat. 'When you off?'

'There's a bus at two.'

He hugged her. 'I'll see you sometime over Christmas. Don't worry. She'll come out the other side soon. Happy Christmas.'

'Happy Christmas, Dave. I hope next year is a bit less eventful.'

As he drove to work, he worried about Jemma. Although he'd had a few girlfriends in Dorset before he met her, none of them had lasted. It was good to be with someone he really cared about, even if she was stubborn at times.

***

Jemma spent most of Christmas on her own sleeping, eating and watching television. She managed to catch up on some of her work but felt torn about not spending enough time with Dave and Ellie. Being alone was helping her to refocus but she felt guilty about pushing away the most important people in her life. However, as the days went by, she started to feel a bit more human and ready to face the world.

On Christmas Eve, she sat alone with a large glass of whisky and Dino by her feet.

'Cheers, Dino, I just want this year to end. Surely things can only get better next year.'

Chapter 38

January appeared with some early snowdrops, which were soon covered in a white blanket that followed their arrival. Jemma sat with a cup of whisky-laced tea going through some student dissertations. She still seethed about the ban on field trips, it was so unfair. Outside the snow had fallen for several hours and was settling well.

Ellie sprawled on the sofa wearing her pyjama top and shorts with her long legs hanging over the edge. Jemma looked on enviously, *Oh for the toned skin of the young.*

'You OK, Mum? You're staring.'

'Yes, I'm fine. Any plans to go out?'

'No, I've seen the weather, so I fancy grabbing some food and having a duvet day.'

'Sounds nice.' There was a ping as a text came in on her mobile. *I bet that's from Dave, he's probably stressed out with his inspector's exams.* She picked up the phone and her heart raced when she saw a message from Brad.

'I'm bored on my own if you fancy a coffee. Or a tea.'

'Who's it from?' Ellie asked.

'Brad. He fancies a cuppa and some company'

She smirked. 'Wow. Dave goes on a week-long training course and you're planning afternoon drinks with your ex.'

'He's not my ex. Well, he is but he isn't. He's a colleague now. I'll pop round for a bit because I bet he wants to talk about Chrissie or something.'

'Are you driving?'

'No, my van won't make it back up the hill in this snow. I'll walk.'

'You better tell your bodyguard outside.'

'Oh, it's not fair to drag him out in the snow. I'll go out the back door and across the fields. I'll be back in a couple of hours.'

'Well, well. Sneaking out and trying to lose the nice policeman. He's watching for your benefit, you know.'

'I know but I hate being followed everywhere.' Jemma picked up her phone and sent a text to Brad. '*I'll be round in fifteen and I'll come bearing chocolate.*'

A reply came straight back. '*Perfect, see you soon.*'

Jemma slipped on her boots, hat and coat and set out. The fields were deserted and silent under their blanket of snow, which deadened any sounds. She reached Brad's cottage twenty minutes later, knocked and waited. The door opened revealing a grinning Brad and she immediately wished she wasn't still attracted to him.

'Feeling better?'

'Yep, healing up slowly,' he said.

'Great!'

'Come in, it's cold outside.' They hugged awkwardly and Jemma followed him into his lounge. The cottage looked small from the outside but the inside was surprisingly spacious. With the small windows and oak beams it was quite dark even with the light on.

Jemma raised an eyebrow towards a large dining table

covered with towels. 'Am I disturbing something?'

'No, I've got a massage booked after lunch.' He smiled. 'Helps with the muscles.'

'Sounds heaven.'

He limped through to the kitchen. 'Coffee?'

'Tea, please? I could do with a shot of whisky to warm my bones as well,' she replied.

'Yep, I can manage that. A bit too early for me though. Jack Daniels OK?'

'Yes, lovely.' Jemma sat on the sofa while Brad made the drinks, adding a generous glass of JD to the tray. She called through to him. 'Can you carry everything?'

'Yes, I'm good, thanks.' He brought the drinks through and sat next to her. Their knees touched and Jemma jumped and pulled her leg back.

She brought a bar of chocolate from her pocket. 'Here you are, help yourself.'

Brad's phone rang. 'My masseuse. Excuse me one second.' He walked through to the kitchen and took the call.

While he was out of the room, Jemma drained the glass and picked up her tea, gradually relaxing as the alcohol kicked in.

After a few minutes, he returned and sat down. 'Cancelled. She doesn't want to drive in the snow. Dammit. Setting up the table was a pain in the ass and I really need a massage. Starting to feel desperate.'

Jemma looked at him. 'I can do one.' *Why the hell did I say that? Can't be the whisky talking yet.*

'What?' he said.

'I said I can do it. Give you one.' *Oh my God. What am I suggesting? I haven't given a massage in fifteen years. What will Brad think?*

He frowned. 'I never knew you could do massages.'

'I know the basics.' She tried to look confident.

'You sure?'

'Yeah, I'll try.'

'What? Now?' he said.

She shrugged. 'Why not?'

He paused, waiting to see if she'd take back her offer. 'OK, I'll go and get ready.' He disappeared upstairs.

What am I doing? I can't trust myself!

Brad came back down in a dressing gown holding a bottle of baby oil, which he handed over. 'Here you are.'

'Thanks. Now get your kit off and lie down.'

He removed the gown and stood next to her with a towel around his waist. 'This is weird,' he said.

Jemma grinned. 'Nothing I haven't seen before. We can stop if you want?'

He laughed. 'No. It's been a long time and I've got some new scars.'

'Just lie down on your front.'

As he lay on the table with the towel covering his modesty, Jemma poured some oil on his back.

He jumped. 'Shit. That's cold.'

'Don't be a wimp,' she giggled. She rubbed his shoulders and, as he closed his eyes, worked on the knots she found.

'That feels so good. Where did you learn this?'

'Oh, I did a course years ago when I was married to Liam.'

'Lucky guy.'

'He did like it, although he used to complain my hands were too rough.'

Brad grinned. 'Rougher the better.'

Jemma finished his back and moved on to his legs. She deliberately avoided going anywhere near his towel as she was starting to enjoy the experience way too much. 'OK then, roll over. And keep the towel over your bits!'

'You're no fun,' he laughed.

Jemma bit her tongue as she worked on his legs. She moved her way up his thighs and had to stop herself from going too far up his legs. Her heart beat faster and, as her excitement level rose, so did her temperature. She hoped she wasn't blushing too obviously. *Phew, lucky with all the baby oil he can't tell my palms are really sweaty. Even with all his scars, he's still a bloody attractive man. Maybe it's the scars that do it for me.*

'Getting hot in here,' Brad said, his voice huskier than before.

'Is it?' Jemma asked. She finished his legs and started on his chest, and as she stood behind his head and reached down towards his stomach, she realised her breasts were pressing against his face. 'Excuse me!' she croaked, quickly standing up.

He grinned. 'I'm not complaining.'

She tried to distract herself. 'How are all the injuries coming along?'

'They've healed well but I need to keep strengthening the muscles. Lots of PT and massages.'

'Hope this helps!'

He swallowed. 'You're certainly reaching the spot.' There was a moment's silence as she worked on his chest. He moaned under his breath. 'My usual masseuse doesn't touch my chest or stomach. She said she can't as they're considered erogenous zones.'

Jemma stopped and lifted her hands off his chest.

He grabbed her hands and put them back where they'd been. 'Don't stop,' he whispered.

Her mind wrestled with the turmoil of what was

happening. She tried to think of Dave but instead could only see the oiled body before her on the table. *I've got to stop before something happens that I'll regret.* She continued and worked down towards his abdomen, trying to ignore the twitching movements under the towel. She paused. 'Do you want me to stop?'

Brad closed his eyes. 'You're kidding. This is awesome.'

Jemma was getting carried away and felt beads of sweat form on her forehead. *I must stop. I can't stop. I must stop. I can't stop.* Next thing she knew her hands were moving under the towel, onto Brad's abdomen, and then lower.

Brad's entire body jumped. 'Jemma, are you sure?'

'Shut up and kiss me.'

They kissed and Jemma pulled the towel away before slowly taking off her own clothes. She climbed upon the table and knelt over him.

'Are you up to this?'

'Depends what this is, but yeah, I'll give it a go.'

Jemma woke up naked on Brad's sofa, snuggled against his chest. *Oh, my God. What have I done? I should have had more self-control. What's wrong with me?*

Brad stroked her hair. 'Well, that was a surprise.'

'I'm so sorry, Brad, I don't know what came over me.' She jumped up and snatched her clothes from the floor.

'It was me the second time.'

Jemma let out a sigh as she dressed as quickly as she could. 'This was a massive mistake. It should never have happened. Can we forget everything?'

'Forget it?' he said. 'How can I forget that?'

'You must. That was never meant to happen.'

'But it did.'

'No. It didn't.' Jemma said. 'I must go.'

'OK. But come back soon, Jemma, won't you? I always hoped our relationship would have a happy ending.'

'Shut up, Brad. I have to go. See you around.' Jemma put on her boots and her coat before fleeing from the cottage.

Walking back across the field the snow was now deeper and had covered her earlier tracks. Her head was spinning in a turmoil of doubt, uncertainty and guilt. She couldn't believe what she'd done and was torn between thinking "wow!" and "bloody hell, I'm so stupid!" *This is another complication I don't need right now.* She arrived back home and noticed the police car still parked outside. *Never spotted me at all.*

She opened the back door and walked in. The warmth of the kitchen hit her after the cold of the snowy fields. 'I'm home.'

Ellie came wandering downstairs. 'Well, how's the invalid?'

Jemma paused. 'He's alright. Getting much fitter. So he says,' she blushed.

Ellie frowned. 'What's up, Mum? Why are you going red?'

Jemma stammered and imagined the word "GUILTY" tattooed on her forehead. 'Um, erm. Nothing. I'm a bit warm after the walk back.'

Ellie's mouth dropped open. 'Mum! You haven't!'

'Haven't what?'

'You've shagged Brad! I can tell!'

'Don't be silly,' she said. 'Of course, I haven't!'

'Don't lie to me, I'm not stupid. The guilt's written all over your face.'

Jemma started crying. Ellie reached over and hugged her.

'What's going on? You complained about Dad when he had an affair.'

'This isn't an affair.'

'What is it then?'

'I don't know, Els. A fling? A moment of weakness? Don't worry, it won't happen again.'

'I can't believe you've done this to Dave after all he's done for you. It's lucky he's away for the week or you'd have some explaining to do.'

'I know.'

'What's wrong with you and Dave?'

'Nothing, Els. We're really happy. That's what's so weird.'

'But why do the dirty with Brad?'

'I don't know. It just happened.'

'What are you going to do?' Ellie said.

'Just forget about it.' Jemma walked over and poured herself a whisky.

Ellie watched her. 'Booze isn't the answer, Mum.'

'I don't care anymore.'

'I'm worried about you. Have you talked to Dave?'

'Yes, we talk a lot.'

'Don't bottle things up, will you?'

'No, Els. I won't.'

'Something's wrong, Mum. I'm sure you've lost weight. Aren't you eating?'

'Don't be daft, you know I love my food.'

Ellie tugged at her hair before heading back upstairs.

Jemma watched her go and returned to her whisky. She swirled it around in the glass before draining it. As the burn hit her throat, she put her head in her hands and shut out the world.

Chapter 39

Keith Fletcher walked into the office with its dirty walls, dusty shelves and grubby neon lights. He looked around. 'We should have a better office than this, you know, we're property dealers.'

Reggie didn't even bother looking up from his phone. 'It's good enough for what we need. Decent offices cost money and we haven't got much spare at the moment. Did you swap the plates on the van?'

Keith held out a piece of paper with the registration. 'Yes. This is the false number.'

Reggie snatched the note from him.

Keith sniffed. 'Can't we leave Dorset and go back to London? Much nicer than Lulcombe.'

'No, we can't! We've invested a lot of the money we made in London and from the Hillside housing estate into buying the site for the casino project.'

Keith stared at the poster for the hotel project on the wall. 'There must be some left.'

Reggie rolled his eyes. 'There's enough left to buy the other properties and start the building. After that, we'll need the bank loan. All we need to get started is the museum and the first two houses on Seaton Road. If we don't obtain them, we might struggle to sell the other land and then we're in a big mess. If Jemma's gone, we can buy the museum and her house, and we're ready to rumble.'

Keith pulled up his chair. 'OK. What do you want me to do?'

There was a note of excitement in Reggie's voice. 'Right. First I'm going to send her daughter a message from her old phone. We can then meet her in the car park round the back of the Red Lion behind the college. I'll text her the details of the van and the false plates. All we've got to do is wait. When she gets near us, you grab her. Then you can pull her into the back, tie her arms and legs, and we'll be off.'

Keith grinned. 'Sounds good. When are we going?'

'This afternoon, hopefully. The college has a lunch break at one o'clock so I'll try to arrange a fake meeting for her with her mother. Once we grab her, we can use her to get hold of Jemma. Go fetch the cable ties and some cloths to make a gag.'

'Will do.'

Keith left the office and Reggie took out Jemma's mobile from the desk drawer and typed out a message.

***

Ellie sat daydreaming in her lecture when a text came through from Mum.

'Fancy lunch today? I can pick you up in Swanbourne. Love Mum X.'

She replied, *'Great, I finish at 1. Where do u want to meet? X.'*

A reply pinged straight back. *'Meet you in the car park round the back of the Red Lion, behind the college. I'm in a white van reg XPR65PZ as mine's in the garage. See you later.'*

Ellie replied, 'OK', and grinned. *A bit newer than Mum's usual piece of junk. I wonder where she's taking me.* She put away her mobile and tried to regain some sort of interest in the lecture. Most of her lecturers were great but this morning's was boring with a monotonous voice that droned on and on like Uncle Colm from the TV show *Derry Girls*.

She had been really worried about her mum recently. Jemma had been struggling with everything that had happened and Ellie had noticed that the whisky bottle seemed to be in a different place every time she walked through the kitchen. Her mum had never been one to show her emotions but Ellie got the feeling that all was not well.

Her last session before lunch was to go through some earlier exam questions. However, when she arrived at the room, she found a note on the door saying the tutor had gone home ill so all students should use the time for private study.

Ellie reached for her phone. *Sod that, I can meet Mum early.* She selected the number and rang it. The call rang out with no answer so she rang off and checked the number. Her list of contacts contained a 'Mum' and a 'Mum 1', which she couldn't understand. She tried the second listing and, this time, Jemma answered.

'Hello, Els, you OK?'

'I'm alright, Mum. How are you?'

'Fine. I'm doing some marking in my office at uni. How's your day?'

'Bit boring so far but I'm looking forward to lunch.'

'Why, what are you doing?'

'You muppet, I'm seeing you.'

'What?'

'We're meeting today!'

Jemma sounded confused. 'Are we?'

'What d'you mean? You texted me earlier about getting together for lunch and I told you I finish at one. I'm ringing to say we could meet before then if you wanted.'

'Ellie, I didn't send that text!'

Chapter 40

Jemma turned pale as she tried to process what Ellie had told her.

'Are you sure you didn't send it, Mum? It came from your phone?'

Jemma whispered 'What number was it from?'

'Let me check,' Ellie said and there was a pause. 'The message came from this number.' Ellie read out the digits.

Jemma thought for a moment. 'Els, that can't have been me. That's my old phone that somebody stole.'

Ellie didn't respond straight away. 'Oh, Mum.'

'Don't worry, where were you due to meet?' Jemma said.

'In the car park of the Red Lion, round the back of the college, at one o'clock.' Ellie gave her the details of the van, which Jemma wrote on a pad.

'Stay where you are. Don't leave until I call you again. I'll ring Dave and tell him.'

'OK, Mum. Don't do anything silly.'

'Speak soon, bye, Els.'

Jemma rang off and called Dave. He answered on the first ring.

'D.S. Gill.'

'Hi, Dave.'

'Hello. You alright?'

'I'm fine but they've tried to snatch Ellie.'

Dave's voice raised. 'What? Who?'

Jemma started talking quickly. 'Whoever stole my phone sent her a text, offering to pick her up for lunch at one in the car park behind the college.'

Dave interrupted. 'Slow down, you're gabbling.'

Jemma attempted to calm down. 'Someone in a white van is planning to grab Ellie in the car park behind college at one.' She gave him the registration number.

Dave paused. 'OK. It's ten to one. I'll send a car up there straight away and put out an alert for a vehicle with those plates. You stay where you are. I'll call you in a bit.'

***

Reggie parked at the end of the large car park by the back entrance with an easy escape route if Ellie didn't turn up within a few minutes. There were numerous other vehicles around so he wasn't in full view of the entrance. He had his police scanner on and heard a message alerting a car to go to the Red Lion car park. He shouted at Keith to hold tight and drove out just before a police car with its blue lights flashing pulled into the other entrance.

After rushing down through Swanbourne, he drove into an estate to swap the plates back to the old ones and they were soon driving to Lulcombe with Keith back in the front. Reggie stuck rigidly to the speed limits and drove to the industrial unit beneath the office. Breathing calmly again, he locked the van, closed the shutter and together they walked up to the building.

***

There were only a few cars about as Dave drove in and parked next to the police car, which still had its lights flashing. He approached his colleague. The driver saw him and got out.

'No joy, sir. No white van with those plates anywhere to be seen.'

'I was sure they'd be here. I'm not sure why they didn't show.'

'I got here at twelve fifty-nine, sir.'

'Bloody hell.' Dave slammed his hand on the roof of his car.

The policeman turned off his emergency lights and drove off.

Dave took out his phone and rang Jemma.

She answered on the first ring. 'What's going on?'

'Nothing. A patrol car got there before one, but nobody showed up. Can you tell Ellie I'll pick her up outside the main entrance to the college? I'm in my car, which she knows.'

'Will do.'

***

Jemma felt sick as she called Ellie. 'Hi, Els, the police got to the car park but nobody showed up.'

'Oh.'

'Can you meet Dave? He'll wait at the front of the college in his silver Mondeo. You know his car, don't you?'

'Yes. Is he waiting now?'

'If you go down, he should be outside. He'll bring you home and we can decide what to do next.'

316

'OK, Mum. Thanks.'

Jemma breathed out. 'I'm so glad you rang.'

'Me too. I can see Dave's car now. Love you, bye.'

'Love you, Els.'

***

Keith followed Reggie into the office. His lips parted but his brother raised a hand to cut him off.

'Don't say a word.'

'But....'

'Be quiet. The brat tried to ring on this phone but I didn't want to answer. She must have realised something was wrong.'

'Can they trace the call?'

Reggie jumped up. 'Bloody hell, I never thought of that!' He threw the mobile on the floor and stamped on it until all that remained was a heap of broken plastic. He tore out the battery and chucked the lot in the bowl of water sitting in the sink. 'That woman's living a charmed life! I've got to have a rethink and try to sell the pile of old bones instead.'

'Who's gonna buy them?'

'My contact is putting some feelers out to see if anybody wants them.'

'Good, let's hope somebody does.'

***

Dave dropped Ellie off at her mum's and told them to stay inside with the door locked until he got back around six. Before he left, he spoke to the policeman sitting in the car outside Jemma's front door. After he explained what happened earlier, he drove back to Swanbourne Police

HQ. He'd always thought Dorset was a quiet place with low crime levels, but the events of the last few months had made him think differently.

***

Jemma buried her head on her daughter's shoulder.

'I'm getting scared by all this, Mum. What's going on?'

'I don't know, Els. I haven't got a clue.'

Jemma put the kettle on and opened the pack of chocolate digestives she kept in the cupboard, in case of a stressful day, and together they sat with the tea and biscuits. The atmosphere in the kitchen was not a happy one as they both wrestled with the implications of what had happened.

'What are we going to do?' Ellie asked.

Jemma sipped her tea. 'I'm still trying to think of a way to find out who's behind this.'

'All of this started when you found Plessie. Could someone be jealous?'

'I've been racking my brain thinking who might gain by stealing Plessie but I can't figure out who. If only it was as simple as obtaining her, why murder Chrissie and cut my brake pipe afterwards? Surely, once they stole Plessie, they wouldn't need to come after me.'

Ellie frowned. 'Nothing makes sense but I wonder if it's all connected to Plessie. Maybe she brings bad luck.'

Jemma thought for a moment. 'A dangerous fossil! No, that's stupid, but Plessie might be the link.'

'What does Dave think?' Ellie asked.

'Oh, he just keeps talking about the ongoing investigations, but they're getting nowhere. I feel I should be doing something myself.'

'You can't, Mum. That's too dangerous. Dave wouldn't let you.'

'That's why I won't tell him yet.'

'Just be careful. Please.'

Jemma smiled. 'I will.'

'Talking of telling Dave.' Ellie looked down at her cup. 'Are you going to tell him about your fling with Brad?'

'No.' Jemma replied.

'Don't you think you ought to?'

'No. I was totally stressed out and not thinking straight. I'd had a few drinks and things just happened.'

'But won't they happen again?'

'No. I'm going to go and see Brad and tell him that I can't have anything to do with him anymore.'

'Better fit a lock to your knickers when you go. Can't you borrow that chastity belt that you showed me in the museum storeroom?'

'Ha ha, I've got more self-control than that.'

'Have you?'

Jemma scowled at her. 'Yes! Now can we just leave the subject?'

Ellie held her hands up. 'OK. OK. Oh, Mum, I need to forget about all this shit going on. Can we find something on TV? Perhaps a comedy? Anything to take our minds off the real world.'

Jemma turned on the TV. 'What do you fancy watching?'

They spent a few minutes looking for a film and chose *The Blues Brothers*. Jemma fetched a bottle of wine and they snuggled under a blanket on the sofa to watch it. She tried to lose herself in the film but the American accents kept reminding her of Brad.

Chapter 41

Jemma sat alone in her kitchen reading through a dissertation. She yawned and put it down. Picking up her phone, she typed out a message to Brad. *'Can I pop over for a chat?'*

'Only a chat?'

She sent a curt reply. *'Yes. Just a chat.'*

'OK, whenever you want, I'm not going anywhere.'

She sneaked out of her back door, figuring the policeman outside the house wouldn't spot her. It felt wrong to not tell him that she was leaving but she didn't want anybody to know she was going to Brad's. For all she knew, the police might be keeping a log of her movements and she didn't want Dave to see that.

Her mind was in turmoil as she walked down to Brad's cottage. *I can resist Brad. I'm in a happy relationship. I can resist Brad.* She arrived at his door and knocked.

'Come in, it's open.'

She opened the door and found him on his sofa with his legs up.

'How ya doing?' he said.

'I'm good thanks. You?'

'Yes, the PT is helping a lot. And the massages.' He gave her a grin.

Jemma blushed as she recalled the one she gave him that had a rather happy ending. 'I bet they are.'

He stood slowly. 'Drink?'

'I'll have a whisky, please. With ice.'

He walked over to the sideboard and poured two generous measures before placing them on the coffee table and returning to the sofa. 'Here, come and sit down.'

Jemma sat next to him and picked up her drink before taking a sip. Heaven. She drained the glass and placed it back down.

'Easy, girl!'

'I needed that.'

Brad edged closer. 'What's going on between us, Jemma? I thought we'd finished years ago, but that's not how it seemed last time you were here.'

Jemma swallowed and wondered why she was at Brad's. 'That was a moment of stupidity. I've been under a lot of stress with everything going on. I needed a release.'

He smirked. 'Three times, if I remember.'

She blushed again. 'Stop.'

He leant over and put his arm around her. 'What do you really want, Jemma?'

Jemma sobbed. 'I want things to go back to how they used to be.'

'What? Like when we were back at uni?'

'No. How things were six months ago, when it was just Ellie, Dave and me.'

'Before I came back?'

'Yes.'

'I'm not sure you know what you want.'

'I just want to be happy.'

'Aren't you happy with me?' Brad asked.

'No... Yes. Oh, I don't know.' Jemma put her head in her hands.

Brad sat back in his chair. 'We should both just disappear and go hunting fossils around the world.'

Jemma tried to grin through her tears. 'Sounds tempting but I can't leave Ellie.'

He raised his eyebrows. 'And Dave?'

'And Dave.'

'You're sending out some weird signals Jemma.'

'Not intentionally,' she said.

He leant towards her and brushed her lips with his. Jemma's resolve dissolved instantly and she returned his kiss hungrily.

Two hours later she woke with a start and couldn't work out where she was.

The wall facing her was covered in old-fashioned wallpaper, and there was an arm wrapped around her chest.

Oh no. This can't go on.

She looked around and noticed that, like the sitting room downstairs, the bedroom was devoid of any pictures, ornaments or any items of a personal nature. It was as if he wasn't planning to stay long.

'Back to the land of the living?' Brad said.

She turned to face him and pulled the duvet up to cover her nakedness. 'This must stop, Brad.'

'You're the one who keeps jumping me.'

'I don't care. It has to finish.' She gazed around the room. 'I can't go on like this. Why don't you go far away?'

He tensed and removed his arm. 'Can I ask one question?'

'What?' Jemma replied.

'Do you want to be with me? All the time, not just when you want to make out.'

Jemma thought for a moment. At that point she knew

that this all had to stop. 'I'm sorry Brad. I don't.'

He sat up. 'That's it. I'm going back to the States. I can't stand this blowing hot and cold.'

'Do you mean that?'

'Yes.'

'I'm glad. I was happy in my life with Dave then you showed up and unleashed something I didn't know was there. But I thought you'd bought this house and were staying here for a while?'

'I was, but this isn't for me,' he said.

'Aren't you still in trouble with the authorities?'

'Not anymore. My collection has checked out, mostly. Other than confiscating the T. Rex I found on federal land, they're handing the rest back.'

Jemma smiled. 'Well, that's great news.'

'Yep. Sure you don't want to come back with me?'

'No, Brad, I can't. I want to go back to me, Dave and Ellie.'

'Life won't be the same when I'm not around.'

She shrugged. 'I'll manage.'

'What about the big thing you'll be missing.'

A grin. 'Boasting again.'

He laughed. 'That's it. I'll book a flight and go back. I should be able to rent this place out.'

'Aren't you going to sell it?'

'I might keep it in case I ever decide to come back.'

'Please don't, Brad, not again. You always cause trouble when you come back.'

'Talking of which, you know when I came back nineteen years ago?'

Jemma paused, 'Yes?'

'Well, you know when we met up in London in my hotel and... certain things happened?'

323

Jemma looked away. 'Look, can we forget about that as well? Please.'

'Why?'

'Because I was with Liam at the time and I was so guilty about what we did.'

'You shouldn't feel guilty. You can't resist your American beefcake.'

She scowled at him. 'Shut up.'

'No, I won't. I had a thought last week. How old is Ellie?'

Jemma paused. 'She's eighteen.'

'When's her birthday?'

Her mind was spinning as she thought back to the concerns she had nineteen years ago about who Ellie's father actually was. 'That isn't important.'

He persevered. 'It might be. When is it?'

Jemma looked down. 'February the fourteenth.'

'Well, we got together in May, nineteen years ago.'

Jemma picked up her bra and t-shirt and started getting dressed. 'Can we change the subject?'

'No. I want to know.'

She stopped and stared at him. 'Know what?'

'Is Ellie my daughter?'

'No. She's not.'

'But she could be, couldn't she?'

She blushed. 'No, she couldn't. I was, er, using a coil when we got together. When you went back I removed it as Liam and I had talked about starting a family.' She wasn't happy about lying but to mention her suspicions to Brad would open up a whole new can of worms.

Brad stared at her. 'I'm not convinced. The timing fits.'

Jemma shouted. 'It doesn't fit! Forget it all, for God's sake. She's not yours.'

Chapter 42

Over the next week Jemma couldn't stop thinking about Brad. She hadn't told him that there was a fifty-fifty chance that Ellie could be his daughter. It was something she'd always put to the back of her mind until he turned up again. It worried her that she still had such strong feelings for him. She told herself that it was understandable as he was an attractive man, but she'd thought she was happy with Dave. She couldn't wait for Brad to go back to America and remove all the temptation.

She was working through some student dissertations when a text came in from Brad. She'd heard nothing from him, since her last visit hadn't ended well. She opened the message.

'I'm going back to the States today.'

'Good.'

'Just one problem though. The taxi has let me down and I need to be at Heathrow by eleven. Any chance of a lift?'

Jemma checked her watch. *'Can do I suppose. I'll pick you up in fifteen minutes.'*

She got changed, drove down to Brad's cottage and parked her van.

The front door opened and Brad appeared with an enormous case. 'Hi. Thanks for this. You're a star.'

'You're welcome,' she said. 'It'll be good to see your plane actually leave so I can return to a normal life.'

He grinned. 'No temptation?'

'No bloody temptation.' She heaved the case into the back of the van and they set off. For a while, they drove in silence.

'How's Ellie?' he said.

Jemma's hands clenched the steering wheel. That was one subject she didn't want to discuss at all. 'She's OK.'

'Would you mind if I kept in touch with her?'

'Yes, I would. Leave it alone, she's not your daughter.'

'I still think she could be.'

'Well, she's not.'

They drove the rest of the way in silence.

They arrived at the airport and walked through to departures.

Brad joined the check-in queue. 'Guess this is goodbye again.'

'Bye, Brad.'

They hugged awkwardly. He moved in to kiss her.

'No. Don't,' she said.

'I only want a kiss? We can't get carried away here.'

She frowned. 'I said no. This is hard enough without kissing.'

'It's never too late, you know.'

'What's never too late?' she asked.

'For you to come to the States.'

Jemma sighed, 'Oh Brad, don't start this again. My life is here and I'm happy.'

'Really happy?'

'Yes. Now piss off and don't come back.'

Brad laughed. 'Not quite as romantic as a Casablanca goodbye.'

'Sorry,' she said. 'Here's looking at you kid.'

He started to walk away but then turned back and kissed her. She responded briefly before pushing him away. Even though she tried to look determined, inwardly she was desperate to fling her arms around him.

'Bye, Brad. Don't come back, please.'

He smiled and turned away. 'See ya, Jemma. This could have been the start of a beautiful friendship. Still, we'll always have Plessie.'

His case wobbled across the tiles as he struggled to pull it along. She watched him dragging it down the queue and walked away rubbing a tear from her eye.

After a tiring journey back to Lulcombe, she parked the van and went inside for a cup of tea. Dave was sitting at the kitchen table reading a paper.

'Got rid of him at last then?' he said.

Jemma looked down at her mug. 'Yeah, he's gone.'

'Did he 'ping' going through security?'

She shrugged. 'No idea, I left him at departures.'

'Oh, well. One less complication.'

She looked up. 'What? Why a complication?'

He looked straight into her eyes. 'I'm not stupid, Jem. I know you still have feelings for him.'

Jemma bit her lip. 'I'm fond of Brad and I still feel guilty about what Phil did to him.'

'That wasn't your fault.'

She frowned. 'I know but Phil did it because he was stalking me.'

Dave's voice raised. 'For God's sake, Jem. There was nothing you could have done.'

Ellie wandered in as Dave was shouting at Jemma.

'Mum, can I-'

Jemma interrupted her. 'Can you give us a few minutes, Els? It's not a good time.'

'Sorry, I'm sure!' She turned and flounced out.

Jemma turned back to him. 'Brad's gone and he's not coming back.'

He raised his mug of tea. 'Here's to that.'

She looked at him. 'Dave, there's something I've got to tell you.'

He put down his drink and tilted his head. 'What?'

She paused. Her inner turmoil was growing so much that she almost confessed what had happened with Brad and faced the consequences of her guilt. Within that split second, she decided that Brad was over the Atlantic and she should just forget about him. 'I love you.'

He kissed her. 'I've got something to tell you too.'

She looked up. 'What's that?'

'Well you know I've always wanted to try for Detective Inspector?'

She hesitated. 'Yes...'

'I've been offered a DI role.'

She hugged him. 'Oh, that's brilliant news.'

He didn't smile back. 'Only one small problem.'

'What?' she said.

'It's in Birmingham.'

Chapter 43

The next day Jemma had the morning free so she tidied her workshop. She was still thinking over Dave's bombshell news about being offered the Birmingham job. It was with a mixture of relief for herself, and disappointment for Dave, that she'd heard him say he'd turned it down. She felt selfish about holding him back from a major promotion but he'd said he was happy to wait for something more local.

After breakfast, her mobile rang. It was Jeremy Lovell, the fossil dealer who'd tried to buy Plessie before she was stolen.

'Morning, Jemma.'

'Hello, Jeremy, how can I help?'

'You remember that I tried to buy your plesiosaur on behalf of one of my clients?'

'Yes,' she said hesitantly.

'Well, he's been back in touch and wishes to try to help you recover it.'

'Who is he?' she asked, astonished.

'He wishes to remain anonymous for the moment.'

She paused. *That's strange. Why won't he reveal his identity?* 'What does he have in mind?' she said.

'He plans to put the word out to some of the dealers

who are less reputable than I am. His words were, "Let's go fishing and see what we catch." It could work, you know.'

She struggled to contain her excitement. 'What happens next?'

'He's asked me to organise a meeting over a meal.'

Jemma frowned. 'But he doesn't want to reveal who he is. I'm confused.'

'He'll reveal his identity when you meet,' Jeremy said.

'That's strange. I don't think my police minder will be very happy if I don't know who I'm meeting.'

'He's happy to meet in a public place and I can personally vouch for him and his intentions.'

She thought for a moment. 'Ok. I suppose so. Where does he want to meet?'

'He suggested the restaurant at the Cliff Hotel in Lulcombe. Thursday evening at seven.'

'That's a bit beyond my price range for a meal, I'm afraid,' she said.

'That's not a problem. He insisted that it would be his treat.'

'How will I recognise him?'

'He'll be in the bar and will look out for you.'

'Very mysterious. I'm nervous about meeting a complete stranger with everything that's been going on but I've got to do something to help.'

'That's good,' he replied. 'I hope it's a successful meeting.'

She ended the call and stared at the phone. *Am I taking a big risk? It will be a public restaurant and the policeman will be outside. Hopefully, I'm not being stupid.*

After a full day of lecturing at the university, Jemma came home and showered. Dave was working late so she hadn't told him about her dinner plans. It might be best to keep these investigations from him to start with in case he tried to stop her. She could tell him afterwards, once she'd decided if the mystery collector might be able to help.

In the kitchen, the whisky bottle was calling at her as she walked past. *No. I can't. I'm driving with a police car following.* She reached for the bottle and opened it. The smell reached her nostrils and she inhaled deeply. *No. I don't want a drink. I can beat this.*

She walked over and emptied the whole bottle down the sink. The smell filled the kitchen, so she ran the taps until all traces had been washed away. A few sprays of air freshener completed the task. The empty bottle was thrown into the recycling bin after which she stared down at it with a feeling of satisfaction. *That's me and whisky done.*

After locking up, she spoke to the policeman in his car outside to let him know she was meeting a colleague in the restaurant. He said he'd wait in the car park while she had her meal and then escort her home.

This intrusion into her life was unwelcome but she appreciated their concern and efforts. The last few weeks had been crazy, and she wanted it over and the guilty party behind bars. She had never lived in fear before and she didn't like it at all.

The drive down only took a few minutes. She could have walked but the heels she wore with her dress were higher than she was used to. Driving in a pair of pumps and changing when she arrived was much safer than trying to drive in her stilettos.

As she parked up, she waved to the police escort who

pulled in alongside her, put her heels on and walked towards the entrance. Her scruffy van looked out of place next to all the posh cars but she shrugged and continued up the stairs. The front door opened automatically and she carried on through to reception.

Behind the polished, dark wood counter, an elegantly dressed young lady saw her and smiled. 'Good evening and welcome to the Cliff Hotel. May I take your coat?'

'Thank you. I'm Jemma Thorne and I'm meeting someone for dinner. It's rather strange, I'm not sure who I'm meeting yet.'

'Oh, yes, your friend has arrived and is waiting in the bar.' She pointed. 'Through that door on the left.'

'Thank you, I'll go through and find him.'

Jemma walked through and saw a man sitting on his own at the bar. He turned around and smiled as she walked up.

She gasped. 'Brad?'

Chapter 44

Brad stood from his bar stool and limped over to Jemma, kissing her on the cheek as she stared with an open mouth. 'Hello, Jemma,' he grinned.

'What the hell are you doing here?'

Brad straightened up. 'We're going to get Plessie back.'

She started gabbling. 'But you flew back to America. I saw you in the queue. You can't be here.'

He held her arm. 'Calm down. Come and have a drink and I'll explain everything.' They walked over to the bar and Brad spoke to the barman. 'Bourbon for the lady, please, and an orange juice for me.'

'Just a tonic water for me please,' she said. 'I'm driving.' She turned to Brad. 'OK then, you've got five minutes before I'm out of here. What's going on?'

He smiled. 'I was at the check-in queue and had the sudden feeling I was running away when you really needed me. I've never been a quitter and I'm not going to start now. I cancelled my ticket and here I am. Ready to help you find Plessie.'

Jemma flopped on the bar stool as her head sank into her hands. 'Oh, no.'

'Don't worry, I only want to help. That's why I called Jeremy to get him to arrange a meeting.'

'Why wouldn't he tell me it was you?'

'If you'd known it was me, would you have come?'

'No, but…'

He interrupted. 'That's why.'

'Wait a minute.' She paused. 'So it was you who tried to buy Plessie through Jeremy a while ago?'

'Guilty. I wanted him to try to buy her anonymously.'

She ran her hands through her hair and totally messed up her earlier attempts at styling. 'I'm so confused. That's bloody deceitful.'

He smiled sheepishly. 'I thought you might sell to somebody else.'

'That failed miserably,' she said.

He shrugged. 'I know that now.'

She shook her head again. 'But why get involved now?'

'I did a lot of thinking in that airport queue.'

'And?'

'I felt guilty about not helping you look for Plessie.'

'You were lying injured in hospital,' she said.

'I know but when I came out, I didn't help at all.'

Jemma sighed. 'I know I'm going to regret asking this, but how are you planning to help?'

The waiter appeared, showed them through to the restaurant and took their order for food.

The dining room was swanky with a copper-topped bar surrounded by blue leather stools. At the far end was a wall covered in shelves full of old books. If she wasn't with Brad right now, Jemma would've loved to browse through them.

They sat at the table with their drinks and Brad continued to explain his idea.

Jemma put down her glass. 'So to get this straight,' she began, 'you're going to ask around some shady dealers and collectors and tell them that you're looking for special fossils, no questions asked, and you have plenty of money to pay for them.'

He nodded. 'That's it so far.'

'Then you're going to look at what's on offer and hope someone out there is trying to sell Plessie.'

He looked serious for a moment. 'I wanna do this, for you and for Plessie, but I need you to sign off on it?'

Jemma paused. 'I don't want you to put yourself in any danger, but yes, why not.'

'Don't worry. I've dealt with some shady people in the past so I know how to take care of myself. Besides, you know what a cautious fellow I am.'

'I'm sure you are but we should involve the police before anything gets dangerous,' she said.

Brad looked at her. 'Talking of police, what do you reckon Dave will make of your investigations?'

'I'm not going to tell him yet. If we find out anything useful, I'll tell him then.'

'He won't be happy when he finds out.'

Jemma shrugged. 'He'll have to stomach it. The police don't seem to have any useful leads so it's good to try something to help.'

'Why don't you just let him know what I'm planning?'

She frowned. 'He'd try to stop us.'

'It might be dangerous,' Brad said.

'I know but two of my friends are dead and my daughter nearly went over a cliff.' Her voice rose. 'I want to get the bastards responsible.'

'Then let's nail the sons of bitches,' he said.

They raised their glasses and tapped them together. Jemma felt excited about the prospect of finally doing something about Plessie.

***

The following night Jemma sat with Dave watching TV and catching up on the day's events.

She hadn't told him about her meeting with Brad. Although she felt guilty about not telling him, she knew they'd end up arguing if he knew of her plans.

'Any news about the investigation?' she said.

'Fraid not. We keep hitting dead ends. No prospect of tracing the old explosive, nothing on any CCTVs, and nothing from any of the locals CHISs.'

Jemma turned and looked at him. 'The whats?'

Dave laughed. 'Covert Human Intelligence Sources. We're not allowed to call them grasses anymore.'

'This is no good.' She paused. 'I better start investigating myself.'

Dave's body twitched. 'Don't bother, it's too dangerous. We'll have a breakthrough soon, I can feel it.'

'I'll just ask a few discreet questions. See if I can find out anything useful.'

'Don't, Jem, please. There are some bad people around.'

'I'll be careful. I promise.'

Dave pulled away and looked at her. 'Look, Jem, I'm serious. These people want you dead. You should be keeping a low profile, not going around like a bull in a china shop with your own enquiries.'

Jemma turned her back to him. 'You don't tell me what to do.'

'OK then, get yourself killed. See if I care.' He grabbed his coat and left through the front door, slamming it after him.

Chapter 45

At around one a.m. a dark figure with a fuel can in his hand walked along the back of Jemma's garden and up the path. Because he came in from the fields, he was hidden from the policeman parked outside the front of her house. The night wasn't pitch black, as there were breaks in the cloud where the moon peeped through and with the patchy moonlight he was easily able to find his way without the use of a torch.

After reaching the back door, he leant against the wall listening for a few minutes to the sound of his beating heart. He'd show his brother he was the clever one who didn't need to be told what to do.

Opening the can, he splashed petrol all over the step, trying to pour as much as he could under the door and into the kitchen. The smell of fumes was strong.

He removed a lighter from his pocket and lit one of the Molotov cocktails before throwing it at the door, which immediately burst into flames. Satisfied it was well alight, he ran out of the garden and back across the fields.

***

Dino roused and barked as the fire licked the door. A second later the smoke alarm activated, and Jemma and Dave leapt out of bed snatching at their clothes.

'That's smoke,' Dave yelled. 'Let's get out.' They ran along the landing and down the stairs.

Dave opened the kitchen door and Dino ran through the crack frantically wagging his tail. The flames had spread to the inside of the back door so Dave grabbed the fire extinguisher from the wall and attacked them.

Jemma ran out barefoot through the front door, waving to the policeman who seemed to be dozing in his car. Pavement stones jabbing at her feet, she banged against his window. 'Fire!' she shouted.

He woke up with a start then radioed into HQ before grabbing his extinguisher and following her back across the road.

Jemma ran around the back of the house and unravelled the hosepipe she kept on the outside wall. She turned on the water and sprayed the back door which by now was well ablaze, the flames climbing the wooden door and flickering high at the wall above. The policeman saw what she was doing and dashed inside the house to help Dave.

With the three of them attacking the fire, they gradually got it under control, and by the time the fire engine arrived, it was all but fully extinguished.

Dave and the policeman came out coughing and spluttering and rushed around to check on Jemma.

She was standing on the patio, barefoot in her jeans and jumper, soaked to the skin but otherwise unhurt.

Dave ran up to her. 'You OK?'

'Yes, I'm fine. What happened?'

'Well, by the stink of petrol, I think someone tried to fry you in your bed.'

Oblivious to her wet clothes, she held Dave. 'I don't think I can take this any longer. What's happening?'

'No idea, but it has to stop. I said these people were serious.'

***

Across town in a flat above some offices, Keith made himself a coffee.

His brother walked into the kitchen, sniffing. 'What's that? Why can I smell smoke?'

Keith hesitated. 'I did something last night.'

Reggie glared at him. 'What?'

Keith grinned. 'I showed some initiative and set fire to Jemma's house.'

'What?'

'I said I set...'

'I heard what you said! What happened?'

'I poured some petrol over her back door and lit it.'

'Tell me Jemma is no more?' Reggie said.

'I don't know. I got out quickly once the flames started.'

Reggie turned on his trusty police scanner and settled down to listen. He stared at his brother. 'They're standing down the fire engine and they said the only injury was smoke inhalation. What were you thinking?'

Keith sat down. 'I wanted to do something myself.'

'That ended well.'

'I tried though.'

Reggie scowled at him. 'I don't care about trying, I want success.'

'Sorry, bro.'

Reggie tutted and stormed out.

Keith sat seething. 'I'm going to kill Jemma Thorne if it's the last thing I do.'

***

Jemma took a day's holiday to thoroughly clean the kitchen. 'Any news?' She asked Dave who'd returned early from work.

'Nothing useful. Your camera shows a man lighting the fire and running off. We've got CCTV from town showing him walking past with a can at twelve forty-five a.m. He returned at one-thirty without the can.'

'Can you see who he is?'

'No, he's wearing a hoodie.'

'No clues?'

'Not really. There were no footprints in your garden. We found the can but it had no fingerprints on it and it's a common make.'

'When's it going to stop?' Jemma sighed.

'Soon, Jem. We've got to get a break soon.'

***

The next few days were hectic as Jemma dealt with her insurers, trying to organise a replacement door. The stress was getting to her and she tried to deal with it by keeping busy. That worked during the day but at night she couldn't sleep. Then came the phone call she'd been hoping for.

'Hi, Brad.'

'Hi, Jem. Good news.'

'What?'

'I've had a response.'

'Go on...' she said.

'I got a message that somebody might be selling a quality fossil. No more information but they want a meeting to show me the goods. If I'm interested, I need to leave ten thousand pounds in cash as a deposit, with a further forty thousand due on delivery.'

'Do you know what it is?'

'No, they just said it's a once-in-a-lifetime chance to buy an incredible specimen.'

She felt herself getting excited. 'Where will the meeting be?'

'Everything's very secretive at the moment. If I want to proceed, I have to send a text to a phone that will only be turned on for a minute at six p.m. each night. I'll be given instructions on what to do next.'

'OK. Great. When do we go?' Jemma said.

Brad sounded shocked. 'We?'

'Yes, I need to come, so I can check whether they've got Plessie.'

'No way, José. This could be dangerous. Don't forget, somebody has been trying to kill you. Anyway, I'll be able to recognise Plessie.'

'Ah, I suppose so. I know, I could hide on the rear seat of your truck and be ready to call the police.'

'Might work if you don't get out. My windows are tinted so no one will see you.'

'OK. What's the next move?'

'Leave it with me for a couple of days while I sort out the cash. I assume I'll have to show it to them to prove I'm serious.'

'This is exciting. Once you confirm it's Plessie, I'll call the police and they can grab the bastards behind all this!'

'We'll have to be careful.'

'I know that. Are you sure you're happy to play the buyer?'

'Of course, I am. I'll call again once I know anything else.'

***

That night Jemma planned to meet Ellie in Swanbourne for a meal. She invited her police minder to join them but instead he settled for a takeaway in his car.

They sat in Pizza Hut working their way through a pile of food. 'What's happening with the hunt for Plessie?' Ellie asked.

Jemma dropped her pizza down to her plate. 'Well, there's a story.' She told Ellie about Brad's abortive departure and his plan to help.

Ellie frowned. 'Sounds dangerous.'

'It shouldn't be.' Jemma said. 'They won't do anything to Brad as they'll want the rest of the money. Once he lets me know it's Plessie then I can call in the police and they can arrest the baddies, rescue Plessie and retrieve Brad's money.'

'Mum, you can be so naive at times. I'm sure it won't be that simple. You need to call the police as soon as you suspect anything.'

'I will, I promise.'

'Can I come?'

Jemma shook her head. 'Course you can't! There's no need for you to endanger yourself. The police will sort it out if it's Plessie.'

'Are you telling Dave?'

'I can't. He wouldn't let me do it,' Jemma said.

Ellie frowned. 'Will you tell me when you're going and where you're meeting him so I can act as a remote backup if needed?'

'No probs, Els, I'm sure this is going to be sorted soon so we can go back to how we were.'

Chapter 46

Brad was excited about the prospect of engaging in some amateur detective work, not to mention helping Jemma. He was a bit worried about what Dave would say when he found out, but decided it was worth the risk. As he hadn't decided yet how long he was remaining in England, he was staying at the Cliff Hotel. His cottage had been emptied prior to letting out so he couldn't stay there.

At six p.m. he was sitting in his room reading when a text came through from an unknown number.

'Arrangements confirmed for tomorrow afternoon. Be in Lulcombe Beach Car Park at 3:00pm and you'll receive directions. Make sure you come alone with no tracking devices. You'll be watched and scanned. Bring the deposit in cash. Unmarked £10 or £20 notes. Do not involve the police or attempt to track the mobile sending this message.'

His heart beat faster as he read and re-read the message. *So, this is happening. Still time to back out... No, let's go!* He forwarded the text to Jemma. Ten minutes later, his phone rang.

'Hi, Brad.'

'Hi, Jem. Still up for this?'

'Of course, I am. I want to nail these bastards.'

'Don't let this get personal. You've got to keep a clear head.'

'Don't worry, I'm thinking perfectly clearly. I want to see whoever did this being led away in handcuffs,' she said.

'OK. This is the plan. At two-thirty, I'll park my black truck in the Beach Car Park. Can you lose your bodyguard and come down to me there? You can hide under a blanket on the back seat and we'll wait for instructions.'

'Do I need to bring anything?'

'Just some binoculars and a flashlight in case it's dark.'

'Have you got the cash for the deposit?' she asked.

'Yes, took a while though. I don't know why banks are suspicious and ask so many questions these days. I mean, doesn't everybody need fifty thousand in cash every now and then?'

Jemma paused. 'You sure you're still OK to go through with this?'

'Oh yes, I haven't felt this excited in years.'

'Right. I'll see you in the car park at half two.'

As Jemma stared out of her window, the early morning mist was hanging over the fields. *So today is the day.* She was gripped with a mixture of excitement, nervousness and guilt about not telling Dave. She picked up her phone and called Ellie.

'Hi, Mum.'

'Hello, Els. How are you?'

'I'm fine. Any more news?'

'Yes. We're on for this afternoon!' Jemma said.

'Wow! When and where?'

Jemma sounded excited. 'Two-thirty in the Beach Car Park. We're going in Brad's vehicle.'

'Make sure Gareth from the Café doesn't spot you or he'll think you're being abducted!'

'Good point, Els. I'll make sure I'm out of sight.'

'Can I help in any way?'

'I did have one idea. Can you drive over and talk to the policeman parked outside the house? I don't think he'll notice me coming out of the back and down the garden path but it might be safer if you're distracting him.'

'OK. I'll come over after two.'

'Perfect. See you later.'

'Bye, Mum. Oh, and one other thing.'

'Yes?'

'Don't forget to ring the police as soon as you can.'

'Course, I will.' Jemma put her phone back on charge and grabbed her coat to take Dino for a walk. The fog was thickening and her concerns about the day ahead were growing.

***

Reggie and Keith Fletcher stood in a disused quarry between Swanbourne and Axminster going over their plans. The yard was full of dirty puddles of stagnant water dotted with rainbow patches of old diesel. Several Portakabins and decrepit buildings formed a U-shape around the yard. Behind the buildings, an imposing cliff face was scarred with several tunnels that looked like giant mouse holes.

Reggie looked around. 'Seems such a long time ago we were helping Dad run this bloody dump.'

Keith sneered. 'I remember, I usually got the heavy work. When did this place shut down?'

Reggie thought for a moment. 'Must have been in nineteen eighty-five 'cause it had been closed for fifteen years when Dad died. It was when the stone ran out that I decided we needed to turn to crime to support us and Dad when he couldn't work anymore.'

Keith paused. 'I'd forgotten about that.'

Reggie grinned. 'It will be nice to become respectable businessmen after selling the new hotel. No more crime.'

Keith gestured at the quarry. 'Will you sell this place?'

Reggie shrugged. 'It's not worth anything. A disused quarry with no stone left? I'll probably just keep it; it's always useful to have a quiet place to store stuff.'

Keith laughed. 'And dinosaurs!'

'You managed to lift the fossil into the back of that dumper truck?'

'Yes, all sorted'

'Good.'

They walked over to the Portakabin that had acted as the office for the quarry. Keith went first, pulling open the rusty door that creaked and complained as it moved.

Reggie turned on the light and surveyed the room. 'I thought we could do any business in here. We'll check the colour of his money, show him the fossil and, if he wants to buy it, we'll discuss how and when we can swap cash for bones.'

Keith smirked. 'I like the sound of that.'

'I want you to park out of the way near the old telephone box at the top of Swanbourne Road in Lulcombe at two o'clock this afternoon. You can leave the first set of instructions in the phone box somewhere.' He handed Keith a brown envelope with "*Directions*" written on the outside. 'When he leaves his car to collect this, you can check to ensure he's on his own and not being followed by the police. You can use this sweeping device to make sure there aren't any trackers on his vehicle. This will pick them up from thirty feet away so you don't need to open his car door.'

'Got that,' said Keith.

He gave Keith the scanner. 'It's fully charged.' He showed him a button on the side. 'This is how you turn it on.'

'OK.'

'Oh, and one other thing,' Reggie said. 'I've acquired a couple of guns in case anything goes wrong. I'll park the Range Rover on the back road out of the quarry, with a pile of rock in front. If we need to skedaddle then that can be our escape route.'

He handed Keith one of the guns, which he put in his jacket pocket.

'OK,' said Keith. 'What do you know about the punter with the readies?'

'Absolutely nothing other than he's loaded and after top fossils. Also, he's not afraid to buy them through unofficial channels.'

'I like being unofficial.'

'OK. Off you go and sort everything out. Don't forget to wear black and bring your balaclava for when we meet him here. Make sure you keep it on this time.'

***

At around five past two, Brad drove his pickup into the Beach Car Park at Lulcombe and parked at the far end. The sea wall hid the vehicle from the prying eyes in the café. He wasn't really expecting to get Plessie back but he had put some old carpet and a tarpaulin in the load space in case he had to retrieve her. That's if it was her they were selling.

The weather was conducive to remaining hidden. A mist blew in, which reduced visibility and made the temperature feel colder than it was.

Brad got out and limped over to watch the sea while he waited for Jemma. His injured leg and arm were gradually improving but were still painful in the cold weather. With the mist coming down, he couldn't see the waves but he stood there breathing in the salty air whilst shivering with a mixture of nervousness and excitement.

Chapter 47

Ellie arrived at ten past two and parked outside her mum's house, the rear end of her car facing towards the front of the police car, and stepped around to open her boot. Wearing her tightest jeans, she blushed at the thought of what she was about to do.

After opening the boot, she leant over and dipped her head inside to check the tyre lever was still in place. She could feel herself blushing as she stretched. *Hope he appreciates my butt.*

***

In the police car, the young constable definitely appreciated Ellie's butt and long legs. He recognised her car and knew it was Jemma's daughter. He checked his notepad for her full name. Ellie May Thorne.

He was tempted to get out for a chat but instead decided he ought to stay in his vehicle in case his radio went off.

***

Ellie straightened up, grabbed two carrier bags and slammed

the boot shut. Looking round, she pretended to spot the policeman for the first time. She waved at him and walked along the pavement towards his car. 'Hello, constable.'

He wound down his window. 'Afternoon, Miss Thorne.'

Ellie tried to look shy and demure and was sure she failed on both fronts. 'Ooh, you know who I am.'

'My job is to identify everybody who comes and goes from your mum's.'

'Well, that puts you at an advantage then.'

'Why?'

'Because you know my name but I don't know yours.'

'Oh, I'm PC Hawkins.'

She gave him a killer smile. 'No, silly! Your first name.'

'Ben.'

'Well, Ben, I hope you're watching out for any baddies hanging around.'

'Oh, yes, Miss Thorne.'

'Ellie, please.'

'Yes, Ellie, but it's been quiet today.'

She started to enjoy her cameo as a scarlet woman and he was quite a handsome young man. 'In that case, you might be able to help me out,' she said.

'Of course, Miss... Ellie. What's the problem?'

'Er, I've brought my mum a tyre lever she wanted to borrow and it's slid right to the back of the boot. I can't reach far enough, no matter how hard I try.'

'Oh, I noticed you reaching in.'

She blushed. 'Did you? Would you mind terribly getting it for me, please, so I can leave it for her?'

'My pleasure.' He got out of the patrol car, donned his cap and followed Ellie to her car.

She unlocked it and bent over again. 'I just can't get it,'

her muffled voice came out from the boot.

He had been somewhat distracted for a second time by her denim-clad rear. He jumped and replied. 'You just move out of the way and I'll get it for you.'

She stretched out, stood beside him so that he faced away from her mum's drive and placed her hand on his arm. 'That would be lovely.'

Reaching in, he retrieved the wrench and moved to hand it to her but he wasn't looking down so his hand, not the tyre lever, ended up in her hand. 'Oh, sorry,' he said as this time he was the one to redden.

'Thank you so much,' she purred and reached up to kiss him on the cheek. Beyond him her mum was crossing the garden and gave her a thumbs up before disappearing out of the gate and into the field. Ellie brushed his chest. 'Anyway, I can't chat all day. I need to drop this in and shoot off, lots to do.'

'OK, Ellie. Nice to meet you.'

'Lovely to meet you too. I'll tell you what, when you've solved my mum's case and you're no longer watching her house, give me a call and we can go for a drink.'

'Oh, yes, right. That would be great. What's your number?' Ben held up his mobile and, as Ellie read it out, he added her to his contacts.

'Don't forget, you have to solve the case first. I'm sure there are police rules about going out with witnesses or something.'

'I'm on to it.'

'Good.' She gave him a tight hug and walked back down the drive, amazed at what she'd done.

When she reached her mum's back door, she scanned the fields and could see her disappearing into the distance.

I thought mothers were supposed to worry about their daughters. With me it's the other way round. I wonder if that's a sign I've started adulting!

***

While Ellie did her Mata Hari impression, Jemma trudged across the fields on the path that led down to the beach. The recent rain had made it muddy and she worried Brad might not appreciate dirt on his seat.

Halfway across, she discovered a heavy weight in the pocket of her coat. She stuck her hand in and pulled out a black and yellow geologist's hammer. *Bugger, I didn't mean to bring that. Must have left it there after a field trip.*

She checked her watch, wondering whether she had enough time to pop back and leave it in her garden. It was two-twenty so she thought she'd best make haste to the car park. She returned the hammer to her pocket and walked on.

Her new coat was a bit stiff and uncomfortable, but, as her old one was in the evidence room at the police station, she'd had to buy a new one. Thinking about her old coat reminded her of Chrissie, who'd been wearing it when some bastard pushed her over the cliff. *I'm going to find out who's behind this and end the nightmare.*

At two twenty-five she arrived at the car park and walked along the sandy concrete until she saw Brad's twin cab pickup at the far end. The fog was thicker and, as she reached his truck, she couldn't see the café or the other end of the car park at all.

Brad turned away from the waves and embraced Jemma. 'You ready for this?'

'As ready as I'll ever be.'

'Nervous?'

She nodded. 'A little. You?'

He stared out into the mist where the sea should be. 'Nah,' he said, a little too confidently. 'Well, yeah, maybe a bit.'

Jemma didn't know whether she was scared about what might happen or that nothing would happen.

Chapter 48

Ellie left the love-stricken policeman looking in his rear-view mirror and trying to clean the lipstick off his cheek. She put the carrier bags and tyre lever in her mum's kitchen and returned to her car. After unlocking it, she got in, made a three-point turn and headed back down towards Lulcombe town centre. After parking by the Anchor Inn, she slipped on her black coat and walked to the Beach Car Park.

A thick mist rolled in off the sea preventing her from seeing any vehicles. As she crept around the edge of the car park, she tried not to look like a furtive car thief but failed miserably.

Reaching the far end, she crouched behind the wall near the truck. Ignoring the graffiti left by bored teenagers, she peeped over as her mum stood talking to Brad further along the sea wall.

At this point, Ellie realised that she didn't have much of a plan. She knew her mum only wanted her to distract the policeman but she'd feel so helpless waiting at home. She'd thought she might be able to follow them in her car, keeping a safe distance, so they wouldn't notice her. However, with the mist making visibility a nightmare, she decided she needed an alternative.

She edged along the wall and moved closer to where they were parked. When she felt she was near, she jumped over. In the mist she was confident they wouldn't spot her and as she crouched on the ground her heart thumped hard. Staying low, she dashed across to the tailgate of the truck. A few moments later, she checked the cargo bed and found a tarpaulin covering most of the floor.

Trying to be as quiet and nimble as she possible, she climbed into the back while regretting that she was still wearing her tight jeans. *If I ruin these I'll be furious,* she thought as she burrowed under the tarp. When she was underneath, she used the torch on her phone to check her surroundings and found she was lying on a piece of old carpet. *I better hide under this as well,* she thought, *in case anybody checks out the tarpaulin.*

She burrowed further down and, once she was under the damp and smelly carpet, she lay still and waited for the truck to move.

***

Brad and Jemma returned to the pickup and talked about what might happen when he met with the thieves or their dealer.

He glanced across at Jemma. 'Happy with the plan?'

She shrugged. 'I think so but we need a signal.'

'OK. How about when I go to check the fossil, you watch through the binoculars? If I'm sure it's Plessie, I'll hold my hands behind my back and look upwards as if I'm stretching.'

'Got that,' Jemma said.

'That's your sign to call the cops.'

'OK.'

'If it isn't Plessie then I'll try to leave with my suitcase of cash.'

'Sounds good,' Jemma said. 'How about if you feel threatened at any time, put both hands on your head and I'll call them straight away.'

'OK.'

She touched his arm. 'The thing that concerns me is how long they might take to arrive.'

He smiled. 'I'll have to use my natural charm and keep talking.'

By two-fifty they'd been over all the possible scenarios several times so they chatted for a while about nothing in particular. Ever since Brad had returned they hadn't mentioned their recent fling. Jemma felt that not discussing it was probably worse than talking about it but neither of them seemed keen to face up to the elephant in the room.

'Thanks for doing this, Brad, I hope we can find Plessie and help catch the culprits.'

'That's OK. I'm enjoying it. I just want to see her back where she belongs. I won't pretend that I don't want you to come back to the States with me, but, if getting Plessie back makes you happy, then I'm cool with that.'

They waited in silence as the dashboard clock displayed the minutes slowly creeping by.

***

In the back of the pickup, Ellie was already having second thoughts. Her hair was full of dust and grass, and she struggled to keep the smelly carpet away from her face. Whenever the damp coarseness touched her skin, she recoiled.

What am I doing here? She panicked that she'd said it out loud.

Carefully, she wriggled onto her side and moved her arm over her head to shift the dirty carpet away. She wondered how long it would be before they started moving.

***

Brad's phone pinged. He tried to contain his excitement. 'Incoming text from an unknown number!' He picked up his phone. 'Right, the first instruction is; Drive out of Lulcombe on Swanbourne Road and stop at the old telephone box on the brow of the hill. Wait there for five minutes and the next instructions will be given.'

'I'd better keep out of sight once we get going in case anybody's watching,' Jemma said and clambered onto the rear seat. She placed the binoculars next to her, lay down and covered herself with the blanket.

Brad started the engine, which for a massive truck was very quiet. 'OK, let's go.' After driving out the car park, he turned left up Swanbourne Road past the museum, fire station and playing fields. It didn't take long to reach the old red phone box at the top of the hill where he parked and checked the time to start counting off the minutes.

Jemma sat up. 'I'll come and have a look with you!' She reached for the door handle.

'Don't get out!' he hissed.

She jumped. 'Why?'

'They might be watching to check I'm alone.'

'Ah, right,' she said.

After five minutes, another text came through. *'Walk over to the telephone box and collect the brown envelope. Read the contents, replace the envelope and follow the instructions.'*

Brad climbed out of the pickup and limped over to the phone box. On a shelf there was an envelope with the word "Directions" written on it. Opening the envelope, he used his phone to take a photo of the instructions and returned it to the spot where he'd picked it up.

***

While Brad was busy in the phone box, Keith came out from where he was hiding and scuttled over to the black pickup. He turned on the scanner and checked all around the vehicle for tracking devices. The machine didn't bleep so he turned it off.

His balaclava-clad reflection peered back in the tinted window. Pressing his face against the glass he could just make out the empty seats inside the vehicle.

After checking Brad was still in the box, he quickly glanced in the cargo space of the truck but saw nothing other than a dirty old tarpaulin. Raising the edge, he saw some scruffy carpet beneath, but nothing else. Satisfied, he beat a hasty retreat back behind the hedge. The man who'd left the pickup seemed familiar from somewhere, but he couldn't be sure.

***

Brad jumped back into the pickup anxiously checking over his shoulder. 'Nobody opened the door while I was out, did they?'

A muffled voice from the rear seat said, 'I didn't hear anything.'

'That's good. When I went to the phone booth, somebody

checked the truck out. I'm glad I told you to stay hidden.'

'Had you better check your brakes?' Jemma said.

'No, he only looked through the windows and in the load bed.'

'Phew, that was a bit close. Where next?'

Brad scrolled to the picture on his mobile. 'Go to the car park behind the supermarket in Axminster. Off we go again,' he said as he put the truck in drive and headed off.

***

Keith watched him leave and rang Reggie. 'Target has left the first stop,' he said. 'No tails.'

'Right. Watch for another ten minutes then come straight to the quarry. I'll send him some more instructions to keep him going around in circles for a bit so you've time to get back here first.'

***

It took Brad around fifteen minutes to drive to Axminster. Every market day the streets thronged with people and stalls. He drove to the supermarket but took a while to find a space. 'OK in the back?' he asked.

A muffled reply came from under the blanket. 'Just about!'

A few minutes later there was another ping as a text came in. He read it out loud. 'Head south towards Lyme Regis for three miles and stop in the lay-by beneath the 'Jurassic Coast' sign.'

He set off again. 'I think they're trying to make us dizzy.'

'It's working,' said the blanket.

Leaving the car park, he drove back through the busy

streets and headed for Lyme.

The next ping came through well before he reached the intended lay-by though he couldn't check it until after he'd pulled up.

'Hopefully keeping up so far. Turn right in half a mile onto a dirt road and follow it for a mile until you arrive at some gates. Get out of your truck and open them. Drive through and park in the middle of the yard and wait for more instructions.'

Brad drove off and turned onto a small track that was dowsed in dark shadows. In the swirling mist it appeared to lead nowhere, the sort of road you'd miss if you were driving past at normal speed. 'This might be a little rough,' Brad said to his back seat passenger.

The truck bumped along the single-track road until it reached the gates. A faded sign read 'AXMINSTER QUARRY - CLOSED.'

He climbed out and approached the gates whilst trying not to step in the muddy puddles. The rusty old hinges squeaked as he pushed. He got back in the pickup, drove into the centre of a big area of rough gravel and pulled up, turning off his engine.

He whispered. 'We're here.'

'Where?' asked the voice from under the blanket.

Brad looked around. 'We're parked in an old quarry near Axminster, awaiting further instructions.'

'OK, I think I know where we are. This used to be a quarry for limestone but it shut down years ago.'

Brad jumped when his phone rang and he pushed the button to switch to the car's speakers. 'Hello?'

'Leave your vehicle and stand in front of it. Place the money on the floor and I'll come over and check it. I hope for your sake it's all there.'

Chapter 49

The smells and sounds of a working quarry were long gone as Brad picked up the briefcase containing the cash and stepped out into the yard. Everything was peaceful in the swirling fog. The buildings around the edge were difficult to pick out as the last of the light faded.

A voice shouted out from the mist. 'Walk forwards fifteen paces towards my voice, put down the case, go back and stand by your driver's door.'

'OK.' He limped over and left the case on the floor. His leg was becoming more painful and his limp was getting worse. Stepping backwards, he retreated and leant against the door, the bulk of his truck obscuring the briefcase and anybody who went to retrieve it.

'Stay where you are,' boomed the voice. 'I'm checking the money.'

Brad squinted through the two sets of tinted side windows but couldn't make out anything from where he stood.

'It's too dark to count it. We'll check it in the office in a few minutes. Wait there while I fetch the merchandise.' Footsteps diminished into the darkness and Brad waited, breathing deeply to bring down his heartrate as he suddenly felt very nervous.

A heavy engine fired and ticked over. An unseen driver revved it, and gradually a massive dumper appeared out from the gloom and parked in the yard. A figure emerged from the truck and walked over to one of the buildings, returning with a ladder. Brad couldn't distinguish any characteristics as the person was wearing black and had a balaclava covering their face. The ladder was placed against the back of the lorry and the figure retreated.

The voice boomed again. 'Walk over to the dumper and take a look.'

'OK,' Brad said.

He hobbled over to the lorry and held the ladder with both hands. Perhaps this wasn't the right time to say he'd injured his arm and leg and didn't know if he could get to the top. He decided not to complicate things further so he gulped and began climbing.

***

Jemma waited a little longer and slowly sat up in the seat, partly out of caution but also because her joints had seized up after being concealed for so long. *Too many hours kneeling on the wet ground. I hope I don't need to run and fetch help!* She tried to stretch out her knees in the back.

In the murky mistiness of the darkening quarry, she could just make out Brad on the ladder. She checked her phone for battery life and signal. Both OK. She put it on mute, grabbed the binoculars and watched. Her hands were shaking which didn't help her view through the lenses.

***

In the back of the truck, Ellie checked Google maps and tried to work out where they were, failing to notice her phone battery was down to four per cent.

***

Brad slowly climbed the ladder and held on tightly despite the pains in his arm and leg. Reaching the top, he breathed out and peered over the lip of the dumper, but couldn't see anything in the darkness.

He shouted over. 'It's too dark, I can't see the fossil.' *I told Jemma to bring a torch but forgot mine.*

The voice didn't boom this time. 'Give him the torch.'

'Here,' said the darkly clad man in the balaclava as he held up a silver torch.

Brad slowly descended a few rungs, until the man on the ground lost patience and climbed up the shaking ladder before handing the torch up like a vertical relay baton swap.

Brad put it in his coat pocket and climbed back up, switching on the torch after reaching the top and peering into the dumper.

Inside was a jumbled mass of bones that had been roughly arranged into the shape of a plesiosaur. Brad shone the light along the length of the skull and thought *that's Plessie.*

Sweat trickled down his back as he realised this confirmed that the people he was dealing with were murderers.

Leaning forwards on the ladder, he held the torch in one of his hands and clasped them behind his back in the pre-arranged signal for Jemma.

***

On the back seat of the truck, Jemma used the binoculars in an attempt to discern what was happening. It was much darker than she expected so she could only make out the dumper and a torch waving around at the back of it.

Bugger! We should have made a backup plan.

***

The voice boomed out. 'Have you seen enough? Interested?'

'Very!' Brad replied, conscious he should play for time now that Jemma had called the police and help was on its way.

'OK, we'll go to the office and count the deposit. We can arrange the main payment and delivery as well.'

Brad carefully climbed down the ladder and stood back on terra firma. *The more firma, the less terra.*

'Here, pass over the torch and follow me.'

Brad handed it back and followed the beam dancing over the muddy floor towards the place where the lights had been on earlier. He hurried after the torch, hoping he wouldn't step into one of the deeper puddles of rank, oily water.

They walked across the yard, and a Portakabin light came on. Arriving at the door, the man in the balaclava pointed for Brad to go first. 'After you and no funny stuff.'

'That is not my style,' said Brad.

'Shut up and get in.'

'Please be courteous to our customer. Come in,' said a shorter man in the office, who also wore a black balaclava. 'Right, down to business. Are you happy with the merchandise?'

'Yes, a lovely specimen,' Brad said.

'OK. How long will it take for you to source the other forty thousand?'

'Give me five days and I should be able to organise the full amount.'

'Right, Mr…?'

'Jones.'

'OK, Mr Jones. Five days. Obviously, you'll leave your non-refundable deposit with us. We'll contact you again beforehand to arrange the details of how to pay the balance and the delivery of the fossil. We won't be coming here again so don't think about rushing back with the cavalry.'

'No problem.'

'Delighted to do business with you, Mr Jones. Now, how about a glass of single malt to celebrate our successful transaction?'

'OK,' Brad said. Despite the cold, droplets of sweat formed on his forehead.

***

Outside in the truck, Jemma thought that, as she hadn't been able to see Brad, she needed to go and check out the contents of the dumper for herself. She could then decide whether or not to call the police.

She slid along the seat and climbed out of the truck. As she got out, she was hit by the cold wind, so she grabbed her waxed coat and slipped it on.

On the way to the lorry, several rats ran across the yard but she reached the ladder and climbed up carefully. At the top she took the small torch from her pocket and shone it into the back, ensuring no light showed over the lip.

As soon as she saw the bones, she had no doubt what she was looking at.

Plessie!

She reached into her trousers for her mobile but it wasn't there, so instead she checked the pockets of her coat. All she could find was her geologist's hammer.

Shit, it must be in the car.

***

Back in the office, the shorter man stared out the window. 'The lights should have come on earlier when you were in the yard. I don't know what's wrong with them.' He checked a switch on the wall. 'Ah, my mistake, the master was off.' There was a click as he turned it on. 'That should illuminate the way back to your vehicle.'

***

Jemma slid down the ladder and ran for the car but she was suddenly blinded by a floodlight that lit the yard and highlighted her in the gap between the dumper and Brad's truck.

Oh, bugger!

Chapter 50

Dave arrived at Jemma's and nodded to the policeman sitting in his car outside. Seeing her van parked on the drive, he pushed the back door expecting it to be open. However, it was locked and his forward momentum brought his shoulder thumping into the wood.

'Ouch,' he said out loud and called, 'Jemma.'

He didn't receive an answer so he used his key to unlock the door. Dino came bounding out, waiting to be stroked before running off down the garden to water some bushes.

'Where is she, Dino?' He rubbed the dog's neck as it came back to him. Dino gave him a doggy look which translated as, 'I've peed, I'm happy now. Where's my food?' and ran back inside.

That's funny. She usually asks if she wants me to let Dino out.

His anxiety level grew as he stepped into the kitchen and shouted up the stairs, 'Jemma, you in the bath?'

Nothing. He checked the whole house before taking out his mobile and ringing her number. It rang for a while before going to voicemail. After the bleep, he left a message, 'Hi, Jem. Where are you? Just wondering. Give us a bell.'

He reviewed the front door camera feed on his phone, but, other than Ellie going past twice, it had recorded nothing since he left for work that morning. He then watched the CCTV footage from the camera covering the back door and garden, which showed Jemma locking the door, walking down the path and then out of the rear gate at around two. She was on her own and walked purposefully but he still felt very uneasy. He wandered across the road to where his colleague was sitting in his car.

The window opened as Dave approached. 'Afternoon, sir.'

'Hi, Ben, have you seen Jemma?'

The young policeman glanced at the house. 'She's inside. Ellie called in earlier and left some stuff, but Jemma's not been out of the house all day. Is everything OK?'

'Well, I can't find her. The CCTV shows her leaving the house by the back door and going off down the garden at two twenty. Let me ring Ellie and I'll let you know if there's any problem.'

'Oh, she didn't tell me she was going anywhere.'

Dave paced back into the house and dialled her number but again there was no answer so he left another message and sent a text as well.

He thought that something didn't feel right. Confused, he tried to decide what he could do to find her. Possibly young Freddie might be able to track Jemma's phone. He didn't have a number for Freddie or his mum so he decided to call on them instead. As Dave rushed out to his car, the policeman called out.

'Do you want me to stay here or start searching for her?'

'Wait here for now. I'm going over to her sister's. If I need anything, I'll call in.'

'OK,' Ben replied and wound up his window.

Dave sped to Sue's semi-detached house, parked and banged on the door.

She opened it. 'Hello, Dave, this is a surprise. Everything OK?'

He smiled. 'Hope so, I was wondering if you've seen Jemma. We may have a problem.'

Her mouth tightened. 'What's the matter?'

'I can't find her. Her van and Dino are at home and her mobile's ringing out.'

'Oh, my God, do you think she's in trouble?'

'I don't know.'

'Wasn't she being guarded by some dishy young copper?'

'I thought she was but he didn't see her leave. Is Freddie in?'

'Yes. Come in, don't stand on the step.'

He entered and waited in Sue's narrow hall. She yelled upstairs, 'Freddie, come down a minute, please.'

There was a loud stamping noise as her youngest son came running down the stairs. 'What's up Dave?' Freddie asked.

They went into the lounge and Dave said, 'I can't contact Jemma and no one seems to know where she is.'

Freddie selected an app on his phone. 'Let me track her mobile.'

The app opened and a map appeared on his screen. 'She's there, near Axminster.'

'Whereabouts?' Dave asked.

'Don't know but we can follow the signal,' said Freddie.

'Sorry, Freddie, I daren't take you in case there's any trouble. Can I just borrow your phone please?'

The lad's shoulders slumped. 'I suppose so.' He handed his mobile to Dave. 'The dot on the screen is Jemma's phone. You can zoom in and out.'

'Thanks, Freddie,' said Dave. 'I'll bring it back in one piece, I promise.'

'Can't I come? Please.' Freddie pleaded.

'Sorry, mate, I'd lose my job if I put you in danger.'

Sue followed Dave out to his car. 'Be careful, won't you? Are you calling the police in?'

'Not yet,' Dave said. 'Don't want to be the laughing stock of the station if we find she's got bored and gone off somewhere.'

She touched his arm. 'You've got me worried now. Let me know when you find her please.'

'Will do.'

He unlocked his car and attached the mobile to the dashboard holder then, checking the display, he drove north, resisting the urge to put his magnetic blue lights on the roof. No, if he did that then he'd need to explain later why he considered it an emergency.

As soon as he left the thirty-mile-an-hour limit of Lulcombe, he hit the accelerator pedal and his two-litre Mondeo shot up the hill.

***

In the Portakabin, Keith noticed the lights turn on in the yard. 'That's funny,' he said. 'What's triggered them?'

'Go outside, Keith, and check we haven't got any company. Don't forget your piece.'

Keith tapped his jacket and felt the reassuring weight of the Walther PPK in his pocket.

Brad turned pale at the mention of the weapon.

***

Before going outside, Keith pulled his gun out and flicked

off the safety. As he stepped out through the door, he saw Jemma running back towards the truck and shouted.

'Stop! Hands up!'

Jemma froze and slowly raised her arms.

'Stand still. Don't turn around 'til I say.' Keith strode over to her, grabbed her arm and turned her to face him. 'Bloody hell! I wasn't expecting you,' he exclaimed. 'Walk over to the Portakabin and don't try anything funny.'

Jemma moved past him in the direction of the cabin, up the ramp, but didn't go inside. Keith came up behind her and gave her a rough shove with the muzzle of the gun. She half walked, half stumbled into the office. Brad gasped as she was pushed in.

Keith followed her, still in his balaclava. 'Guess who I've found in the yard. Only Jurassic Jemma herself! After everything we did to try and dispose of her, she's done us a favour and come to us!'

Reggie pointed his gun at Brad. 'Better sit down with Jemma. It appears the deal's off.'

Keith grinned and pointed at Brad. 'It's been bugging me where I've seen you before. You were at the museum with Jemma for the press day.'

Brad attempted to save the situation. 'I'm still happy to go through with the transaction.'

Reggie sneered. 'Ah, but this changes everything. We can now get rid of you both and sell the fossil to somebody else.'

Brad glanced towards the quarry entrance and raised an eyebrow in Jemma's direction.

She shook her head faintly and slumped down into the chair.

Reggie held the gun steady. 'I suppose, as we're going to kill you, we don't need these anymore.' He removed his balaclava and ran his fingers through his hair.

Keith tore his off and threw it on the floor. 'Thank God for that, the bloody thing itches like mad.'

Jemma stared at them both and suddenly realised who they were. 'You? But why?' she stammered.

Reggie smirked at her and perched on the desk. 'Still haven't got it?'

Jemma frowned, but then it dawned on her. 'Your hotel, casino and the museum. This is all to do with that, isn't it? You want me out of the way so you can buy the site.'

Reggie slowly clapped his hands together, causing Brad to squirm as the gun was pointed all around the room. 'Got it in one! Well done!' He taunted. 'Shame it's too late and you're going to be shot.'

'So, you killed Anna and Chrissie because of greed.' She spat. 'You evil bastards.'

He shrugged. 'Sometimes in business, you need to remove certain obstacles to proceed. I thought stealing the fossil might finish off the museum. The woman who interrupted us just happened to get in the way. A simple case of the wrong place at the wrong time.'

'You bastard!'

'Oh, it was my little brother who delivered the coup de grace. He doesn't realise his own strength. Poor Chrissie found out the dangers of impersonating a wanted woman. So unfortunate she looked like you and wore your coat. That should've been you going for a one-time flying lesson.'

Jemma's mouth dropped open. She slumped in the chair with the confirmation they'd been trying to kill her and Chrissie was just an innocent bystander.

Reggie continued. 'You see, with you gone we'll be able to buy the site. We'll also have the added bonus of acquiring your house. I'm sure your family will be happy to get rid of it. Of course, accidentally disposing of Chrissie means her house will shortly be coming on the market too, which will make our site much bigger with another road access.'

'Ellie will never sell to you.'

'I bet she will when she receives a very persuasive offer. I might even discuss it with her personally… when I give her my condolences about her missing mother.'

'You stay away from her, you piece of shit!'

'Now, now, your language is quite foul for a lady. And you, Mr Jones, I'm afraid you've also involved yourself in something you should have stayed clear of. Unfortunately, your attempt at snooping today will turn out to be somewhat fatal and…'

'Can't you just tie us up and make your getaway?' Brad interrupted.

Reggie tutted. 'Oh, no, that won't do at all, not after we've invested so much into Lulcombe and its future.'

Keith waved his gun. 'Shall I shoot them now?'

Reggie held up his hand. 'Not here, you'll leave traces of blood and brains everywhere. Oh, this is all ending so well. We get rid of Jemma, once and for all; we can keep the ten grand and sell the fossil as well. Quick, give me your phones.'

Brad stood and patted his pockets. 'Mine must be in the truck, probably on the dashboard.'

'Don't know where mine is,' Jemma said. 'Must be on the back seat.'

'Go and check, will you Keith? On the way back, pop into the stores and fetch a couple of canisters of explosives, a detonator and a fuse.'

His brother gave Jemma a look which sickened her. 'OK.'

***

Keith went out to Brad's truck, the lights flicking on as he crossed the yard. The two phones were inside so he shoved them in his pocket and made his way to the stores where he collected the explosives, and the other bits, before strolling back to the office unable to hide his grin.

***

Ellie lay in the back of the truck and held her breath. Someone opened and then shut the doors. She expected to start moving again but everything stayed quiet and nothing happened. Lifting up the edge of the tarpaulin, she saw it was dark in the yard, so remained in the truck. *This place is so creepy. Why don't people have lights?* She checked her phone and found the battery had died.

Oh shit! She thought. *Meant to recharge it.*

Chapter 51

Jemma's mind raced as Keith stepped back into the office. *What can I do? How can we get out of here?* Her eyes frantically darted about the room for ideas.

Keith gave the mobiles to his brother and stuffed the explosives in a carrier bag.

Reggie held the phones. 'Better dispose of these in case anybody tries to find you.'

He dropped them to the floor and crushed them with the heel of his boot before kicking them under the desk and turning to Keith. 'Time to rock and roll. Please take our guests right to the back of Tunnel Seven.'

Keith frowned. 'Isn't that the one that's about to collapse?'

Reggie sneered. 'It's fine. It just won't take a lot of explosives to bring it crashing down.'

'You sure it's safe for me to go in?'

'Well it is for you, just not our visitors.'

Keith laughed. 'Not safe at all.'

'When you reach the end room, shoot them both. Then set the charges on a long fuse and leave quickly. That will give Jemma and Mr Jones a lovely rocky tomb. Ideal for two fossil hunters who stuck their noses where they shouldn't.'

'I'll look forward to the shooting bit.'

Reggie grinned. 'Bet you will, you animal. Tell you what, if they behave themselves in the tunnel and go quietly, I'd recommend a shot to the head. Nice and quick. If they cause you any trouble, I think gut shots are called for. That way, they'll feel the explosion as they're buried alive.'

Jemma's eyes flicked across to Brad who by now was shivering uncontrollably.

Reggie continued. 'I think we'll leave the truck on Lulcombe Beach Car Park. Everybody will think Mr Jones has done a Reggie Perrin and gone for one last swim.'

Brad looked across at Jemma and mouthed, 'Who?'

She shrugged and mouthed silently, 'Doesn't matter.'

Brad jerked up to his feet.

Reggie was quick and pointed his gun at Brad's chest. 'Don't think about it.'

'I'm not thinking about anything at all. Another suggestion, how about I send two hundred and fifty thousand pounds to an offshore account somewhere and you can both disappear without having more cases of murder on your hands.'

Reggie spat. 'We're not disappearing with a miserly quarter of a million. The profit on the hotel, casino and spa resort will be a cool fifteen million. You can keep your pathetic offers and prepare to meet your maker. Take them away, Keith, I'm getting sick of their faces.'

Keith waved his gun. 'OK you two, off we go.'

He pointed at the door and Brad and Jemma shuffled out. Tears rolled down her cheeks as she contemplated her life ending in this godforsaken place. All she could think was, *Ellie and Dave don't know where I am. They might never find out what happened to me.*

***

Keith pushed Jemma and Brad across the yard and into the darkness of a cobwebbed tunnel. He flicked a switch and some basic lighting came on.

The tunnel had been cut into the rock but the walls and ceiling appeared to be crumbling. Water trickled down over the light fittings, and a narrow rail track ran down the middle.

He pushed them onwards. 'Start moving, it's freezing down here.'

Jemma noticed a sign on the wall. *Danger, risk of collapse.* She looked at Brad who read it and shrugged.

Keith ignored the sign and waved his gun at them. 'Off you go then. Don't try anything funny.' He was careful to keep them at a distance so they wouldn't have a chance to jump him.

They continued to shuffle through the tunnel. A couple of times Brad and Keith had to stoop under the pipes that crossed from either side as dust crumbled from above.

Jemma glanced up. *It wouldn't take much to bring this whole roof down.* Her fingers closed on the geologist's hammer in her pocket. *Could come in useful,* she thought as her brain raced and her plan began to take shape.

Brad stumbled against a stone, falling with a cry.

Keith remained back. 'Help him up.'

Jemma leant down and pulled Brad back to his feet, whispering, 'Do that again in a minute but stay down hurt.'

'Come on, keep moving,' snarled Keith.

'I'm trying,' Jemma sobbed. 'But he's heavy.'

Brad brushed himself off. 'Thanks, Jem. I'm struggling with my leg.'

***

In the back of the truck, Ellie decided she finally needed to take some action and crawled out from under the tarpaulin. Stretching her cramped legs, she peered out over the side and was shocked to see a man holding a gun entering an illuminated tunnel. She crouched back down and waited for him to disappear inside.

What's going on? She shook her useless phone and tried to turn it on, though without success.

Now, what do I do?

She had to do something so she grabbed her bag and climbed down from the back of the Hilux.

Everything seemed quiet as she waited behind the truck, trying to get her bearings. The lights were on in a building over to her left. Across the yard, she could see the illuminated entrance to the tunnel that the man with the gun had gone down earlier.

She crept around the side of the pickup and crossed the yard in the darkness. Suddenly, all the lights came on and all she could do was stand motionless.

A man came out from the office. 'Who's there?' he shouted. 'Is that you Keith?'

Ellie dropped to the ground and crawled under Brad's truck where she remained trembling, as a large pair of filthy boots crunched close to her nose.

Go away, she thought, concentrating on breathing silently until something touched her head. She put her hand up to feel what it was and a rat sank its teeth into her finger. She screamed and scrambled out from beneath the truck, straight into the path of a man grasping a gun. 'Shit!' she cried and held up her hands.

'Well, well, well. The day that keeps on giving! I do believe Jemma's brat has come to join our little party.'

Ellie was close to tears. 'Where's my mum?'

'She's accompanying my brother on her farewell tour,' he said.

'On her what?'

'Oh, he's taken her with Mr Jones for a little walk to their final resting place.'

'No!' she cried.

'Yes, I'm afraid they will soon be shot and buried in a very long tunnel.'

'You bastard!'

'Dear, dear young lady, you're as foul-mouthed as your mother. Let's go and have a seat inside. When Keith comes back, he can take you on your own final wander into another tunnel. I'd take you myself but somebody has to keep an eye out in case of any unwelcome visitors.'

'I won't go.'

'Oh, how tiresome. If you won't cooperate I'll shoot you in the knees and Keith can take you in a wheelbarrow. Imagine how painful that would be. Oh, I think you'd prefer to go under your own steam. More dignified.'

After they entered the office, he made her sit behind the desk. He took some cable ties and bound her wrists and ankles together.

Chapter 52

In the tunnel, Brad fell over again. This time he shouted in pain and held his leg.

Keith stopped and raised his gun. 'I'm getting annoyed now. Looks like you're heading for the gut shot Reggie suggested.'

'Sorry,' Brad said. 'Twisted my knee and can't get up. Old football injury.'

Jemma struggled as she tried to lift him. He played the role of a dead weight very well.

'I should shoot you both here but I'm sure Reggie wants you right at the back of the tunnel so I can blow it up and seal you in forever.'

Jemma gave up trying to lift him and stood back. 'Help him up will you, please? I'll be able to pull him along once he's on his feet.'

Keith snarled and waved his gun towards them. 'Just get up or crawl if you must. It's not far to the end of the tunnel.'

Brad looked up pleadingly at Jemma. 'Please help me up.'

She tried again but couldn't lift him off the floor. 'I'm sorry, Brad, you're too heavy.' She looked to Keith. 'Please help him, he's badly hurt.'

Keith grunted and pushed past her, leant over and attempted to lift him.

As he did, Jemma grabbed the geologist's hammer from her pocket and using all her strength, she smashed it against Keith's skull.

He cried out and tried to protect himself with his hands but she hit him again. The gun fired and a bullet struck the wall behind Jemma. The noise reverberated through the stale air of the tunnel, and she fell backwards against the wall in a shower of rock and debris. A terrible pain shot though her side.

Struggling to her feet, she swung the hammer again at Keith's head. 'That's for Anna,' she yelled. 'And that's for Chrissie.' After what seemed like an age she stopped and collapsed to her knees, sobbing.

'Help me get him off.' Brad called out from beneath Keith's inert frame. 'There's blood dripping all over me.'

Jemma helped him push the huge man off his chest and checked for signs of life. 'I think he's still alive.' She picked up the gun from the ground beside him.

'Do you know how to use it?' Brad asked. 'I'm still struggling with my right arm and couldn't lift it.'

'Yes, I reckon so.' She stared at the gun in her hand. 'I went to gun club a few times when I was a teenager. It's so tempting to empty it into his head.'

'I wouldn't do that. It could bring the roof down and I think you've done enough damage already.'

'I honestly don't care,' Jemma said. 'Let's get out of here.'

'Wait a minute,' Brad said. 'He might have some more bullets in his pockets.' He searched Keith's pockets and found some extra bullets and cable ties. 'Let's tie him up.' They secured his wrists on either side of a drainage pipe. 'Right, he's not going anywhere now.'

Suddenly, a chunk of rock came down from the ceiling followed by a shower of dust.

Jemma tugged on his arm. 'Quickly, let's get out of here!'

They started scrambling back down the tunnel. Luckily, there was only one main branch, so they wouldn't lose their way. As they ran, they heard more rumbling sounds followed by a loud crash as a section of tunnel collapsed behind them and a rush of air knocked them off their feet.

Chapter 53

Sitting in the cabin, Reggie and Ellie felt a rumble shake the yard.

'That will be him now, sealing up the grave.'

The effort of trying to be brave caught up with Ellie and she screamed. 'Mum!' She put her head in her hands and sobbed.

'Oh, shut up girl, any more blubbering and I'll have to gag you. If you really annoy me, I might even suggest to Keith that he has some fun with you when he takes you on your final journey.'

'You're evil.'

He laughed. 'I like them high-spirited. I'm tempted to have some fun myself before I let my brother loose on you. Might be pleasant, as long as I have the first go.'

He stared out through the window. 'Come on, Keith, what's keeping you? I want to party with this sexy lady.'

Ellie was shaking as she tried to work her hands free from the cable ties by rubbing them against the corner of the desk, but it only made her wrists sore and had no effect on the plastic.

'Let's have a celebratory drink while we're waiting,' he said with a leer.

Ellie could only glare at him.

He sauntered to a box on a shelf and removed a bottle of whisky and some plastic cups. After pouring out three generous measures, he placed one in front of her. It was difficult to hold with her cable-tied hands, but she pretended to take a sip regardless. He swigged from his own while the final cup waited on the far side of the desk for his absent brother.

A gasp. 'Wow, that's strong stuff. Now, now, young lady, not drinking? Go on and neck it. You never know, it might make you relax a bit more when we're partying. Cheers.' A smile crossed his face as he held up his drink towards her, but she flung the contents of her cup in his face. Stumbling back, he growled, wiping at his eyes. 'What a silly thing to do, bitch.'

Before she could react, he punched her in the face and a sharp pain rushed through her head, sending her to the floor where she lay sobbing. 'Back on the chair, you bitch, you're going to regret that.'

She climbed back up and sat with her head bowed.

After composing himself, he peered out the door. 'Where's my brother?'

**

Back in the tunnel Jemma and Brad had picked themselves up, brushed down their clothes, and were heading for the entrance.

Stumbling along, the pain in her side worsened. 'I reckon I've cracked a rib or something,' she groaned.

Brad panted. 'That sucks.'

They staggered into the yard and Jemma thrust an arm

in front of Brad. 'Let's try to get the car keys from the office.' Remembering the lights from before, she pointed, 'but walk round the edge that side.'

Jemma carrying the gun and Brad holding the bloody hammer, they sneaked around the outside. They had to be careful as there were piles of old equipment and broken blocks of stone strewn all over the place. Creeping along in the near darkness, Jemma prayed the lights wouldn't turn on and give them away. Approaching the office, she peered inside through the window trying to spot the keys for Brad's truck. Her heart missed a beat when she saw who was in there with Reggie.

Pulling Brad close, she whispered, 'Ellie's inside. I can't see her face but I'd know her hair anywhere.'

'Oh, shit,' he croaked.

'We're going to have to dash in with the element of surprise.' She held up the gun. 'I'm prepared to use this.'

'OK,' Brad said. 'I'll ride shotgun with this.' He brandished the geologist's hammer as his face tightened.

'Right then, let's go,' she said.

***

Lit by Dave's headlights, the road to Axminster unfurled like a black ribbon in the misty early evening darkness.

He screeched to a halt as he flew past the dirt track that marked the entrance to the quarry.

The mobile on the dashboard had stopped flashing but he was sure the signal had been coming from this direction. There was no sensible reason for Jemma to be in an old quarry in the dark, so he made the decision to ring the station.

'Swanbourne Police Headquarters.'

'Evening, sarge, Dave Gill. This is important. Can you scramble some units up to the old quarry? Just off the A358 three miles south of Axminster. Jemma's gone missing and I'm tracking her phone. The signal brought me here.'

'OK, Dave, I'll radio the nearest cars.' After a few minutes the sergeant returned. 'They're on their way. You should wait 'til they arrive before going in.'

'Right, I'll keep an eye on the place.'

'Yeah, I bet you will,' the sergeant said.

Dave cut the call, slammed the car into gear and screeched down the track.

Chapter 54

Jemma hobbled into the Portakabin pointing the gun. 'Hands up!'

Reggie had left his gun on his desk and his eyes instinctively flicked towards it as he held up his arms. 'Now, now, Jemma, let's not be hasty. I'm sure there's a way out of this for all of us without using a gun.'

Jemma stared at him and held the gun steady. 'Oh, yes, there is a way out. You're going to put your hands behind your back and Brad is going to cable tie you to that filing cabinet. Then we're going to fetch the police and you're going to rot in jail.'

Reggie sneered. 'That's not going to happen.' He made a sudden lunge for his gun and Jemma fired a shot, hitting him in the leg. The noise made everybody jump as it echoed through the confined space. He screamed and fell clutching his thigh. 'You're dead, bitch!' he yelled as he rolled on the floor.

Brad pushed past her and grabbed Reggie's gun from the table. After limping over to Ellie, he tried to loosen her cable ties but they wouldn't budge. There was a pair of scissors on the shelf so he used them to cut through the plastic before embracing her.

Reggie sat up, still holding his leg that oozed blood. 'Where's Keith?'

'Well, I'm afraid he fired his gun in the tunnel,' Jemma said, 'and, as we were leaving, everything collapsed behind us.'

'No!' he wailed. 'You've killed him.'

He lifted himself up, grimacing at the pain in his leg. A pickaxe handle leant against the wall so he grabbed it and swung at Jemma.

There was another bang, the noise deafening in the small cabin and Reggie stopped and stared down at the blood bubbling from his chest.

Jemma shouted, 'This one's for Ellie!' She fired again and he slumped to the floor, his glassy stare showing he no longer needed to worry about buying museum sites.

Her ears ringing, Jemma remained motionless as the gravity of what had happened registered. Finally, she rushed around the desk to Ellie, who stood in shock, rooted to the spot by what she'd witnessed. Brad's arm was held protectively around Ellie's shoulders, Reggie's gun in his other hand. Jemma joined them for a hug.

'Mum!' Ellie cried as she squeezed Jemma and Brad.

'Ouch, that hurts.' Jemma winced. 'Don't worry, you're safe now. It's all over.'

'I hope so, I really hope so.'

***

Dave's car entered the yard and he swung the headlights around, trying to see through the misty gloom. He saw the Portakabin lights so jumped out, dashed closer and peered inside. To his amazement, Jemma and Ellie were hugging a man holding a gun.

Dave shouted. 'Drop the gun!'

Brad and Jemma both jumped and dropped their guns on the floor.

Dave's eyes widened when he realised who the man was. 'Brad? What are you doing here?'

Brad grinned. 'I decided I needed one last adventure with Jurassic Jemma.'

Dave's brow furrowed as he tried to think why they'd all been hugging. *Maybe it was just a reaction to whatever happened.* He then noticed a man lying in a pool of blood.

'Bloody hell, Jemma, what have you been up to?'

Jemma gestured to the chaos about the room and could only mumble an incoherent response. 'We've… had…a slight incident.'

'Wow, you're not wrong. Are any of you hurt?'

'Just a bit winded but we appear to have two dead Fletcher brothers.'

Dave hesitated. 'Two?'

'Yes, Keith took me and Brad into a tunnel, intending to kill us, but I managed to stun him with a hammer. Unfortunately, for him, he fired a bullet into the wall and the roof collapsed. Luckily, we were able to escape, but I think he was a bit flattened when the mountain came down on him.'

'A bit flattened. Right,' said Dave, not knowing what to expect next.

Jemma gabbled. 'Reggie came at me with a wooden handle so I had to stop him.'

Dave glared at the body on the floor. 'Permanently.'

She continued. 'Oh, and you'll find Plessie in the back of the lorry parked in the middle of the yard.'

***

Two police cars sped in through the gates, their blue lights flashing and sirens screaming. 'Nobody move, and don't touch anything else.' Dave said before running out to meet them.

He approached the nearest car. 'Radio in, two suspects down, everybody else seems OK but there's a bloody shitstorm here to sort out. Can you get an ambulance down to check everybody out?'

***

Dave helped Jemma from the office as one of the policemen secured the crime scene. She sat on an oil drum but suddenly felt short of breath and the pain in her side worsened.

Dave stroked her arm. 'You Ok? You're white as a sheet.'

'Yeah, just a bit winded but I'm fine.'

'Here, let me see.' Dave helped remove her coat.

Jemma glanced down to her stomach, saw her sweatshirt covered in blood and collapsed to the ground.

EPILOGUE

ONE MONTH LATER

Lulcombe was basking in some thin spring sunshine and the braver leaves and plants were considering putting in an appearance. Dave walked downstairs and sat at the kitchen table. Dino got out from his basket and stretched before padding closer for some attention.

Dave stroked his head. 'You miss her don't you, Dino?'

The dog looked up with doleful eyes.

'I'll take that as a yes.'

He continued stroking Dino while he sat there. He heard footsteps coming down the stairs and looked over as the door opened. 'Morning, Ellie.'

She hugged him. 'Morning, Dave.'

'You OK?'

She shrugged her shoulders. 'Yeah, I'm alright. It's just a bit weird not having Mum around.'

'I know, I keep expecting to see her sitting here.'

She sat. 'Suppose I should have some breakfast, though I'm not very hungry.'

Dave pushed a box of cereal towards her. 'Looks like it's cereal or toast anyway, nothing exciting.'

She got up to fetch a bowl, spoon and some milk. The sink was full of takeaway containers. 'Suppose I'd better clear this up,' she said.

Dave stared at the pile. 'It's a shame Jemma never taught us her lasagna recipe.'

Ellie opened the bin and dropped some of the containers inside. 'Yep. Should have got her to show me.'

He put the kettle on. 'How did the date go last night?'

She smiled. 'It was a good film and I really like Ben.'

'You must be daft going out with a copper. They're nothing but trouble.'

'I'm sure Mum said that a few times.'

Dave looked at her and smiled. 'Don't know why, she certainly got lucky with me.'

Ellie nodded. 'She did, you know. She may not have appreciated it but she did.' They hugged again.

'You've grown up a lot over the past few months, Ellie. You're quite sensible... for a teenager.'

She smiled gently. 'You're making me feel old now. It's probably just a reaction to what's been going on around me.'

He grimaced. 'I'm afraid that happens when people close to you die. It's part of the coping mechanism.'

'Maybe that's it.' She checked her watch. 'I'm just popping down into town to get some bits. I've got some lectures this afternoon.'

'You want a lift to college?' he asked.

'That'd be great thanks.'

She grabbed a coat and left.

Later that morning Dino jumped up and ran to the door. It opened slowly and a cardboard box was pushed through. After a short gap a wheeled suitcase followed.

Dave shouted. 'You need a lift with anything?'

Jemma stepped into the kitchen. 'No, I'm good thanks.' She walked over, followed by a very excited Dino, and kissed Dave.

'How you doing, Jem?'

'I'm fine, just don't hug me too tight. It's still a bit painful, although the bullet wound has healed' She pulled up her shirt to show him the neatly stitched wound in her side just above her waist. 'Cool hey? It's a lot better now most of the pain has gone but I still get a few twinges.

'You're so lucky, you know, going off playing hero and gunslinger.'

'We caught the baddies, didn't we?'

'Blew them away, more like. How was the conference?'

'It was great. Not only was I guest speaker but I got loads of sympathy and congratulations as well. Sold lots of Plessie posters too.'

'I bet nobody argued with your theories.'

Jemma laughed. 'Funnily enough, everybody was as good as gold. What's it been like living here on your own for a week?'

'Pretty easy. Ellie's been here for a few days so I've not been on my own. I've just had to fight for the bathroom, that's all.'

'Oh well, you've got me now to contend with, although it doesn't take me long to put makeup on.'

They kissed again and Dave smiled. 'Good to have you back.'

'It's good to be home. The hotel was nice but it's never the same as your own bed. I'm so glad you moved in. It felt right after everything that happened.'

'So it wasn't just to get a free dog sitter while you were on your jolly.'

'Nah,' she said with a grin. She sat in her usual seat at the kitchen table.

Dave grinned, 'Dino's been staring at that chair all week. He couldn't work out where you were.'

She stroked the dog who had started to calm down. 'I just want to relax a bit and try to forget what happened.'

Dave held her hand. 'Hopefully you can now.'

Jemma frowned. 'But then I don't want to forget about Anna and Chrissie. It didn't end well for them.'

'We won't forget them,' he said.

She sat up straight. 'Oh, any news about Plessie?'

'Nothing definite yet but I think they're going to give her back soon.'

She smiled. 'Fantastic!'

'They usually hold that sort of evidence for years but she's too large to keep in storage. Word is they're planning to release her to the museum, as long as they can access her if required.'

'No problem with that.'

'I must admit I'm a lot happier now the coroner's inquest is over and Reggie's body has been released to his family,' Dave said.

Jemma exhaled. 'It was quite stressful having to give evidence about the two deaths, especially as I caused them.'

Dave looked over at her. 'There was never any doubt over the verdicts, you know. Keith's, accidental due to the roof collapse. Reggie's, a lawful killing after he ordered his brother to kill you both.'

'It was still an ordeal,' she said.

'I know.' Dave replied. 'It helped having Brad as a witness to corroborate your version of events.'

'Thanks to him for that,' Jemma agreed. 'What are they

doing about Keith's body?'

'Absolutely nothing! They decided it would be too dangerous to try digging down to retrieve his remains. The DNA from the mask found at the scene matched up with Keith's so that shuts down the first murder cleanly.'

Jemma wiped away a tear. 'Not for Anna.'

'I know but at least the culprits won't be doing it to anyone else.'

'So true,' replied Jemma, although her mind was still on Anna.

Dave sipped his tea. 'It was useful that Freddie could identify a photo of Keith Fletcher as the man who tampered with your brakes. Also, the explosives found in the stores at the quarry were the same type as those used to destroy the cliffs.'

'What about Chrissie's murder?' Jemma asked.

'Unfortunately, despite Keith admitting to killing Chrissie, there's no evidence to prove he or Reggie actually murdered her. It will probably stay on record as an accident.'

'That's awful. We all know it wasn't an accident,' she said.

'Unfortunately, it all revolves around evidence.' He paused. 'How are things at uni?'

'All fine now. I'm fully reinstated and can take field trips out again, although I better keep an eye on Sally. I know she's after my job but at least she's not a psychotic killer.'

He laughed. 'Hopefully.'

'Don't joke about such things. I just want life to go back to normal.'

Dave looked at her. 'Is Brad really going back to America next week?'

Jemma shrugged. 'So he says.'

He grinned. 'I always knew he'd be trouble.'

'That's cruel.' She smiled. 'He did help me find Plessie and take down the Fletchers.'

'I suppose so.' Dave conceded. 'Still be glad to see the back of him though.'

Jemma put her hand to her stomach and grimaced.

Dave looked worried. 'You OK?'

'Yes, just another twinge. Any news jobwise?'

'Not really. It's all gone quiet since I told them I didn't want to move away from you and Ellie, so I'm going to hold the DI idea until something comes up locally.'

She squeezed his hand. 'Thanks, Dave.'

Her stomach churned at the thought of giving Dave her big news. *I daren't tell him I'm pregnant, especially as it might not be his.*

Her phone rang. It was Jackson Carter from the University Archaeology Team.

'Hello, Jackson.'

'Hi, Jemma, how are you doing?'

'I'm great now, and you?'

'I'm good, everything back to normal?'

'Yes, touch wood. Now the local psychopaths are no longer trying to kill me.'

'Cool. I've had an interesting phone call from the TV company that filmed the GPR survey.'

'Oh, no, they're not after costs because it wrecked their plans, are they?'

'No, quite the opposite. They thought you and Ellie were naturals on screen and they want you both to front a new television series.'

'You what?'

'Yep, it'll be called The Rock Detectives.'

ACKNOWLEDGEMENTS

I'm extremely grateful to Kate Thomas, Clare Kimble and Amy Fearn, whose feedback on early drafts was invaluable and to Randall Krzak, Tony Torzillo, Tim Bartlett, Erin Byrd and Donna Sundblad for their help as beta readers.

Thanks especially to Pauline and Sara for their multiple reviews, insights, help and typing.

Thanks for the professional assistance of Shaun Baines (structural editing), Damian Jackson (copy editing and proof reading), Ken Dawson for the book cover design and Kate Coe for formatting.

Special thanks to author Wendy Holden for her advice and suggestions at the early stages of the books conception.

Thank you for buying this book. I hope you enjoyed it. If you did, may I ask a small favour please?

As a new author reviews are very important to getting established so, if you could leave a review on Amazon, I would greatly appreciate it.

Thanks for your support.